FACE DOWN
IN RISING SUN

Live a good story!

K.D. Nelbauf

FACE DOWN IN RISING SUN

A missing small town girl and the crime that shocked the world.

A novel
K.D. ALLBAUGH

Battle Ridge Rising Sun Press

Published by: **Battle Ridge Rising Sun Press**

Printed in the United States of America

ISBN paperback: 978-1-7360809-0-0
ISBN eBook: 978-1-7360809-1-7

Book Cover and Interior Design: Creative Publishing Book Design
Cover Art: Bogdan Maksimovic

This book is dedicated to my husband.
Of all the love stories I have ever heard, ours is still my favorite.

INTRODUCTION

We all have a story that compels us to tell it. The story of Clara Olson, a beautiful, young, Norwegian woman born in the early 1900's in Southwest Wisconsin, could be like thousands of others, but it isn't. Something happened to this beautiful girl. Something shocking and awful happened to her and for a short while much of the United States talked about it. The newspapers were full of stories about her, some of them true and some of them untrue. The citizens of Crawford County, Wisconsin, all had various versions of what happened and why it happened. Like most tragedies, people stopped talking about it after a time of shock and disbelief, but her story still needs to be told.

As I look at a picture of Clara the first feature that I notice are her eyes. They are beautiful dark eyes and they hold an expression of wonder and possibly more. Clara wanted more in her life, more than the mere existence of a farm girl born into a large family and the day in and day out chores that would lead to a life that was "settled down". Her expression has hope and determination. I can tell that she would have told her own story if she had been given the chance.

I have read and heard countless reports about Clara in my research for her story. What I felt was lacking was the "fullness of the first person" as if the various characters could each tell parts of this story, especially Clara herself. As a mere storyteller, I find I must draw upon the actual details and then add to them with a fictionalized account of telling Clara's story. I do not even begin to imagine that I tell this story as Clara would have been able to do for herself.

PROLOGUE

The Hill Country of Crawford County, Wisconsin, has a beauty all its own. The ridges and valleys that run along the banks of the Mississippi River hide the secrets of the Driftless Region and the people who reside there. Mist often gathers in the valleys and over the ridges and shrouds the area in an almost mystical quality.

This Hill Country was originally called "Little Norway" because of the large population of Norwegian immigrants who came to the U.S. and saw this little spot of Heaven. They decided to work this fertile land and make a life here for their families. The chief crop they planted was tobacco and, at the time, this area was known for its tobacco production due to the black soil rich in nutrients and due to the industriousness of the Norwegian settlers.

The great Indian Chief, Black Hawk, came here to fight one of his last battles in 1832 on a place called Battle Ridge. In September of 1926, a secret hastily deposited in the earth of that same Battle Ridge just south of Rising Sun, Wisconsin would change this small community forever.

Chapter 1

JUNE 25, 1925 –
SENECA, WISCONSIN

The morning dawned early and bright. The air was crisp, as the summer heat comes later to the Hill Country of Seneca, Wisconsin. The grass was still wet with the dew of the previous night and it caught the early morning sunlight and scattered it like a brilliant carpet of diamonds. Clara Olson grabbed a light sweater as she left her family farmhouse to help milk the cows. "Up with the cows" as Clara's father, Christ Olson always said, Clara trudged towards the barn with her father and her brothers Adolph and Bernard. They didn't really need Clara's assistance, but she enjoyed the time outside with her father and there were plenty of sisters to help Clara's mother Dena prepare the breakfast. Christian Botolf Olson (or Christ for short) often told those around him that he might not be a wealthy tobacco farmer, but he was rich in children, nine in fact, and they were more important. Clara at age 21 was right in the middle of the birth order and she was unmistakably one of her father's favorites.

Clara was pretty with dark brown wavy hair and the most beautiful dark brown eyes. She had a slim build that wasn't even in need of the corset that young women her age were forced to wear. She had a ready smile with white and even teeth. She was healthy with a glow about her that drew people to her. Clara could be shy with people she did not know but with her family and close friends she was fun and creative. She was a devout Lutheran, having been confirmed a few years earlier in the Utica Lutheran Church near Mt Sterling. Although Clara was the "catch of the litter" as Christ often said, she had not had a single beau as she was chaperoned by several older brothers and sisters every time she went out in public.

But Clara wanted to go to new places and meet new people. She had visited the small cities of LaCrosse and Prairie du Chien only once each, and she had visited friends of her brother Arthur's once in the larger city of Milwaukee. She had enjoyed the sounds and sights of the cities and the mysteries of the unknown that they promised. Clara kept dreaming of finding a life that might take her away from the hills of Crawford County: the tobacco farms, the old country Norwegian customs, the outhouses, the houses without electricity, and the harsh life that took a woman's youth long before her time. She wanted to see the distant places she found in magazine pictures that she purchased at the Mt Sterling general store. She tried to replicate some of the beautiful dresses she saw in those same magazines. She had just finished a new yellow cotton dress with white polka dots to wear to the basket social at Peter Severson's this afternoon...

"Och! Clara! Are you still sleeping or are you gathering wool?" Christ's voice broke through Clara's reverie just as the cow she was milking began to kick the pail. Clara snatched the pail from the cow's hooves as the warm foamy milk sloshed about inside it. Some of the milk had sloshed over the top, but Clara had rescued the main portion of it. She patted the cow's side gently and said, "Vaere Stille" ("Be still" in Norwegian). The cow turned back to her breakfast and Clara resumed her milking.

"Sorry, Papa. I guess I am a tad bit excited about the box social." Clara turned her pleading brown eyes towards the stern countenance of her father. He paused, and then his face softened looking at her hopeful face. He had such a difficult time telling this daughter no or scolding her like the others. His wife Dena had said many times that they needed to be firmer with Clara.

"Yah, well, I guess there is no crying over the spilt milk." Christ winked at Clara as he moved on to the next cow and began milking. He could hear her musical laughter that sounded so much like his own mother's and he smiled to himself as he leaned against the cow's side. No sense letting his boys see him act daft over his precious girl.

Clara's brother Bernard stood up from his milking stool and turned towards his sister. "Are you excited about the quilt raffle or the homemade ice cream that the Reverend Martin always makes?" One could tell that Bernard was excited about the latter the way his voice lingered over the words. Clara smiled at her older brother. Bernard had found his true calling here on their father's farm on Stoney Point Road, and he did not seem at all concerned with life outside of it. He wasn't even interested in "sparking" with the young ladies of the community as he was a little backwards in social graces. Clara adored her most loyal and protective brother, but she did not want the same things in life and at least the box social was a change in the daily routines.

Adolph, Clara's other brother, came from mucking the stalls nearby. "I'll bet my eye teeth that Clara is more interested in who will be buying her box lunch. I saw her bake a pie and cookies and do the whole box up with a fancy yellow ribbon. I will probably have to buy hers as I surely do like Clara's cookies best." He laughed and the gleam in his eye foretold the mischief that he had in mind for his little sister.

"Oh Adolph, NO!" Clara shouted a little too loudly and the cow shifted again almost upsetting the milk pail. "Please don't do that, Brother. You aren't supposed to know whose box you are buying." she added quickly. She thought to herself, "And I don't wish to have lunch with one of my own brothers again!" When would they understand that they needed to stop following her all the time? She wanted to find a beau of her own and a young man would not show interest if her brothers were constantly with her. Her older sisters, Minnie and Emma, were already well on their way to spinsterhood and Clara could not stand the thought of that for herself. Only her younger sister Alice seemed to understand what Clara was feeling, but Clara was not certain that she wanted to go to the lengths that Alice did to entertain young gentlemen. Clara had heard Alice sneak out of the house at night and Alice had told her of dances and house parties in Seneca where there was even illegal liquor during this age of Prohibition.

"Let's get this here job done afore we worry about this afternoon," Christ broke into the exchange between the brother and sister. "Clara, as soon as you finish up with Boss you head to the house and help Ma and the girls finish breakfast. Ma will have our hides if we are late again." Christ's Norwegian accent seemed as strong as when he had immigrated to the United States from Norway in 1885. He had married Dena in 1892 after she had arrived from Norway in 1891. They had made their way to the Stoney Point Road tobacco farm and, through hard work and sheer determination, they had made a life for themselves and their children.

Clara handed the bucket to Bernard and turned towards the old farmhouse. She knew that her mother thought it was "high time" for her to settle herself and not be such a tomboy out milking the cows and planting the tobacco, but Clara enjoyed being outdoors and her father continued to allow it. Clara climbed the small stairs leading into the front screen porch. She was careful to scrape her shoes on the rug as she went through to the front door. She did not want to risk her mother's ire today as it might result in her having to stay home from the social later. While she was already 21, she was still an unmarried girl living in her parents' home so Dena's rules would continue to be followed. Clara dreamed of a day when she might have a house and family of her own. Her daughters would not have to follow the old country customs. They could work out of doors or they could go to school and possibly a college. There were so many possibilities for the future.

The smells of breakfast greeted Clara as she opened the front door; scrambled eggs, lefse, brown cheese, salami, and oatmeal were ready to be put in serving dishes and placed on the large wooden table in the kitchen. Clara's older sister Emma was slicing some tomatoes as their father loved them with his breakfast, lunch, and dinner. Clara's younger sisters Alice, Cornelia, and Inga were gathered around a small table laden with baked goods talking about the box social. They sounded much like the hens in the hen house as they talked and laughed together. At this thought Clara suddenly remembered that she had forgotten to check for eggs, and she turned to exit back out of the door just as Bernard walked in. He handed her the forgotten eggs quietly but not before their mother noticed from across the room.

Dena Olson sighed to herself. Once again Clara had flitted off with her pa and brothers and then forgotten the one errand she was sent to do. If it were not for her brothers, Clara would be in more trouble with her. It was not that Dena did not understand what it felt like to be a young woman with many dreams. She had come with her parents from Norway as a young woman and she had dreamed of what life in this country might be for her. She had met Christ only a few months upon arriving in the U.S. and within a year they had been married. Their first daughter Minnie arrived only a few months later. Dena realized that she had been lucky to find an honorable man such as Christ who would marry her and give their baby his name. They had made a life and a large family together, but she had left behind many of the dreams that she brought from Norway. Dena saw so much of herself in this middle daughter and it made her worry for Clara. Dena realized with a start that she was the one who was mentally "gathering eggs" when breakfast needed to be finished. She shook her head slightly at Bernard and Clara and turned back towards the stove.

"Clara, apron…" Dena reminded her daughter to don her apron and come help her sisters set the food upon the table. Clara smiled her thank you at Bernard and went to the hook where the apron hung. She tied the apron around her slender waist as her father and Adolph entered through the front door carrying milk pails. There was a flurry of activity from the Olson women to set the food out as Christ and the boys washed their hands and sat down at the table. When everyone was settled, Dena brought the coffee pot and poured Christ's cup of coffee for him. He promptly poured the scalding hot black liquid into his saucer to cool it. Then it was time to say grace. They all said the Norwegian blessing in unison,

"I Jesu navn går vi til bords

(In Jesus' name to the table we go

Og spiser, drikker på ditt ord

(To eat and drink according to his word.)

Deg, Gud, til ære, oss til gavn

(To God the honor, us the gain,)

Så får vi mat i Jesu navn.

(So, we have food in Jesus' name.)

Amen."

Chapter 2

JUNE 25, 1925 –
RISING SUN, WISCONSIN

Erdman Olson opened his bleary bloodshot eyes. The morning sun and fresh farm air poured in through his open bedroom window. Instead of finding them invigorating, Erdman found them like everything else on this hick farm—a nuisance. It did not help that last night he had imbibed too much of his own synthetic gin. He kept bottles of it in the trunk of his Ford Roadster to sell to the eager young farm lads at the dances in Seneca.

Erdman did not consider himself like one of the farm lads who flocked to buy his illegal liquor. His father, Albert, owned one of the most successful tobacco farms in Crawford County and had made certain that his wife Anna, his older son Erdman, and his younger son Arvid had the better things that his money could buy. This included the new Ford Roadster and a college education at Gale College for Erdman. The college education had been Anna's idea as Albert would have preferred to see his son follow in his footsteps and someday inherit the family farm on Lone Pine Lane. Albert even had to hire a young man, Edwin Knutson, to help with the farm work and tobacco crop as Erdman was often gone at school.

Erdman tried not to listen to the pounding in his head as he threw his legs over the side of his bed and stood up beside it. He put on the pair of pants that he had flung to the floor last night. He slowly padded down the hallway and down the back stairs to the kitchen below. His mother Anna was still in the kitchen cleaning up from the breakfast she had served the rest of the family over an hour before. Anna looked at her oldest son, ignoring the signs of the raucous night that Erdman had once again indulged himself in. It was Anna's usual behavior to create excuses for her son and to overlook some of the more alarming signs of his frequent outbursts. He was such a handsome and charming boy, and so bright; at only seventeen years old he had already attended college for one year. Anna had come from a wealthy family in Norway and she knew that Erdman could be very successful and live in one of the bigger cities like Chicago or New York City, instead of putting his life into this farm as his father wished him to do.

"I saved your breakfast for you," Anna turned towards the oven where she had placed a plate to keep it warm.

"No. Just coffee." Erdman replied as he sat at the table. The brilliant sunlight from the windows seemed to explode in his head and it made his habit of blinking his eyes even more pronounced.

Anna sniffed loudly as it was her habit of doing. She removed the plate from the oven and grabbed the coffee pot simmering on the back of the stove. She poured the black coffee into one of her china cups and put it on the table near Erdman. She then returned the coffee pot back to the stove.

"Be careful. It's hot," Anna reminded her son as though he were a lad of only five or six. She sat at the table beside Erdman and reached for the china sugar bowl in the center of the table. She carefully scooped a spoonful of sugar and put it into Erdman's coffee cup then stirred it and gingerly moved it back in front of her irascible son. He took it without further comment and began to drink.

"Your pa and the help started early today. Even little Arvid is out there trying to help. He is so excited about going to your Uncle Peter's for the box social this afternoon. Pa told Arvid that he could have a fifty-cent piece to use for the raffles and games. Why my brother Peter hosts a box social for the Utica church instead of for the one that we attend I will never know, but your pa says that we must go." Anna cautiously studied her son's rough appearance as she spoke.

Erdman laughed to himself. Anna had a way of saying "the help" as though something smelled bad besides the scent of cow dung wafting through their open windows. He drained the coffee from the cup and shoved it back towards her for a refill. His mother's high-pitched prattle was doing nothing to help rid him of the pounding in his head.

Anna stood to refill the coffee cup and repeat the process of adding the sugar. She placed her hand on Erdman's shoulder as she said, "I have pressed a good shirt and pants for you to wear to the social. I don't think you need to wear your suit coat as it will get warmer this afternoon. Besides, many of these people will show up in their farm clothes." She shuddered at the thought of the "farm folk" dressed in their dirty overalls and dresses made from feed sacks and used tobacco cloth.

Erdman turned to look at his mother. "What do I need clothes pressed for? Who said that I am going with you?" His look held a challenge and a threat that an outburst might be forthcoming. At first, he thought his tactics would work, but then Anna glared back at him and threw her shoulders back as she sniffed loudly again. Erdman came by his outbursts naturally as his mother mastered the art of manipulating others by her willingness to scream and wail to get her own way. Erdman knew he had mere seconds before the piercing shrieks began.

"All right, already! I guess that there's nothing better to do today." Erdman consoled himself with the thought that he might be able to sell some more of his gin if he were discreet enough. And there was always the chance of a finding a fresh young green hick girl to trifle with if her papa wasn't looking. At least this would be a different church community than the one his parents usually pushed at him. He had worked his way through some of the lovelier young girls in his parents' church and didn't need any of them showing up today trying to lay claims on him.

Albert Olson chose this moment to enter through the kitchen door. He stood looking at the scene before him. He could tell from the looks on both his wife's and his son's faces that there had been yet another altercation of some level. He had not heard the piercing screams or thunderous shouts on his approach, so he hoped that the two had called this one a stalemate. He was also grateful that his younger son Arvid had been outdoors this time and away from the melee. Arvid was more like his father in personality and both were distressed when they had the misfortune to be caught in the middle of one of these battles.

Anna had been staring at her older son without blinking and Erdman glared back at his mother with rapid blinking. At the sound of Albert's entrance Anna seemed to break from her trance-like state and she turned towards her husband with a stunningly sweet smile. Albert was able to determine that Anna felt that she had won this round by her complete change in demeanor. He also knew that Erdman would be planning a way to circumvent his mother's ploy. Albert would have loved to take this son to task but the greatest irony was that Anna would then defend Erdman to Albert and undo any discipline he would try to enforce. Albert knew at this point he needed to be happy that a crisis had been adverted at least for the time being.

Chapter 3

PETER SEVERSON'S FARM
NEAR UTICA, WISCONSIN

There were several major events in the social calendar of the Hill Country people: threshing time, the Christmas program, and the annual summer box dinner social for the local church. The Peter Severson farm was overflowing with the traffic of horses, buggies, and the occasional automobile arriving for the Box Social for the Utica Lutheran Church.

This would be an afternoon and evening of fellowship, games, music, and food. A raffle would be held for a quilt made throughout the winter months by the ladies of the church. There would be chicks and ducklings for sale for the youngsters and many games to play. The main event would be the evening meal. Most of the food would be brought by everyone attending but special box dinners prepared by the young ladies could be purchased at an auction by the interested young men. The winning bidder of each box dinner would also receive the company, while eating the dinner, of the young lady who made it. To top it all off, the minister made homemade vanilla ice cream fresh from the pail turned with a crank and set in troughs of ice from the icehouse. The ice cream would pair with newly picked fresh strawberries, and no one could resist such a treat.

Christ and Dena Olson had brought their horses and wagon to accommodate the entire family. Clara sat in the back of the wagon with her sisters and brothers as they laughed and talked along the way. She was glad that she had finished the new yellow polka dot dress as she had a new white hat and she had attached some of the matching yellow ribbon to it. Though several of her sisters and her mother had worn their aprons over their dresses, Clara had conveniently forgotten hers on the kitchen hook. She even wore her strand of imitation pearls on this special day. The pearls were a gift from her parents on her Confirmation Day. Dena had thought a cross necklace would have served her better, but Christ had selected the ivory-colored pearls himself. Clara was thrilled with his selection and she wore them only on special occasions.

As Christ pulled his team to a halt beside the numerous other wagons and buggies already assembled, Clara helped her sisters gather the dishes of food and finally the boxes that the sisters had prepared for the social. Only Clara, Alice, and Cornelia had prepared boxes for bidding. Emma had declared herself too old for such things at age thirty, and Dena had told Inga that at thirteen she was still too young. Clara had made an apple pie and her special fattigman cookies along with generous ham sandwiches, cheese, and fresh fruit. She had wrapped more of the yellow ribbon around the box as a small "hint" for the bidders. She was not like Alice who had told several of her suitors what her box looked like and planned to let them have a bidding war for her box and her company. Clara just hoped that someone would outbid her brothers for her box this time.

Clara followed her mother, father, and sisters across the field and into the large yard with shade trees all around it. Christ would find a shady spot among the menfolk and trade stories. Adolph and Bernard would throw horseshoes and look at the various cars that the other young men had brought. Dena and Emma would bustle about with the other women setting out the copious amounts of food on the long planks erected for the occasion. Inga joined the large group of children surrounding the minister as he labored to make pails of ice cream. The minister gave the kids chances to turn the cranks and saved some of his arm strength for scraping the frozen portion from the sides of the pails into the center so that all the liquid in the pails would turn into ice cream.

Clara and her sisters carried their box dinners over to the place beneath a large shade tree that had been decorated with blankets and flowers. Each girl was to surreptitiously place her decorated box upon the blankets and then retreat to the throng of spectators gathered at the wide front porch. Each young man in the crowd was supposed to politely ignore the process but a few were craning their heads to see the girl of their choice place her box among the others. Alice laughed gaily as she made a show of placing her box dinner down on the blanket. Clara and Cornelia quietly followed their sister in placing their boxes and joining the group.

Clara had known a good share of these young people most of her life. She smiled and greeted them as they called out welcomes to her and to her sisters. She walked to the end of the long porch and looked out towards a machine shed where another group of young men were gathered. She recognized more familiar faces in that group including Edwin Knutson, a shy young man who had asked to take Clara home from church once last year. Edwin had been sweet, but very awkward and ended up not really speaking to Clara during the ride home.

Edwin looked in Clara's direction and immediately took off his cap and smiled while blushing furiously. Clara smiled and waved to him. Edwin then started to walk towards the porch where Clara stood. He kept smiling and blushing all the way up to his ears.

"Hello… Miss…Clara…" Edwin stammered with a hopeful look on his face. He came to the ground beneath the railing of the porch. The thought struck Clara that it reminded her of the balcony scene from *Romeo and Juliet*. She had read that play many times and knew it by heart. The thought of Edwin as a Romeo made Clara smile even more, which Edwin took as a sign of encouragement.

"Why, hello Edwin! It is so nice to see you again. Isn't it a beautiful day for the box social?" Clara smiled at Edwin and her beautiful brown eyes sparkled with excitement. Edwin stared at her in wonder and his mouth remained partially open. It made Clara think of a trout from the stream, but she knew that this young man was sweet and kind. She would not hurt Edwin's feelings for the world even if he was as awkward as could be.

Edwin cleared his throat several times before speaking again. "Yes, it is a very nice day. A very nice day. Did you happen to pack one of those boxes, Miss Clara?"

Now it was Clara's turn to blush. So, that was what he was wondering? Well, eating a dinner in Edwin's company certainly beat eating dinner with one of her brothers.

"Well, Eddie, who do we have here?" A deep male voice a few steps away made Clara turn her head towards the speaker. The well-dressed young man stood there smiling at Clara. He had dark brown hair that he had parted in the center and slicked to the sides much like the style of Rudolph Valentino. His blue eyes sparked with a form of mischief and there was a tiny scar in the shape of a v under his right eye. He held a flask in his one hand that he kept down at his side to conceal its presence. Clara felt a small intake of breath before she could stop it, and she hoped that she had not made a sound with it.

Edwin sighed as he began the introduction. "Erdman Olson, this is Miss Clara Olson." Both Erdman and Clara laughed at the shared surname even though they were not related. Erdman tucked the flask back in his hip pocket and turned to walk up the porch steps, through the throng of people, and straight towards Clara. Edwin stuck his cap back on his head and looked dejectedly towards the ground. Clara stood momentarily frozen in place with dozens of thoughts wildly careening in her head at the same time.

Clara regained her composure just as Erdman stopped beside her. He was close enough that she could smell the spicy mingled scent of his cologne and Murray's hair pomade. There was also a slight scent of alcohol that most likely originated from the hidden flask. Clara usually found the smell of alcohol distasteful but at this moment it didn't seem to bother her. Her senses were still reeling from his proximity to her, when Clara realized that she had not answered Edwin's question about packing a box dinner.

Clara turned her attention back to Edwin, who was still looking down at the ground with his hands in his pockets and his shoulders slumped. "Edwin. Edwin" Clara had to call his name a couple of times to get him to look back up at her face. She smiled sweetly at Edwin again and continued, "Thank you for asking after me. I most certainly did pack a box dinner for this evening. I hope that someone will want to bid on it among the glorious other ones the other girls have brought. My brothers like to tease me about bidding on my box, but a girl doesn't wish to have such a fine dinner with her brothers." Clara hoped that Edwin understood that she would like for him to bid on her box dinner. Edwin returned to his state of blushing and stammering and staring at her. Clara could sense the pair of blue eyes next to her still looking at her as though she had spoken only to them.

"That would be a terrible waste indeed." His low voice was so close to her ear that she could feel his breath tickling her. "A waste of a good dinner anyways," Erdman continued and chuckled as he slowly moved away from her and back towards the porch stairs. "C'mon, Eddie. These young lads are looking mighty thirsty and we wouldn't want to disappoint them." Erdman walked back towards the machine shed without looking back.

"I decorated the box to match my new dress and hat," Clara whispered towards Edwin and he nodded dumbly. He turned and followed Erdman back towards the machine shed where the loud laughter had increased substantially since Erdman's return to the group.

Alice appeared beside her sister and grabbed Clara's arm gently, "Clara! Who is that boy with Edwin Knutson?" Clara's heart was still beating so rapidly that she could not answer her sister right away.

Chapter 4

THE BOX SOCIAL

Clara was chagrined at herself for her earlier reaction to Erdman Olson. She admonished herself to ignore him, but she kept glancing in the direction of the machine shed and the group of young men still gathered there. For his part, it was as if Erdman had never met Clara; he did not glance her way nor act the least bit interested in the gathering of young ladies who made their way to the center of the yard. The box dinner auction was ready to begin. That was that, Clara reasoned with herself as she stood with the other young ladies and Peter Severson who would serve as an auctioneer.

The auction began and the crowd enjoyed the good-natured ribbing of the young gentlemen as they bid on various boxes. Alice's box dinner went for a steep price to a young man named Frederik from Mt Sterling whom Clara did not know but Alice obviously did. Cornelia's box dinner also went for a respectable amount to a young man who attended the Stoney Point School with her. Bernard and

Adolph had bid on several boxes, but they had not been the winning bid yet. Clara wondered if Edwin Knutson would be bold enough to bid against her brothers for her box. Then she had a thought. What if Erdman decided to bid on her box? Her heart began to beat rapidly again, and she missed Peter Severson holding up her box for the next bid.

"And here is a very nice box. Why, it is fastened with a pretty yellow ribbon even," Peter Severson's words brought Clara back to her senses. Clara had the usual anxious thought that perhaps no one would bid for her box dinner, so she was relieved when one of the boys from her Confirmation class was the first bid. Bernard and Adolph also bid on it as they smiled at her. Clara looked through the crowd telling herself that she was trying to find Edwin Knutson and encourage him to bid, but her brown eyes were searching for another face.

"I bid five dollars!" the voice came from the crowd as people gasped at the extravagant amount offered. Clara blinked several times sure that she had not heard the sum correctly. That amount alone would be two days or more wages for Edwin. Or, had it been Edwin who had bid?

"I guess he likes the yellow ribbon! SOLD to… Edwin Knutson," Peter Severson's voice boomed as the crowd clapped their hands. Edwin made his way through the crowds of men clapping him upon the back and remarking about the yellow ribbon. Clara noticed one lady who stood away from the crowd as she stared harshly at Clara and whispered loudly to the gentleman standing next to her. The gentleman looked uneasy and offered his arm to the lady to escort her away from the yard and towards the field and buggies. The woman kept staring at Clara with her bold blue eyes as she allowed the man to lead her away. They stopped once to speak with someone, and Clara realized that they were speaking to Erdman Olson. Erdman nodded a few times and walked away from them brusquely. He turned back to face Clara and only then did he seem to notice her again. Clara was certain that she saw a wink from those piercing blue eyes.

"Miss Clara, where would you like to sit for dinner?" Edwin's tremulous voice caught Clara's attention as he stood before her holding the box dinner with the yellow ribbon. Clara found herself happy that Edwin had been bold enough to bid against the others and she told herself that it really was the very best outcome she could have hoped for. She looked around as the other couples were settling in here and there throughout the yard. She saw her father grinning at her and her mother with a more concerned expression but a faint smile. Clara smiled back at her parents and looked to see where her brothers had sat down in the yard. She knew that poor shy Edwin would fare better away from the teasing comments of Adolph and Bernard. She noticed that Alice had taken her beau to the other side of a tree facing the field further away from the large crowd. There was space near Alice, and Clara felt she could serve two purposes: she could count on Alice to fill in the empty spots in a conversation with Edwin and she could keep an eye on her flirtatious sister. She held out her hand to Edwin and he reached for her with his trembling hand. Clara led Edwin through the crowd towards Alice, determined that she would not glance again to see if anyone else might be watching.

When they reached the chosen spot, Clara handed Edwin an old quilt to lay on the ground. He handed the box dinner to Clara and carefully spread the quilt out, smoothing the edges as if he were preparing for the queen herself to sit upon it. Clara's heart was warmed at his kind and gentle attentions. Edwin reached again for Clara's hand and helped her to sit down on the quilt. Clara busied herself with unpacking the items from the carefully packed box as Edwin returned to the porch to bring cups of ice-cold lemonade. Clara looked at the feast she had spread out before her and she was glad that she had packed plenty as she was starting to feel quite hungry.

"Miss Clara, would you mind terribly if my friend Erdman joins us? He doesn't really know many of the other folks here today." Edwin stood at the edge of the quilt holding the cups of lemonade. Beside him stood Erdman who had donned a light gray fedora and a pair of sunglasses with dark lenses. His white button up shirt was now open at the collar and his shirtsleeves were rolled up to his elbows. He was in stark contrast to Edwin who still had his best shirt with the shirtsleeves down and buttoned tightly at the wrists, and a bow tie that was slightly crooked at the top button of his shirt. There were large marks where the sweat had shown through his shirt, possibly from the heat or his nervousness or both.

Clara felt a caution mixed with the excitement of knowing more about this handsome stranger. She smiled encouragingly at Edwin as she replied, "Well, I am sure that since you paid for the box dinner Edwin, we can share it with anyone you choose. There is more than enough food as I am used to making a lunch fit for the appetites of my brothers," she laughed gaily and slid over to make more room on the quilt. Clara almost did not recognize her own voice, and her comments made Alice stop her own hushed conversation to look at her sister.

"Will you look at my sister with beaus buzzing about her as bees to the honey?" Alice winked at Clara and resumed her conversation with her beau. Clara knew that Alice was teasing her as it was always

Alice who had multiple suitors instead of Clara. But this day would be different, and Clara intended to make it the very best, one she would always remember.

It seemed to Clara that it was a matter of minutes instead of several hours that passed as she sat listening to stories and telling her own stories and enjoying the company around her. Even Edwin seemed somewhat animated as though he were vying for Clara's attention. She tried to listen raptly to each of Edwin's stories as he launched into one after another. Was this the same young man who had driven her home in virtual silence last winter? Clara would smile and nod at Edwin to encourage him, and yet she was acutely aware that Erdman was sitting opposite them on the quilt, facing her with a polite smile on his face. He had reclined back and was leaning against the tree at his back. He sipped at his lemonade occasionally while watching her. Clara was sure that he had poured some of the contents of the hip flask into his lemonade and possibly into Edwin's as well. Alice and her beau had both borrowed Erdman's flask to "add punch" to their lemonade but Erdman had not offered any of the flask's contents to Clara. She did not care for strong spirits, but she was confused why he would exclude her from the partaking.

The sun was setting over the hills, and the brilliant colors made everyone pause to enjoy the view. A hush began to descend as the revelers seemed to understand that soon the party would end. They would depart to their own homes with the memories of another box social to brighten their daily lives. The ladies had put away the leftover food and they were now herding tired children towards the buggies in the field. The menfolk had snoozed and eaten and talked and eaten some more. It was time to harness the horses and head for home as chores came early in the morning.

Clara did not want the evening to end. She could not remember a time when she had enjoyed herself more. She repacked the few items left from the dinner back into the box and secured it with the yellow ribbon. She knew that perhaps she should offer the ribbon to Edwin as a token of their day well spent, but she wanted to keep the ribbon herself, tucking it away with a few special keepsakes in the small trunk under her bed.

Alice knelt beside Clara and whispered next to her ear, "Clara, I asked Papa to allow me to ride home with Frederik and he said that I may if you will ride along. Will you please come with us, Clara? Frederik's brothers will be driving the buggy so there will be a few of us."

Clara didn't feel like playing third wheel to her sister's date, but she also knew how difficult her parents were about escorts. She turned to Alice and replied, "Yes, I will go with you, Alice but we need to get straight home this time." Clara turned towards Edwin who was seated next to her. "Thank you for such a lovely time, Edwin. I hope that I might see you in church again soon?"

"Oh yes, Miss Clara. I hope to see you again soon." Edwin scrambled to get to his feet so he could assist Clara to her feet. He stumbled at the first attempt but righted himself and held out his arm to Clara. "You make the very best sandwiches and cookies I ever rightly had." Edwin added in his clumsy attempt to compliment her. Clara took his proffered arm and stood to her feet. She glanced back to where Erdman was still leaning against the tree. The dark lenses of his sunglasses obscured whether he was sleeping but he made no comment or movement. Why didn't he just remove the silly sunglasses as it was almost dark? Clara decided that he was of no concern to her, so she turned to leave with her sister and the waiting Frederik.

"So, Freddie, what do you say we both see the gal home with a little more style? I brought my Roadster and it is a sight more accommodating than the back of your brother's buggy." Erdman spoke as he removed his sunglasses and stood in one swift movement. "These pretty ladies deserve that after listening to you boring fellas all afternoon. What do you say to that Alice?" He directed the question to the more willing sister.

Alice's eyes sparkled with excitement. "Why I think that idea is just grand! Don't you agree Clara?" Alice turned pleading eyes towards Clara, willing her to agree with the plan. "After all it isn't every day we get to ride home in a car with such handsome gentlemen," Alice added when she saw the guarded look on Clara's face. "Or maybe Clara would like to see if Bernard or Adolph are available to come along?" Alice knew that Clara would not want their brothers to tag along.

"There is no need for our brothers to come with us, Alice. We are not children," Clara blurted out. "Thank you for your very kind offer, Erdman," she added. "Isn't Edwin going home with you also?"

"No. Eddie has to take my little brother Arvid back home. My parents had to leave earlier because my ma was getting one of her headaches. Pa left instructions for Eddie to look after Arvid as the boy loves him so much. Speaking of which, don't you think you best go find the boy, Eddie?" Erdman glanced at Edwin who looked surprised at this turn of events.

"Don't worry about me none, Miss Clara," Edwin looked nervous again as he glanced around. He reached out and grabbed Clara's hand and shook it heartily. "I need to go find the boy right away. Mrs. Olson gets real nervous about young Arvid." Edwin picked up the quilt he had placed so carefully and thrust it into Clara's arms. Then he handed her the box and before Clara could react Edwin was gone.

Erdman reached out and took the quilt and the box from Clara's arms. "Shall we?" he asked as he shifted the items to one arm and held out his other hand for Clara. She went to take his arm politely and he slid her hand down into his own clasping it and bringing it protectively to his side. "I wouldn't want to see you trip over the tree roots in the dark. Don't worry, I have you safe and sound."

They made their way across the field to the almost new Ford Roadster. Erdman made sure that Frederik and Alice were in the rumble seat. Then he held the passenger side door open for Clara. He handed her the quilt and the box. He went to the front of the car and gave a few turns of the crank. The engine started with a roar as he opened the driver's side door and sat down.

"Ready to go, Bright Eyes?" He flashed the exact same grin as the first moment she saw him that morning. Clara's stomach was doing flips. She did not know if it was due to the car ride on the curvy Black River Road or that suddenly Erdman was giving her his full undivided attention. He told her about Gale College, being a member of the rowing team, and his aspirations of going into business in Chicago or New York City. He kept commenting about how pretty she was and how especially pretty her brown eyes were. It only took the fifteen-minute ride from the Severson's farm to Stoney Point Road for Clara to fall head over heels in love with Erdman Olson.

Clara was sure that Erdman probably had many girlfriends. She did not want him to know that she was far more naïve than he was as she was 21 and he was 17. She kept quiet for the most part as they drove along. When Erdman parked the car out in front of the lane leading to her farmhouse a quarter of a mile away, he slid from behind the driver's seat and came to her side of the car. He opened the car door for her and took her hand in his again, leading her out of the car and down the lane a short distance. Alice and Frederik stayed behind in the car.

"I am glad that you finally decided to give me a chance after I waited all day to talk to you," Erdman stopped walking and faced Clara. "I sure hope that I don't have to wait as long to talk to you again." He leaned towards her, gently placing a kiss on her forehead and then another on her lips. It was Clara's first kiss.

"You waited all day to talk to me?" Clara was still breathless from his kiss. He seemed to not even have noticed her for most of the day, but he had been waiting for a chance to talk with her.

His response was a chuckle as he traced the side of her face with his fingertip. He stopped his finger just under her chin and lifted it slightly so he could see her eyes in the moonlight. "Who do you think gave Edwin Knutson five dollars to buy a box dinner?" With that he walked back to the passenger side door, picked up the quilt and the box from the seat, removed the yellow ribbon and put it in his pocket. He smiled as he handed the rest to Clara and called over his shoulder, "Okay, Freddie. Give your gal one more kiss and let's be on our way."

Chapter 5

RISING SUN, WISCONSIN

The day after the box social Edwin Knutson was up before dawn. He was tired after enjoying the afternoon with Clara followed by a harrowing search for Arvid. He searched for over an hour and finally found the lad fast asleep in the hay mow of the Severson's barn. Arvid had purchased three ducklings with his fifty-cent piece from his father. He had taken his ducklings and curled up to keep them warm, oblivious to the fact that Edwin was searching frantically for him.

Edwin was relieved to find the boy safe. He quickly bundled Arvid and the ducklings in a blanket borrowed from Mrs. Severson and put them in the buggy. Edwin knew that Mrs. Olson would already be fretting about him being so late with the boy. That woman could shriek loudly (enough to wake the dead) when she went into one of her rages. Edwin appreciated the job and the living arrangements from Mr. Olson, but there were times that he considered leaving the place and never returning.

Needless to say, Edwin had brought the boy home right away handing him off to Albert Olson. Albert seemed surprised to see Edwin with the boy and even asked where Erdman was. Edwin surmised from this that Erdman had been instructed to bring his brother home, pushing the task off onto Edwin. He didn't really mind as Arvid was a nice boy and they got on well, but he didn't like being fooled by Erdman once again. Erdman was more like his mother than his father, so Edwin was careful not to rile the young man and would not mention this incident to anyone.

Edwin had made a place in the corner of the barn for Arvid's new ducklings so that the boy could see them as soon as he came out to the barn. Edwin had done all the morning chores with Albert. Edwin was just finishing his work in the barn when he noticed the shadow of someone standing in the doorway. Erdman stood there in just his undershirt and pants casually watching Edwin work. Erdman walked over to the corner, picked up one of the ducklings and held it out to inspect.

"Yesterday was quite a day, wasn't it, Eddie? Nothing like spending time with a pretty girl to make a young buck like you feel like quite a man. That Clara would make any buck feel more like a man." Erdman laughed as Edwin began his inevitable blushing.

"Oh no, Erdman. Miss Clara isn't like that at all. She's a real nice girl. I took her home from church once and we were very proper and nice," Edwin protested seeing what appeared to be a leer on Erdman's face. He had to make Erdman understand that Clara was not like the myriad of other girls that Erdman sweet-talked and then dumped when he was done with them.

"Proper and nice eh?" Erdman laughed harder at Edwin's protestations. "I wouldn't say she was proper and nice when I was kissing her in the moonlight last night. You see, Eddie a gal like Clara will only allow you to be her friend while she wants me for much more than that. Believe me, I will give her what she wants."

Edwin felt a rage building inside him that he had never experienced before. His hands curled into fists at his sides as he tried to keep from punching Erdman square in his foul mouth. He knew that Erdman was a liar. Clara would not allow Erdman to kiss her or do any of the other things he was suggesting to her. Clara was not like those others, she couldn't be like them. Edwin also knew that he had to contain himself and not respond to Erdman's cruel taunts.

"What's the matter Eddie? You look a little riled." Erdman continued. Erdman would shift from one foot to the other and rapidly blink his eyes when he was about to fly into one of his rages that rivaled those of his mother. He still looked relatively calm to Edwin, but Edwin did not wish to push the matter farther at this point. There was a long tense silence as the two stood there staring at each other.

Erdman finally broke the silence, "One last thing. There will be no more rides home with Clara for you. Don't cross me on this Eddie, or bad things will start to happen around here and you know I will blame them all on you." There was the sickening crunch of bones breaking as Erdman crushed the neck of the tiny duckling in his hand and threw it against the wall. Edwin stared in disbelief as a wave of anger mixed with fear and nausea washed over him.

Erdman went back out the barn door and called to Albert who was over by the house, "Pa, come see. The dogs must have got to one of Arvid's ducklings. This stupid moron of a hired man didn't even think to put them out of reach. Poor Arv is going to feel real sad about this." Erdman cast one more glance at Edwin and walked out of the barn leaving Edwin to lose his battle with the waves of nausea washing over him.

Chapter 6

SEPTEMBER 1, 1925 – SENECA, WISCONSIN

The Wisconsin weather was beginning its preparations for Autumn to arrive. Each day grew shorter by a few minutes and the winds that blew were filled no longer with bursts of heat, but with spicy coolness. The leaves on the trees also began their transformation from the variety of lush greens to the darker golds, oranges, and crimson reds. The harvests were almost ready and the corn, soybeans, and especially the tobacco looked healthy and abundant. Gardens were overflowing with vegetables that would be preserved for the cold winter months ahead. The apples from the trees that lined the ridges in nearby Gays Mills were ready to pick and can or dry. There was much work to be done on the Christ Olson farm and each family member was expected to do their fair share.

Clara sat at the large kitchen table with her sisters snapping beans to ready them for the canning jars. It was a tedious task, but it was one Clara could do without concentrating on it very much. Her thoughts were on all the changes in her life in the past two months since the box social. Clara was certain that this time with Erdman had been the happiest of her young life so far. In fact, she couldn't believe that she had ever been happy before falling in love and knowing that Erdman loved her too.

Erdman wrote many love letters to her, usually at least one each day. He would come to her house to take her for rides in his car all over the Hill Country. He had even taken her to Prairie du Chien for his favorite picture show, *The Sheik* with Rudolph Valentino. Clara had been a little shocked at the movie as the main character abducts a young woman and forces his attentions on her, but Erdman assured her that in the world outside little Crawford County that was the way of things. She readily accepted Erdman's opinions because she did not want him to think that she was "backwards" and be embarrassed by her. Clara knew that Erdman could have his pick of many girls; she needed to be the sophisticated woman that he would want to marry someday. He told her in his letters that they could live in Chicago in a big house with fancy cars and servants. Clara just knew that she wanted to be with him wherever in the world that was.

Christ and Dena had their reservations about Clara's new beau. Christ had told Clara to invite the boy into the house for supper or dessert numerous times, but Erdman always had an excuse as to why he couldn't visit with them. Christ thought it was disrespectful to Clara the way the boy would pull over to the side of Stoney Point Road and make Clara walk the quarter of a mile down the lane to meet him. Sometimes Erdman would pull his car into the part of the yard farthest away from the house; he and Clara would sit there together for hours on end.

Dena would whisper to Christ, "Pa, those aren't Sunday School lessons out there" as a stern reminder of the possibilities. Anytime Christ would try to bring up his concerns about Erdman to Clara she would start to cry and tell him that he just didn't understand. Christ trusted that Clara was a good Lutheran girl and he would drop the argument with her. He just wanted his little girl to be happy and hopefully, the young couple would settle down once the romance was no longer new.

Clara's brothers and sisters had varying opinions of Erdman. Bernard and Adolph were wary. Many of the local fellows told stories of Erdman's escapades selling illegal liquor. While this was common among the locals (many a farmer had a moonshine still somewhere), Erdman was also known for brandishing a pistol that he kept hidden in the trunk of his Ford Roadster. Emma would chastise Clara for going out to meet Erdman in his car. She reminded her sister that "Men only want one thing, Clara, and then they don't want you anymore." This piece of advice coming from Clara's thirty year-old virginal spinster sister made Clara more determined not to end up like Emma. Clara's youngest sisters Cornelia and Inga thought that Erdman was dashing and handsome; they thought Clara was so lucky to have Erdman as her beau.

Alice broke into Clara's reverie by whispering, "A penny for your thoughts Clara?" Clara smiled at her sister as they both knew what or rather who Clara was thinking about. Alice asked her mother if Clara could help her bring in the next batch of beans from the side yard. When Dena gave them permission, Alice wasted no time rushing Clara out the front door and into the yard so they could have a more intimate chat.

"Sister, I know that you fancy yourself in love with Erdman," Alice began. "Have you considered what will happen when he returns to college this month?" Alice set down the basket of beans to take Clara's hand in her own. "I don't want to see you making decisions towards him that he might not return towards you when there is a distance between you. Sometimes a boy like Erdman…"

"What do you mean 'a boy like Erdman'?" Clara snapped. She started to withdraw her hand from Alice's, but Alice held it firmer.

"I only mean that while Erdman has been your first and only beau, he has had many girls that interested him. Sometimes a girl can feel pressured to do certain things to keep him interested in her. You don't need to do those things, Clara, if that is all that will keep him." Alice looked into the angry eyes of her most beloved sister. "You are wonderful and beautiful and so very smart Clara. You can do anything that you put your mind to, so just don't settle for something less."

Clara laughed, "You would think that **you** are the older sister, Alice. Thank you for all of your wisdom little sister, but I don't think that I am needing it right now." Clara withdrew her hand and stooped to pick up the basket of beans from the ground. She faced Alice again and glared at her.

It was Alice's turn to be angry, "Clara, if you know so powerful much can you please tell me why your Erdman Olson is seen dancing at the Seneca Dance Hall every Thursday night? It seems that he enjoys the company of multiple girls and you are nowhere to be found! Folks are saying things, Clara, and they ain't good things."

Clara reached across and slapped Alice's face in response. Clara had never struck one of her siblings before and both sisters stared at each other in shocked amazement. Clara saw the angry red mark start to form on her sister's face. Everything in her cried out for her to hug Alice tightly and beg for forgiveness. Clara felt torn between the little sister whom she adored and the fierce loyalty to the man she loved. Why did her sister have to try to ruin the one good thing Clara had? Was Alice just jealous or was she speaking the truth? Before Clara could reach for Alice again, Alice ran towards the barn with her hand covering the red mark upon her cheek. Clara stood there as if she were frozen trying to decide what she should do next. Tears of remorse welled up in Clara's eyes. She knew that she had to find Alice and apologize.

Clara was grateful that her father and her brothers were out in the tobacco fields, so they had not witnessed her loss of self-control. Clara stepped into the cool shadows of the barn's interior. She listened carefully for the tell-tale sniffling cries of her favorite sister. The sounds led her from the barn floor to the hay mow above her head. Clara climbed the ladder and stood at the top. She saw Alice's crumpled form in the corner. Regret now sliced through her like a knife knowing that it was she who had made Alice cry with her deplorable behavior.

Clara knelt beside her sobbing sister, "Alice, I am so sorry. I should not have ever struck you. Please forgive me, Sister." Clara reached out to pat Alice's back as the girl was still shaking with muffled cries. Alice turned to her sister who sat beside her. Alice's eyes were swollen and red as she looked back at Clara. Her hair was disheveled with small bits of hay sticking out here and there. She would have been a comical sight if she had not been so mournful.

Alice shook her head. "No, Clara, it is I who am sorry. I should not have blurted out those things to you. I never want to see you hurt and I thought that I might prevent it somehow. I want you to be happy and if Erdman makes you happy then I won't say anything more." She hugged Clara tightly.

Clara handed Alice a handkerchief to blow her nose as Clara replied, "Say no more, Alice. I have some questions to ask of Erdman tonight."

Chapter 7

VIROQUA, WISCONSIN

Erdman had surprised Clara that evening with tickets to a movie at Temple Theater in Viroqua. The movie showing was *Little Annie Rooney* starring America's sweetheart, Mary Pickford. Clara knew that she should be laughing with Erdman and the rest of the audience at the antics portrayed on the screen, but the comments that Alice had made niggled in the back of her mind. Why would Erdman continue to attend dances without her? Did other girls still hold his interest in ways that she had not? What would happen to them when Erdman returned to his college life next week? Would he remain true to her or would she be another summer romance; a flower picked in bloom and then discarded when summer had come to an end?

Overall Erdman had been a sweet gentleman to her. They often engaged in "necking", kissing and embracing each other, but there had not been overtures of a more intimate nature. Clara had enjoyed this just as much as Erdman; she certainly had not stopped his advances.

In fact, she longed for the times that he would kiss and embrace her, whispering the most wonderful sweet nothings in her ear. Surely, Alice had just overheard the vicious gossip of girls who knew that Erdman was Clara's beau and not theirs. This was creating a "tempest in a teapot", and Clara decided that she would not let it ruin one more moment of her remaining time with Erdman before he left for school.

The audience laughed as Mary Pickford's little rogue character threw bricks at the villains. Erdman leaned in close to Clara's ear, kissing and nibbling it, causing Clara to laugh as well. His hand had rested on her knee and he slid it up further to her thigh. Clara's heart began a staccato rhythm. She felt an excitement and yet she knew that there were limits to their caresses, especially in a public place. She put her hand on top of his and clasped it to hold in her own as she smiled at him. Erdman sighed aloud and turned back to watch the movie again. Clara felt another stab of doubt assail her. No, she just simply would not accuse him of any inappropriate behavior with other girls. She turned her attention towards the movie, but even as she joined in the laughter, doubts like tiny gnats, flitted around in her mind.

When the movie ended, Clara and Erdman followed the crowd out of the theater. Erdman would often hold Clara's hand close to his side just as he did the first night they met, but tonight he walked a small distance in front of her with his hands stuck in his pockets. There were warning bells joining the doubts in Clara's head as she tried to keep up with his pace to the car. Had she hurt him by stopping his hand? Was he angry enough to just leave her for college girls who would welcome his attentions?

Erdman walked to the passenger door to open it for Clara. She paused before him, grasping his head with both of her hands, and pulled him to her for a passionate kiss. There she was, Clara Olson, devout Lutheran girl, kissing a boy on a public sidewalk. Clara was sure there would be many gossips tearing up the telephone lines with her wanton behavior, but she did not care for any of it as much as she cared for Erdman. He smiled down at her as he gently led her to her seat in the car and closed the passenger door. He started the car with the crank and jumped in the driver's seat beside her. Clara could sense that their relationship had just changed in a major way.

Erdman drove the car back down the Black River Road towards Clara's home in Seneca. The night was clear and cool with a multitude of stars in the sky outside the car window. Clara pulled her new sweater closer around her. "Are you chilly, Honey?" Erdman asked with concern in his voice.

"I am just a little chilly. My sweater will help warm me. Thank you for asking." Clara replied. Erdman grinned at her and said," Well, right now I am wishing that I was that pretty new blue sweater of yours, hugging you so tight and keeping you warm." Clara's eyes grew wider at his boldness and yet she knew that he wanted her to be as flirtatious as she had been when she kissed him earlier.

"Then maybe you should be hugging me instead." Clara laughed lightly as she said it, but she was unsure of what she even meant by it. Erdman threw his head back and laughed, delighted at what he perceived as her bold invitation. They were approaching his home near Rising Sun when Erdman turned left off the main highway onto an old logging road. The old road was rather desolate and led to a copse of trees on the top of Battle Ridge. Here they were hidden from the highway and had a beautiful view of the starry sky above and the dark valley below. Clara knew that this spot hidden away from all prying eyes was different from the spot in her parent's farmyard where they usually parked the car.

Clara saw a farm not more than a quarter of a mile as the crow flies. The house had gas lights unlike the ancient kerosene lanterns in her own home. Clara thought this might be the farm that belonged to Erdman's parents. Maybe he wanted to show it to her or take her there and introduce her to his parents. After all, it was only a matter of time before he proposed marriage to her, wasn't it? A rush of love for him washed over her again erasing the earlier doubts and fears.

Erdman turned off the car engine and reached to pull Clara close. She laughed as the sensation of his muscled arms around her really did seem to warm her much better than the sweater. Clara tilted her head back just as Erdman claimed her mouth with his own. His kisses were more passionate and his caresses more intense than ever before. There was a new boldness in Erdman that was exciting to Clara but as he continued his amorous petting, she felt an underlying urge to escape his grasp. Instead of a gentle and gradual build to love making Erdman was becoming more and more aggressive with almost a ruthless quality in his urgent attempt at consummation. Erdman shifted his weight so that he was almost pinning her down on the seat, and Clara felt as though she could not breathe.

"Erdman, PLEASE!" Clara began to struggle against him. His breath, hot and rapid, was in her face as he tried to silence her with another kiss. Tears began to form in Clara's eyes as she tried to turn her head away from him. "Erdman, You're hurting me," Clara begged and the tears that had formed were now flowing freely. Clara braced her hands against his chest and pushed with all her might.

Erdman suddenly stopped and the silence in the car was palpable. Erdman shifted his weight off Clara and the air that rushed into her lungs escaped back out as a sob. Clara looked down at herself to see her dress torn open at the neck and the new sweater ripped on the right shoulder. The bottom hem of her dress was almost at her waist. Clara felt the burn of deep embarrassment as she tried to adjust all her clothing back to its original state. She glanced at Erdman at her side. He was still breathing heavily. He gripped the steering wheel with both hands and bent over so that his head lay upon it while his eyes were closed. Then Erdman struck the steering wheel so hard that the entire car shook. "Never do that again!" he bellowed at Clara as he opened the car door, left the driver's seat, and slammed the door behind him. Erdman walked off into the darkness, leaving Clara alone, bewildered, and shocked at the turn of events.

Clara wondered where Erdman had gone. She knew better than to get out of the car and try to search for him. She could hear the faint cry of wolves in the distance, which added to her feeling of desolation. She put her fingers to her swollen lips to see if they were bleeding and again tried to fix her clothing so that no one else would notice her appearance. Papa and her brothers must never find out what had happened here tonight. There were still Old Country traditions such as a shotgun wedding where the groom was forced to marry by having a shotgun trained upon him. Clara was concerned that her brothers might try to use the shotgun on Erdman without the wedding if they knew what had happened. And yet... Clara recalled her mother's adage "If you play with fire you might get burned." Clara suddenly felt guilty for her brazen behavior with Erdman. Surely, she was the one responsible for what happened? She must protect Erdman from the rage of a father and brothers who did not understand the situation at hand.

What if Erdman had walked off and left her not planning to ever return? She knew he had been furious at her and perhaps he had decided to call it quits, leaving for Gale College in a few days and never looking back. Clara's sense of concern heightened to panic as she began to look around to see if she could see Erdman anywhere. She had to make him understand that she loved him beyond reason and that she would do anything for him. She knew now that he had not meant to ever hurt her while showing her his passion. If only he would give her another chance.

Clara thought that she saw movement at the base of a tree several yards away down the logging road. She strained her eyes to see if it was indeed Erdman sitting there and not an animal of some sort or just shadows playing tricks with her eyes. The clouds shifted, revealing moonlight that lit the ground around the base of the tree. There was Erdman sitting against the tree with his hands covering his face and his knees pulled up to his chest. He looked so distraught that Clara left the car without another thought for her own safety.

Clara walked quietly to where he sat. He did not look up at her nor did he speak. Clara reached forward, her hand shaking slightly, to touch the hair that he had obviously tousled in frustration. He started at her touch, but he still did not look up at her as she knelt beside him. Clara leaned forward until her forehead touched his temple as she continued to stroke the hair on the back of his head, soothing him.

"Clara, you can't ever do that to me again," Erdman spoke as he lifted his head to look at her. "You do not realize what you do to me. I have waited for you for months, Clara. I have tried to be patient with you. When I told you that I loved you I thought that you loved me too."

"Erdman, I do love you! I love you so very much," Clara gasped as she wrapped her arms around him hugging him tightly.

"No, Clara. I don't think that you do love me. I never would have suspected that you are a tease. You have tried to lure me these past few months then when I try to show you how much I love you just push me away as though I do not matter to you at all." Erdman began to remove her arms from around him. "Maybe it is best that this happened now since I will be leaving soon, and we should part ways."

Clara felt as if the wind had been knocked out of her. She gasped for breath as she cried in great wracking sobs, "Please don't say that, Erdman. I do love you. You are my first and only love. I just don't understand all the right ways yet, but I can learn. Please, you can teach me. You can show me what you want me to do. Don't leave me, Erdman. I love you." Clara knew that this moment would decide her future happiness. She would do whatever it took to make him love her again.

Chapter 8

SENECA, WISCONSIN

Several hours later Clara walked slowly towards her family's farmhouse. The house was dark with a solitary light in the front window. Clara knew that her father had left that light for her to return to, lighting her path to her home and family. Clara paused in the pathway, saying a quick prayer that her family especially her father had already gone to bed. She just didn't have words for them right now as she was consumed with emotions that crashed against her soul like the waves of the ocean.

The house was quiet as Clara made her way in the front door, extinguishing the kerosene lamp set out for her, and silently climbed the stairs to her bedroom. She could not help but wonder if she were a very different person than the girl who had come down the same stairs earlier that morning. She just needed to get to the sanctuary of her own room and take stock of what was left of her troubled mind, bruised sore body, and especially her disillusioned heart.

There was a small lamp burning in her room, casting a faint glow across the room. Her nightgown was laid out upon her bed and a wash basin of fresh water along with a towel and hairbrush stood on the nightstand. Alice had thoughtfully laid these things here earlier to let Clara know that all had been forgiven from that day's argument between them. Clara's eyes welled with fresh tears at Alice's thoughtfulness. Clara walked over to the wash basin and began to remove her dress and underclothing. She knew that she would have to hide them as they were stained with the clay ground of Battle Ridge as well as the previous rips she had noted. She shoved the clothing underneath her bed to deal with later and turned to the wash basin. She longed for the metal bathtub filled with steaming hot water from the stove that the family used for bath nights. She would love to immerse her entire body, washing away some of the scents that clung to her and the memories that were associated with them.

She washed her face, arms, and torso first. Even in the dim light she could see faint bruises forming on her arms and legs. She knew that it should hurt more than it did, but she was clothed in a numbness that seem to block some of the physical pain. The worst of the physical pain was at her very core. She looked to see the blood on her underclothing and legs as a telltale sign that what had occurred was not just her imagination. She was confused as it was far from time for her monthly courses, but she decided to get out the belt and cloths that might be necessary to prevent more staining. Clara continued to wash in the water from the basin, then after tenderly drying her body, she put on fresh underclothes.

There was a light tapping on her bedroom door as Alice entered the room behind her. Clara quickly reached for the nightgown to put it on, but not before Alice had seen the bruises and marks. Clara winced at Alice's gasp. She continued to put the nightgown on as though nothing were awry, but it became stuck midway on her back. Alice turned Clara towards her to look at her sister more carefully in the dim light. Clara could not speak. She saw Alice's horrified expression as Alice examined her thighs and torso.

"Clara, are these bitemarks?" Alice's eyes narrowed looking closer at the injuries on Clara's torso and thighs. "**He** hurt you…" Alice's voice was a mixture of grief and rage. Alice pulled the nightgown down over Clara's battered body. A single sob was loud in the quiet of the house around them. Alice hugged her sister tightly to herself. "Can you tell me what happened?"

"Not yet." Clara whispered through a throat that had constricted so tightly she could barely breathe. The numbness that had enveloped her was receding, leaving her weak and helpless. Clara's legs buckled underneath the weight of the emotions that continued to assail her. Alice eased Clara onto her bed and laid down beside her stroking her hair and whispering, "I'm here Clara, I'm here." Clara shut her eyes against the tumult knowing that Alice would keep watch over her until morning dawned.

Chapter 9

RISING SUN, WISCONSIN

The farmhouse at the end of Lone Pine Lane was still ablaze in lights and Erdman could hear the music from the radio as he turned off the car's engine. His mother must be having yet another one of her "all-nighters"; she would come out of the morose state she had been in for days and suddenly busy herself with everything that had been neglected for weeks. His father would certainly be sitting nearby at the kitchen table making certain that she did not burn the house down trying to clean it. Hopefully, his father would have a bottle of Kentucky bourbon out as well as Erdman could use a stiff drink. Albert stored an illegal supply of the bourbon so that he could tolerate all of Anna's episodes.

The evening had taken some unexpected turns even by Erdman's estimation. Clara had boldly kissed him in public, pushed him away in the car, then came to find him underneath the tree, determined to show him that she loved him. He had been reluctant to initiate more after her first cruel refusal, but she had been so insistent that soon his passions fueled by lust took him over again. He had attempted to be gentler with her, caressing and whispering the words of love that seemed to always delight her.

Her lack of responses confused him; she no longer pushed him away or even cried out as he attempted to escalate his actions to elicit a reciprocation of passions. She remained silent throughout only gasping once, the moment of the initial junction. She reminded him of a lifeless rag doll. Her seeming disinterest angered him prompting him to replace the gentle caresses and kisses with raucous groping and even biting. He wanted her to respond to him as she had when she kissed him on the sidewalk. How dare she humiliate him? She was only a green hick of a girl while he had many lovers, past and present, who had always appreciated his passions.

When he had finished, he looked at her closely to see if she had fainted. She looked back at him with eyes full of pain and fear. There was a tremulous smile on her face as though she were seeking his approval. He knew that he should probably feel sympathy towards her, but he only felt more anger. Erdman scrounged around on his hands and knees looking for the clothing he had discarded so rapidly. He found his coat above Clara's head where he had placed it after removing one of the prophylactics he always stored there. He found the flask of gin he had been searching for and took a large swig. He then handed the flask to Clara. "Here, this will help."

She hesitated for a moment and then took the flask from his outstretched hand. She sipped the gin and began to cough violently, then she sipped some more. He could not tell if the tears running down her face were from the strong spirits or from her own emotions, but he did not comment on it. It was always best when his mother had fits of tears to ignore them. She handed the flask back to him. She just kept looking at him as if she were searching his soul for something she could not name. Erdman found that he liked this even less than the tears.

He had busied himself with collecting the rest of the clothing and then he had turned back to help her to her feet. She swayed several times and seemed to experience pain upon standing but she had not made a comment. Erdman had taken a few steps towards the car when Clara stayed him with her hand upon his arm.

"Erdman will you please hold my hand?" her voice had sounded small and pleading. He had taken her hand in his and held it to his side.

"Don't worry, Clara. I have you safe and sound." He had decided then and there that he only had to be more patient with her next time. He drove Clara home and kissed her lightly. He had promised to write her the very best of love letters and then he had watched her walk slowly towards her house. It had been a very unexpected turn of events. And now he had to face his mother.

As Erdman entered the kitchen, he found his father Albert seated at the table just as he had anticipated. His mother Anna sat in Albert's lap kissing him amorously. Erdman sighed to himself. This was when Anna was at her very worst; she would ignore Albert for months on end with an icy contempt and then suddenly she would play the harlot, her wanton behavior embarrassing Albert and Erdman and confusing poor little ten-year-old Arvid.

Anna glanced up at Erdman and screamed in delight. "My baby boy! Where have you been all this time Erdman? Come dance with your ma. I want to dance!" She threw her arms around Erdman and attempted to dance to the music blaring on the radio. An outsider would mistake her behavior for drunkenness, but Erdman knew that at least drunkenness would wear off after a few hours and Anna could continue like this for days on end. Erdman tried to dance with her as he knew she would throw a fit if she were denied anything in this state of mind. Erdman looked over her shoulder at his father who had the bottle of bourbon and was pouring himself another drink. Albert nodded at Erdman to get a glass from the cupboard and join him.

"Anna, I think Erdman will want some of that pie you were making. When is it going to be finished, Honey?" Albert was trying to divert Anna's attention from their son much as one would show a small child a new toy to distract them.

"Oh, my gracious! The pie! Shame on you for making me come over there to you to perform my wifely duties when I need to finish this here pie for my baby boy!" Anna winked at her husband, patted Erdman's cheek, and spun away from her son towards the counter where the mess of utensils, flour, and fruit was strewn everywhere. Erdman walked to the cupboard, took down a glass and joined his father at the kitchen table. Albert took the glass and poured a generous serving of the bourbon, handing it back to Erdman.

"I even gave a small nip of this stuff to the lad before sending him off to his bed," Albert whispered as he glanced towards his wife across the kitchen. "I thought it might help him to fall asleep and stay asleep through all of the noise she makes. I remember doing that for you when you were a lad too." Albert sighed as he poured another glassful for himself. "Poor Edwin is hiding somewhere in the barn after your ma lit into him for simply walking into the kitchen as she was 'doing her wifely duties' as she so delicately puts it. I am afraid that I will have to hire another farm hand if she scares this one away like the others. At least she doesn't seem to be attracted to Edwin like some of the others. That's always bad business to deal with, I tell ya."

Albert pushed the half empty bottle towards Erdman, leaned back in his chair and continued to sip the deep rich amber liquid.

Albert continued to watch his wife flit about the kitchen, spilling ingredients more than mixing them together as she sang heartily to the music on the radio. His speech began to show the effects of the several glasses of bourbon he had already consumed. Albert raised his glass, "To bourbon whiskey, amber liquid, sweet and dear, not as sweet as a woman's lips, but a darn bit more sincere," he quoted. Albert chuckled to himself over the toast's appropriateness to his own troublesome marriage.

The events of the evening coupled with seeing his parents stuck in this recurring interval of pandemonium pricked at the underlying rage Erdman had experienced earlier with Clara. He knew that there should be some feeling of love for his own mother and yet shutting all the emotions off had served him best throughout his formative years. The only emotion strong enough to break through his long-established barrier was rage and he took his example from Albert in subduing it with alcohol. Perhaps if he allowed her to, Clara could learn to help him subdue the rage as well. She seemed so willing to love him even after tonight.

The thought of Clara reminded him of the promised love letter. Erdman stood and walked to a small desk in the corner. He removed some paper and a pencil, returning to the kitchen table with them. He poured another glass of bourbon for himself as he did his best writing of love letters after consuming strong drink in excess.

"Oh, Erdie! Are you writing another letter to that sweet girl of yours at Gale? What is her name? That's right, her name is Luanne; such a fine girl from a fine family." Anna screeched from the counter area where she still stood. She was nowhere closer to making a pie than when she had started, but it kept her happy and occupied for the time being.

"Yeah, Ma. Fine girl," Erdman shouted towards Anna. "If you like a girl with a face like a horse and the teeth to match," Erdman whispered to his father seated next to him. "Her laugh even sounds more like a whinny," he added. "Go ahead and go on up to bed, Pa. I will stay up with her tonight. You're looking beat tired."

"Thanks, Erd boy. I might just do that. Just be sure to keep turning the oven off if she lights it so's there's not another fire." Albert stood and patted his son on the back. He blew a kiss towards his wife and stumbled towards the stairs. Anna was so engrossed in her culinary endeavor she did not even notice that he left the room.

Erdman often wrote love letters to various girls including the Luanne his mother had mentioned. Luanne was from a wealthy family in Minnesota and after meeting her at their first year Convocation at Gale College, Anna had been insistent that she was the perfect match for Erdman. Luanne was very shy, painfully so, and usually Erdman was just expected to escort her to various social functions. He would write to her occasionally when he returned home to keep in her good graces. Luanne always answered him immediately, her letters just as painfully awkward as she was, but it was a good indication that there were no other suitors vying for her.

Clara was an entirely different matter altogether. Erdman found that in the last two months, he enjoyed much of the time that he had spent with her. She was beautiful but that wasn't it; he had dated many beautiful girls before her. Her beauty came from within her as well. She seemed willing to love him no matter what happened. Erdman knew that he should have run off after the first night that he took her home. He didn't want to feel anything for Clara or any other woman ever because look where that had left his father, but with Clara he just couldn't seem to help himself. He put the pencil to paper,

My dearest C,

It is often hard for a fellow to tell what is in his heart. Sometimes the fellow must show his love in other ways. It is when I hold you and kiss your sweet lips that my heart can show how I truly feel. Sometimes this love can be overwhelming, and this same fellow is not able to control his passion for you. Never doubt anymore my beautiful Bright Eyes how deep and abiding both my love and passion for you are.

Though it has been only a few hours since we parted, I long to hold you once again and show more of the depths of my love for you. I only wish that we could have stayed together where we were, laying in each other's arms until morning light. There will be a day in our future when we will not have to part ways but stay together always.

Soon I must go back to school and I cannot go without seeing you again, to show you my love and receive your love to take with me. I will stop by on Thursday night after I stop in Seneca. Leave a light in your window if you are willing to come to me once again or you will leave me as brokenhearted as any fellow can be.

Yours ever and always,

E

Erdman folded the letter carefully and put it in an envelope. It concerned him more than a little that perhaps some of his letter was true and not the made-up fodder he usually offered a conquest. He would have to guard himself so that he would never fall into the same trap that continued to plague his father.

He looked up to see Anna sitting on the floor against the counter. She was fast asleep. Erdman crossed over to her, picked her up, and carried her to the couch in the parlor, covering her with an afghan. He laid down on the floor in front of the couch so that Anna would have to step on him to get off the couch waking him in the process. Erdman shut his eyes knowing he had only a couple of hours of rest before she started again.

Chapter 10

THURSDAY, SEPTEMBER 3, 1925 – SENECA, WISCONSIN

The midday sun radiated through the freshly washed windows of Christ and Dena Olson's farmhouse on Stoney Point Road. Every window had been opened to embrace the fresh air and the remnants of the summer's heat, fluttering the white flour sack curtains in the breeze. The kitchen was in a state of repose between the bustle of breakfast and lunch. Christ and the boys had gone to the field hours ago, Cornelia and Inga had left for the schoolhouse, and Dena and Emma went to visit a sick neighbor after preparing a lunch of chicken and dumplings to simmer on the back of the stove.

Clara and Alice had been left with instructions to make some of Clara's famous fattigmann cookies. As Clara gathered the ingredients and utensils, Alice disappeared up the staircase. Alice returned a few minutes later carrying a bundle which she took out the side door towards the wash tubs set up in the yard. Clara followed her sister out to the yard wondering why Alice had left the kitchen so abruptly and not returned. She found Alice furiously scrubbing the dress Clara had worn two nights before on her date with Erdman. Alice looked up from her labor to see Clara standing there watching.

"I think the dress will come out alright. I mended the sweater yesterday while you slept. I had to cut up the underclothing because those stains were just too bad…" Alice trailed off as she resumed her scrubbing on the washboard. "It's good that you took to your bed with a headache yesterday so that Ma didn't ask too many questions. You still look a little pale today. Why don't you go in the house and start the cookies? You don't have to watch this, Clara" Alice rubbed at her face with the back of her hand, and Clara could not tell if it was from the sweat forming on her brow or the unbidden tears she could hear in Alice's voice.

"I'm ready to tell you now." Clara's simple statement caused Alice to stop her scrubbing and look up at her sister. Alice's eyes softened and her lip trembled. She nodded at Clara and held the dress up to the sunlight to examine it one more time. Alice took the dress to the clothesline and hung it among the other clothes already drying in the breeze. She came to take Clara's hand and led her back into the house.

Together the sisters set about the task of mixing the ingredients, rolling out the dough, cutting each cookie, frying them in the oil already heated on the stove, and finally sprinkling them with powdered sugar as they dried on cheesecloth. They worked together quietly each knowing that one would have a hard time with telling and the other would have a hard time with hearing, but they were sisters and best friends always.

As they finished the last of the cookies Clara took her pointer finger, pressed it in the remaining powdered sugar, and dabbed the sugar on Alice's nose. They had done this ever since they were little girls and were first allowed to help Dena and their older sisters make the cookies. Alice knew this was another way that Clara used to express the words, "I love you." Alice pressed her finger in the powdered sugar and dabbed it on Clara's nose in response, "I love you too."

The two sisters made their way up the stairs to their bedroom. Alice quietly closed the two windows in the room. No one else need ever hear what Clara was about to say. Alice sat beside her sister on the edge of the bed and waited patiently for her to begin.

"This wasn't what it looked like to you," Clara began slowly as she kept her gaze trained on the braided rug beneath their feet. "I love Erdman very much and I know that he loves me too."

Alice vehemently shook her head. "No, people who love you don't hurt you! They don't leave marks on you! They don't…"

"Please just hear me out, Alice. This is difficult for me to explain because of my behavior that led up to what happened. I kissed him boldly in public, Alice. I led him to believe that I wanted much more than I was willing to allow. He had stopped when I asked him to stop. It was my idea to continue, but I didn't know what to do because it was my first time. I think it was just so frustrating for him that his reactions became rougher than he intended." Clara continued to stare down at the rug as the tears flowed down her cheeks. "I thought it would be so romantic, but it wasn't. I just want him to love me." Clara's voice broke as her tears flowed harder.

"So, you want me to believe that what happened to you is your fault?" Alice asked incredulously. "Clara, no matter what you did leading up to this, he doesn't have the right to hurt you or even make you feel that you must prove your love to him somehow. You remember Mrs. Severson down the road? It is well known that Mr.

Severson hits her when he has been drinking. Do you honestly think that it is her fault that he hits her?" Alice took Clara's chin and gently lifted it so that she could look into her eyes.

"No, of course it is not her fault." Clara replied slowly. "I just meant that I want you to understand. I love Erdman and now that we have had relations, I intend to marry him someday. You do not see all the times that he is kind and gentle to me. I know that I am lacking in understanding certain things, but I will learn, and we will be fine."

"Clara, he does not hurt you or misuse you because **you** are lacking something. He does it because **he** is lacking something. I do not want to see my favorite sister become the lady that everyone knows is being hurt, but no one ever does anything about it, because we don't talk about such things. You know that I would do anything in this world for you. Please don't ask me to stand by and do nothing." Alice stood and walked to the window, looking out on the farmyard below them.

"Alice, please listen to me. I love him with all my heart. I am asking for your promise to be silent about this one time and nothing else. I know that he can change and that we will be very happy together. Will you do this for me?" Clara pleaded. Alice's response was a nod as she continued to look outside. She did not think it was her imagination that she felt a sudden chill go down her spine even though she had closed the windows.

Later that afternoon when lunch had been served and all the dishes had been washed, Christ announced that he was going into town for some nails while the boys returned to the field. Alice asked him if she could have a ride to her friend Sophie Torgeson's house. She would stay for the evening in Seneca and have Bernard return for her later that night.

Christ smiled at Clara, "Would you care to ride along and keep your old pa out of trouble? Or maybe you are still feeling a mite poorly and you would rather just rest?" He looked at Clara with obvious concern on his face and then to Dena to see what she thought. Dena quietly assessed Clara and nodded at Christ with her approval.

Clara knew that she needed to reassure her parents that she was fine. "Of course, I will go with you Papa, but I don't know of anyone alive who can keep you out of trouble." Clara replied. Even Dena laughed in amusement as she settled into her rocking chair with a pile of mending at her side. It was comforting to Clara to see little things like her mother rocking in her chair with busy hands still at work and the occasional humming of a tune. Clara knew that Dena would remain there working until the girls came home from school, the boys came in from the field, and she and her father returned from their errands.

Christ dropped Alice off first and drove into downtown Seneca. He would drop Clara off at the Post Office and then she would meet him at the general store. He stopped the wagon in front of the Post Office so that Clara could jump down safely. Clara leaned over and kissed Christ's weathered cheek, "Thank you, Papa." She jumped down quickly and walked away. Though Clara was the most affectionate of his children, she surprised him at times with her random expressions. Christ chuckled to himself and continued on his way.

Clara asked the young man behind the counter for the family's daily mail. He smiled at her as he handed her the packet of various missives. Clara smiled back at him out of politeness and started to look through the individual pieces of mail. In the middle of the pile was an envelope addressed to her with familiar handwriting. Erdman had written the letter he had promised, and he must have done so right away for her to receive it so promptly. Clara was certain that it was just as she had tried to convince Alice; Erdman loved her, and they would get married and be happy together. Suddenly Clara realized she was still standing in front of the young postal clerk, beaming at him and she had missed most of what he was saying to her.

"I am not from the area and I would love to have someone show me where the best places to picnic would be," the postal clerk added hopefully. "Perhaps sometime if you," he began. She really did have to pay more attention to things, because now she needed to escape from this conversation in the most gracious way possible.

"Why I do know of several young ladies who know the local geography much better than I do," Clara interjected before he could finish his question to her. "I would be very happy to suggest a group get together and introduce you to them sometime very soon." She promised half-heartedly. She could tell by the look on his face that had not been what he intended at all. She excused herself quickly and left the post office promising herself to not engage in a conversation when she was not paying attention again.

Clara walked to the end of the block and found a small bench. She knew that Christ would be trading stories with some of the other farmers at the general store, so she would have time to read her letter from Erdman. Her hands shook slightly as she opened the envelope and smoothed the page out on her lap. What she read left her breathless as she saw the words of love and his intentions to marry her right there on the page. He wanted her to meet him that night, to leave a signal for him that she would come to him, to show him that she loved him and trusted him. They would be together always.

Clara folded the letter carefully and put it in her pocketbook for safekeeping. She would add this letter to her most treasured things as it was the promise for her future she had hoped for. She was glad that she had put some extra pin money in her purse so she could go and buy something pretty to wear when she met Erdman later that night.

Chapter 11

LATER THAT EVENING –
SENECA, WISCONSIN

That September evening was cool with small gusts of wind that pushed the leaves from the trees and swirled them around on the streets in front of Grace Tolefson's hotel. The establishment was respectable enough to house guests on the first floor and daring enough to host a pool hall and a dance hall on the second floor. Many of the local youth ignored the repeated warnings of the Lutheran ministers about the combined evils of dancing and drinking, enjoying the entertainment of dancing inside the hotel and the purchasing of illegal liquor outside on the street.

Since the Volstead Act of 1919 (which led to the 18th Amendment in 1920) made the distribution and purchase of alcohol illegal, there was a new form of salesman who profited enormously from the sale of illicit liquor. Rum was brought in from the Caribbean, whiskey was brought down from Canada, and many local entrepreneurs had the corn mash, copper wires, and homemade stills to make gin. Gangsters like Al Capone in Chicago made this industry look rather glamorous and very profitable. Young Erdman Olson envisioned himself as one of these liquor distribution magnates in Crawford County.

Erdman's Ford Roadster was a common sight on the streets of the various small towns up and down the Mississippi River. He had established a growing trade of selling synthetic gin from several nearby stills to the thirsty lads who sought his enterprise for their procurement. There was even the occasional thirsty young lass who bought his liquor and kept it in a small flask held on by a garter hidden under her skirt. Erdman had found plenty of his former conquests this way; he attributed his acts as a libertine as a necessary part of conducting business.

Erdman parked his car in the back alley adjacent to the Tolefson hotel/dance hall. He always began by offering a drink to the young men who traveled towards the hotel so they would know his hooch was quality. He then followed up by making his presence known in the dance hall, flirting and dancing with the local ladies. Men and women would then follow him back to the roadster in small groups to make their purchases. He had a revolver in the trunk of the car to dissuade anyone thinking of robbing him of the large amounts of cash that accumulated.

There were fewer people than normal on the streets of Seneca this evening, probably due to the wind that had increased as the evening began. Erdman decided to join the company of revelers inside the dance hall earlier than usual. This was more than acceptable to him as he anticipated meeting Clara after he had conducted his business. Erdman found himself whistling as he took the stairs to the second floor two steps at a time.

A popular dance band from across the river in Iowa was set up and playing to a large crowd in the dance hall. The sounds of shuffling feet and loud laughter mixed with the music greeted Erdman as he opened the door. He glanced about the room to find familiar faces as well as a few new ones. Erdman saw a group of pretty, young ladies sitting around one of the tables on the perimeter of the room. These ladies had attracted a large group of admirers and Erdman knew this group would prove advantageous to his sales.

Erdman sauntered over to join the group. He heard a vaguely familiar voice among the crowd as she flirted with several of the young men nearest to her. There was laughter for a moment and then the storyteller continued.

"I tell you that it is a serious dilemma for me and my sisters. Imagine having big brothers who are not only protective of their sisters, but the one is also a decorated war hero for having shot so many men in the Great War. One look at my brother has most young men running for the hills! What is a girl to do for entertainment?" Alice Olson sat laughing among many admirers telling her woeful tale. She turned slightly, when she noticed Erdman, another brilliant smile illuminated her face.

"Speaking of entertainment! If it isn't my sister's charming beau, Erdman. He usually has some entertainment of the liquid nature lying about." Alice laughed and turned back to a young man who had leaned in close to her pretty face. "Perhaps you had better get some of that liquid entertainment as it also suffices for courage, Darling." she cooed at him. "It is my war hero brother Bernard who shall collect me this evening and heaven help the fool who trifles with his sisters." Alice threw her head back in laughter, and the rest of the group joined her. Erdman joined in the laughter as some of the group started to rise and exit out to the alley with him. As Erdman held the door open for the group, he noticed that Alice was looking intently at him. She was not laughing anymore.

Erdman was in the roadster heading out of Seneca for Stoney Point Road only thirty minutes later. Alice's endorsement had proven very successful for the evening, but her words were also disquieting. Erdman felt a small sense of relief that he had sold his supply before Bernard Olson had appeared to fetch his sister. He did not need the inconvenience of protective older brothers about. He reassured himself with the thought of the revolver hidden among the blankets in the trunk. There was not an older brother anywhere that could match a pistol being brandished at an opportune moment. Erdman being a subjugator himself considered his mindset of cowardly domination to be the foremost disposition of others as well.

As Erdman slowed the car for the left-hand turn from Highway 27, a sudden thought overtook him. What if Clara had told her family about what had happened two nights before? What if her brothers were waiting for him rather than Clara? His first impulse was to find a driveway and turn the car around as the sides of the road were often muddy and it was easy to get stuck if one drove off the road. He realized with chagrin that the nearest driveway was the one leading to Clara's farmhouse. He slowed down even more and then he saw it: a bright light from the second story window of the house. Clara had set out the signal and she would come to meet him soon.

Erdman pulled the car into the driveway and turned off his headlights turning them back on and then back off quickly. He had given his signal to her as well and now all he had to do was wait for Clara. He decided to go and get the revolver from the trunk and put it on the floor of the rumble seat for an added sense of security. He had just returned to the driver's seat when Clara appeared next to the car. Her sweet smile assured Erdman that there was no threat of irate brothers in his future.

Erdman hopped out of the car to open Clara's car door. He embraced her as she approached him to enter the car. "Someone has a pretty new hat that goes with her beautiful brown eyes," he whispered in her ear as he held her close to him. "I missed you, Clara," Erdman declared and realized that he was telling her the truth.

Erdman had decided yesterday to take Clara to a beautiful spot overlooking the Mississippi River near Ferryville. It was a fifteen-mile drive to the overlook. As Erdman drove, he took Clara's hand in his own and held it. She was quiet although she would laugh at his stories and smile at him when he glanced her way. She was not as flirtatious as she had been the last time they were together, but at least she was not crying as she had been when he drove her home two nights ago.

They arrived at the outlook situated upon one of the bluffs just as the sun was setting. The brilliant rays of the sun radiated off the glistening water of the river, and they sat in silence watching the sun disappear behind the horizon. The October moon was already high in the sky and was almost full; it replaced the brilliance of the sun with a glow of its own. Erdman watched as Clara looked up at the sky in rapt attention to the beauty displayed. He reached behind her in the rumble seat and brought out a bouquet of fall wildflowers he had gathered just for her. It wasn't his usual habit to pay such close attentions to a girl that he had already sullied as he did not want them to form attachments to him, but he had felt compelled to gather the flowers including some plumes of purple mountain pampas grass. He had remembered a day earlier that summer; Clara had walked through a field of the tall purple grass touching the plumes with her outstretched hands, with a delightful smile on her face.

Clara gasped in surprise at his offering. She took the bundle of flowers and daintily poked and prodded at it for a few moments to make a stunning arrangement out of it. She selected a single black-eyed Susan from the bunch, broke off the stem, and put it in the buttonhole on Erdman's lapel. Her beautiful large brown eyes were luminous in the moonlight as she leaned towards him and kissed him.

"Thank you. They are so beautiful. I have never had anyone give me flowers before. I love them, Erdman, and I love you." Clara reached up to remove her hat, carefully placing it along with the flowers in the backseat. She turned back towards him and continued, "I had never done other things before either and I am sorry if it made you upset because I didn't know what to do. I want to make you happy, Erdman. I am willing to learn if you are willing to teach me what you want." She looked bashful and desirous at the same time.

Erdman knew that this should be his exit cue. She had put her trust in him, and her feelings of love for him were genuine. She had marriage and a life together in mind. He should leave her now and never look back. Erdman's only response was a long slow sweet kiss that held promises of his own. Only Clara brought out this gentleness in him and he was not willing to part with that or her just yet.

Several hours later Erdman and Clara sat in the driveway of her farmhouse on Stoney Point Road. There was a tenderness between them now that had not been present before. He held her in his arms as he promised to write to her every day while he was away at school. The tears she shed this time were for his pending departure. Erdman wiped her tears away and replaced them with gentle kisses and whispered promises of their future together. Finally, he reluctantly gathered her hat and her flowers from the back seat and placed them in her arms.

"I love you, Clara. Wait for me to come back to you. When we get married, we won't have to say any more goodbyes." Erdman kissed her one last time before Clara turned to walk towards the farmhouse.

Erdman got back in the roadster and backed out of the driveway. He turned the car to travel back down Stoney Point Road and out to Highway 27 towards his home in Rising Sun. As he glanced in his rearview mirror, had he really seen the figure of Clara's brother, Bernard, standing in the road watching him drive away or was it just his imagination?

Chapter 12

SUNDAY, SEPTEMBER 6, 1925 – RISING SUN, WISCONSIN

Erdman sat at the kitchen table finishing a letter he was writing to Clara. It was almost evening and the hired hand Edwin was designated to drive Erdman back to Galesville to begin his second year of college. It would be a three-hour round trip for Edwin who had already been working almost non-stop for days helping Albert and Erdman harvest the tobacco, but Edwin welcomed the relief from the chaos that Anna's latest woes had brought on the household.

It had begun on Friday morning when Anna had found the flower on Erdman's discarded jacket. Anna had questioned Erdman closely as to who had put the flower there and when Erdman tried to evade answering, she flew into a rage. She reminded Erdman that he was practically engaged to dear Luanne and the time to see other girls had come to an end. She had screamed and cried, trying every form of manipulation within her repertoire, he had still withheld the unfortunate girl's name. Erdman knew that in her current state Anna might bring some form of harm to Clara. He did not anticipate that Anna could do any physical harm, but she was an expert at character assassination with anyone with whom she found herself at odds.

Anna had reduced herself to such a state that by Sunday she had taken to her bed telling Erdman that she never wanted to see him again. Albert had sent young Arvid to Anna's brother who lived on the farm adjacent to theirs, sparing the boy some of the more violent outbursts. Anna had broken numerous items by throwing them at Erdman and Albert. She had clawed at Albert with her fingernails when he tried to restrain her from hurting herself or the others. Albert's face still bore the angry red marks she had left there.

Albert sat down at the table next to Erdman. He pulled several twenty-dollar bills from his pocket and laid them on the table beside his son. This was his typical method of alleviating his guilt and remorse about the abuse Erdman had just endured at the hands of his own mother. "I figured there will be some new clothes and such for you to buy. I have set up a checking account so that you can also write checks when you need more." Albert explained. "Make sure your ma doesn't come back down here to see you writing a letter to your gal. I think we have all heard enough on that subject."

Erdman sealed the envelope and put it in his coat pocket. "Pa, why don't we try a hospital somewhere for her or at least hire a nurse to take care of her? I am afraid if we don't do something soon, she will be the death of us." Erdman picked up the money, putting it in his pants pocket; he was accustomed to his father's form of apology.

"You know as well as I do that last time we tried hiring a nurse your ma just about killed the poor soul, thinking I had replaced her with a second wife. As tempting a thought as it might be, I can not just stick your ma off in an asylum either. For one thing, her family continues to send large amounts of money to me for her care and for another, she would most likely end herself if we sent her away. Try to recall her good days and try to forget her bad ones." Albert rose from his chair and looked out the kitchen window at Edwin loading Erdman's suitcases into the car.

"Just make sure your gal understands that your ma must not know about the two of you. I ain't telling you not to sow your wild oats while you can cause goodness knows that is what I did at your age. Just be careful not to get any gal in the family way because that is also what I did and here you are and here we are too." Albert had just blamed Erdman's existence for the lifetime of misery his father now faced.

Erdman did not bother to reply as he had heard this so many times before. The emotions that threatened to overtake the barrier he had set against them pummeled him from every direction. Rage led the assault and Erdman knew that he needed to leave before he followed Anna's example of succumbing to them. He nodded at his father and left the house without another word.

"You drive." Erdman barked at Edwin who was standing beside the roadster waiting for him. "I need a drink." He went to the shed, bringing back several more bottles of gin for their road trip. He climbed in the passenger side and opened the first bottle, taking a large drink. Edwin prayed silently that Erdman would drink enough to fall asleep quickly.

Erdman drank half of the bottle of gin before he fell into a drunken sleep. He sought the numbing effects of the liquor to evade the thoughts of rejection and bitterness that battered his wounded mind. Once the drink had begun to take effect his thoughts shifted to something much more pleasant; like a shining beacon she drove the darkness of his mind back to the recesses where it belonged. He loved the thought, the feel, the sight of her. And so, in his drunken sleep, Erdman poured out his heart for Clara. He relived their intimacy and her willingness to love him. What Erdman did not realize was that he was speaking it aloud so that Edwin could hear.

Erdman had begun with a few intelligible mumbles that assured Edwin the alcohol was insuring a more pleasant drive. Then Erdman kept repeating one word, Clara. Edwin winced at the reference to the one girl who had captivated him from the moment he met her. Erdman then began drifting in and out of sleep, speaking out the very details of his intimate relationship with Clara. Each word caused an increase of pain to Edwin until he felt he could not endure any more. Edwin even considered stopping Erdman from ever speaking another word; he could overcome this drunken sop in his current state and dump his lifeless body in the river that was just to the side of Highway 35. Surely anything dumped in the mighty Mississippi would never be seen again. Then Edwin realized the utter depravity of his dark thoughts. Edwin knew he could not harm this drunken young man snoring beside him, but he could not allow Erdman to ever hurt Clara again.

Chapter 13

NOVEMBER 19, 1925 –
FAIRVIEW, WISCONSIN

Clara had spent the time since Erdman had left for Gale College beginning to prepare for their future together. She started a quilt for their own bed in their own home; this was a standard practice for young ladies who were about to be betrothed. Dena, Emma, and Alice all understood the meaning of what Clara was doing even though it had been overlooked by her father. Christ only noticed that the one daughter who had longed to be outside doing the chores with him now much preferred to stay indoors working on more feminine pursuits. While he was slightly saddened by this transformation, Christ knew that it was the inevitable conclusion of Clara's childhood and the emergence of her young womanhood.

While Dena had been hoping and praying for this change in Clara's pursuits, she was now more than a little concerned as to why this sudden change had occurred. Dena was secretly glad that Clara's beau Erdman was far away in Galesville. She hoped that one of the local boys would soon catch Clara's eye and take her attention away from Erdman's pursuit of her. The boy was very persistent as hardly a day went by that Clara did not receive a letter from him in the mail. Clara would secret the missive off to her room and when she returned, she would be in almost a trance-like state of bliss as she sat and worked on the quilt for hours on end. Dena knew that she should be happy for Clara but her concerns for this daughter overshadowed most of her joy about the transformation.

Dena had spoken with a few of the ladies in the church and several had suggested allowing Clara to "hire out"; a young unmarried lady would stay with families in need of a caretaker for their young children while the mother of the household was recuperating from childbirth. Clara could then learn the rigors of taking care of children and running a household. It was often during this "hiring out" that a young woman like Clara would meet many of the local boys who were seeking a wife. Clara would even receive wages for her efforts. Dena found a nice family in desperate need of help in the nearby town of Fairview. It was decided that Clara would live with them for a month or so.

So, at the beginning of November Clara had moved in with the Lars Bjornstad family, including Lars, his wife Birgit, ten-year old son Harald, eight-year old son Jorg, five-year old daughter Rebekka, and newborn twins Karl and Karina. Birgit Bjornstad had not been able to carry a baby to full term for several years after Rebekka's birth and the doctor had fully expected to lose Birgit and her twins in childbirth. Clara was extremely busy taking care of the recovering mother, the newborn twins, and the rest of the household.

Clara embraced the challenge that she faced. She had always loved babies and children and she had a natural way about her that endeared her to them as well. Clara soon had the Bjornstad household settled into a well-managed routine that amazed the family and the ladies of the church community. Even the gruff old country doctor praised Clara's abilities, telling anyone who would listen that Clara was probably named after Clara Barton because she was such a good nurse. The doctor encouraged Clara to pursue a nursing career, but Clara already knew what she wanted for her future, a life with Erdman.

It had already been almost a month since Clara had come to stay with the Bjornstads. Clara had settled Birgit in the rocking chair with the babies in a basket close by. She was busy preparing a stew for the family's evening dinner while putting pans of bread dough to rise on the back of the stove. Lars had taken the day to go to Prairie du Chien, so Clara was to take a lunch for Harald and Jorg to the nearby Tully School at noon. Lars had left a small buggy ready for Clara's use and little Rebekka had the important task of helping her ma for the fifteen minutes that Clara would be gone.

Clara packed the metal lunch pail with sandwiches, fruit, and cookies for the boys. She checked on Birgit and the babies and set off for the mile trip to the country schoolhouse. As Clara approached the school, she saw the schoolhouse door open and the children walking out for lunchtime. She had arrived just in time as the boys only had twenty minutes to eat and then run off some of their energy in the schoolyard. Harald came up to hold the horse and tether it to the hitching post as Clara climbed down from the buggy. Little Jorg came to hug Clara shyly and get his lunch from the pail. Harald came over to thank Clara for the lunch and take his from the pail as well.

Clara noticed a young boy standing beside a tree just a few feet away. He was looking wistfully at Harald and Jorg enjoying their lunches. Clara whispered to Harald, "Who is that boy standing by the tree? Doesn't he have any lunch to eat?"

"His name is Arvid Olson. He is a real nice boy. He usually has one of the best lunches of anyone but sometimes his ma forgets him. The rest of us make sure to share with him when that happens." Harald motioned for Arvid to join him. Harald handed the boy half of his sandwich. Arvid accepted the offered meal and happily began to eat it. Clara made up her mind that there would be an extra piece of dessert that night for Harald because of his generosity.

Clara smiled at Arvid. "Be sure to check the lunch pail as I always pack extra fruit and cookies. Have a good day at school, boys. Harald, please make certain you bring the lunch pail home with you so I can fill it with more cookies for you and your friend tomorrow." Suddenly it occurred to Clara, this boy was probably Erdman's little brother as their home was less than two miles away. Was Erdman's mother ill and in need of Clara's help? She determined that she would ask Erdman about it in her next letter.

As Clara turned towards the buggy Arvid took ahold of her hand. "Thank you. I hope you will bring lunch to Harald and Jorg again, you have very pretty eyes." Clara smiled at Arvid and squeezed his hand, then she climbed into the buggy. She needed to return to Birgit and the babies and finish the evening meal. While she drove back to the Bjornstad farm she formulated a plan to have Harald invite Arvid for some boys fun next Saturday afternoon. It would be nice to get to know this sweet boy who would be her little brother someday. She couldn't wait to tell Erdman all about her plan.

Later that afternoon as Clara rocked one of Birgit's beautiful babies, she decided to tell Birgit about Arvid and discuss her plan. Birgit listened carefully nodding her head. "Yes, Harald and Jorg have told me about several times that Arvid had nothing for lunch. I am so glad that Harald shared what he had. We do not have the money that the Olsons do, but we can be rich in kindness. Please pack an extra sandwich for the next couple of days as usually this happens several days in a row."

Clara was shocked to hear this. "Has Arvid's mother been ill so that she can't help him with his lunch? Is there something I could do to help her? Maybe I should go to visit her?"

"I think that Mrs. Olson has troubles. I don't like to repeat the stories that some people tell so I won't say any more than that. Mr. Olson seems very nice. He even helped my Lars with some extra work when I was so sick. Arvid is a sweet boy, he would be welcome to come here anytime. I am just not certain that his parents will allow him to visit us. We can try and see if they will. Clara, you are rocking that baby to sleep before she has eaten, and we can't have that." Birgit laughed as she handed Karl to Clara and took Karina to her breast. "You will be such a good mama someday, Clara."

Clara patted little Karl's back until he burped, sighed, and drifted off to sleep. She imagined herself holding Erdman's baby someday in a house of their own. She decided that out of all her dreams that one was her very favorite. Perhaps in tonight's letter she would share that dream with Erdman as well.

Later that night after the children were all put to bed and the chores were done Clara sat down to write a letter to Erdman.

My dearest Erdman,

I was so happy to receive your letter today. It is good to hear the happenings that keep you busy at school. I would love to visit you there someday and see for myself all the wonderful things that you describe. I am anxiously awaiting your visit home for Christmas. I want you to hold me in your arms once again and tell me more about our future together. Yesterday I took the boys their lunch at Tully School and I met your little brother Arvid. He is sweet just like his big brother. He even told me that I have pretty eyes, a lot like his brother I guess. Harald mentioned that your mother may be unwell. I do not want to alarm you about this. I wondered if I should visit your mother to offer her my help. I want her to know that I will love her like she was my own mother and I wish to help her like a daughter. Please advise me as to what you wish for me to do.

Just this day as I sat holding one of Birgit's sweet little babies, I imagined holding our own babies someday. I felt such a love for you and such a hope for our life together. Please know I love you more each day. I cannot wait for you to return to show you just how much. I will see you in my dreams this night and every night until we are together again.

With my love,

Clara

Chapter 14

NOVEMBER 22, 1925 –
GALESVILLE, WISCONSIN

*E*rdman had spent a busy Sunday escorting Luanne to church and then to a poetry reading. He continued to write letters to Clara professing his love for her and promising her a future together. When Erdman had first returned to Gale College in September, he had considered breaking all romantic ties with everyone except Clara, but as time wore on, he returned to his old habits including his weekly liaisons with Lilla.

Erdman had met Lilla at a speakeasy in Galesville during his first month of his freshman year. She was unlike any other girl he had ever met; Lilla swore and drank like a sailor, she lied when it was convenient for her, she enjoyed intimacy with Erdman, but she never asked him about other girls. Lilla kept company with other men as well and she expected Erdman not to object. For the most part Lilla was perfect for Erdman and initially he imagined himself in love with her, but after a time it bothered him that she did not expect his faithfulness, nor could he expect hers. Had Erdman thought more about the matter he might have discovered that he could not love Lilla because she was too much like him.

Erdman had taken Luanne home after paying all his due respects. Then he headed straight for the speakeasy to meet Lilla. After they had danced and drank too much, they ended up in Erdman's dorm room. Erdman had to bribe his roommate to leave for a couple of hours, but it was an arrangement that had worked well for over a year. Lilla always managed to sneak into his room without any issues; Erdman suspected it was because she had other male friends in his dormitory, but he knew that she would neither confirm nor deny it if he asked.

Erdman opened his eyes to find himself face down on his bed. He often fell asleep after being with Lilla, but she refused to sleep afterwards. She also refused to let him hold her in his arms or kiss her when they were finished. Erdman lifted his head to see Lilla sitting on his roommate's bed across from him. She still wore her black satin slip as she sat with a glass of gin and a cigarette in one hand and a sheet of paper in the other hand. She pursed her pretty, red lips as she read the paper and laughed to herself. She glanced up to see Erdman looking at her, leaned forward to hand him the glass of gin and the cigarette, then sat back up to continue her reading,

Erdman rolled over and sat up facing Lilla who did not speak to him as she was preoccupied with what she was doing. He rubbed his free hand through his hair, a habit he had when frustrated or concerned. While Erdman liked that Lilla was not as smothering as many girls, her callousness often irked him. He took a drink from the glass of gin and began smoking the cigarette. Lilla used her free hand to hand him an empty glass to use an ashtray. Lilla chuckled as she put the paper down beside her on the bed.

"You know you probably shouldn't lead little Miss Wholesome from down off the farm to believe that she is going to have your babies and live happily ever after. I mean it doesn't make any difference to me what you do, but that misguided little girl is offering to go take care of your poor sick mama." Lilla picked up the paper she had been reading and read aloud in a sing song voice *'I imagined holding our own babies someday. I felt such a love for you and such a hope for our life together. Please know I love you more each day. I cannot wait for you to return to show you just how much. I will see you in my dreams this night and every night until we are together again.'*

Erdman realized that Lilla had opened his most recent letter from Clara. He was instantly angry; Lilla had encroached on an area of his life where she had no dominion. He was also shocked hearing from Lilla's pouty red lips that Clara wished to have his babies; it was as if those same painted red lips that only an hour ago he found tantalizing were now vulgar, contaminating the pure thoughts of someone that Lilla could never endeavor to be. Erdman extinguished the cigarette under his foot, stood, and threw the glass of gin against the nearest wall smashing it into thousands of shards. He grabbed Lilla by the shoulders pulling her to her feet. Lilla glared defiantly at him trying to mask the fear that was now in her eyes.

Erdman shoved Lilla back onto the bed behind her. "Get your clothes and get out. You make me sick." He walked to the door, opening it, forcing Lilla to pick up her clothing in a haphazard fashion and exit the room. She left without a word as Erdman slammed the door behind her. Erdman crossed to the bed Lilla had just been sitting on and snatched up the letter to read it for himself.

In reading the entire letter he realized that Lilla's intrusion was only the beginning of his quandary; Clara wanted to go and meet his crazy she-devil of a mother.

Erdman left more cash on his roommate's bed to compensate for the damage done and hastily gathered a few of his things. His Christmas vacation would begin earlier than expected. He would catch the last bus to LaCrosse and call on Edwin to drive all night to meet him there. Erdman knew he had to get to Clara before she attempted to go and meet his mother. Clara's love for him was the one thing he needed to preserve at any cost.

Chapter 15

NOVEMBER 23, 1925 –
FAIRVIEW, WISCONSIN

It was Clara's last day with the Bjornstad family. Birgit's health was progressing steadily, and Birgit's younger sister Elsa was arriving from North Dakota the following day. Since it was the week of Thanksgiving it had been decided that Clara would return home and spend the holiday with her family. The Bjornstad children had been so sad to see Clara leave that Clara had promised Harald and Jorg she would walk to the Tully School on their lunch break to tell them goodbye. Clara would then return to the house to bid Birgit farewell and wait for Lars to take her home in the afternoon.

Clara was happy to return to her family, but she knew that she would miss Birgit and her beautiful children. She packed extra cookies in the lunch pail in case she saw Arvid and set off for the school. She had been a little surprised that she had not received a daily letter from Erdman, so she hoped that his mother had not taken a turn for the worse. Clara was sorely tempted to walk from the school to Erdman's parent's farm, but she had not heard back from Erdman and she had promised to wait for his advice on the matter.

The sun was shining, but the wind was cold with the bite of frost in the air. Each morning there was more and more frost on the grass and the trees gave the appearance of a world covered in frosting. It would not be long before the first snow. While many detested the appearance of snow and the bitter cold that accompanied it, Clara loved being outdoors in the fresh snow with air so cold it would take her breath away. She was glad that she had thought to wear her rubber boots with her heavier coat and mittens as she walked the mile to the schoolhouse.

Clara was within sight of the schoolhouse when she noticed a familiar car approaching her from the opposite direction. The car slowed down and pulled off to the side of the road. Clara could not believe her eyes as the driver's door flew open and Erdman came running towards her! How could this be? Why hadn't Erdman told her he was coming to visit? Oh no… what if something dreadful had happened to his mother? These thoughts flooded her mind in the few seconds that it took for Erdman to run to her and throw his arms around her. He peppered her face and lips with kisses as he laughed at her reaction.

"Hello, Bright Eyes! Fancy meeting the most beautiful girl in the world walking alongside the road! I was just coming to try and find you and it seems you found me." Erdman laughed as he kissed Clara again. "I have missed you so much. Where were you headed, Honey?"

Clara began to regain her sense of speech after her initial shock in seeing Erdman standing there in front of her. "How did you..? I didn't know.. Oh My! I am not making any sense at all am I? I was taking the boys some lunch at the school. Now you are here. Oh Erdman! I am so happy to see you!" Clara threw her arms around his neck and pressed her head against his warm chest. She drew back to look at him cautiously a few moments later. "I hope there hasn't been a tragedy has there?" she whispered seeking his eyes for an answer. He answered her by kissing her again slowly. "The only tragedy I have had is not being able to do this every day."

They stood alongside the road for several more minutes when Clara realized that she was still holding the metal lunch pail for Harald and Jorg's lunch and it was probably already lunchtime at the schoolhouse. Erdman took her hand in his and led her to the roadster. They hopped in the car and he turned it around heading back the way he came, towards the school. The children were in the schoolyard as they pulled up to the front. Clara waved at the Bjornstad boys as she hopped out of the car and walked quickly towards them. She did not notice that Erdman stayed behind in the car until she saw Arvid run for the driver's side of the car with a huge smile on his face. Clara gave Harald and Jorg huge hugs, letting them take extra cookies with their lunches as they said their farewells.

When Clara looked back towards the car, she saw that Erdman had gotten out and was leaning against the side panel while hugging his little brother tightly in his arms. Arvid had buried himself in Erdman's hug; Clara was touched at the sight of the two brothers. She approached them slowly and quietly, not wanting to disturb them. As she came closer it sounded as if Arvid was crying while telling his brother, "and then Ma just stayed in her bed for days and she wouldn't come out for nothing. She wouldn't even eat this time Erd, it was really bad." Clara stopped walking towards them as she realized what Arvid was saying. She knew she needed to help them if she could.

Erdman looked up to see Clara standing there. He replied to his brother, "I know, Arv. I'm home now." He adjusted Arvid in his arms to shield him from Clara seeing the boy's tears as he handed him his handkerchief. "What's this I hear about you telling my girl that she has pretty eyes? A fellow goes away for a bit and you try to take his best girl?" Erdman chuckled as he punched Arvid's shoulder slightly. Erdman looked back at Clara with a smile on his face as Arvid turned to see who Erdman was talking about. "Clara! Did you bring more cookies?" Arvid exclaimed.

It was Clara's turn to laugh, she came towards them offering the rest of the cookies in the pail to Arvid. "You know, I have been wondering about which one of the Olson brothers is more good looking than the other and I guess I still haven't decided. I think that I will need more time with both of you to come to any conclusion." She was rewarded with a smiling face covered with cookie crumbs from Arvid; he hugged her quickly and ran off to play with Harald and Jorg.

Clara held out the final cookie from the pail to Erdman." I still have a favorite Olson boy. Would he be willing to take me back to the Bjornstad's to pick up my things and then take me home?"

"Nothing would make him happier than to have the chance to be alone with you." Erdman took the proffered cookie and shoved the entire thing in his mouth. His grin made Clara's heart skip a beat. He walked over to open her car door and helped her inside.

Clara went into the Bjornstad farmhouse to say her goodbyes and collect her things while Erdman waited for her in the car. Inside the house Birgit could not help looking out the window at Clara's beau. "Och, Clara he is very handsome. He is good to you, no? You deserve only happiness min venn (my friend)" Clara hugged her friend, kissed the babies and little Rebekka goodbye and joined Erdman who had approached the house to carry her bags to the car.

Erdman drove the roadster down the long driveway leading out to Highway 27. Clara wanted to ask him to take a left-hand turn towards his home in Rising Sun instead of a right-hand turn towards her home in Seneca. She wanted to offer to help his family, but he had not brought up the subject of his mother at all. When he reached the end of the driveway he asked, "Will you be needing to get home right away?" Clara shook her head no, Erdman took a left-hand turn towards Rising Sun.

Clara thought for sure that he would tell her about his mother, why he had to come home so suddenly, and why his little brother had been crying. Erdman held her hand in his, quietly driving the few miles to Rising Sun. Clara remembered that the turn for his home on Lone Pine Lane was to the right just past the curve they had just negotiated. Erdman drove past the turn and took the next right onto the old logging road. Clara looked at Erdman with a slight frown forming across her brow. Why was he taking her here instead of to his house to help his mother?

"Don't frown, Clara. I promise we came here just to talk this time. I will be on my best behavior although it will be difficult when I have missed you so much, Love." Erdman pulled the car over in the same area as the first night they had been here. Erdman shut the engine off and reached into the back seat for a blanket. He covered Clara with the blanket tucking it in around her with meticulous care. "No sense in you catching cold out here." Erdman settled his arm around Clara's shoulders. He looked out at the copse of trees in front of him and seemed lost in his thoughts. Clara waited for him to speak, sensing that he was struggling to find the words.

"I am glad that you met my brother Arvid. He really is the best part of our family. He seems very taken with you too. He needs to have more friends around him especially when I am so far away from him." Erdman removed his fedora and traced the brim with his fingertips, contemplating how to proceed. "I received your letter about visiting my mother. I appreciate your concern for her Clara, but you need to trust me when I tell you that going to meet my parents right now would not be a good idea."

"I don't understand. Are you ashamed of me, Erdman?" Clara's eyes filled with tears. This thought had not occurred to her and the pain it brought was searing. How could they ever be married if she could not even meet his parents? "I know that my family does not have everything that yours does."

"I am not ashamed of you. I am ashamed of my own mother." Erdman blurted out the statement; it hung in the air between them for a few moments. "She has a sickness of her mind and soul that causes her to inflict pain on others. She has been this way all my life. I can try to bear it, but I could not ask you to shoulder a burden that is not yours. I came back to try and explain; to ask you to not be ashamed of me." Tears coursed down his face.

Clara reached up, gently wiping at his tears. She kissed his eyes, his cheeks, and finally his mouth with a gentleness that ripped at the barriers Erdman had placed so fiercely around his heart. He sobbed as she held him against her heart. "We have each other now Erdman. No matter what else happens, we have each other."

Later when Erdman was returning to Rising Sun after driving Clara home, he was able to reflect on what had transpired between them. He had taken a risk by telling Clara a partial truth instead of his usual bold face lies. He had needed her to understand that she had to stay away from his mother, so it seemed reasonable to tell her about Anna's unbalanced mental state. He did not anticipate Clara's reaction; instead of being repulsed by him and his family as he expected, she had held him and caressed him while whispering her love for him. There had been no further intensification of physical intimacy between them that afternoon, but Erdman had never felt such gratification from any of his former trysts.

Erdman knew that he would have a price to pay for leaving the college before completing his exams. His parents would offer to donate money for the latest charitable college foundation thereby effectively bribing the administration to let Erdman retain his standings. It was worth it to him to bring what had been a possible catastrophe to a peaceful resolution. He decided to bring a beautiful Christmas present for Clara when he returned home in late December.

Chapter 16

DECEMBER 20, 1925 – UTICA LUTHERAN CHURCH

Clara had immersed herself in assisting with the church Christmas pageant since she had returned home from the Bjornstad family. The Christmas pageant would be held on December 24th. Like the box social, it was one of the major events of the year. There would be music, decorations, recitals, food, and of course, the nativity. An evergreen tree would be cut down and brought into the church vestibule. The tree would then be decorated in candles, garland and Julekerver (small heart-shaped boxes made of paper).

Clara and Alice had volunteered to stay after the Sunday church service and help decorate the church for the coming week. Dena had packed a lunch for them, and Bernard had promised to return for them later in the afternoon. They were gathered with a group of young people looking forward to the activity of working together. Edwin Knutson had also been invited to help as he had arrived that morning for the church service unexpectedly.

The group enjoyed their noon meal together in the church basement. They decided to divide into small groups, each group having specific tasks to accomplish. Clara was put in a group with two of the other girls and Edwin. Their tasks included stringing festive red wooden beads into long garlands and then placing the garlands on the tree that the boys had already set in place. It took two people to carry each garland and place it around the tree, Clara and Edwin were paired together to complete their task. They fell into light-hearted conversation as they worked; Clara was relieved as she had not talked to Edwin since the box social and she had wondered if resuming their friendship would be awkward for them both.

Clara and Edwin had placed numerous garlands on the tree, and they were just returning to the storage room for another when Edwin pulled Clara aside. "Miss Clara, will you please follow me for a moment?" He gently took her arm and steered her towards the side door leading to a small staircase outside. Clara looked around to find that the others had gone inside to the vestibule and she and Edwin were alone. Edwin took off his suitcoat and handed it to Clara encouraging her to put it on for warmth. Clara accepted the coat, placing it just around her shoulders. She turned to Edwin with a curious look on her face.

Edwin began, "Miss Clara I have been very concerned for your well-being. I have tried several times to find a moment to speak with you. Please don't think me too forward if I ask how you are faring as of late?"

"I am well. Thank you for asking, Edwin. May I ask why you are so concerned?" Clara shivered. She didn't know if it was from the cold air or from what he might say. What was she to do if he were to declare his love for her or ask her to be his girl? She did not want to hurt Edwin, but she was very much in love with Erdman and there would never be anyone else for her.

"I am glad you are well. I have been concerned because I know that you have been seeing Erdman Olson ever since the box social and there are things about him and his family of which you are not aware. I do not wish to distress you in any way, but I felt it very important to tell you about this if you will allow me." Edwin grasped Clara's cold hand in his. She noticed he was trembling and wondered if he were cold too. She quickly removed her hand.

Clara's brown eyes flashed in anger. "I do not think there is anything for you to tell me, Edwin. I have been seeing Erdman and he has told me many things about himself and his family including some that were very difficult for him to share. I think that it is very rude of you to assume that Erdman would be dishonest with me. If you will excuse me, I am returning indoors now with the others." Clara climbed the stairs hastily, opened the side door, and entered the vestibule. Her cheeks were bright red from the cold air outside and from her outburst of anger. She realized as she stepped inside that she had forgotten to give Edwin his suitcoat in her haste to leave him. She looked across the vestibule to the group of young people staring at her entrance with Edwin just steps behind her.

Alice was the first to speak. "Clara! We were wondering where you had gone. Were you looking for more of the supplies in the shed?" Alice gave Clara a look trying to get her to agree to Alice's suggestion of where she and Edwin had been. Clara nodded and took the suitcoat off her shoulders, handing it back to Edwin without looking at him. Alice continued, "I thought so. Well, look who else was able to join us, Clara." Alice smiled as she looked to the opposite wall by the front door. Clara's gaze followed her sister's. Erdman was standing there, still in his coat and hat, staring at Clara with a grim look on his face. His look turned murderous when he saw Edwin behind her. "I will wait for you at the car." Erdman nodded to the others and left out the front door.

The group broke up soon after as the tasks had been completed. Bernard had arrived as he promised, and Alice left with him reluctantly. Clara walked to where Erdman leaned against the passenger car door of the roadster. His hat was pulled down with the brim covering his eyes; it was difficult for Clara to read the expression on his face, but she could guess that he was still upset at seeing her and Edwin together. Clara approached him and tilted the hat further back on his head by pushing the front of the brim upwards. She brushed her lips against his as she clasped her hands behind his neck. He stood still for a moment then he circled her waist with his arms drawing her closer. His responding kiss was hard and fierce, with an unspoken anger, but Clara continued with feathering light kisses across his eyes, nose and cheeks while kneading the back of his neck gently with her hands. He broke their embrace and opened the car door for her. As she sat down, she noticed that Edwin was still standing across the driveway staring at them. When Erdman entered on the driver's side, Clara purposefully reached for Erdman's coat lapels pulling him to her to kiss him again. She wanted Edwin to see what she was doing so that he would never try to poison her mind against Erdman again.

They were quiet for a few minutes as Erdman drove towards Clara's home. Erdman finally spoke. "I was trying to surprise you, but I guess I was the one to get surprised. Do you want to explain to me what you were doing with him?" He had asked a question, but Clara knew he was giving her a command.

"We had been setting garland on the tree and he asked to talk with me outside. I didn't think about being out there alone with him because I feel about him as I feel about Bernard or Adolph. It wasn't until I came back in just a few minutes later that I realized it might look like something else to others. Please believe me, Erdman. I would never do anything to shame you." Clara's eyes were voluminous as she pleaded with him.

"I do believe you Clara, but I want you to tell me what he said to you. He didn't put his hands on you, did he?" Erdman gripped the steering wheel so hard his knuckles on both hands were turning white.

"I will tell you anything you want to know but could you please pull the car over here in Mt. Sterling so that we can talk?" Clara was nervous about Erdman's reaction to her conversation with Edwin. She did not want him to be driving the car as she told him. Erdman turned onto a deserted side street in the tiny hamlet and parked the car. "Now, please tell me Clara."

"As I said, Edwin asked to speak with me. He gave me his coat because it was cold. I put it on myself, he didn't."

"So, he didn't touch you at all?" Erdman persisted.

"He did take my hand at one point because he was trying to convince me of something, but no, he did not touch me otherwise." Clara knew that she risked more of Erdman's anger, but she would not lie to him about anything. "I removed my hand because he made me angry and I told him that."

"What did he say to you?" Erdman leaned in closer to her face. His voice was almost a hiss, a small amount of his spittle leaving a spray across her face. Clara knew she needed to continue to tell him the truth.

"He tried to tell me that there are things about you that I do not know. He said it would be for my best interest if he told me about you and your family. I told him that I did not wish to hear anything that he had to say. I also told him that anything I needed to know you had already told me and that he is extremely rude. I left him standing there with his mouth open like a fish. I was so angry that I forgot to remove his coat and throw it at him, and I came back inside. I am so sorry, Erdman. I ruined your surprise and now I have made you angry with me." Clara's voice caught with emotion as she tried to suppress the sobs that shook her body.

Erdman was still silent. He put his hand under Clara's chin and lifted it so that he could look into her eyes. "I want to believe you, Clara. Don't ever go anywhere alone with him or any other man again and never ever lie to me about anything. Do you understand?" His angry eyes bored into hers and the pressure of his fingers on her chin increased.

Clara winced and nodded at him. "I promise, Erdman."

He let go of her chin and trailed his hand down her neckline. "Good. Now slide over here and give me the greeting I should have had in the first place."

Relieved, Clara slid over to him, closed her eyes, and gave way to his amorous desires.

Chapter 17

DECEMBER 23, 1925 – SENECA, WISCONSIN

The day before Christmas Eve was known in the Norwegian community as "Little Christmas". There were many chores to be done for the celebration on the 24th and in the evening the Christ Olson family would gather in the parlor to decorate their Christmas tree. Although it was a hectic time it was also one of merriment for Clara's family. Dena insisted that the first chore to be accomplished was to clean the house until everything in it shone.

Emma, Clara, and Alice had donned their aprons along with kerchiefs to wrap around their hair to keep the dust and cobwebs out. Wash buckets full of soapy water and rags were lying everywhere as they worked their way from room to room cleaning, laughing, and singing Christmas carols. Dena was hard at work in the kitchen beginning preparations for the large family feast they would have after the Christmas pageant at the church. It was traditional to make at least seven types of treats: there were Smultringer (donuts),

Sandkaker, Sirupssniper, Goro, Krumkaker, Berlinerkranser, and of course, Clara's famous Fattigmann. Cornelia and Inga were in the barn preparing a stall for the dinner for the Nisse; it was Norwegian tradition to leave a special dinner of rice porridge and beer for the little gnomes who watched over the farm and promised a good harvest and health for the following year. The Nisse would come in the night and eat their meal and leave gifts for the family. To ignore the Nisse was an omen of ill tidings.

Clara had always loved the traditions of Christmas and this year seemed even more special to her. As she cleaned, she imagined having her own home filled with her children and Erdman laughing and celebrating together. Clara had saved some of her money and sent away for a gift for Erdman. She had selected a beautiful brown silk necktie etched with gold fleur delis. She could just imagine Erdman wearing his new tie with his dapper brown suit and matching brown fedora to important business meetings. She wanted him to know how proud of him she was, and she could hardly wait for him to open his gift.

Inga came running into the house calling for Clara, "Clara! Your beau is waiting outside for you. He asked me to come and get you. He's so handsome!" Clara looked out the front window to confirm that Erdman was standing beside his car in the usual spot down the lane. Clara gave Alice a horrified look, "How can I go out there like this? I look terrible!" Clara looked at her old dress and apron and the kerchief on her head in the hall mirror. She would never have time to do the primping she normally did before Erdman arrived.

Alice laughed, "You have no idea what an absolute beauty you are do you Sister? Here put on your new coat and wrap a pretty scarf around the kerchief. Good as new." Alice said while she assisted Clara in donning the mentioned garments. "Your eyes sparkle as beautiful as always and I believe I have heard him mention your bright eyes?" Alice kissed Clara's cheek.

Inga took Clara's hand. "You are beautiful Clara. Guess what? I saw your beau holding a pretty package and I bet it is for you!" Inga finished her sentence with a squeal of excitement. Clara hugged her youngest sister and ran quickly up the stairs to her room to fetch her present for Erdman. She came back down the stairs and opened the front door. She paused to catch her breath at the door and then walked out of the door and down the lane. She was so excited that she did not notice her sisters gathered at the front window watching her walk towards Erdman. Dena did notice the group and shooed them away back to their tasks. Dena also paused long enough to say a little prayer for her Clara.

Erdman met Clara halfway down the lane. He hugged her tightly and then took her hand in his and held it to his side as they walked; it was so comforting to Clara whenever he did this. Clara touched the gift that she had stored in her coat pocket and smiled to herself in excitement. The snow crunched underneath their feet as they walked together. Erdman opened the passenger side door for Clara, and she looked at him quizzically.

"Did we make plans to go somewhere today? I am sorry for the way I look as I was in the middle of house cleaning." Clara sat down on the car seat and Erdman walked around to the driver's side without starting the car.

"No, we didn't make plans, but I couldn't wait because I brought something from Viroqua for you." He kissed Clara gently and handed her a long flat ivory satin box with a yellow ribbon tied around it. "Do you remember the ribbon?" He smiled and slid closer to her putting his arm around her.

Clara looked at the beautiful box and saw that the ribbon was the very one she had used on her box dinner the first day they met. He had taken it that evening and put it in his pocket after giving her a first kiss. Clara ran her finger across the ribbon and nodded her head. "Yes, this is my ribbon from my box dinner."

"Well, it was your ribbon, but I am pretty sure that it is mine now. I am taking it back with me after you open your gift, but I thought you might like to see that I still have it." Erdman whispered as he nuzzled the side of Clara's face. "Go ahead and open it."

Clara had never had anyone give so much thought to a gift for her. This was the Erdman that she knew and that she wanted Alice and her family to know. Suddenly she remembered his gift in her coat pocket. "Oh! I almost forgot after looking at this pretty package! I have something for you too." She shyly reached into the pocket, pulled out the tissue paper package and handed it to him. Erdman seemed surprised that she would have a gift for him. He held it in his hand and turned his head to kiss her again.

"You get to open your gift first, Clara and then I will open mine," Erdman insisted. Clara took the ribbon off the box, carefully handing it back to Erdman with a smile. He tucked it back into his pocket while continuing to watch her. She opened the box; there on a bed of ivory satin lay a beautiful pearl handle hairbrush and tiny matching hair combs for her hair. Clara gasped in surprise, her eyes filling with tears.

"This is the most beautiful thing I have ever seen. Oh, Erdman, I love my gift and I love you!" she exclaimed as she leaned to kiss him. His hand came up behind her neck as he returned her kiss. "I wanted to think of my hairbrush being the last thing to touch you at night and the first thing to touch you each morning. The combs are for you to wear so that I am with you even when I am away at school," he said quietly against her ear as he gently rubbed the back of her neck. "I love you, Clara."

"Now it is your turn to open your gift. I hope you like it." Clara nodded at the tissue wrapped package still lying on his lap. Erdman smiled at her and moved his arm from her shoulders to open the gift. The brown silk tie glided out from the tissue as he tore it away gently. He picked the tie up with both hands, holding it out in front of himself so that he could see the beautiful design. "This is the finest tie I have ever owned. I will only use it for very special occasions like our wedding day." His eyes were so earnest, and Clara thought her heart would surely burst. He had written to her many times about getting married, but this was the first time he had spoken it aloud to her. Clara could not remember ever being so happy, but she was certain that her future with Erdman would be filled with happy moments such as these.

The following day was Christmas Eve, the center of the traditional Norwegian celebration. Clara wondered more than once what Erdman might be doing as he celebrated the day with his family. She hoped for the day that they could celebrate "God Jul" together with both of their families. She knew that once she was a married woman her celebration with her father, mother, and siblings here on Stoney Point Road would never be the same, so she decided to savor this day as it might be the final one she would have with them.

The traditional rice porridge had been prepared for the family to eat with milk, cinnamon, and sugar after they returned from the church service. Clara had to arrive at church early to help everyone with the last-minute costumes for the nativity. She had put on her best black silk dress with her pearl necklace from her parents and the beautiful hair combs from Erdman. Adolph whistled at her as she entered the front hall for her coat and hat. "I thought the only angels were in the nativity." He said as he helped Clara and Alice with their coats. Clara smiled at her brother, trying to capture each one of the precious moments this day and store them as memories. Inga held Clara's hand as they walked together to the buggy where Bernard was waiting. Inga was excited as she had been chosen to be Mary in the nativity, and her happy chatter as they rode to the church warmed Clara's heart.

The interior of the Utica Lutheran Church was awash in candle-light. Clara just knew that Heaven would look like this someday with the glistening light of hundreds of candles. She looked out the window at the cemetery to the side of the church. Many of the parishioners had lit candles in memory of their loved ones buried there and stuck them in the white snowy ground. There was a peace that Clara recognized only came from the One whom they celebrated this Christmas Eve and she stored this along with the memories of the day in her heart.

At five o'clock in the evening all the church bells from the different parishes began to ring calling the people to the various services. The pageant was performed, and the nativity was presented to the congregation. Clara joined with the choir at the front altar to sing the final song, Silent Night. The hymn was sung without instrumentation, the beautiful mix of voices adding to the reverence of the words. Clara closed her eyes and sang with all her heart as the entire congregation joined for the last verse.

When Clara opened her eyes again, she noticed that just to the side of the door leading to the vestibule, Erdman was standing with his hat in his hand. He wore his brown suit and his new brown silk tie. Clara was so overjoyed at seeing him that she barely noticed the numerous people congratulating her on the success of the program as she made her way to where he stood. "God Jul, Clara. I was hoping that I could drive you home. I can't stay very long as I must get back for my family, but I couldn't miss seeing you on Christmas Eve. You were so beautiful up there singing." He had made the trip just to see her for a few minutes.

Clara stepped away long enough to gather her hat and coat and whisper her intentions in her mother's ear. Moments later she was back at Erdman's side and they slipped out of the door quietly amidst the throng of joyous revelers. Erdman led her to the car, and they were soon on their way. Their time together that evening was brief as Erdman had to get back. They were soon parting on the lane in front of the farmhouse. Clara gave Erdman one passionate kiss to remember their first Christmas Eve by and another as a promise of many more to come. Then as suddenly as he had appeared, he was gone again into the snowy night.

Clara enjoyed the rest of the family festivities that evening including their porridge dinner (Clara was the special one who found the almond in her porridge), exchanging gifts with her family, and finally holding hands with her brothers and sisters around their decorated tree. She helped Inga and Cornelia take the dinner for the Nisse into the barn to ensure a good year to come, but Clara was already certain that the coming year would be her best yet.

Chapter 18

DECEMBER 26, 1925 –
RISING SUN, WISCONSIN

The period between December 25th and January 1st was known as Romjul in the Norwegian community of Crawford County. This was a festive time set apart for family parties and merry making. There were often ice-skating parties and toboggan sledding down some of the best hills in Wisconsin. The young men of the community would select the girls that they fancied the most to escort to the many festivities.

Christmas Eve had been quiet and uneventful at the Albert Olson house. Anna was festive, giving numerous extravagant gifts to Albert and the boys. The day had been celebrated without any of her infamous outbursts and Albert and Erdman considered this her best gift to them. Arvid had enjoyed opening his many gifts from his mother including a Louisville Slugger baseball bat and a Babe Ruth leather baseball mitt. Erdman had brought his brother a metal race car that wound up with a key and Arvid sent the toy car back and forth across the dining room floor repeatedly.

Edwin Knutson had left for a visit to his family in Stanley, Wisconsin, a few days prior (right after his Sunday evening with Clara at the Utica Lutheran Church), so it had been just Albert, Anna, Erdman and Arvid to celebrate together. Albert had taken Anna and Arvid to the South West Prairie Lutheran Church for a Christmas Eve pageant. Erdman had left the house briefly, returning by the time they had supper together after the church service. Anna was in a subdued frame of mind and had not asked Erdman about his absence so there had been no further arguments.

An elderly neighbor had been hired by Albert to portray "Julenisse" or Santa Claus. He came to the house after their Christmas Eve dinner with his red stocking cap and long white beard bearing a sack of gifts for the family. It was the tradition for Julenisse to ask each member of the family if they had been good that year; Erdman sighed inwardly as his parents responded that they had been very good. When Erdman was asked the question, he responded, "Of course."

Albert had given the old man a bottle of their best gin in replacement of the customary beer. They had forgotten all about the rice porridge, so Albert had given the old man a second bottle of gin declaring, "the hooch is much better than old porridge anyway." But Arvid had been concerned about the bad luck it might bring to not leave the porridge for the Nisse.

Anna's brother Nels who lived on the farm adjoining theirs, had asked their family to join his family for a dinner on December 25th. It had been a large feast and again Anna had been very calm, so Erdman had enjoyed the occasion. Erdman found himself wondering what Clara might be doing with her family; he wished that he might be able to bring her to his uncle's party, but he knew what trouble from Anna it would bring for them. This was the first time that Erdman had thought of bringing a girl to meet his family, so he knew that he was getting more than fond of Clara. He tried to remind himself that he should begin to distance himself from her, but he could not bring himself to do that. Instead, it caused him to think about Clara even more.

Erdman had asked Clara on Christmas Eve to accompany him to a sledding party in Fairview on December 26th. The Saturday afternoon sledding party would be hosted by some of Erdman's old classmates from the Tully School. He knew that there were probably more sledding parties that Clara had been invited to nearer to her home in Seneca, but Erdman had considered Alice's admonition about their protective brothers as a valid reason to bring Clara nearer to his home than hers. Erdman had also been asked by these same former classmates to bring bottles of gin for the large bonfire in the evening after the sledding. He knew that he could make a lucrative profit selling the gin and enjoy the company of his best girl at the same time.

Erdman parked the roadster in his usual spot at the beginning of the lane leading to Clara's farmhouse. Sometimes he felt a little bad about having Clara walk the quarter of a mile distance to him, but he did not want to risk meeting Christ Olson for a "little talk" as many fathers with beautiful daughters were in the habit of doing. Erdman did not want Christ to ruin things by asking about his intentions towards Clara or what his prospects for the future were. He certainly did not plan to be an old green hick like Christ or Clara's brothers and raise cows, kids, and tobacco on a little piece of land in the middle of nowhere.

Erdman glanced up to see Clara heading towards him. She was stunningly beautiful even though she had traded her fancy hat and coat for a heavy red woolen knit cap and an older coat, scarf, and red mittens. She also wore large black boots over her shoes so that she could navigate the snow drifts while sledding. She was holding an extra blanket and a basket of food she had brought for their dinner. Even the scantily dressed ladies on the risqué postcards hidden in the drawer of his bureau could not match Clara's ability to make his heart race at the sight of her.

He jumped out of the car to meet her. His hug was so intense he nearly knocked her off her feet, catching her as she began to slip on the snow. Clara laughed as she handed him the basket and stood on her tip toes to kiss him. Her warm and inviting lips made him forget that they were standing in the middle of the lane in broad daylight with several of her brothers possibly lurking somewhere nearby. She tasted like cinnamon and gingerbread; he wanted to just continue to kiss her right there on the spot not caring who else might be around them. The noise of another car passing by on Stoney Point Road brought Erdman back to some of his senses. He pulled back from their embrace long enough to take her hand in his and lead her to the car.

He placed the basket of food in the back seat and resumed his place behind the steering wheel. Clara's brown eyes were sparkling as she asked him, "Can you guess what dessert I just took out of the oven for you? I will give you another kiss if you can." She giggled in anticipation and caught her lower lip with her teeth as she waited for his answer. The desire to kiss those lips again made him grin.

"I would have to guess, gingerbread. It is my favorite thing in the world right after you." He laughed as her eyes rounded in surprise and a shy smile played across her lips. "I would also venture to guess that I just won my kiss. I will collect it once we are alone tonight so that I don't drive off the road in my mad distraction over you, Bright Eyes." The beautiful blush that warmed her cheeks told him he had been correct, and this was going to be a wonderful day.

The cold sunny day was perfect for sledding. The gentle sloping hill to one side of the barn was the for the less enthusiastic and the steeper hill to the other side was for the more daring of the men gathered. Erdman appreciated that Clara did not react as a few of the other girls gathered had; they had only been out a short time and were already whimpering about the snow and the cold wanting to return to the warmth of the barn. Clara rode on the toboggan with Erdman down the gentle slope again and again and laughed as she trudged back up the hill through the deep snow. She seemed invigorated by the cold fresh air. She looked like a snow angel as the snow that sprayed back on them from the toboggan runners had formed a layer on her dark eyelashes and rings of black curls below her cap.

They had been out in the cold for a considerable amount of time when Erdman suggested that they warm themselves with some coffee in the barn. Many of the young couples had wandered in that direction and several of the young men had hinted to Erdman that they were interested in adding something stronger to their coffee. Erdman sent Clara on ahead towards the barn as he stopped at the car to gather a couple of the bottles of gin, concealing them in the extra blanket Clara had brought. He picked up the basket of food and smiled again at the thought of her promised gingerbread kiss later.

Erdman returned to the barn to find Clara hesitating at the sliding doors, still more outside the structure than she was inside it. He was puzzled as to why she had not joined the others in the warmth emanating from the interior of the barn. He reached for her arm and she flinched at his touch looking like a skittish young deer in the path of a predator. Erdman looked beyond her into the barn to try and determine what had caused this response in her. A few of the young couples were gathered around sitting on hay bales chatting and drinking coffee. There were quite a few of the other couples engaging in various stages of necking unfazed by the crowd around them. Erdman turned back to see Clara's big brown eyes looking at him in confusion.

One of the young men from the group seated on the haybales approached Erdman. "Did you bring some of your entertainment, Erd?" he asked looking at what Erdman held in his arms. Erdman brought the bottles from underneath the blanket and handed them off with the basket, nodding his permission for the young man to open them. The young man took the bottles over to the coffee and poured some of the liquor into one of the cups nearby. "Erd brought his party!" he exclaimed to the others, and many of them rose to join him.

Erdman watched as Clara's eyes traveled from the amorous couples to the drinking and carousing, beginning with the gin. Her eyes widened slightly as she seemed to realize what was happening. Erdman felt an irritation towards her much like what he felt their first night of intimacy together. What was wrong with her? These couples were not doing anything they hadn't already done together. Why did she have to ruin what had been an otherwise perfect day? He felt his grip on her arm tighten with his rise in frustration.

Clara regarded Erdman and instead of a look of disbelief, fear, or abhorrence for him and his companions, she glanced down at the ground briefly, gathered her courage, and turned to put her hands around the back of his neck. She whispered, "Were you wanting to collect your kiss now?" He saw the look of submissive adoration in her eyes and he knew that he should be ecstatic at her response, but he wasn't. He realized that while Clara had given in to intimacy with him, she had done so as an act of loving him; it had been for him alone to witness and not this group of people around them. She anticipated being his wife not his next lustful conquest. She was not accustomed to his world of speakeasies and common women and the decadent practices of the others surrounding them. He also realized that he did not wish for her to become accustomed to any of it.

Erdman encircled her waist with his arms, touching his forehead to hers. "Not just yet, Love. I would rather have you all to myself. I think we have had enough sledding for today. Let's go get some dinner in Viroqua and see a movie." His heart warmed at her smile that held a hint of relief as she nodded her head. He approached the bottles of gin, paused, and then picked up her basket lying discarded on the floor.

"They can keep the hooch, but I want my gingerbread," he winked at her as he took her hand and led her out the door. She had been willing to change yet again for him, but he had made a deliberate change for her, sacrificing his gin profit and possibly much more in the process.

Chapter 19

FEBRUARY 13, 1926 –
SENECA, WISCONSIN

The snow piling up outside the parlor window of the farm-house on Stoney Point Road left Clara feeling sad and a little frustrated. Usually Clara loved the winter snow; she loved to build snowmen with her younger sisters, and she made numerous attempts at making the perfect snow angel throughout the winter season. But it had been snowing most of the weekends after Erdman had left her to go back to Gale College and he had finally promised to come home to her for Valentine's Day tomorrow.

Since the holiday for sweethearts had landed on a Sunday, Erdman was to come home today and stay through Sunday evening. The current weather had all the makings of yet another blizzard, and Clara knew that she could not expect Erdman to risk the trip on hazardous roads just to see her. Tears welled up in her eyes as she watched the wind blow the falling snow into deep drifts covering the lane until it was almost impassable. What good was it to have a beau if she couldn't even have his attentions on their first Valentine's Day together? Clara chided herself for her childish pettishness; she had a wonderful beau and she just needed to make the best of the day. She would put the combs he had given to her in her hair, and she would write a long love letter to him this evening. Still, it just was not the same.

She realized that Inga was standing beside her when her youngest sister took ahold of her hand. "You look so sad, Clara. Isn't being in love supposed to make you happy?" Clara brushed the few tears that had escaped down her cheeks with the back of her other hand. Inga was right in her sweet honest way. She needed to be happy that she had someone as wonderful as Erdman to love her. Clara smiled and squeezed Inga's hand in her own.

"You are right, Inga. I am the luckiest girl in the world. Thank you for reminding me. As soon as we finish our morning chores, let's go and play in the snow, and then we will make some heart shaped cookies and some gingerbread men for everyone."

Inga nodded in agreement and the two went to finish their assigned tasks. They asked Emma, Cornelia, and Alice to join them outside and soon Clara felt much better as the sisters laughed and played in the snow. Clara attempted yet another snow angel by plopping in the snow drift and moving her arms up and down and her legs outwards. Bernard was enlisted to help Clara out of the drift without leaving the tale-tell marks that ruin a perfect snow angel. Bernard gently scooped his sister straight up and stepped back. There was the perfect outline of the angel with wings in the snow. Clara cheered when she saw it, as she had tried so many times before and this was the best one by far.

They had decided to go into the house to bake cookies and drink hot chocolate when they heard a horse and sleigh approaching on Stoney Point Road. Who in the world was out traveling in weather like this? Clara's heart thudded rapidly as she wondered if Erdman had made it through to her. She tried to not look as disappointed as she felt when a young store clerk from nearby Mt. Sterling got out of the sleigh. He greeted Bernard and then reached back into the sleigh for a large box.

"This here is for one Miss Clara Olson of Stoney Point Road, Seneca. The sender was insistent that it be delivered today. I had to borrow a horse and sleigh as the regular buggy and even the cars could not get here. It came in on the last train to make it through last night. It must be pretty darn important." He held out the box and Clara stepped forward to take it. "Well, now that I see how pretty she is, I can see why it was so darned important. Ma'am." He took his hat off for Clara and grinned at her. Clara blushed and hurried away with her sisters following close behind her. Bernard stood shaking his head slowly at the clerk as the young man climbed back into the sleigh.

There was so much commotion over Clara's delivery as they entered the kitchen that even Dena, who was never nonplussed over the chattering of her brood, rose from her rocker to see what had happened. Clara set the box on the kitchen table and then hesitated to open it, looking around at the crowd that had gathered.

Cornelia was the first to ask, "Well? Aren't you going to open it? I know if I had such a package, I would have opened it long before this!" She giggled as Inga nodded her head in agreement.

Alice intervened on Clara's behalf. "Cornelia, we will all remember that you said that when a package from your beau arrives someday. Perhaps Clara would prefer to open it by herself?" Alice looked to Clara for confirmation and at her sister's nod, Alice began to shoo the rest of her siblings out of the kitchen into the parlor. Dena still stood beside the table watching Clara and the box on the table. Dena walked to the coat tree in the hall and took down a heavy coat along with her boots and put them on. She was heading for Christ who was in the barn, leaving Clara by herself with the package still unopened.

Clara's hands trembled in excitement as she took out a pair of shears from the drawer to cut the cords around the box. As she opened the box, she saw a dozen yellow roses and a large candy box shaped like a heart. It was also yellow with numerous yellow ribbons and bows. A small note was on the bottom of the box.

My dearest C,

 I am so sorry I could not be with you as we planned. I was barely able to get this package through to you. Please accept this token of my affection until I can be with you again. I have the real yellow ribbon next to my heart as you are in my heart. Be Mine as I am Yours.

 With all my love, E.

Clara felt a rush of love for him stronger than ever before. She would write the best love letter and bake more gingerbread to send to him as soon as she could reach the post office again. Inga had been correct; you were supposed to be happy when you were in love.

Christ listened as Dena described the package sitting in their kitchen and their daughter's response to it. "A young man does not go to this length for a gal he is just fond of; there is more between them, Pa. It is as plain as the nose on your face. It is time to get them married and settled down. Has he spoke to you at all?"

Christ shook his head slowly as he closed his eyes and let Dena's words soak in. He had hoped that the boy would come and speak with him already. Christ knew that Dena was right and if the boy would not come and speak to him, he just might have to go and speak with the boy soon.

"Don't say anything to Clara just yet. Let her enjoy her gift." Christ admonished Dena. He could just imagine the look of bliss on the sweet girl's face right now. He hoped and prayed that her look of bliss would not turn to one of sorrow and betrayal later. He made up his mind that he and young Erdman were about to have a chat one way or another.

Chapter 20

FEBRUARY 14, 1926 –
GALESVILLE, WISCONSIN

The St. Valentine's Day blizzard raged on in Galesville, Wisconsin. The wind that howled and raged outside mirrored the emotions that Erdman battled internally. He had sent the package to Clara on Friday when he found that there was no way he would be able to make the trip to Seneca. All the trains and buses had shut down for the following two days, quarantining the Gale College students in the little town instead of sending them south to LaCrosse or north to Minneapolis, Minnesota. There had been various celebrations in houses and dormitories and Erdman's gin sales had skyrocketed. Erdman should have been very satisfied to sell out his current stock and to go and find a feminine distraction to keep his mind off Clara, but his dark mood had scared any prospects away.

It began with more of his nightmares the previous night. His dreams had begun with Clara, fresh and sweet and inviting, the ways she looked at him and the soft sighs of contentment she made when she curled up in his arms and rested her head upon his chest. The dreams had then shifted to the darker night terrors that had plagued Erdman since he was a young boy; visions relived of unspeakable acts by a siren who held him in her utter control. The deeds done to a young boy so shameful that they could never be seen in the light of day, only pushed to the utter darkness of his soul where they resided with the turmoil of emotions they produced.

Erdman woke to the screams of his roommate cowering in the corner as Erdman stood over him brandishing an oar from the rowing team. Erdman was never sure how he ended up in the various places he was located after one of his nightmares; he only knew that he wanted to obliterate the siren, sending her back to the abyss for good. After he woke from one of these night terrors it would be days before he felt safe enough to succumb to sleep and risk encountering the torment again. Not even the anesthetizing effect of alcohol alleviated his agony.

If only Clara were there. She would singlehandedly keep his dark purgatory at bay with her selfless love for him. Erdman knew that seeking the company of any other female at this juncture would be to no avail. Erdman knew he needed Clara like the air that he breathed, and the knowledge of his dependency on her only compounded his wretchedness. He would not, he could not, love her or any other human being ever. Love was a word tossed about to achieve his conquest and then discarded at will. To truly love someone was to give them control of your heart, body, and mind, and no one could ever have that from him again. He knew that he should have taken his own counsel months prior by discarding Clara heartbroken, but wiser, like all the other girls in his past. Erdman felt that he could not live without Clara and yet he detested the feeling of being trapped or controlled by her love.

Suddenly the walls of his dorm room felt as though they were closing in around him. He grabbed his overcoat and hat and headed for the door, not even thinking about where he would go. He did not have to think because he knew his habits of drowning everything out would take him to the speakeasy and to Lilla. If he consumed enough alcohol, he could imagine Lilla was a poor substitute for Clara. Even if he couldn't make that leap in his imagination, Lilla would accept whatever dark place he was in; she seemed to enjoy his darkness because it matched her own.

Erdman headed into the basement of a warehouse where the speakeasy was concealed from the prying eyes of law enforcement. He walked right past the large guard stationed outside, as his presence there was a very common sight. Erdman walked to the bar to order the first of many drinks. He felt the touch on his shoulder that ran down to his forearm; he did not have to look to know that Lilla had already located him in the busy room of carousing strangers. He signaled to the man behind the bar to bring Lilla her usual drink as he knew she was continually thirsty.

"Well, aren't you a sight for sore eyes?" Erdman was not certain if she meant him or the drink that she accepted from the bartender. Either way it wasn't of any consequence to him. Lilla sat down beside him and lit a cigarette. Erdman motioned for the bartender to pour his second drink and to leave the bottle for him.

"What's the matter with my baby? You can't still be angry with me are you, Lover?" Lilla crooned as she leaned to kiss the side of Erdman's face. He glanced at her face, and the heavy makeup to cover the dissipation from alcohol and lasciviousness. Erdman wasn't sure if the nausea he suddenly felt was from his sleep deprivation or from her proximity to him. This was going to take a lot more alcohol than he had anticipated.

"You are in a bad way aren't you, Honey?" Lilla turned Erdman's face towards her. Even in the very dim light she could see the haggard appearance that denoted "his spells" as she called them. Lilla slipped off the bar stool putting Erdman's arm around her shoulders, bringing him to his feet. Lilla grabbed the bottle from the bar and steered Erdman towards the exit.

"Don't worry Baby, Lilla has got you." Why did that phrase sound so familiar to Erdman? There was some distant memory about it that he thought was pleasant if only he could make his muddled brain remember it. The memory of it and a yellow ribbon flitted about him for a moment before the utter darkness came to claim him once more.

Erdman awoke the following day in the strange surroundings of a flophouse down the street from the speakeasy. He lay on a narrow cot in just his skivvies, his clothing strewn all over the floor. The stench of urine and vomit permeated everything in the room including the thin scratchy blanket that had been placed over him. The combination of repugnant odors and after-effects of his alcohol consumption made Erdman more than a little queasy. He sat up quickly to find a basin in which he could retch, when the door opened and Lilla entered the room.

"You are finally awake. You scared me a little this time, Baby." Lilla carried a paper bag which she set down on the bed beside Erdman. "Usually when we party you are ready for more in a few hours. You got in here and was screaming and crying until you passed out, so I took off your clothes and let you sleep. Even in your sleep you called out so many times for help that the people around us in the other rooms was complaining. Only you could make too much noise for a flophouse, Erd." Lilla sighed as she sat down beside him pressing against him on the narrow cot. She reached into the paper bag and brought out a bottle of gin and two glasses.

"Here, have some of the hair of the dog," Lilla chuckled as she opened the bottle and started to pour him a drink. "I had to use some of your cash from your wallet to get another bottle. I also had to get some gin for the people next door so's they didn't call the cops on you. I had a little money left over so I brought something pretty for me from you." Lilla watched his face closely for signs of one of his temper tantrums that often followed close on the heels of his blackouts.

Erdman knew that he should feel disgust at the filth around him, anger at Lilla for stealing from him again, and remorse for his own degraded state, but he felt absolutely nothing. He knew that in this present state he could sleep unencumbered for several days and that was what he needed the most. He slowly put on his shirt, pants, and shoes, handed Lilla the rest of the cash in his wallet, and stumbled out the door. College and the rest of the world would have to wait until he could see straight again. He left without another word to Lilla, knowing that she would be waiting for him again the next time the dreams began.

Chapter 21

FEBRUARY 22, 1926 – SENECA, WISCONSIN

It had been over a week since the large St Valentine's Day blizzard. The snow and wind had finally abated, but the arctic cold that took their place did little to alleviate the very hazardous road conditions. It was now the final week of February and Clara had not heard anything else from Erdman. She surmised this was due to the fact that much of the transportation between her home in Seneca and Gale College in Galesville was almost literally at a frozen standstill.

Monday morning had dawned sunny and warmer with a high in the 30's, unlike the sub-zero temperatures of the previous week. Clara had written one love letter to Erdman on Valentine's Day. Then she had gradually added three more letters as the days wore on. She knew that Christ would soon decide to make the trip into Seneca for supplies and to talk with the other farmers who might be gathered there. Clara baked some gingerbread early that morning and had it packaged in a box to send to Erdman, hoping her father would return from his chores in the barn to announce that he would make the trip into town.

Christ had just put down the saucer from which he drank his cooled black coffee when he announced that he intended to make the anticipated trip into Seneca that afternoon. He had exchanged numerous glances with Dena throughout the course of the noon meal that prompted him to ask, "Clara, would you be wanting to go along?" Dena had nodded and smiled at his offer as if she were the one to have posed it in the first place.

"Thank you, yes Papa. I was hoping that you might ask. I just have a package to get upstairs and then I will be ready whenever you are." Clara took off her apron she had worn to help clear the noon dishes and turned to head up the stairs to retrieve her package for Erdman.

"Oh, Papa! I would love to go too! It has been awful being cooped up in the house for so many days," Alice exclaimed as she came to the table to pick up the cup and saucer her father had just used. Christ sent a bewildered look to Dena who sat in her rocker with her mending.

"Alice, I need you to help me pick out the colors for the quilt squares on the Swenson's baby quilt. No one else has the eye for matching the very best colors like you do. Emma will take over the mending for me and we will work together this afternoon." Dena invented a strategy to divert Alice from going with her father and Clara. Christ had promised to have a talk with the girl and no one else was going to waylay the plan if Dena could help it. After seeing Alice's disappointed look as she nodded at her mother's directive, Dena added, "Pa, please bring home the latest Ladies' Home Journal and a couple of bottles of Dr Pepper for Alice and Emma to enjoy." Both girls stared at their mother in astonishment; while Christ was known to bring home various treats, it was almost unheard of for Dena to direct him to do so.

Christ and Clara were soon on their way unaccompanied by anyone else. Christ drove the team of horses slowly as there was still considerable amounts of snow and he needed the time to think of exactly how he wanted to start. He finally decided that it was best to go straight to the subject.

"Clara, your ma and I have been wanting to know what your plans with the Olson boy are? It has been quite a few months now and we have yet to meet him ourselves. I know that you are a little older and I certainly don't have any strings on you as to what you decide to do, but every papa wants to know that his daughter will be settled and happy in her future. Has he spoken to you about the future?" Christ had started his speech very quietly, but as he talked his voice had increased in volume with his confidence. He was far from yelling at Clara, but he still had the brusque mannerisms of the Old Country, and she was grateful that the road to Seneca was basically deserted other than the occasional bird or squirrel.

Clara knew that she had to answer her father carefully. While she wanted to defend Erdman in every way, even she did not understand why Erdman had not made any attempts to speak with her father. "Papa, I know that you and Mama love me. I know that you only want the best for me. I am certain when I tell you that Erdman and I are in love and he is the very best for me." Clara turned her luminous brown eyes to look at her father and Christ could see in their reflection that his little girl was in love.

"I see. I want to be happy for you my dear girl, I really do. If your mama were here, she would be quick to remind you that when people are in love, they get married so everything can be proper." Christ's gruff voice dropped off for a little bit as he tried to think of what he could say about the topic without saying it. "Has he spoken to you about getting married, Clara?"

"Yes, Papa. We plan to get married. I think Erdman wants to ask you but maybe if Bernard and Adolph were not always about? It can be a mite intimidating or so I would think if it were me. Were you nervous to ask Bestefar Abraham about marrying Mama?"

Christ chuckled. "I would say so. It was a good thing your mama had enough nerve for the both of us. She insisted I talk to her papa, and no one turns down your mama when she insists. Perhaps you can suggest to your Erdman that it is good to talk with your papa and I will make certain that your brothers are scarce at the appointed time. Otherwise, your mama might get insistent with Erdman and none of us want to see that happen to him, do we?" Christ and Clara laughed together. Christ could now honestly tell Dena that he had "the talk" with Clara and that things were going to get sorted very soon.

The little town of Seneca was bustling for a Monday afternoon. It seemed that many of the other inhabitants of the area had become stir-crazy from the days of blizzard and cold and now everyone wished to be outside. The clerk at the post office was very busy with all the people posting letters and checking to see if they had any mail delivered. When he looked up to see Clara standing in front of him with her beautiful smile in place, he adjusted the tie he was wearing. "Hello, Miss Clara. What brings you out in this heat wave?" He laughed awkwardly and stared into her beautiful brown eyes. Clara laughed quietly with him, just enough to try and be polite without encouraging his flirting any further.

"Hello, Ansgar. Yes, it is much warmer outside today, isn't it? I have a package to be sent out to Galesville." Clara put the wrapped box containing the gingerbread and her letters on the counter in front of the postal clerk. "How much will that be please?"

"That should go easily for ten cents." Ansgar took the package from Clara and stamped it. He tried again. "Have you heard the newest program, *Sam and Henry*, on the radio yet? It is great fun to listen to. There is a bunch of us who gather here in the back of the post office to listen on Tuesday nights if you would ever like to join us." He looked hopefully at Clara trying to will her to accept his invitation. He handed her a stack of letters touching her hand as he did so. Clara knew that she needed to let him know nicely that she had a beau so that he could find a girl who would be interested in him. She smiled at him again.

"That does sound like fun, but I am not certain my beau would appreciate my attending. He is the one I send all the packages to in Galesville. I am certain that there are plenty of nice girls around here that would love that invitation from you, Ansgar. Thank you for the help with the package." Clara turned to walk towards the door when she heard the voices of several of the ladies from the town whispering to each other.

"Turn down that nice boy for that delinquent boy from Rising Sun. I hear she is out to all hours of the night with him and that is up to no good I tell you."

"I never imagined that a girl of Christ and Dena's would behave in such a way. She ought to be ashamed of such carrying on and no engagements mind you. It will be a bad end to that business for sure."

Clara gasped. She felt as if she had just been slapped repeatedly by the two women. She shut the post office door with a bang and began to make her way to where her father waited for her at the general store. The tears welled in her eyes as she heard the nasty words over and over in her head. She was angry to be made the topic of the town's gossips and hurt that people would think ill of her and Erdman. Then another thought occurred to her. If these two women were bold enough to say such things in her presence what might people be saying to her parents, her siblings, and even to Erdman's family? Was that the reason that Papa had talked to her about Erdman's intentions? Did he and Mama hear the nasty stories as well? Clara would do anything not to bring grief to her family, especially her gruff but loving papa.

Clara was torn between confronting the reprehensible gossip-mongers and confronting Erdman for putting her in this position in the first place. Papa was right. Their future needed to be settled, and perhaps Clara would have to acquire a few of her mother's tactics when it came to insistence with Erdman. She hoped that the roads to Galesville were cleared soon as she needed to talk face to face with Erdman and the sooner the better.

Chapter 22

MARCH 3, 1926 –
LA CROSSE, WISCONSIN

The bitter Wisconsin winter was giving way reluctantly to warmer weather and less snow. The city streets of La Crosse, Wisconsin were still a quagmire of mud, slush and other debris left by animals that occasionally still roamed the streets. This beautiful city flourished among the rocky bluffs that edged the Mississippi River, and sat at the junction of the La Crosse River and the Black River. The grandest bluff facing the city was named Granddad Bluff. At its summit, one could see the states of Iowa and Minnesota as well as Wisconsin.

In an unexpected turn of events Clara had been hired by Mrs. Lena Hutchins of Soldiers Grove to be a companion for the elderly widow on her trip to the city. Lena's maiden name had been Knutson before she married Samuel Hutchins, one of the founders of the town of Soldiers Grove, Wisconsin. Lena as a young girl from Norway and had been Samuel's second wife, marrying him when he was well into his middle-age years. Samuel died leaving his wife a great amount of wealth but no children to watch over her in her twilight years. Lena had asked at several local churches for a young woman, a good Lutheran girl, to become her companion and travel with her. The minister of the Utica Lutheran Church had felt that young Clara would be perfect, and Christ and Dena felt a change of scenery in the company of Mrs. Hutchins would do their Clara a world of good. Mrs. Hutchins had fallen in love with sweet Clara at first sight, immediately employing Clara to accompany her to La Crosse the following week.

Mrs. Hutchins, like many women her age, adored the various sanitariums that offered restorative treatments such as Turkish baths, Electric, Sulphur, and Vapor baths, and deep tissue massages. Mrs. Hutchins had long been a patron of the sanitariums in Prairie du Chien, as they offered baths from natural artesian wells. The fashionable ladies were traveling to La Crosse to the new Kunert Sanitarium, so Mrs. Hutchins decided that she and Clara would book fine rooms at the new Hotel Linker (which boasted steam heat and electric lights) and Mrs. Hutchins would spend time at her treatments. Clara would have ample free time to explore the city and even to visit her older sister Minnie who lived in La Crosse.

Clara had been struggling with her emotions since the day that she overheard the women discussing her in the post office. To compound the issue, she had heard very little to nothing from Erdman since his extravagant Valentine's gift. Clara knew that her trip to La Crosse would distance her from some of the small-town gossips and divert her attention from Erdman's inattention. She had sent a note to Erdman before leaving with Mrs. Hutchins, to explain where she would be so that he would not return to Seneca and find her gone.

Mrs. Hutchins herself was a healing balm for Clara's heart. The sweet elderly woman was adventurous and fun loving, much like Clara envisioned herself when she reached her eighties. Mrs. Hutchins had insisted on her chauffeur calling for Clara in her private car instead of having Clara take the bus to Soldiers Grove to join her for the trip. The two enjoyed each other's company immensely, even finding their quiet times companionable.

It was midday when Clara left the hotel for a walk. She had assisted Mrs. Hutchins with getting settled in her suite, as the matron had decided to take a long nap before taking a late afternoon treatment and then a leisurely dinner with Clara. Mrs. Hutchins had rented an entire suite for herself with an additional large room for Clara. The additional room had an adjoining door to the suite and a private entrance so that Clara might come and go as she pleased. Clara was amazed at her good fortune in being employed by the generous woman.

Clara left the hotel on Main Street and walked along the wide sidewalk towards the Riverwalk that followed the contour of the Mississippi River. Large barges traversed up and down the river and an occasional paddlewheel boat chugged along, taking its passengers towards Minneapolis to the North and as far as New Orleans to the South. Clara once again felt the stirring of wanderlust that had been within her since childhood; she wanted to see new places and meet new people as she traveled far and wide. A thought of Mrs. Hutchins still traveling at her advanced age made Clara smile and yearn for the ability to see the world with Erdman until they were too old to travel anymore. Thinking of Erdman made Clara wonder where he was at that moment and if he had received her note.

Clara decided to return to Mrs. Hutchins at the hotel. She turned to walk back along the Riverwalk the way she had come. The smell of chocolate increased as she neared the Charmant chocolate factory on State Street, causing her stomach to protest the small lunch she had eaten earlier. She decided to stop at the shop located at the front of the warehouse to purchase a few chocolates to share with Mrs. Hutchins after dinner and possibly have a few before dinner herself. As she rounded the corner, she almost collided with a group of young people gathered on the sidewalk outside a warehouse door on the same block.

"Pardon me. I didn't see you." Clara apologized as she stepped out of the way of a well-dressed young man who had his back to her. He turned at the sound of Clara's voice and she could see his grey eyes widen with interest as he looked at her. He took off the straw boater hat that had been jauntily perched on the crown of his head and tipped his head and hat at Clara.

"The apologies are all mine, Miss. I should have noticed you earlier. I hope that we didn't alarm you." His eyes roved casually over Clara as his smile brightened. "Were you waiting for entrance?" He indicated the door to the back of the warehouse. "I would be happy to assist you in getting past the lookout. My name is Oscar Mikkelson and my band of miscreants and I are from Galesville. We come here to La Crosse to run away from the monotony that is Gale College."

Clara blinked as she heard the young man introduce himself from Gale College. She was confused as to why the chocolate shop needed a lookout, but she did not want to appear foolish to someone who might be a friend or colleague of Erdman. "Did I understand you to say that you are from Gale College? I have an acquaintance who attends there as well. Do you happen to know Erdman Olson?"

Oscar gave a snort as he answered, "Everyone knows Olson, especially the ladies. In fact, Lilla here is probably the expert on good ole Erd." He indicated the young woman he had been leaning against when Clara bumped into them. She was a beautiful girl, dark hair in the latest style, full red lips, and green eyes that narrowed as she assessed Clara carefully. She reminded Clara of a Hollywood starlet and a stab of jealousy prodded Clara to know that this woman knew Erdman well enough to be considered an expert.

Lilla feigned disinterest as she asked Clara, "What did you say your name was, dearie? I don't recall seeing you around Gale before."

"I'm sorry. How rude of me not to introduce myself. My name is Clara Olson. You say that you know Erdman?"

Lilla stared at her momentarily. "Clara." She drawled the name slowly, then Lilla smiled brilliantly at her. "Why, yes. I do think I remember Erdman mentioning you before. Any friend of Erdman's is a friend of ours, right Oscar?" Lilla pushed at Oscar's chest with her hand, getting him to back up a few steps so that she could take a better look at Clara.

"Oscar's suggestion is good. You should join us inside for drinks. Erdman would never forgive us for ignoring such a dear friend of his." Lilla's green eyes glittered as she lifted a cigarette to her lips for Oscar to light. "I am sure that Erdman would prefer to be here himself, but he has been so unwell lately."

Clara's concern for Erdman overrode the distinct feeling of dislike she had for Lilla. "Erdman has been unwell? I didn't know. He hasn't written to me lately. Would you be able to tell him that I am here in La Crosse when you return to Galesville?"

"Oh, Sweetie, I will do better than that. I will tell him you are here and bring a note back from him when we return Friday evening. He is much too sick, or I am sure that he would come to see you himself. Shall we meet here around seven on Friday evening?"

Clara nodded. She needed to excuse herself and return to Mrs. Hutchins right away before she was missed. She was devastated to understand that she had blamed Erdman for not paying enough attention to her when he was ill and obviously could not respond. She would wait for his note on Friday and then try to find a way to Galesville after that. He needed to know that she loved him and would take care of him.

"Thank you. I will meet you here on Friday evening. It was nice to make your acquaintance." Clara excused herself and made her way across State Street back towards Main Street and the hotel.

Oscar watched Clara cross the street and walk away before he turned back to Lilla. "What game are you playing at, Lilla? Olson isn't sick."

Lilla pressed herself against Oscar and kissed him. "Never you mind what I have planned for little Miss Fresh off the farm, Sweetie. That is between Erdman and me, understand? Now get me a drink before I die of thirst." Lilla laughed and guided Oscar towards the door of the speakeasy as she glanced back to see Clara disappear around the corner.

Chapter 23

MARCH 4, 1926 – LA CROSSE, WISCONSIN

"What do you think my dear, the blue or the ivory?" Lena Hutchins held up the two pairs of gloves for Clara to inspect. "I realize that women my age should reconcile themselves to the fact they are expected by society to be dignified and mature, so it should be the ivory. I do so love the robin's egg blue ones, however." She sighed as she placed the blue gloves back in the pile that the store clerk had brought for her to try.

Clara picked the blue gloves back up and handed them to her employer who was now more her friend. "Society does not always know what is best for each person, and the blue ones match your eyes." Clara smiled at the elderly woman's sigh of delight as she accepted the blue gloves, adding them to the large pile of items to be purchased from Doerflingers Fine Department Store.

"Such wisdom from one still so young. If only I had your wisdom at your age, Clara. I allowed all the old biddies of society to tell me what was expected as the wife of a very influential man. I believe my Samuel married me because he truly loved me for who I was, a simple girl from Norway, and not for my status as his wife. I should have let those people talk as they would and make myself and my Samuel happier, if only, I had known better. Remember this quote, Clara, 'To thine own self be true'. I wonder what your heart is telling you, my dear? You look a little downcast this morning."

The perceptive lady was correct; Clara was more than a little downcast and exhausted from a restless night of tossing and turning. She could not get her conversation with Lilla to stop replaying itself over and over in her mind. She was very worried about Erdman, what his ailment was and how long he had been sick. She was concerned that Lilla knew so much more about Erdman's current state of being than she did and what the real nature of Lilla's relationship with her beau might be. She even revisited the ugly gossip from the post office and how it affected her entire family. Clara was weary and anxious.

Lena regarded Clara with a quizzical look, as if she were asking the young woman to unburden her heart to the elderly dowager. Clara felt that it might be improper to tell her employer of her current woes, but she looked back into the compassionate eyes of a friend and a true confidante. At Clara's nod, Lena waved the clerks from the department store away, leaving them alone in one of the store's private salons for its wealthiest patrons. Clara began slowly, "I have found my version of your Samuel. I love him with all my heart."

Lena listened as Clara unburdened her heart to her. She held Clara's hand firmly in her own, nodding occasionally and closing her eyes as if in deep thought. Clara omitted the most intimate details of her relationship with Erdman, but Lena understood Clara's commitment to marry Erdman and spend their lives together. When Clara had finished there was a lengthy pause of silence. Clara was worried that Lena might join the others in condemning her for her love for Erdman and for her choices prompted by that love. Lena gently put her aged, weathered hand upon Clara's smooth cheek as she smiled through the tears in her eyes.

"I know that your love for him is genuine and I hope that his love for you is just as real. Wait for his note to you and then we can decide what you should do next together. If you need to go to Galesville to see to him, then we shall both go and stay there, so that not even the Pope himself might seem so virtuous. I hope he knows what a treasure he has in you, my sweet girl, and that he proves himself worthy of your love for him."

"I could never think to ask you for such a thing. You have been too kind and generous with me already." Clara began to protest. Lena held up her hand against Clara's objections and stated firmly.

"You have asked me for nothing. I have freely given this to you as it is my prerogative to do so. You must accept my offer to pacify an old lady in her final years. Just remember, Clara, that if he proves unworthy of you in any way you do not have to settle yourself with him. You will always have a place with me whenever you might need it. Now, let us call those clerks back in here and choose some new things for your wardrobe. Do you like blue as well?" Lena's laughter sounded like the chiming of small bells, and it did everything to lift Clara's spirits.

The following evening at fifteen minutes before the appointed time, Clara left the hotel with Mrs. Hutchins' admonition to allow the chauffeur to accompany her still ringing in her ears. Clara had assured Lena that the meeting place was only a block and a half away and there was no need for an escort. She promised to send word if she required further assistance. Clara steeled herself against the thoughts about Lilla that pricked at her like a scorpion's sting. She had decided after talking with Lena that it was better for her to know the whole truth about Erdman and Lilla than to live with possible lies, no matter how heartbreaking that might be for her. She knew that Erdman had a past and thought she could live with that if she were his only future.

As Clara rounded the corner and crossed State Street, she realized that Charmant's Chocolates had been on the opposite block; her meeting place with Lilla was in the back of another warehouse further down the block. A sense of apprehension tickled at the tiny hairs on the back of her neck. She should have accepted Lena's offer of an escort, but it was too late to turn back now. Clara approached the doorway where she had last seen Lilla, but she was nowhere in sight. A handsome young man opened the door at the bottom of the stairway and grinned up at Clara.

"You must be here to see Lilla. Geez, no one mentioned how pretty you are." He whistled in obvious appreciation, which heightened Clara's apprehension. The young man climbed the stairs quickly and doffed his cap in greeting. "I am Alvin Larson, one of Erdman's buddies from Gale. He has mentioned you, Clara, but he did not tell us what a beauty you are. Keeping that to himself, I guess."

Clara was growing impatient with his attempt at flirtation. "Erdman has not mentioned you or Lilla to me. May I ask when Lilla will be joining us?" Clara glanced around again, searching for any signs of Lilla's arrival.

"Actually, it is you who will be joining Lilla. She is waiting for you inside with an important letter from Erdman. She asked me to bring you straight to her and I promise that is all that I will do. Shall we?" He turned sideways, motioning his arm towards the door at the bottom of the stairs. Clara was in a quandary about what she should do; she wanted to get Erdman's letter from Lilla, but she felt wary about following Alvin despite his promises. Certainly, Erdman would not send nefarious people to meet Clara, so she decided there was nothing left for her to do but follow the young man.

Clara had to pause just inside the door to allow her eyes to adjust to the darkness of the speakeasy. There were faint traces of red lights here and there but most of the room was enveloped in darkness. The overpowering smells of alcohol and body odors assaulted her nose. Clara walked slowly in the direction that Alvin was leading, so that she would not stumble over anything or anyone.

Clara stopped just in front of a small round table at the end of the room. It was set apart from the large bar next to it and the dance floor at the other end. Lilla was seated at the table casually watching as Clara had made her way across the room to her. It made Clara think of a spider lying in wait and the thought made Clara shudder involuntarily. Lilla noticed and smiled around her cigarette.

"So, you did decide to show after all. I admit I had my reservations about your dauntlessness, but you have proven a worthy contender. Although, I guess we both know Erdman likes his girls adventurous." Lilla laughed but the merriment did not reach her eyes.

"I came out of my concern for Erdman. If you will please give me the letter he sent, I will be on my way. I do not wish to cause you any further inconvenience." Clara sounded bolder than she felt. She was almost relieved that the room was so dark as it might cover some of her tremulousness.

"You are so polite, Clara. Sit down and I will order a drink for you."

"No, thank you, I don't care for strong spirits. You have a letter for me?" Clara persisted.

"You might need a drink by the time we are through, Clara. Sit down." Lilla asked the bartender nearest her for another round and an additional drink for Clara. The man eyed Clara with obvious interest as he brought the drinks to the table. Clara took a small sip from the glass; it was a cola with something stronger mixed into it. The concoction burned her mouth and throat slightly as she swallowed it, but she felt slightly steadier, so she took a few additional sips waiting for Lilla to speak again.

"That's more like it. I think we can learn to appreciate each other Clara. It is old fashioned to vie for Erdman when he obviously needs us both. I told him that you were here, and, despite his recent illness, he insisted on coming here tonight to see you himself."

"Erdman is here? Where is he now?" Clara tried to see in the dark room full of moving people. Her stomach lurched and she didn't know if it was because of the strong drink or the thought that Erdman had sent Lilla to meet her instead of finding her himself. "I wish to speak to Erdman now."

"That's just the thing. Erdman doesn't know how to tell you how things are and that is where I come in. I thought if you could see for yourself then you can make up your mind whether you can accept it or not." Lilla extinguished her cigarette and stood. She motioned for Alvin to take his place beside Clara virtually pinning her in her chair against the wall. Clara looked towards the door and saw Erdman enter the room. She knew it was he as she recognized his familiar coat and fedora outlined against the red light behind him.

Clara's heart hammered against her chest as she watched Erdman embrace Lilla. Even in the dim light she could see the two figures meld into one and remain there. She suddenly knew the bitter taste of betrayal as she reached for her drink to wash it from her mouth. She took several rapid gulps allowing the burning sensation to alleviate the greater pain raging inside her. The room spun around her, and Clara knew that she was going to be sick. She had to get away from them and from this place. She grasped Alvin by the arm.

"Please. I just need to leave this place. I never want to see him again." Tears choked her voice as she closed her eyes.

Alvin glanced at her in pity. "Come on. We can go out the other entrance. Follow me." He put his hand under Clara's elbow and helped her to stand. He led her away from the sight of Erdman and Lilla still kissing and towards a small door in the farthest corner. The door led to another stairwell and suddenly Clara was in an alley gasping for fresh air. Alvin still held her at the elbow as he tried to push her against the wall of the nearest warehouse. Clara tried to fight against him, pushing her hands against his chest.

Just as suddenly as Alvin had thrust Clara against the wall he was gone, having been grabbed from behind and thrown down onto the ground. Clara kept her eyes closed and struggled against the arms trying to pull her forwards. Her face connected with a strong chest; she continued to cry and scream against her attackers. She had paused long enough to take a breath when she heard a familiar voice.

"Clara, it's me. You are all right now, I've got you." Erdman stood in front of her holding her close so that she could not struggle. She opened her eyes and relief flooded through her, followed closely by her new sense of betrayal, grief, and rage. She tried to push Erdman away but only managed to lose her footing and slowly sink to the ground. He eased her into a sitting position on the wall behind her as he knelt in front of her.

"Honey, what in the world are you doing here? Clara, did he hurt you?" Erdman gathered her into his arms, kissing her hair. Clara pulled away, looking at him closely. He was wearing a different coat and a new hat. Suddenly she was very confused.

Clara looked up to see Oscar Mikkelson standing over Alvin who laid bleeding on the ground where Erdman had thrown him. Oscar shook his head, "I told you, Olson, that she was up to no good, but not even I would have guessed that Lilla would send a letch like this after your girl. It's a good thing we showed up when we did." Oscar hoisted Alvin to his feet and waited for Erdman to help Clara stand.

"So, you weren't inside with her? It looked like your hat and coat from across the room; I thought it was you and her." Clara stammered. Everything continued to whirl around her, so she put her face against Erdman's chest and held him close. The relief that it had not been him was almost more than she could bear.

Oscar grimaced. "It appears as though Lilla is the reason for your missing apparel among other things. Take the keys to my rooms over on Front Street. I will take this troublemaker back to Galesville before Lilla finds him and us. Meet you back at Gale on Monday. It looks like Clara can use some strong coffee and some rest. I am sorry for all this, Clara. I tried to prevent it."

"Thanks again, Mikkelson. I owe you one for this. I will deal with Lilla later." Erdman held tightly to Clara as he whispered, "Can you walk? If not, I can carry you. We can hail a taxi when we get to the street."

"I think that I can walk now if you help me." Clara realized that she couldn't leave with Erdman and not let Mrs. Hutchins know that she was safe. She reached for a scrap of paper in her purse and hastily scribbled a note to be sent to the hotel.

'*I am in safekeeping. Erdman is here. All is well.* – Clara.'

Chapter 24

MARCH 6, 1926 –
LA CROSSE, WISCONSIN

"The past is in the past. Leave it to me." This had been Erdman's repeated answer to many of Clara's questions about Lilla and the nature of his relationship with her. Erdman had taken Clara to Oscar's rented rooms on Front Street, getting her hot black coffee to reverse the effects of the large amount of rum and cola she had consumed. He brought fresh water and towels from the water closet down the hallway so that she could wash her face and hands, putting her rumpled appearance back into order. Most importantly, he had sat in one of the large overstuffed armchairs and taken Clara onto his lap, reassuring her that she was now safe and that all would be well again.

While Clara had been immensely relieved that Erdman was not at the speakeasy making love to Lilla, she was still very confused and hurt over the many events that had occurred. Erdman had explained that he had been unwell right after Valentine's Day, but he had improved soon after. He had not received her package with the gingerbread and the love letters, nor had he received her latest note about her arrival in La Crosse. Erdman had looked very irate when Clara had wondered aloud what could have happened to them, leaving her the uneasy feeling that Lilla had been involved in their disappearances. Clara continued to ask how Lilla could have access to Erdman's private items including the hat and the coat she had used in her subterfuge with Clara. Erdman evaded most of these direct questions with his statement about the past, but it caused Clara real concern whether Lilla was truly just a part of his past or of his present as well.

It was late in the evening when Erdman asked, "Have you recovered enough to allow me to see you back to your hotel?" Clara stared at him for a moment before responding, "I thought I would stay here with you." She did not understand why he would send her away when it had been so many months since they had been together. Doubts again edged in close. Had his feelings changed for her? Was Lilla replacing her and he didn't want to tell her as Lilla had suggested, or did he really desire them both? She would never share him with anyone else. Clara's brown eyes were filled with hurt as she asked," Don't you want me here with you?"

Erdman kissed her gently. "Of course, I want you with me wherever I am. You have been through quite a trial this evening and I only want you to go back to your hotel and try to sleep. Your employer, Mrs. Hutchins, sounds very nice, but she probably would not approve of you staying here all night. I will pick you up at the hotel tomorrow afternoon after you have assisted her for the day. We can spend the afternoon and evening together and most of Sunday as well. Believe me, Clara, it is hard enough for me to send you away after only being with you for a couple of hours. I have missed you way too much."

Those were the words that Clara so desperately needed to hear. She threw her arms around him, kissing him with abandon, putting each thought and feeling of love from the last few months without him into the caress. Erdman responded with an intense passion that left them both breathless. "I need to take you back now before I change my mind." He stood, holding her in his arms and carried her to the door.

The next morning Clara awoke with excitement about the time she would spend with Erdman. She knew there were still serious issues including the questions of their future together that her father had addressed, but she also knew that her Erdman still loved her. Clara explained to Mrs. Hutchins that Erdman had come himself when his friend had told him Clara was here, and that he was feeling much better. Their trip to Galesville would no longer be necessary although Clara was still very grateful for the offer. Lena listened with a smile to Clara's recounting of some of the events from the last evening. She continued to pat Clara's hand as she listened.

"Oh, Clara, I am so happy for you. You know, this would be the perfect time for the two of you to start making some of those plans that your father mentioned. Please allow me to assist you in any way that I can. You are already like the daughter that I always wanted. Maybe you and I can pick out some beautiful things for a wedding trousseau?"

Clara hugged Lena tightly. She would start making plans just as Papa and Lena had both suggested. Hopefully, this afternoon would be the perfect time for Erdman to participate further by giving her some idea when they would get married.

Erdman was waiting for Clara at the hotel front entrance when she arrived that afternoon. He took her hand in his and held it to his side as they walked down Main Street together. Clara glanced up at the upper level windows of the hotel; there was Mrs. Hutchins smiling down upon them and waving her hand to Clara. Clara waved back and then turned to look at Erdman. He was immaculately dressed, freshly shaved, and groomed. Just the sight of him always took her breath away as it had the first time she saw him. They strolled slowly together, nodding at the passersby who were also out for a stroll on the beautiful Saturday afternoon.

"They are all jealous of the beautiful girl I have on my arm." Erdman whispered in her ear as they nodded at some gentlemen passing by. "Your new hat is very becoming, but you make it look even better." Clara beamed up at him as he smiled down at her. Lena had insisted that they begin her trousseau by purchasing a new dove gray dress with a dove gray hat in the latest cloche style. The flowers and ribbons that adorned the hat as well as the perfectly fitted coat over her dress were robin's egg blue. Clara felt like a fairy princess. She did not mention to Erdman that Lena had insisted on an ivory satin and lace dress as well as it would be the perfect wedding dress.

They had walked several blocks down Main Street when Erdman stopped in front of a shop. The elegant sign in the window read,

Irvine's Jewelers
Diamonds, Watches, Jewelry,
Wedding Ring Headquarters

"Shall we go in and see what we like?" Erdman held the door open for her. Clara's eyes widened in surprise and elation as she looked at the glass counters full of glistening jewelry displayed on beds of black velvet. A young man in a suit and tie stepped forward and asked if he could assist them. Clara blushed as Erdman replied, "We would like to see your wedding rings. Do you have anything that can compare to the beauty of my girl here?" The young man ushered them to the counter containing a myriad of different wedding rings.

"You should try on the ones you like." Erdman suggested. "Of course, you can't see the one I choose until it is time." After selecting a few choices Clara held out her hand for the clerk, but Erdman took the ring from him at the last moment.

"I believe this is where I come in." He slid the band onto her slender finger and held her hand, admiring it. "I know that you have had some questions as of late, Clara. Hopefully this answers many of them." He kissed her hand and then placed it back on the counter. She tried on several more rings at Erdman's insistence; each one of them he placed on her finger the way he had the first. When they were finished, he thanked the clerk and asked for the shop's card which he tucked in his jacket.

Clara was now certain that this was his way of telling her everything she had wanted to know. She did not need to concern herself over Lilla anymore. Erdman belonged to her; she would wear his wedding ring someday soon. It did not occur to her to ask about a future date for their wedding. She knew that Erdman wanted to surprise her with the ring he had chosen, and she did not want to ruin that. She felt that their hearts were already one and the rest of it would now be a formality.

They took the boardwalk to Riverside Park and walked along the Mississippi River. The late afternoon sun glistened off the water, sending radiant shards of colors to the sky above. It seemed to mirror the joy in Clara's heart perfectly. As Erdman paused on the walkway, she wrapped her arms around the back of his neck and placed her head just under his chin. She wanted to remember every moment of this day for the rest of her life.

"Are you ready for dinner yet? I thought we would try the River-front Restaurant and then take in a movie at the Riviera." Erdman asked, his breath tickling the top of Clara's head as she nuzzled against him. Clara moved her arms from the back of his neck to encircle his waist pulling him even closer.

"Not just yet, Erdman. That sounds wonderful for later this evening, but right now I want to go back to Oscar's rooms so that we can be truly alone." She felt rather than saw his reaction of surprise at her bold suggestion. He leaned away from her slightly and held her face in his hands. "Are you sure about this, Clara? I need to know that you mean it this time." He looked into her brown eyes and her answer was there for him. This time there would be no hesitation or regrets.

Chapter 25

APRIL 4, 1926 –
SOLDIERS GROVE, WISCONSIN

The morning of Easter Sunday dawned bright over rural Crawford County. The deep snow of winter had melted, leaving new buds of brilliant green on the trees and the emerald blades of new grass on the rolling hillsides. The spring that brought new life to the vegetation and the animals, touched the air with the scent of daffodils and tulips. The adage of "March coming in like a lion and going out like a lamb" had proven accurate yet again. The winds of March had roared and wailed but were now subdued and gentled for April's entrance.

Clara had returned from La Crosse with Mrs. Hutchins after having two glorious days with Erdman. All her fears and doubts about their future together had vanished as they had shared so much together in that short time. Clara knew that it might have been the wiser choice to not give herself over wholly to him, but she justified this by imagining that even in God's eyes they were already united in their declarations of love and commitment. She was not foolish enough to believe that Christ, Dena, and Erdman's parents would accept her reasoning, so it was more of a matter of "act in haste and repent at leisure". Their official wedding ceremony would put an end to the gossip that had generated, and Clara could not help but think that it would all happen in the next six months. She had agreed to Erdman's suggestion that they have a simple ceremony with just the two of them and possibly a celebration for her family later. Clara knew Erdman was still concerned about his parents, especially his mother, so he wanted to keep things very quiet until after they had wed.

Clara wanted to spend the Easter weekend with Lena, as the elderly woman had no other relatives with which to celebrate. Clara knew that she could still leave on Sunday evening to join her family for their celebration in Seneca. Erdman had written to tell her that he planned to come home for a few days over the Easter break. Clara had invited him to attend the Easter services in Soldiers Grove and the lunch celebration afterwards as Lena had insisted that she extend the invitation.

Clara enjoyed the view of the green hillsides as she rode along with Lena to the Franklin Lutheran Church. She had chosen her silk yellow dress with the white polka dots and her matching hat with the yellow ribbons to wear. Yellow was a traditional color chosen on Easter as it was the sign of Spring, but Clara knew it also held a special meaning for her and Erdman. She had worn the dress for the first time when they met, and he had kept the yellow ribbon from the box dinner that day; she was hopeful that he would remember it as she had.

Erdman was waiting for her when they arrived at the church. He was resplendent in a light blue suit and tie with a newly fashionable Homburg style hat in light gray. Lena gasped aloud when she saw him and whispered to Clara, "What a handsome beau! Aren't you lucky Clara that I am not sixty years younger?" Lena's musical laughter heightened the joy in Clara's heart at seeing Erdman again. Clara clasped Lena's hand, whispering back, "I am very glad. I wouldn't stand a chance." As Erdman opened the car door for the ladies, Lena assured her, "My dear, that young man only has eyes for you."

Clara took Erdman's arm as they walked together to the church door. "The same beautiful yellow dress as the first day I laid eyes on you. You took my breath away that day, Clara. You are more beautiful than ever." He still remembered their first day together. Clara could hardly wait for their next beginning.

That afternoon Clara sat with Erdman in the parlor of Lena's home. They had feasted on a sumptuous lunch that had featured lamb with mint jelly and many different types of eggs. The eggs along with chickens were the symbols in Norway for fertility and many a young bride was encouraged to eat more than her share to ensure a new arrival in the coming year. Clara had enjoyed the lunch but as the afternoon wore on her stomach became more and more disagreeable. She hoped that whatever was causing her upset stomach would soon pass as she looked forward to her mother's traditional Rakfisk dinner, a fermented trout dish served with raw onions and lefse later that evening.

As Lena handed Clara another one of the Norwegian Easter traditions, a fresh orange, Clara suddenly rushed from the room. Erdman found her a few minutes later returning from the water closet looking very pale and drawn. Clara made her apologies to Lena for departing earlier than she planned and gathered her things for Erdman to take her home. Lena insisted Clara take the fresh oranges to share with her family.

As they drove towards Seneca Erdman kept a careful eye on Clara. Her color had returned, and she seemed to have revived since losing her stomach earlier. He held her hand as she tried to assure him that she was much better, and it was only a little "urolig mage" or uneasy stomach. It seemed to have passed as suddenly as it came. Clara was grateful as she didn't want a silly thing like a sick stomach to put a damper on their beautiful day together.

Erdman insisted on pulling into the yard so that Clara could walk to the house easily. He was relieved to see that most of Clara's family including her father were gathered in a neighboring field enjoying a game of horseshoes together. Their laughter carried over the distance; Erdman saw the wistful look on Clara's face as she smiled at the sound and watched her father and siblings together. He knew that Clara still expected him to speak to her father and ask his permission and blessing for their marriage. That was not something Erdman was prepared to do now or possibly ever. He took Clara's hand in his and kissed her gently on the forehead.

"I am glad we had this day together. I need to get back to see my family before I leave for Gale tonight. Are you sure that you are feeling better?" he caressed her hand with his own brushing lightly against the ring finger of her left hand.

Clara nodded, "I really am feeling much better. I wish that you had a little time to come and see my family before you leave. They will love you like I do, Erdman." Her words full of assurance for him fell on deaf ears.

"Maybe sometime soon. We still have time, Clara. We still have time." He opened the car door for her and kissed her goodbye gently. She seemed to have improved since earlier that afternoon and Erdman felt relieved; he found that he didn't like the thought of her sick or hurt. Erdman had never stopped to consider someone else's feelings before this, so it was a novel realization for him, one that made him uneasy. Clara smiled and waved at him as he drove away down the lane to Stoney Point Road.

Erdman returned to his parent's farm in Rising Sun. Arvid was waiting for him outside the house as he drove in the driveway. Erdman could tell from the tears streaming down his little brother's face that poor little Arvid's celebration of Easter had been one of their usual family disasters. Anna's shrieks from the house punctuated by dishes breaking told Erdman all that he needed to know. *This is what happens when you let yourself fall in love with any woman. This is your real "happily ever after".* Erdman thought as he hugged his brother tightly.

"Don't worry, Arv, I have you. You and I will never make this mistake when we get older, will we? No, Sir. We will never have to go through this again."

Chapter 26

APRIL 16, 1926 –
GALESVILLE, WISCONSIN

Erdman walked briskly along the tree lined street towards his dormitory on the Gale College campus. He passed the courtyard of the Old Main, the central building of the college. The windows in the white brick building were now dark as the regular business of the day had ended. All the important administrative officers of the college were home with their wives and families, unaware of the business Erdman and some of his colleagues were conducting right under their noses.

Erdman was well known on the campus for selling his illegal gin, but he had recently added other attractions to his business that had proven very profitable. Within a few short weeks of adding on to his enterprise, he had made over a thousand dollars in cash. While some young men had to attend Gale College to learn how to run a successful business in the future, Erdman attended so that he could run his successful business at the college in the present.

Erdman opened the door to his dormitory to see a queue of college boys waiting in the hallway. They were sampling the gin that Erdman sold and talking amongst themselves as they waited entrance to the farthest room down the hallway. The room had once served as a large storage space for linens and sundries, but Erdman had commandeered it and renovated it for his purposes. To the unassuming outside population of Gale College, it still appeared to be one of the regular dormitories, but in the evenings and well into the wee hours of the morning it became a major attraction for the decidedly male population of the school.

Erdman nodded at several of the acquaintances in line that he recognized. He turned to go to his room down the opposite hallway when his newly appointed sentinel Erving approached him, a look of concern on his face.

"Hey, Boss. There is a hold up. Things have slowed way down to almost nothing and the help is insisting that you meet. All of these fine gents have been waiting a considerable amount of time already." Erving gestured to the line of boys down the hallway.

Rage burned behind Erdman's eyes, but he answered Erving casually, "Well, we can't have that, can we? Erving, go get these gents some more hooch on the house. Drink up boys, it's on me!" There was a cheer of appreciation from the waiting patrons. Erdman smiled at them while he asked Erving under his breath, "Where is she?"

Erving indicated by the inclination of his head that the help was awaiting Erdman in his own room. Erdman nodded and continued to proceed as if nothing were amiss. Inwardly he seethed at the lost profits from the free gin he had just been forced to dole out. He paused before his door, taking a large breath before opening the door, entering, and closing it again forcefully.

Lilla glanced up warily from the chair next to his bed. She was clad in a red silk robe and high heels. One leg was crossed over the other at the ankle and the top foot was twitching in nervousness, the heel making a clicking sound on the wood floor. She was smoking as usual and she held a glass half full of gin in her hand. Erdman noticed that the hand holding the glass trembled slightly. She glared defiantly at Erdman's arrival, her false bravado making his rage intensify.

Erdman walked past her to his bureau. He took out the keys to the newly installed locks on the bureau from his suit coat pocket. He unlocked the top drawer long enough to stash a huge pile of cash he took from his pants pocket, then he shut the drawer and locked it again. He could hear Lilla breathing irregularly behind him, her anger mixed with obvious fear. He left his back to her as he said in a low steady voice,

"I told you to never come in here again. Get back to work."

"I told Erving I needed to talk with you. I am exhausted and I can't do this anymore. I know that you are still angry at me but there is a better way for me to make this up to you." Lilla rose from her chair and crossed towards Erdman touching his shoulder. "You know I will do anything for you, baby. It's been a long time and I miss you."

Erdman spun to face her, the smack of his hand hitting the side of her face echoing in the small room. The force of the blow sent her reeling as she fell onto the bed across from Erdman's. Lilla started to sit up with her hand across her cheek when Erdman leaped onto the bed forcing her back down and pinning her underneath him.

"You do what I tell you to do when I tell you to do it." Erdman hissed in her face. "You need to remember that you could have it much worse than this, Lilla. Think of poor unfortunate Alvin Larson. You convinced him to help you with your deceit and suddenly he was hit by a car a few days later. I am told he will never be right again and that is your fault too. You tried to take important things from me, and you tried to control me, and I am telling you again, Lilla, no one does that to me and lives to tell about it."

Lilla tried to plead with him, "Don't you care what these other boys are doing? You loved me once, Erdman. I can make you love me again."

Erdman scoffed at her feeble attempts at seduction as he stood and walked away from her. "You have always had this set of talents, Lilla. It was high time that I profited from them. I have never loved you or any woman, and I never will. Now get back to the room before I start breaking things like your fingers or toes, you know, stuff that will hurt but won't keep you from working."

Lilla sat up and eyed Erdman with a calculating expression. "I am sure Clara would be interested to find out that you have never loved a woman and you never will. I can find her, Erdman. I did once and I can do it again."

Erdman turned once more to peer at Lilla. She was partially crouched in front of him as she picked up her discarded glass, reminding him of a cornered animal as her green eyes glittered with malice. He shook his head slowly. "You just don't learn, do you, Lilla? Why do you make me do these things?" He grasped ahold of her hand giving two of the fingers a hard yank at a right angle.

Lilla's screams of pain echoed, and there was a sudden knock at the door. Lilla continued to shriek vile things as she reached to throw the nearby glass at him. Suddenly, the shrieking siren of his blackest dreams was standing there right in front of him and Erdman knew that he had to obliterate her, sending her once again to the abyss.

Chapter 27

APRIL 18, 1926 –
GALESVILLE, WISCONSIN

*I*t was Sunday morning as Albert sat, with his hat in his hand, in the ornate sitting room outside the office of President Lokensgard, Dean of Gale College. A summons for Albert to appear had come early Saturday evening by special messenger. Albert had tried to reach Erdman by phone after receiving the summons, but it was to no avail. He prayed that the ominous news that he was here to receive in person did not include the untimely death of his oldest son. Erdman had struggled with "bad spells" resembling Anna's since he had been Arvid's age of ten or eleven. Albert was accustomed to smoothing over the skirmishes caused by both their behavior.

A small thin man came out of the door leading to the President's office and approached Albert. He nervously greeted Albert and asked him to follow into the office as the President of the college was ready to see him. Albert adjusted his suit and tie and followed the man with a sense of trepidation. He walked into the elegantly appointed office and noted the man seated behind a large mahogany desk. President Lokensgard had a grim countenance as he rose to his feet and walked around the desk to shake Albert's hand in greeting. He then motioned for Albert to take a seat in the chair placed in front of his desk as he resumed his position behind it.

"Mr. Olson, I am grateful that you could attend our meeting on such short notice. I will rarely agree to conduct any form of business for the college on a Sunday, but due to the critical nature of the dilemma we are facing it was paramount to do so." President Lokensgard sat with his hands folded, fingers interlaced, looking as if he were about to lead in a prayer.

Albert was accustomed to the interminable oratory of the collegiate elite; he wished for once that this one could just get to the point. "Is my son dead?" he blurted out, bracing himself for a possible affirmative reply. He looked straight into the eyes of the man seated opposite him and watched as they widened in surprise at his directness.

"Good heavens! No, Erdman is not deceased. You can join him as soon as we have discussed this matter concerning him."

"Well, that's good anyway. Now, why don't you just spell it out for me so we can get to a solution?" Albert continued to stare the man right in the eye wanting a no-nonsense discussion from the dignitary. He doubted that many people spoke to the Dean in this manner, but Albert was certainly not most people.

"Yes, well, as you say, I will try to spell it out then." President Lokensgard sputtered, his face reddening slightly. "Your son Erdman was involved in a very serious incident in his dormitory on Friday evening. The witnesses that have stepped forward attest to the fact that a local girl of no particular standing, one Miss Lilla Rude, was found to be in Erdman's dormitory room scantily dressed."

Albert scoffed, "You brought me all this way on a Sunday to tell me that my son is a healthy young male? I could have assured you that it was the case. I am sure you have some rule about young ladies 'of no particular standing,' as you put it, being in the rooms of the college lads, but this is hardly deserving of this overreaction. Did you intend to sensationalize this trifle, making it necessary for me to give yet another large donation to the college?"

President Lokensgard held up his hand against Albert's protestations. "If I may proceed, Mr. Olson, this is far more serious than the fact that the young lady was found in his dormitory room. Erdman was found by his fellow dorm roommates battering the young woman into unconsciousness. When the other young men tried to intervene on her behalf it took four of them to restrain him. He continued to resist all their efforts to get him to cease the beating. Finally, a strong young lad by the name of Mikkelson had to knock Erdman into unconsciousness and carry him away to the hospital. Erdman has been under a doctor's supervision since that point."

Albert looked down at the floor in front of him. "I see. What happened to the young lady? Will she be alright?" This was far worse than Albert had anticipated, and he knew if Erdman had killed the girl there would be the devil to pay.

"I am grateful to see your compassion for her. She has been hospitalized but the doctor has assured us that she will recover. We have tried to keep the entire matter private so that the reputations of good and decent people are not tarnished. This same young Oscar Mikkelson assured me that the young woman in question had not been invited into the room by your son. In fact, he told us that they had suspected this woman of recent thefts from numerous people in the dormitory including your son. Possibly he came upon her in his room while she was attempting to commit another theft. In any case it has been decided by the Gale Board of Governors that Erdman be asked to leave the university at once to avoid the nasty business of expulsion."

In other words, so the college won't look bad, Albert thought as he nodded in agreement to the solution proposed. "You will make certain that the woman's medical bills are sent directly and discreetly to me?" Albert asked as he rose from his chair. He needed to go and find Erdman and discover just how bad this outburst had been.

"Yes, of course, Mr. Olson. If I might add there were some damages to the room as well." The Dean eyed the checkbook that Albert had been holding in his hand. Albert sat back down at the desk to write. He would make sure the amount was more than enough for them to reinstate Erdman when this had all blown over in a few months.

Albert followed the directions to the hospital given him by the grateful President. He stood in front of a room that was separated from the regular wards. A young orderly stood guard outside the door as if it were a prison cell; he motioned for a nearby nurse to page the doctor on call. Albert waited outside the door and soon an older, balding man in a white coat came forward and introduced himself as Dr. Alexander.

"Mr. Olson, the nature of your son's condition has been very grave. He has experienced several violent fits followed by long periods of crying. Only this morning has he calmed enough for me to examine him properly. I would highly recommend he be sent to a larger hospital that deals with people of this mental inclination. To ignore his condition would be an egregious error."

Again, with the lengthy oratory when a few words would suffice. Albert mused. Instead he remarked, "My son just gets a little overwrought at times. I am sure that some rest and fresh air will be his best medicine. May I see him now?"

"Of course. I will send the information about Eloise Hospital in Westford, Michigan, just in case you change your mind later." Dr Alexander opened the door and ushered Albert inside. Albert could not believe his eyes. A form resembling Erdman lay on the small bed, his wrists and ankles tied to the metal rails of the bedpost. He reeked of body odors and urine, having wet himself repeatedly. His eyes were red and swollen from crying and his skin was mottled with bruises. Albert felt the breakfast he had consumed on the train lurch in his stomach.

Erdman tried to open his eyes; they were narrow slits. He turned his head towards Albert and the young orderly standing there at his bed side. "Pa? Is that you?" he rasped, attempting to sit up but failing due to his restraints.

Albert turned to the orderly. "Take those off of him right now," he demanded in a tone that would not allow argument. The orderly moved towards Erdman slowly to remove the bindings, talking gently to Erdman as he did so. Once the restraints had been removed, Albert knelt beside his son. "Do you think you can sit up, Son? I will help you." Albert gently put his arm under Erdman's shoulders and slid his son's legs towards the edge of the bed with his other hand. He lifted his son into a sitting position and sat beside him on the bed.

Erdman covered his face with his hands as tears fell down his cheeks. Albert waited beside him knowing that Erdman needed time before he could speak. Finally, Erdman stated, "She was here again, Pa, but I made her go away." It was the same story that Erdman had told his father numerous times but this time it had gone much farther than usual. Albert asked the orderly to get a water basin and towels so that he could bathe his son and get him ready to leave on the afternoon train.

Soon Albert had Erdman bathed and dressed, looking somewhat presentable for their travel. He stepped out of the room to sign the discharge papers at the nurses' station. The pretty young nurse handed Albert the papers to sign and asked, "Might I ask what Erdman's mother's name is?"

Albert responded politely, "Her name is Anna. Why do you ask?"

She smiled, "Oh I didn't know if Erdman called her Mother or by her first name. He kept calling for someone in his distress and I thought perhaps it was her."

Albert nodded while thinking to himself that Anna would be the last person on earth that Erdman would ask for. "Do you happen to remember the name?" he asked.

"Why yes. It was Clara." she said.

Chapter 28

APRIL 21, 1926 –
RISING SUN, WISCONSIN

In the three days since Erdman had returned home with Albert, there had been very little change in his mental state. He ate when Albert told him to eat, bathed himself when Albert told him to bathe, did menial tasks as instructed, and kept quietly to himself. He would sit in a chair on their front porch facing Battle Ridge and stare at the horizon. Not even young Arvid was able to rouse his big brother from this deep despondency of soul.

To Albert's great relief, Anna had taken on a role as Erdman's caretaker. She would make sweet treats for him, cover him with her own afghan, and find various pursuits to engage Erdman. She seemed very calm and sympathetic as though she understood the darkness of soul her son was experiencing. Albert knew that Anna's calm would only last for so long, but he appreciated the brief respite as he tried to help his son recover from his malaise.

Erdman would wince at times when Anna approached him, but other than that he did not show any outward evidence that he heard or saw her. Albert was convinced that Erdman would recover his full sensibilities if they only let him rest and rehabilitate. He had received a pamphlet and note from Dr. Alexander regarding the option of treatment at a psychiatric hospital in Michigan, but Albert would only consider it as a final resort if the usual things that revived Anna did not work.

Albert had decided to drive back to Gale College and retrieve Erdman's personal effects from his dormitory room. Anna's brother Nels had come to help at the farm for the day, and Edwin Knutson had the tobacco planting ready for the fields. Knutson had behaved very oddly around Erdman since the Christmas holidays. Even now he kept his distance though Erdman did not even acknowledge Knutson's presence. Edwin was good at the farming aspects of the job, but at times he was a very odd little fellow. Albert was just grateful that the hired hand had not left them after experiencing a few of Anna's outbursts, so he made sure that Edwin had a large and generous paycheck.

Albert arrived at the dormitory midmorning, hoping that it would be almost deserted as the students attended their daily classes. He had found a set of keys in Erdman's clothes and remembered to bring them in case they were needed. He opened the outside door and looked down two different hallways wondering how he could determine which room had been Erdman's. The door he had entered through opened again and a young man stood smiling at him.

Albert asked, "Would you be able to tell me which room belongs to Erdman Olson? I am his father and I came to get a few of his things."

The young man nodded and pointed to a room at the end of one of the hallways. "Yes, it is the one at that end. My name is Oscar

Mikkelson, Mr. Olson. I am one of Erdman's friends. I would be happy to assist you if you would like."

Albert followed Oscar to the room he had indicated as belonging to Erdman. Albert used the key to open the door; it had been untouched since the altercation on Friday night. The room was a ramshackle mess; many items were broken and there was blood spattered against the wall and the floor. Albert was alarmed to see how much Erdman's last outburst had escalated. Albert recalled that President Lokensgard had mentioned young Mikkelson assisting with removing Erdman from the room.

"I was told that you were extremely helpful in getting Erdman out of here. I want you to know that Erdman and I don't forget people who have done a service for us." Albert reached for his wallet in his suit coat pocket, but Oscar stopped him.

"I did what I did to help Erdman and your thanks is not necessary. I only hope that Erdman will come out alright as he is a pretty decent fellow. I gave the Dean a general overview of what happened, but I left out some details that would be inconvenient to Erdman. This young woman, Lilla, had stolen letters and other personal items from Erdman with the help of his roommate. She tried to use these things to harm Erdman and another young woman. Apparently, she had threatened to do more harm to this young woman and Erdman lost control with her. Hopefully she will be wise enough not to make any more trouble for Erdman, but I will be keeping my eye on her just the same."

"Would you happen to know the name of this other young woman you mentioned? Was she of the same ilk as this Lilla?" Albert decided that he was going to have a long talk with his son about loose women and their propensity to inflict damage. Hopefully, Erdman would soon be able to comprehend anything he had to tell him.

"Yes, her name is Clara. She seems to be a very nice young lady and very devoted to your son. She is the type of girl that a fellow might consider marrying someday. When Lilla discovered Erdman was interested in Clara, she tried to claim him when he was not hers to claim. I would say it will be good for Erdman to be absent from Lilla for a little while so that she will find another admirer and move on."

There was the same name that the nurse had mentioned, the girl Erdman had called for when he needed help. Albert needed to find this girl and see if she might help Erdman recover.

"Where might I find this Clara? Does she attend school here or just live nearby?"

Oscar appeared surprised at Albert's question. "Mr. Olson, Clara isn't from Galesville or the college. She lives near you in Rising Sun. I wonder that Erdman hasn't mentioned her as he goes home specifically to see her and sends her letters frequently."

Albert tried to cover for his mistake quickly. "He probably has mentioned her. There have just been so many different girls, I forgot about her."

Oscar grinned slightly as though he did not believe Albert's lie about meeting the girl. "If you met Clara, I doubt that you would forget her," was his simple reply.

Oscar helped Albert gather Erdman's possessions including the large amounts of cash from the top bureau drawer. Albert knew about Erdman's enterprise selling the gin and assumed that recent business at the college had been very good. He insisted that Oscar take one hundred dollars of the cash, make sure any associates of Erdman's enterprise had been paid what was due to them, and pocket the remainder himself.

In the last locked drawer there were several miscellaneous items that seemed out of place with the trappings of his bootlegging son; a brown silk tie, a black-eyed Susan that had been dried between two sheets of paper, some Mary Pickford movie ticket stubs, a business card from a jewelry store, and a length of yellow ribbon. Albert included them in the top of the last box, hoping something might produce a reaction from Erdman and impel him from his present state of melancholy.

Erdman was sitting in his usual spot on the front porch when Albert arrived back at the farm late that afternoon. Arvid sat nearby keeping watch over his brother, ready to run for anything Erdman might need. Albert handed the box he was carrying to his younger son and asked him to take it up to Erdman's room. Albert took Arvid's chair beside Erdman and stretched out his legs after the long drive home.

Albert decided that he would try to get Erdman to talk to him. It was a risk that might send Erdman spiraling back down to his place of darkness, but Albert knew that he had to try something. It had been days and Erdman had never gone this long after his previous outbursts. He leaned close to his son and whispered,

"Erdman, can you tell me about Clara?"

Albert waited. Erdman continued to stare at the ridge on the horizon as if he had not heard his father speak. A sudden urge to breathe in alerted Albert to the fact that he had been holding his breath, hoping this Clara would be an answer. Albert closed his eyes in resignation. He would check for more information on the hospital in Michigan tomorrow morning. It was only a matter of time before Anna slid into one of her episodes, and Albert knew that he could never manage them both at once. He had tried to throw a lifeline to his son, but this time the depths were too deep.

Albert patted Erdman's knee and rose from his chair. He walked back down the front steps and headed for the car. He would bring the boxes of Erdman's belongings into the house and deal with them later. He opened the car door and turned to find Erdman standing beside him. Erdman looked directly at Albert for the first time since he had arrived home again. His hand was trembling as he picked up the length of yellow ribbon from the top of the box Albert held. Albert froze in place trying to decide what Erdman might do next.

Erdman pressed the ribbon to his lips once and tucked it away in his pocket. "How long have I been gone?" He asked the simple question as though he had merely been on a journey and had returned home again. Albert realized in a way that was exactly what had happened as he put the box back down so he could embrace his son. Like the prodigal son, Erdman had returned once again.

Albert remembered his statement to young Mikkelson earlier that day. '*I want you to know that Erdman and I don't forget people* who *have done a service for us.*' Whoever this Clara might be, Albert owed her a debt of gratitude for singlehandedly rescuing his son.

Chapter 29

MAY 7, 1926 –
SENECA, WISCONSIN

It was a warm spring in Crawford County; the frost had already left the ground making the time right to plant the tobacco seedlings. The seedlings had been grown in beds under tobacco cloth until they were about six to eight inches high, and now they would be carefully planted two to three feet apart in long rows in the rich black soil. A good tobacco crop would mean a bountiful harvest and cash for an entire family to live on for the year.

Everyone helped with sowing the tobacco seedlings into the ground on Christ Olson's farm. Christ, Bernard, and Adolph had worked long hours tilling and fertilizing the soil so that the young seedlings could grow deep roots down into the earth. Alice, Clara, Cornelia, and Inga rode on special benches on the back of the wagons, planting the seedlings in the furrows made by their brothers and father. It was tedious and strenuous work, but they knew that the harvest could bring good provision for the whole family.

Clara rode along on the back of the tobacco wagon carefully placing the seedlings in the rich earth below. Alice sat beside her watering each plant carefully after Clara had placed it in the ground. Bernard followed behind them gently tamping the soil around each young plant. The sun was already warm, and the earth gave a moist, sweet, heady smell. Clara normally loved the almost cloying smell of the freshly turned earth mixing with water, but today her stomach was giving her signals that much more of the scent would cause more emesis from her.

Clara had been battling with her stomach since Easter Sunday. Just when she thought that her stomach ailment had improved, she would become queasy and often lose her stomach contents. She tried to not fuss about it as her older sister Emma often did when she experienced cramps from her monthly periods. Emma would take to her bed and act as if she were about to die at any moment when it was something as simple as letting nature take its course. Clara knew it had to be something just as simple and she did not wish to alarm her parents, so she had kept quiet about her indisposition.

Christ had just called a break for their lunch when Clara jumped off the back of the wagon to head for the outhouse again. She could hear her brothers' teasing laughter as Clara had taken her fair share of breaks to relieve herself already.

"There she goes again!" Adolph laughed. "How can one little gal have to pee so often?" he asked Bernard who shrugged his shoulders as he chuckled. Alice glared at her brothers and turned towards them with her hands on her hips.

"Well, that kind of talk is why you two aren't exactly beating back the women chasing after you! Leave her alone for once. Don't you two have anything better to do?" Alice chided as her brothers laughed even harder. Alice headed towards Clara who had just exited the outhouse. Clara looked pale as she sat down on a bench under a large maple tree.

"How about a drink of cold water?" Alice offered as Clara wiped her sweaty face in her apron. Clara nodded her thanks and Alice headed for the hand pump in the yard. She primed the pump and soon fresh cold water from the well flowed out into the tin cup kept there for drinking. Alice took the cup of water into the kitchen and sprinkled a bit of ground ginger into the cold water, then returned with the ginger water for her sister to drink.

"Is your stomach still bothering you?" Alice asked with concern as she gave the cup to Clara. When Clara nodded Alice asked, "Clara, just how long has this been going on? It seems like more than a couple of weeks to me."

Clara admitted, "It has been off and on again since Easter Sunday. I don't think anything is the matter and I don't want to fuss like Emma does about her monthlies. That will really draw the comments from our brothers." Alice laughed in agreement, then suddenly thought of something else.

"Clara, when did you have your last monthly? We haven't washed cloths for you in a while."

Clara blushed at her sister's direct line of questioning. She paused to think as she was certain that it had not been very long, only to realize that her last monthly course that she could recall had been in late February right before she went to La Crosse. She had spent two days with Erdman in La Crosse and now it had been almost nine weeks without the indicator that a young woman was not...

Alice watched as Clara's face turned from a rosy blush to a white pallor and then a greenish cast as she ran for the outhouse again. Alice could hear her sister's retching amid her sobs and knew she had an answer to her question. Clara reemerged and sat down beside Alice on the bench. The sisters did not speak, as the reality of their discovery set in.

Dena came to the back door to call the tardy sisters to the noon meal. "Girls! Your pa has been at the table waiting to say grace. Come in right now." Her tone was stern as she scolded them and motioned for them to follow quickly. Alice acted as though she were going to try to make an excuse for Clara not to attend the meal, but Clara stood quickly and answered her mother.

"Sorry, Mama. I was a little overcome with the heat and Alice brought me a cool drink. We did not mean to make you and Papa wait for us. We are coming right now." Clara pulled Alice to her feet and headed for the back door and the retreating figure of their mother. Clara knew that she must not let her parents know about her condition at the risk of Papa or her brothers doing harm to Erdman. She must try to act as if she felt well for his sake.

Clara regretted that Mama had chosen this day to serve boiled potatoes and sauerkraut with sausage for their noon meal. The odiferous food and her recent revelation coupled to make Clara's stomach rebel and her head swim. She had to quickly excuse herself and make her escape outside. Alice offered an explanation that Clara was suffering under the same symptoms that plagued Emma causing an immediate sympathy from their older sister and a more skeptical look from their mother. Bernard and Adolph lamented that they had teased their little sister when she had been feeling unwell. Alice's diversion seemed to have worked. Only Christ sat staring at the door through which Clara had fled.

Clara walked to the end of their farmhouse lane so that she could be alone with her thoughts. While she was shocked that she was pregnant, she was also happy that she would have Erdman's child. She needed to talk to Erdman rather than write letters back and forth as they had been doing recently. He had written that he had come home to Rising Sun in the last few weeks because of a set of bad tonsils and was facing having them removed. She did not want to tell him before his surgery, but she did not know how long she could wait. If it had already been nine weeks, then a new baby would arrive right after Christmas and they absolutely must be officially married well before that. Clara placed her hand across her stomach for the first time since realizing that her child lay hidden there. A flood of love, powerful and protective, rushed through Clara as she walked back towards the farmhouse. She was a mother now; her child needed married parents.

Chapter 30

MAY 10, 1926 –
VIROQUA, WISCONSIN

The city of Viroqua, Wisconsin, was bustling for a Monday afternoon. The streets were filled with automobiles and the sidewalks and shops were filled with patrons. This county seat of Vernon County was a busy intersection for some major highways— U.S. Highways 14 and 61 and Wisconsin Highways 27, 56, and 82. It served as a crossroads, and the businesses there thrived from the populace moving through.

Albert brought Erdman and Arvid to Viroqua, joining the throng of people in the downtown district that afternoon. Anna had joined two of her sisters in traveling to La Crosse for several days. She visited the expensive sanatoriums and salons taking in restorative treatments that Albert doubted benefitted Anna in any real way, but it distracted her and that was just as good. Albert had worked along with Edwin, Erdman, and Arvid to set the tobacco seedlings for numerous tiring days in the last few weeks and a respite day in Viroqua had been much anticipated.

While Erdman had come out of the catatonic state he was in earlier, he still looked fatigued and sickly. Albert knew there were several good clinics in Viroqua that had helped the veterans of the recent World War with conditions such as shell shock. Albert had taken Erdman to one of these veteran homes several times in the last month, and each time Erdman had shown improvement. He decided that today they would combine another visit for Erdman with some shopping, a movie, and a dinner later in the day.

Albert had dropped Erdman off at the clinic on Walnut Street, and he and Arvid headed for the downtown to find something to occupy their time while they waited. Arvid liked the fountain sodas at Dahl Pharmacy so they headed there first. They entered the busy pharmacy and strolled towards the back where the ice cream counter was situated. Arvid hopped up on one of the few empty stools at the counter and looked at the menu on a chalkboard nearby. Albert left him there to decide which treat to choose while he picked up a few sundries around the store. He had brought a bottle of tonic that the doctor in Galesville had prescribed for Erdman, wanting the pharmacist to suggest something else to replace it as it was almost gone.

Albert waited as two young women consulted with the pharmacist in hushed tones. The pharmacist stepped into the dispensary and brought back a brown bottle, handing it to one of the young women. She thanked him and they turned and walked past Albert towards the ice cream counter. Albert was next to consult with the pharmacist about Erdman's tonic.

After reading the label the pharmacist commented, "This is a very heavy dose of a barbiturate. It can be very addictive and is commonly used to euthanize someone. Has your son shown adverse effects from taking this medication?" After Albert explained some of Erdman's symptoms, the pharmacist suggested getting rid of the current tonic and taking something far less potent. Albert hoped this would help in getting Erdman back to his old form. He thanked the pharmacist and headed for Arvid at the ice cream counter.

When Albert found Arvid, he was chatting happily with the two young ladies who had consulted the pharmacist. Albert noted that they were both very pretty girls and he was amused that already young Arvid had such good taste. Arvid hopped off the stool he had been perched on to hug the young woman who had received the medicine from the pharmacist. Obviously, Arvid had met the young lady prior to today, but Albert did not recognize her at all. Albert walked up to where his son and the young woman stood, nodding at the other young woman who was waiting a few feet away. Arvid was in the middle of telling the pretty girl a story.

"I was able to visit at Harald and Jorg's house just like you said. We had so much fun and Mrs. Bjornstad said I can come back again soon. I was hoping that you might visit too because I haven't seen you since you and Erdman came to bring me cookies. I miss you and your cookies, Clara." Arvid's eyes lit up as he looked at her, and she was smiling at him in obvious affection. She noticed Albert out of the corner of her eye and started for a moment looking concerned that he was standing so close to them. The first thing Albert noticed were her luminous brown eyes as she looked at him with curiosity. This had to be the Clara he had been hearing about.

"Papa. I found one of my friends from Tully School. She took care of the Bjornstads when they had their twins and she brought Harald and Jorg their lunch. She brought lunch for me when Mama was having her bad days." Arvid trailed off as if he suddenly recalled that he was not supposed to mention his mother's condition and he looked anxiously at his father. Albert smiled gently at Arvid encouraging him to continue without correction. "Clara, this is my papa. Well, he is Erdman's papa, too, of course. Clara said she couldn't decide who was the better looking of the Olson brothers, Erdman or me, but I think it's me." Arvid nodded his head knowingly at them both. Albert chuckled while Clara blushed and smiled shyly at Albert.

Apparently, Clara had rescued more than one of his sons. "Clara, I am happy to meet you. I want to thank you for caring for my son while my wife was ill. Arvid, I think it would be a good idea to thank Clara for her kindness towards you by offering to buy both these pretty ladies a treat from the ice cream counter. What do you say?" Albert looked up to include the young woman a few feet away who was now staring at him in shock. Arvid was shaking his head in agreement with his father's suggestion and offered his stool to Clara.

Clara smiled at Arvid's gallantry as she introduced Albert to the other young woman. "Thank you, Mr. Olson. It is very nice to meet you as well. This is my sister, Alice." Alice approached slowly still regarding Albert as if he were a sideshow attraction at the circus. Albert gestured for Alice to take the stool beside Clara as he and Arvid walked to the other side of Clara to sit down. Albert asked the ladies and Arvid for their choices and placed all their orders with the soda jerk behind the counter.

Clara listened as Arvid gave her all the details of their visit to Viroqua, nodding her head at him to encourage him to continue. Albert could not remember when Arvid had been so animated in conversation as he was often a rather shy and withdrawn boy at home. Albert noted Clara's expression when Arvid mentioned that they were waiting for Erdman to be finished with a doctor appointment so they could do more shopping and have dinner. Clara looked confused and then worried when hearing that Erdman was at the doctor again. She remained calm and serene with Arvid but had given Albert several furtive glances over the top of the lad's head looking as if she wanted to know more of Erdman's present whereabouts.

Albert was unsure about how to proceed. He would like to have a lengthier conversation with Clara, but this was not a good setting for it. He thought it was rather heartless to allow her to continue to worry when Erdman was only a few blocks away but he couldn't just scoop her and her sister up and cart them over to the clinic, surprising Erdman and possibly revealing more about his condition then he was willing to share. Albert formed a quick plan in his mind.

"Have you ladies visited the park on the far edge of town? It has beautiful views and it is one of Erdman's favorite places to visit when he is in town." Clara's beautiful eyes softened as she nodded at him. Albert believed the perceptive girl understood his meaning. When they had finished, he stood with Arvid and bade the ladies a good afternoon, leaving the pharmacy to walk back and meet Erdman.

Erdman looked even more restored when they found him waiting outside the clinic. Albert suggested getting dinner from one of the local diners and taking it to the park for a picnic. Albert had asked Arvid to not tell Erdman about seeing Clara at the pharmacy so that they could surprise his brother with the outing. Erdman seemed mildly surprised with the idea of a picnic but agreed to go with his father and brother.

Albert made quick work of ordering food, getting enough for the possibility of extra guests. When Albert pulled the car into the park entrance he watched as Erdman looked up to see Clara standing nearby. The intuitive girl had followed Albert's suggestion hoping she might see Erdman.

Erdman barely waited for the car to stop before he bolted out of the passenger door and ran towards Clara. He embraced her and kissed her hair repeatedly as they spoke in whispers to each other. Albert could see that Clara was crying as she stepped back to look at his son's face. The look of adoration on her face assured Albert that he had just located the best possible medicine for his son.

Arvid asked Albert as they carried the food towards a table where Alice sat waiting, "Papa, aren't we going to go get Erdman and Clara? They will miss dinner."

Albert ruffled the hair on top of Arvid's head. "Not just yet, Son. Not just yet."

Clara smiled up through teary eyes at Erdman as she took in the changes in him since they had been together at Easter. He had lost a considerable amount of weight, he was very pale, and there were dark circles under his eyes. The usual spark of unspoken mischief in his eyes had dulled to almost nonexistence. But he was there, standing in front of her, overjoyed at their meeting, and Clara was so happy to see him.

She ran her fingertips along the line of the chin she had come to know and love so well. Erdman's eyes were closed as if he were afraid to open them and find that she had vanished, a momentary figment of his imagination. She gently kissed his chin several times slowly producing his familiar grin as she assured him that she was very real indeed. He opened his eyes drinking her form in as though he had been dying of thirst, slowly bending his head to graze her lips with his own. Her response to his kiss was immediate; she had been longing for the touch of his lips to hers.

There was a considerable period of kisses, caresses, and murmuring affirmation of love for each other. They knew that Alice, Albert, and Arvid were somewhere close by, but they were alone in their own little world of each other. Clara suddenly remembered that one other person had entered their world as a light flutter swept across her belly. She was thrilled that Erdman was with her the first time she felt their baby move but she was in a quandary on whether to tell him now or allow him to recover more before changing his life forever.

She decided to wait a little while longer for a time when they were truly alone. Alice had come to Viroqua with her to seek a remedy for her morning sickness and to order a maternity corset by mail so that she could get it discreetly. Arvid and Mr. Olson were also waiting politely for Clara and Erdman to join them. She wanted Erdman all to herself so that they could share the love they had for each other and their child and so they could plan a marriage ceremony before anyone else found out their secret.

Erdman and Clara walked hand in hand to where the members of their two families chatted amiably with each other. Clara prayed this was the beginning of good relations between the two Olson clans. They joined in the conversation and enjoyed the dinner with a relish that had not been present for either of them for a long while.

After enjoying their repast, Albert offered to forgo the movie and take Clara and Alice home to Seneca so that their parents would not get concerned at their lateness. They piled their purchases into his car and left for home together. Alice sat in the front seat with Arvid and Albert, leaving the back seat for Clara and Erdman. The two sat close together whispering back and forth and joining in the light-hearted conversation from the front seat. They even sang a few songs when Arvid asked if they could all sing together. The time seem to fly by and soon they arrived at the lane on Stoney Point Road. Albert parked the car at the end of the lane and he and Arvid waited for Erdman to walk Clara part of the way to the house. Erdman kissed Clara goodnight and promised to come to see her that weekend. He was still uncertain as to how all of this had transpired, but he was too grateful to be with Clara again to ask too many questions.

Arvid had fallen asleep sitting between Erdman and Albert on their way back to Rising Sun. His soft snores were the only indicator of his presence in the car on the quiet ride home. The boy had enjoyed himself immensely on one of the nicer days in Erdman's memory of his family. Albert marveled that Erdman already appeared to have regained much of his former stamina after only a few hours in Clara's presence. Albert hoped that the young woman might become a more permanent fixture in Erdman's life if only he could get Anna to see the reasoning of it. He knew that the chances of Anna ever accepting Clara were very slim. They were almost home when Albert brought Erdman back to reality with one statement.

"You know that your ma must never find out about today."

Chapter 31

MAY 15, 1926 –
SOLDIERS GROVE, WISCONSIN

The afternoon sun sent its warm rays through the panes of Lena Hutchins' parlor windows. The sunlight caught the dust motes swirling in the air from the flurry of activity as Clara assisted Lena in sorting through various boxes scattered on the parlor floor. Clara had brought the boxes from the attic as Lena only trusted "her girl" with the treasures she had stored inside each one. Many of the items had been brought from Norway when Lena was a young bride coming all the way to Soldiers Grove, Wisconsin, to marry her husband Samuel.

"That box, please, Clara." Lena pointed to yet another box. Clara bent to pick up the box and brought it to the elderly lady. Lena nodded as she peered inside the box and began to remove several of the items. She produced a large wooden chest with the traditional Rosemaling (floral designs painted in bright colors) on the top. Inside the chest was a Bunad, the traditional wedding suit for a bridegroom, an ivory fan, a silver flute, and a tiara with silver bangles extending off the sides. Lena's hands ran over each item thoughtfully as she recalled her own wedding day so many years ago. Lena turned to Clara and extended her hand. Clara smiled as she took Lena's hand to join her in looking at the remembrances.

"You see, Clara. My Samuel wore this Bunad on our wedding day. He looked like a regal prince standing there waiting for me to join him in the procession to the church. A man playing this flute led the procession and we followed, then our parents, and all the wedding party, family, and guests. I held this fan with a spray of roses that Samuel brought for me and I wore this tiara over my veil. The bangles jingle as you walk, and it chases all of the evil spirits away so that you have only blessings." Lena demonstrated by jangling the small bangles as she laughed, her laughter sounding much like the melodious jingling.

Lena placed the fan and the tiara in Clara's hands as she kissed her cheek. "It is my honor to give these to you. I have a feeling that you might have need of them soon. Use them in good health, my darling girl." Lena beamed with pride at Clara and clapped her hands in delight. "Do you have any idea when it might be?" Lena turned her head to one side looking just like one of the little chickadees she fed in her yard each day.

Clara looked at the precious treasures Lena had placed in her hands. "I am hoping it is soon. We have talked about getting married countless times and I am just waiting for him to set the date." Erdman was coming to pick Clara up this afternoon after she had finished helping Lena. He wanted to take her for dinner in Prairie du Chien, and Clara was hoping that one of the wedding bands that she had tried on at the jewelers in La Crosse would also be present this evening.

"Thank you so much, Lena. I don't know if I should accept such a precious gift from you." Clara was constantly amazed at Lena's generosity, but she did not want to take advantage of it in any way.

"Accept it you shall, as when I am gone no one else will even know that it or I was here. Give it to your own daughter someday and remember me by it my sweet Clara. Do you think Erdman will want to wear the Bunad?" Lena laughed as she held up the ornate suit complete with suspenders, vest, shorts, and hosiery. They both laughed, knowing that many things had changed from the traditions of the Old Country, but Clara hoped for a daughter to pass on this gift from her elderly friend one day. She would keep Lena's memory alive with her own children including the one who lay hidden within her that very moment.

Lena stood on her wide porch outside waving goodbye with her handkerchief as Erdman and Clara drove away a few hours later. She had insisted that Clara take the wooden chest with the beautiful Rosemaling across the top to hold the treasures she had given to her. Erdman had put it carefully into the car looking at Clara with curiosity when Lena mentioned he might want to look inside the box later in the evening.

While Erdman drove, he regaled Clara with many of the details of his rowing team at Gale College. He did not mention that he had been asked to leave the college back in April, because he was certain that his father would get him reinstated with another generous donation. He did not want Clara to be concerned about the situation especially regarding anything to do with Lilla. He tried to keep the details of his recent illness to a minimum as well, blaming the sickness on his tonsils and telling her that he was soon due to have them removed. Erdman had returned to his old habits of omitting details that were inconvenient for his purposes.

Erdman had chosen to take Clara for dinner at the elegant Dousman Hotel, built by the millionaire fur trader Hercules Dousman, and situated with a beautiful view of the Mississippi River. The meal was extravagant with very rich foods served in several courses. Clara was grateful that the tonic the pharmacist had given her for her morning sickness had been working as she did not wish to concern Erdman any more than she already had at Easter time. Erdman looked far healthier than he had a few days before and Clara began to contemplate telling him about their baby that evening. She wished that he might bring up the topic of their wedding date; she did not want him to feel forced to do so after she had told him her news. She would continue to wait and hope for the best possible time.

After dinner they rode the ferry across the Mississippi River that led into Marquette, Iowa. There was a beautiful overlook near the ferry docks, and they enjoyed the view together as Erdman held Clara, resting his chin on the top of her head. This was what he had been waiting for, their time spent alone. Clara rested against him with her eyes closed.

"You know, Minnesota is a better place than Wisconsin or Iowa to elope. In Wisconsin and Iowa, you wait three days for a marriage license, and in Minnesota you don't have to wait at all." Erdman's musing aloud had Clara opening her eyes suddenly and turning her face to look at him. "Winona isn't that far from La Crosse when it comes time for us." Clara smiled up at him her brown eyes sparkling.

"Do you have any idea of when it may be time? I want to make sure that I am prepared after all." Clara looked at him so hopefully that Erdman felt a twinge of regret for having mentioned it. If there was one person he would ever consider marrying, it was Clara. But there were mountains of obstacles including his mother and his own recent mental breakdown standing between them. He needed to have her continue thinking it was a possibility without committing himself to the actual eventuality. Erdman leaned forward to place a kiss on her nose.

"I am thinking that we need more time to plan our future. We can't just get married and not have anywhere to live. While I would love to keep you in my dorm room at Gale, they have rules about such things." He chuckled, forgetting all the former dorm rules he had blatantly disregarded when it suited him. Clara frowned and bit her lower lip as she looked towards the ground. She turned back and looked at the view before them again, her hands clasped together across her stomach.

They took the last ferry back across the river to Prairie du Chien. The sun was just setting in brilliant hues over the river as Erdman opened Clara's car door for her. She had been very quiet and pensive since he had brought up the elopement earlier. Erdman knew he needed to lift her spirits again as he hoped for her eager reciprocation to his passionate intentions. He had been without her for too long.

As Erdman drove along the River Road, he took Clara's hand from her lap and brought it to his lips, kissing each finger and lingering over the ring finger on her left hand. She wanted his full commitment and, while he could not give her that, he could give her more reason to hope for the near future. She loved him and she had proven her devotion to him in numerous ways. He would take another risk by broaching the subject again.

"Honey, what if I check to see if there is a small house we could rent near the college? It might not be much at first, but we would be together when I go back to school in September. We would have to sneak away to Minnesota before then." He heard her gasp, and he almost let go of the steering wheel as she flew across the seat at him hugging him tightly and peppering the side of his face with kisses. He pulled the roadster off to the side of the road and kissed her longingly.

"Let's you and I drive to our place over by the farm and you can show me more of that appreciation, Bright Eyes. Don't you forget where we were just now."

Clara's eyes shined as she nodded eagerly. She curled up against him on the seat with her head on his shoulder. Her news could wait a little while longer as she now had an elopement to plan and it should be in plenty of time, hopefully July or early August. Clara remembered the wood trunk in the back seat with Lena's wedding fan and tiara inside. Lena had been right; she would need them soon.

Chapter 32

JUNE 3, 1926 –
SENECA, WISCONSIN

The town of Seneca, Wisconsin, was set for the customary Thursday night dance at Grace Tolefson's hotel and pool hall. The early summer heat brought many lads from the nearby farms to dance, flirt with pretty girls, and buy illegal gin from Erdman Olson. While the sale and distribution of alcohol were forbidden by law, the consumption of alcohol was still legal, and this legal loophole made a booming business for Erdman.

The past few weeks spent with Clara had returned Erdman to his physical health prior to his breakdown. His mental health was improving at a slower pace, but Erdman was a master at disguising the signs of unstable symptoms so that even his pa had stopped taking Erdman for the weekly visits to the veterans' clinic in Viroqua. Albert had viewed Clara as a cure-all for his son, and he encouraged Erdman to spend copious amounts of time in the company of the pretty young girl with the gorgeous brown eyes. Albert made sure that

Anna was kept unaware of Clara's existence and Erdman's growing attachment to her.

Clara could be seen riding along in Erdman's roadster through the hills and valleys of Crawford County. She and Erdman had even gone on longer sojourns; they went to nearby Richland County to watch the Ringling Bros and Barnum and Bailey Circus parade down Court Street in downtown Richland Center, then ate ice cream at the Blue Bird Cafe. There were concerts in the bandstand at Viroqua and even the occasional baseball game played in Liberty Pole. Erdman was able to sell gin out of the back of his car as they traveled from place to place. Clara's pretty face had attracted many more clientele than Erdman usually experienced outside his home territory of Crawford County. She merely sat in the rumble seat and smiled at the various patrons while they lined up in droves. Erdman didn't allow them to come close enough to flirt with Clara, but they could admire her from afar.

In the times they spent alone Clara had become just as passionate as Erdman. She had fully accepted his ploy of eloping and settling in a small house near the college at Galesville, so she considered herself his wife in everything but name. Erdman knew that he would need to change tactics once they drew near the dates he had suggested for carrying their plan out, but he was selfish enough to enjoy the benefits of being her husband without worrying over her later devastation when she discovered that it would not happen.

Erdman pulled into the alley behind the Tolefson Hotel that Thursday night to conduct his business and then go find Clara. He had resumed the gin sales in the middle of May and by early June he already had a significant stash of cash built up again. He was grateful that his father had thought to bring his money home from his dorm room at Gale since he still had not heard about readmission for the fall semester. He knew it was probably only a matter of time before the college relented and allowed him to return, valuing his father's ready money more than they valued their stuffy old rules of conduct.

He had contemplated what he might do if the college did not allow him to attend again, even considering taking Clara up on the elopement scheme and carrying her off to Chicago or New York City where he was sure that he could make a lively business from the scratch he had already saved. But then he would remember all the times that Clara spoke of her family and knew that while she wanted to be with him, she didn't want to be without them.

Erdman sat in the roadster deep in thought when a group of young people approached him from around the corner. Erdman understood that this was a clear sign that they wished to purchase his gin, taking it back down the street to consume. Erdman recognized several faces in the group; he was relieved to see that Alice Olson was not among them this evening. Alice often gave Erdman shrewd glances when she thought he wasn't noticing. She was very loyal to her sister so she would not reveal to her parents the nature of Clara and Erdman's relationship, but it was obvious that she did not trust Erdman as Clara did.

Erdman was in the middle of selling his hooch when Christine Anderson sauntered up to the car and leaned against it. She had shown signs in the past of having a crush on Erdman, so he flirted with her when it was convenient for him but, lately, he had largely taken to ignoring her. As the other couples made their purchases and strolled down the street, Erdman turned his attention to Christine who was still leaning against the car smiling alluringly at him. A small voice inside him told him to proceed with caution, but Erdman was never good at listening to anyone including himself.

"What is a pretty lady like you doing out here all by herself?" Erdman felt a bit rusty at his flirtation as he realized that he had spoken this way to only Clara for months. That thought irritated him, so he reached to put his arm around the attractive girl. He was not married even if Clara wanted to pretend, and no woman ever was going to control him. He tried again escalating his next overture.

"Are you seeking gin or company or both?" Erdman felt better and her giggling made him sure that he still had the ability to seduce even though he had been out of practice.

"I guess that all depends, Erdman." Christine turned so that her body grazed his lightly. "I mean everyone knows that you and Clara Olson are a pretty hot item right now. I don't really have any designs on you after tonight, but I don't want to get in the middle of a big mess or anything." She batted her eyes at him as she traced her finger across his chest.

"I didn't realize that Clara and I were such a topic of conversation." Erdman's voice sounded gruffer than he intended. Perhaps this little tete a tete was not such a good idea after all. He recalled hearing that Christine and her cousin Marie were both good friends of Alice Olson's, and he did not need any word of his indiscretions getting back to Clara. Why did it seem that Clara controlled his every waking moment even when she was not present?

"Oh, my goodness, Erdman. You two are the talk of the whole town! I have heard the stories of your late-night meetings and your traveling alone together all over the state. The latest story is that Clara is in the family way and you won't marry her. My cousin told me how Clara was sick to her stomach for months and the silly goose didn't even realize why."

Erdman's mind was reeling. "Who in the world is making up these stories? I tell you that none of it is the truth and I don't want you to repeat them to anyone else. Clara is a nice girl."

"Clara used to be a nice girl before you came along. Why, even her ma and sisters have been shunned by a few church ladies who believe the stories about you two. Like I said, Erdman, we can have some fun, but I don't want to get in the middle of any trouble." Christine leaned forward to kiss him, but Erdman stepped back away from her, the familiar rage starting a slow burn behind his eyes.

"If you are looking for gin here it is, Christine. Otherwise I am calling it a night." Erdman handed her a bottle from the back seat. She reached inside her bodice to retrieve her cash, but Erdman waved her away. "Keep your money and keep your mouth shut about Clara. I am telling you it's not that way." Christine accepted the bottle, kissed his cheek quickly and sauntered away.

Erdman took another bottle from the trunk, took a large drink, and crossed to the driver's side door. He needed to get to Clara's house and with her help try to figure out what was going on. As he turned the car's headlights on, he noticed a man standing on the opposite street corner staring at him. He was tempted to stop and see if the man was a possible customer, but for the second time that night the small voice inside him told him to keep going. He listened this time and drove the car quickly down the alley and onto Highway 27, leaving Bernard Olson where he had been standing on the street corner for the last thirty minutes.

As Erdman drove the three miles to Clara's house, he replayed Christine's words in his mind. Clara had never mentioned that she or her family might be suffering from the malicious talk that was obviously going on about her and Erdman. As for a baby, that wasn't even a possibility. He was always careful in using protection with Clara and anyone else. He mulled over his various intimacies with Clara in the past trying to recall that each time he had taken the necessary precautions to prevent pregnancy. The only ones that he could recall being different were the times they spent at Oscar's boarding rooms in La Crosse. He had looked at wedding rings with Clara and she had surprised him with wanting to be together that afternoon. He was sure that he had the normal protection with him as he always kept it in his overcoat pocket, except…

Erdman pulled the roadster off to the side of the road just outside the Seneca city limits and closed his eyes trying to recall through the haze of the various events that occurred before his last breakdown. He always kept the protection in his overcoat except Lilla had stolen his overcoat and he had to borrow one of Oscar's overcoats and hats when they left in a hurry from Gale to intercept Clara at the speakeasy. When he and Clara were intimate the following afternoon, he had not had the protection because he had not had his own overcoat and he had been taken by surprise at Clara's sudden desire to be alone. He had not had the protection….

Obviously, he had been carried away at the time and then had put the possible risk out of his mind afterwards, as that was his usual way of handling risks. Erdman broke out into a cold sweat as panic riddled his mind and body, effectively pushing the rage aside. She could not be pregnant with his child; this could not ever happen to him exactly the way it had happened to his pa. Denial came to him on the heels of panic. Clara had not told him that she was going to have his baby and she would tell him if the baby were his. She had been sick on Easter but that did not necessarily mean that it was a baby. The thoughts chased each other in circles in his mind.

Finally, he decided that he would take Clara to their usual spot, over by their farm on Lone Pine Lane. He needed to choose whether to proceed with their usual intimacies and then ask about the gossip or to start with the gossip and try to make up with her later. Erdman pulled the roadster back on to the road and drove to the lane on Stoney Point Road. He looked at Clara's bedroom window on the second floor and a lamp was glowing brightly, her signal that she was waiting for him. He flashed the headlights on and off and looked to see that she adjusted the shade twice. She would be out in a few minutes and he needed to make up his mind how to proceed.

Another car pulled slowly into the lane from Stoney Point Road. The car crept past Erdman sitting in the roadster and Erdman could see the outline of a young man in the driver's seat. He seemed to have his head turned towards Erdman as if he were studying him. Erdman continued to stare straight ahead not wanting whoever it was to stop and try to talk to him. The car continued up the lane towards the house, stopping one more time as Erdman could see the taillights light up again. It paused there for a minute and then slowly pulled away again. This had been a terrible evening full of unpredictable and ominous events for Erdman; he was tempted to just leave and tell Clara he had needed to go home.

Erdman had been so deep in thought that he had not noticed Clara's approach until she was suddenly standing beside the car. She opened the passenger side door and looked in the car at him; her usual smile was in place but there was a definite look of concern in her eyes. Erdman's heart was hammering in his chest from the sudden scare combined with the panic that still resided within him. Clara sat on the seat beside him, reaching her hand out to touch his cheek as she slowly leaned forward to place a gentle kiss on his lips.

Erdman sat frozen for a few seconds and then responded to her kiss with his own, fiercely claiming her mouth and driving away the doubts that still swirled in masses around him. Clara was here with him now, and she would make all the darkness trying to claim him leave just as she always did. Erdman had made his choice.

A couple of hours later the two lay on a blanket under the now familiar copse of trees facing Erdman's family's farm. Clara had her head on his chest as he lay on his back staring up into the sky. Clara had made most of his dark thoughts flee with her almost magical presence, but Erdman knew that he needed to get some facts straight so that he didn't slip back into the darkness inside his soul once she left him for the evening. Whatever he had to face, he would be able to face it with Clara there snuggled beside him. At times like this, he didn't know whether to be relieved about this fact or irritated at his obvious dependence on her.

"You seem like you are a million miles away even though I can feel you right next to me." Clara nuzzled her soft hair against his chin as she lifted her head slightly to speak to him. Erdman wrapped his arms tighter around her, and she sighed as she settled back against him. He rested his hand that crossed over her against her stomach, and she shifted away from him slightly. He hadn't realized until now that recently she had taken to wearing a fancy corset that was unlike any of her other underclothes before. He had assumed it was something meant to intrigue him but now he wondered if the purpose was to hide in plain view a child, most likely his child.

"Had some stuff on my mind, I guess." Erdman started, wondering where this conversation would lead them both. "Who was it that pulled into the lane when I was waiting for you tonight?" He needed to lead with some minor questions before he hit on the major one.

"Oh, that was Bernard. I think he may have a gal in Seneca as he has been keeping some late nights himself. He asked where we were going, so I just told him we were going for a drive, which is mostly truthful, I guess. I will be happy for the day that I do not need to skirt around the truth with my family anymore. Once we are married it will be a relief in more than one way. Bernard didn't talk to you, did he?" Clara rolled into a sitting position so that she could see Erdman's face.

Why did she always bring everything back to getting married? Erdman was irritated at the thought and yet he knew that he needed to appear calm and relaxed to her.

"No. He just drove past and stared at me as though I were a thief in the night there to steal you away. You know, like Rudolph Valentino in The Sheik." Erdman liked the thought of emulating his movie hero.

Clara laughed softly. "I am not sure that you can steal someone who is so willing to go with you." She reached forward to caress Erdman's hair and push the strands that had fallen into his eyes back into place. "Besides, you're better looking than Rudolph Valentino."

It was Erdman's turn to laugh. In the year since they had met, Clara had turned from a shy young girl into quite an accomplished flirt. His mind replayed his first glimpse of her, their first kiss, and their first time together in almost this exact location. She had trusted him even when she shouldn't. She had proved her love for him even when he didn't. She was far too good for him, when he had tried to make her only a green hick of a girl who didn't matter in his mind.

"I would guess you had fallen asleep, but you have the same grin on your face as the first day I met you. Have I ever told you how much I love your grin?" Clara brought herself to her hands and knees trapping his face between her arms as she leaned down and kissed his chin repeatedly. Erdman opened his eyes to look at her and caught the glimpse of a slight swell to her belly underneath the loosened corset as she leaned over him. He again reached to touch her stomach, and she suddenly stopped kissing his chin. She did not shift away from him as before. She froze in place as if she were willing him to realize what she could not bring herself to tell him. She was only inches above his face, her brown eyes like dark pools, as she searched his eyes for an answer.

"When did you realize?" she asked quietly. He was grateful that she was not dramatic or sappy. He would not have been able to tolerate either one, but she probably already knew that as she seemed to know him better than he knew himself.

"I think the more important questions are when did you realize and when were you going to tell me?" He countermanded her question with his own questions. He did not want her to hear about the way Christine had told him the news as it didn't matter anymore.

Clara resumed a sitting position next to him. She brought her knees up to her chest and wrapped her arms around them. She rested her head against her knees and sighed.

"I started to suspect over a month ago, but you had been so sick, and I didn't want to make you worse again somehow. Then you said we could elope soon, and I thought I would wait until closer to that time. I want you to marry me because you want to and not because you feel that you had to. We love each other, Erdman, and this does not change any of that, but I am sorry if you feel that I misled you. I am actually relieved that you know so we can do this together." Clara's voice was calm and clear as she looked at him. He knew she was telling him the truth; she always told him the truth, when he had told her so many lies.

Erdman expected the panic, denial, and rage to overwhelm him again as they had earlier in the evening. Instead he was amazed at the calmness that washed over him in waves. He would have to come up with answers in the very near future, but he didn't have to come up with them right now. Clara was still watching him just like she had after their first night together, searching him for answers. This time he would not dump her off at her house bereft and alone; he owed her that at least for all the good she had brought to him. As he sat up, he reached out to touch her arms still wrapped around her knees.

"Are you sure you should be sitting like that?" he asked her. "I mean all folded up. Aren't you squishing it?"

Clara's eyes registered disbelief, soon followed by joy. She moved into his lap kissing him gently. She then placed his hand across her stomach with her hand resting on top of his.

Erdman knew that she would need this night to believe in their happily ever after so that she could face what loomed before them, and not even he was selfish enough to take it away from her just yet.

Chapter 33

JUNE 16, 1926 –
SENECA, WISCONSIN

The day began humid. The dark storm clouds that so often gathered along the Mississippi River could be heard rumbling in the distance from Christ Olson's farm. Christ, the boys, and most of the girls had started early that morning trying to do the field work before the storms came that afternoon. While the rains would bring much needed water for the tobacco, the winds and hail of a potent storm could ruin an entire year's worth of crops in less than a day. It was a farmer's lot in life to depend heavily on the chance that Mother Nature would be kind and generous instead of vicious and unrelenting as often was the case.

The family had come in from the fields as the first spatters of rain began to fall. The wind blew in gusts and the lightning cracked in the distance. The last chores were being finished in the barn by Bernard and Clara as the rest of the family had finished and headed for the house and shelter. Clara enjoyed the pattering sound and the fresh smell of the rain hitting the ground in the barnyard. She took a deep breath inhaling the freshness, as she sat on a crate in the barn waiting for Bernard to finish his chores in the haymow so they could walk to the house together. Suddenly, her baby fluttered rapidly causing a moment of alarm in Clara. She put her hand to her stomach as she was in a habit of doing when she was alone in her room, but the corset prevented her from feeling the fluttering against her hand.

Do you hear the noises of the coming storm little one? Clara wondered. The fluttering came again harder and more insistent. Clara chuckled to herself. *Don't worry, your mama and papa will both protect you from harm.* As if the babe could read her thoughts the fluttering subsided. Clara imagined a sweet baby with dark hair sucking its thumb and drifting back to sleep at the assurances of its mother. Now that Erdman knew about their baby, Clara became even more excited about its arrival in December.

While Clara still did not understand how Erdman had figured it out, she was grateful that he had taken the news calmly. She had been concerned that his reaction might be closer to anger or frustration with her even though it had taken both of them to make this baby. Many men saw it as the woman's responsibility, and sometimes a baby before the wedding was seen as the woman's sole mistake. Clara had heard of young women who were sent away by their families in disgrace while the young men went on with their lives as though nothing had happened.

Erdman did not seem happy about the baby like Clara was but that was often common with men too, she supposed. She hoped that someday Erdman would be a father like her own papa, whom she loved and admired so much. Clara wondered if Papa had felt like Erdman about her older sister Minnie, who had arrived only a few months after her parents' wedding. If he had at the time, he had transformed into the most wonderful father to her and to all her siblings later and that was what mattered most. She wanted to suggest that Erdman speak to her father, but she understood that now they would have to get married first and the relations between Erdman and her family would have to be established after they wed. She knew that she looked forward to knowing Erdman's father Albert better; she hoped that Erdman's mother would be accepting of her after the fact. Possibly having a new grandchild to love and hold soon after their wedding would help ease the shock for Erdman's mother.

The crack of lightning hitting the ground nearby and the reverberating rumble of thunder soon after was the sure sign that the center of the storm was upon them. Clara would have to wait it out in the barn with Bernard, as the risk of being struck by the lightning outside was too great. The fluttering began as though the wee one had been awakened from its dreams by the tumult and was sending a protest to Clara.

"Didn't like that noise did you now? Shh, it's alright." Clara crooned to her unborn child as she shifted her position on the crate.

"Are you talking to the cows or to yourself Clara? Careful or people will think you are a little daft like me." Bernard appeared at the opening to the haymow over her head. *Shoot! I need to stop talking out loud,* Clara thought as she smiled up at her brother who was climbing down the ladder to the floor below. She was glad that she hadn't said anything else out loud. Bernard had always been very protective of her and her sisters and explaining this to him would be more than difficult.

"Talking to yourself doesn't mean that you're daft Silly. You're only daft if you answer yourself or argue." Clara laughed. She loved this older brother best of all her brothers. He had gone off to fight in the Great War, and there had been times Clara wondered if they would ever see him again. The brother who returned was the same in that he was still sweet and funny but different in that he grew quiet and serious and sometimes angry. Clara had wanted many times to ask him why he had changed, but like most of the boys who made it home, Bernard never wanted to speak of the atrocities he had seen. Papa seemed to understand Bernard best and helped him through the rough days, but Clara knew that people still considered Bernard a little "touched in the head" and their unfair criticism of a war hero angered her.

"Looks like we are here for the duration, huh?" Bernard found another crate and pulled it over to where Clara sat. "I don't know about you but sometimes I prefer a little quiet." He settled himself on the crate and looked at the storm raging outside the door. "I had been looking for a moment to talk with just the two of us, and in this big crazy family those times don't come very often." He paused and smiled lovingly at his baby sister.

"Bernard, are you going to finally tell me that you have a gal somewhere? I wondered about some of your late nights. I think that is wonderful." Clara teased and assured her brother at the same time. Bernard grinned at her suggestion, but his face turned sober again as he slowly shook his head no.

"Nope. I wish what I need to say was that pleasant. Clara, I need to know what you know of this Erdman Olson fellow of yours." Bernard looked at Clara directly which was unusual because he rarely made eye contact with anyone. Clara was immediately on edge. She wanted to snap at her brother for his nosiness, but his gentle eyes were pleading with her to be patient with him, so she answered his question with one of her own.

"Is there something that makes you ask me about Erdman?" Clara's voice wavered as she asked the question. She loved Erdman. They were so close to eloping, she wasn't sure that she wanted Bernard to answer her question.

"It's just that as I can tell it's been over a year since he started coming around here. I think that you have fallen for him pretty hard, and I am not sure that he is a fellow who is worthy of my favorite little sister." Bernard was still searching Clara's eyes, but she could tell that he was not comfortable with what he was trying to say. Clara loved him for being the protective brother; no one in his estimation would ever probably be good enough so it wasn't just Erdman.

"I appreciate your care for me, Brother. I assure you that Erdman and I are meant to be together. He is far from perfect, but so am I. Papa talked to me a few months ago about this and I will tell you what I told him. We love each other and we are going to get married someday soon." Clara took her brother's hand in her own. "I hope that you will try to like Erdman for my sake."

Bernard put his big hand, calloused from hard work, over Clara's smaller hand. "I see. I would do anything for you, Clara. I think you know that already. I will treat him as he deserves to be treated. If he is good to you then I will be good to him, but if he is not..." Bernard looked down at the ground gathering his strength to finish. "Then he will pay."

The hair on the back of Clara's neck stood up at her brother's threat. She could not imagine what would make her sweet gentle brother talk in this way. Her impulse was to defend Erdman, but she knew that Bernard had always been trustworthy, and she would not stop trusting him now. "Why do you say that?" Her voice showed her vulnerability.

"Well, I guess because a fellow who has the greatest gal in the world should not be out at the dance halls kissing and fooling with other gals. He has been a regular down in Seneca most Thursdays and a few Thursdays ago he was out there in the alley with one of the Anderson gals. He should not be doing such if he is marrying my sister." Bernard shook his head resolutely.

Clara felt the pangs of jealousy stab her. She knew that Erdman sold his gin at the dance halls and she knew that he often flirted with many of his female customers but even she did not know how far he went with his flirtations. On the other hand, if her sweet brother had heard this from one of the town gossips then it might not even be true. "Who told you this, Bernard?" she asked gently.

"Nobody had to tell me. I saw it for myself. Then when he's finished with her, he comes up here and waits for you to come out to him. I drove past him sitting there and I wanted to get out right there and have a talk with him, but I knew I should talk with you first, so I did. He should not ever hurt you Clara. I am telling you I'm not going to let that happen." Bernard looked back at her with distress written across his face. She could not be angry with her gentle giant of a brother.

"Thank you, Brother. I know you did this because you want the best for me. Please let me handle this with Erdman. I promise you that if I need help with him or anyone else you are the first person I will call." She leaned to kiss her brother's cheek and noted that one tear trailed down it. They sat together quietly watching the storm pass, but a new storm raged on inside of Clara. She was rarely ever angry but when she was, she was a force to be reckoned with. Erdman would soon find that Bernard was right in his estimation about how Clara's future husband and the father of her child should behave.

Chapter 34

JUNE 17, 1926 –
SENECA, WISCONSIN

The storm system that had raged through Crawford County on Wednesday had been a harbinger for the rains that continued through the night and well into the next day. Most of the tobacco crops that had weathered the initial rain, wind, and hail now faced another deadly foe: areal flooding. The already saturated ground could not keep up with the amount of rain continuing to fall. Small streams that would simply meander through fields and woods now raged and overflowed, sweeping the ground and whatever it contained along with it. The U.S. Army Corps of Engineers were already stationed at various spots along the Mississippi, building dams and locks, and now they built temporary dikes to channel the deluge back to the river.

While the hearty Norwegian residents of the county did all that they could to keep kith and kin together during periods of flooding, they were not altogether unused to erratic, extreme weather conditions from the Old Country, and they took it as part of everyday living. The same farmers who had watched part of their crops and livelihoods be destroyed in the morning were likely to distract themselves with the social interactions at Tolefson's dance hall that evening. A popular dance band from the local area had been hastily hired for the evening entertainment as other bands could not traverse the flooded and washed out roads in the low-lying areas of the county.

Erdman knew that part of the farmers' diversion would be his gin, so he arrived with a well-stocked trunk in his usual alley in downtown Seneca. There were plenty of people milling about, and soon a discreet line had formed. Erdman was a consummate businessman, trying to hold a brief conversation with most of his clientele as he sold his wares. Many of the regulars had commented on the increased number of people in the dance hall that evening seeking solace and society after the trying day. After selling a fair share of his stock, Erdman decided to check out the dance hall. He would have one of his largest sales days if he sold just a half case more. Spurred on by his greed, he strolled to the hotel and climbed the stairs.

There was a much larger crowd than normal in the dance hall. The band was playing, and Erdman could hardly see the dance floor for all the people standing between it and him. He strolled around the perimeter, stopping to greet people and promising to return outside in short order. As he listened to the music, he had the urge to dance a bit as he enjoyed it and Clara did not. He looked around for a partner and saw Christine Anderson making her way towards him. He cringed inwardly as he recalled their last meeting in the alley and the revelation about his baby that she had given to him. It was too late to avoid her, so he smiled and held out his hand as an offer to dance. Christine surprised him by shaking her head no with a pout on her face. She walked past him without stopping to speak.

Erdman shook his head slightly at the capriciousness of most females. It was then that he noticed people around him staring and whispering to each other. He gritted his teeth against the likelihood that Christine had not kept her mouth shut about Clara as he had advised. Irritation prickled at him; why couldn't people in small towns mind their own business?

Suddenly several people stepped out of his way, and Erdman had a view of the crowded dance floor. There in the middle of the dance floor was Clara, his Clara, dancing with the clerk from the post office. She was laughing as she followed his lead, his hand was at the middle of her back as he held her for the dance. Jealousy slammed into Erdman like a punch to his gut.

Several couples around Clara stopped dancing as they watched Erdman slowly approach Clara from behind. Erdman followed the etiquette of tapping Ansgar's shoulder asking to cut in; the tapping sounding much more like a smack with some force behind it. Erdman locked eyes with Ansgar, his determined look challenging him to refuse the request. Ansgar looked to Clara briefly and appeared ready to accept Erdman's challenge when Clara shook her head slightly at the postal clerk and turned to dance with Erdman.

Erdman expected Clara's usual reaction of submission when he became agitated. He was shocked when he looked into her face and saw what looked like anger igniting in her brown eyes. She held eye contact with him as they fell into step with the dance. This was a Clara he had never experienced, and Erdman was struggling to formulate the words that normally came so easy to him.

Clara spoke first in an icy tone. "Well, darling, I heard that you come here to dance quite often, and I was afraid that I had missed you in this crowd. Bernard brought Alice and me over tonight as he says that he sees you here when I am sitting at home waiting for you. I decided not to wait at home for you tonight."

Erdman reacted to her mention of her brother, but immediately came to his own defense. "You already know that I come here to sell hooch just like we have done together countless times. I did not ask you to come with me because you don't like to dance." He met her glare with one of his own, trying to regain control over the conversation, but she kept him off balance with her uncharacteristic demeanor.

"I don't get to dance because no one has offered before." She corrected him coldly. "I spoke with Christine Anderson earlier and she agreed with me that while she has kept you company on the dance floor in the past, I should probably take over from here. Unless you object of course, Erdman." Clara's meaning was clear, she would not sit at home and tolerate his tomcat behavior anymore.

"What about your recent dance partner?" Erdman glanced towards where Ansgar stood with Clara's sister Alice at the edge of the dance floor. Clara waved at them as she and Erdman danced by; Ansgar looked nervous but Alice had a bemused look on her face.

"Ansgar was only being polite as I was sitting there all by myself waiting for you. Besides, what is that you kept telling me? 'The past is in the past. Leave it to me.' I think that is good advice for both of us, don't you? Now, should I tell my brother that you will be taking me home?"

Erdman knew that he should be angrier than he was, but he was too shocked and too impressed by her bold behavior to protect what she thought of as hers. His meek and mild little Clara had a ferocious side. This had brought out something in her that he could identify in himself and understand. He suddenly grinned at her and nodded his head. He would be taking her home tonight and heaven help him if she decided she wasn't finished yet.

After speaking with her brother, Clara followed Erdman towards his car. Other patrons who had waited for Erdman to return to his car followed the couple as well. Erdman hesitated when he saw the line gathered, but Clara climbed into the rumble seat assuming her usual spot during his sales. She sat smiling and waving like a regal princess addressing her court. Erdman sold his half case of gin and another whole one beyond it.

The rain had stopped earlier in the evening leaving a shiny surface on the ground wherever the headlights of the roadster touched it. Erdman drove quietly towards Clara's home trying to guess where her thoughts were leading her as she sat in silence beside him. She had not spoken directly to him since the dance floor; he could not determine what her present mood was. He determined that he would take the rein back as he did not like the feeling of the loss of control she had caused.

"I have had a lot of women. It is probably best that you do not ask me about them as it will only hurt you more. You already know that Lilla was one of them, but she isn't anymore. I don't know what you heard about Christine, but she isn't either. I warned you about being in the company of another man. I will not share you with anyone ever. If you can accept that, then we can probably continue on." Erdman laid out his ultimatum as he drove into the farmhouse lane expecting Clara's immediate capitulation. He even dared to hope that she might be desirous of him after her fiery reaction earlier had attracted him to her stronger than ever before.

Clara sat quietly for a moment then turned to him as she scooted across the car seat towards him. She kissed him gently but when he reached to pull her even closer, she pulled away. Her voice was clear and unwavering.

"I love you, Erdman. There has never been anyone else for me, and I don't think there ever could be anyone else. Come back to me when I am the only one for you. If you can accept that, we can continue on." With that Clara opened the car door and left him sitting there as she walked away without looking back.

Clara willed herself to continue to walk away though her legs were trembling so badly. Her resolve to not live her life in the shadow of Erdman's indiscretions and lies was the only thing keeping her from turning back and throwing herself at him, begging him for his forgiveness. If it were only her welfare she would have given in at his ultimatum, accepting him because she could not bear to lose him. But she was now responsible for the welfare of another and she would battle anyone, even Erdman, for the sake of her child.

Erdman sat in disbelief as Clara disappeared into the darkness beyond the reach of his headlights. His rage slammed against him, and his first temptation was to run after Clara and haul her back by her hair if necessary. His second thought was of the father and brothers who he knew would come to Clara's rescue if she made even a single cry for help. He jerked the car into reverse and wildly turned it back onto Stoney Point Road. He was so overcome by the rage pounding a cadence in his mind that he narrowly missed hitting another car turning onto the road from Highway 27. The near miss sent him partially into the opposite ditch, but he yanked the steering wheel and the car careened back onto the roadway.

A short time later Erdman found himself in his own driveway having no remembrance of driving the twenty minutes home. *How dare she? Who in the world did she think she was? She was nothing to him. If she thought this would somehow allow her to control him, she had just made the biggest mistake of her life.* Erdman pummeled the steering wheel with his fists until they bled.

Weren't you looking for a way out? She just handed it right to you. All you need to do is not look back. Good luck to her and her little bastard. If she thought that you were taking responsibility for that she is sadly mistaken. This is the best possible thing that could happen, your lucky day. He nodded vehemently in agreement to his own thoughts even as his breaths came in short gasps and there were brilliant pinpoints of light sparking behind his eyes. He struck his own head with his fists trying to knock out the lights now clouding his vision.

He opened the car door and attempted to get out. He steadied himself on the front panel and noticed that he had punctured the front tire, probably during his near miss in the ditch earlier. The tire would have to be patched quickly or it would be completely ruined. Thinking that possibly the manual labor would help him to get his senses back into order, Erdman approached the trunk for the tire iron stored there.

Erdman in his distress had not noticed the loud angry voices of his parents emanating from the kitchen. It was not until he was on the ground in front of his tire that the voices of Anna and Albert arguing registered with him.

"Anna, enough. You need to tell me plainly what happened. Why are you telling me that Erdman will be reinstated at the college with such surety? I gave the Dean a large donation and we still have not heard the results." Albert was tired of his wife's elusive answers to his questions.

"I told you. I only did what I needed to do to get our son off this good for nothing farm and back to his school. You think that you are so big offering him money. You are nothing. I told you I went to La Crosse with my sisters when I went up to that high and mighty college and did what you could never do. I know for certain that Erdman is back in school and he can thank his mama for it like usual." Anna spewed the words in Albert's face

"Anna, what are you trying to tell me?" Albert repeated.

"Not even you can be this dull, Albert. The Dean is a man like any other man, and I offered him what you couldn't. You know that I am very persuasive when I want to be. I don't want my baby boy to end up a dirt farmer like his worthless pa."

Albert grabbed Anna's arm and yanked her into the chair beside him. "You lie. Not even you would stoop this low nor would he have anything to do with you. Go to bed, Anna."

Her loud maniacal laugh was chilling. "He has a large mahogany desk in his office, doesn't he? I told you a long time ago, Albert, do not ever stand in my way. You will never control me."

Erdman stood, still holding the tire iron, bringing it down across the hood of his beloved roadster. The waves of rage crashed over him until he was underwater and could no longer breathe. Instead of sending the Siren to the abyss he was now at the precipice himself, unsure that he would ever return.

Chapter 35

JUNE 21, 1926 –
WESTLAND, MICHIGAN

The afternoon air was warm and humid. A small occasional breeze fluttered the flags in the courtyard of the Eloise Mental Hospital in Westland, Michigan. The prestigious brick building had been built on the original site of a pony express stop between Chicago, Illinois and Detroit, Michigan. There were three hospitals within the grounds, the Eloise Infirmary (better known as the poorhouse), the Eloise Sanatorium (better known as a TB clinic) and the Eloise Mental hospital (better known as a psychiatric clinic and insane asylum). The very wealthy and prestigious were often referred to the Eloise Hospitals for treatment of various disorders. The discreet manner in which the clienteles was diagnosed and treated, especially for mental conditions, made this the ideal location for someone who needed treatment without anyone else ever knowing about it.

Albert sat waiting in the shady courtyard watching swans glide across a lake situated to the hospital's side. He had brought Erdman to Westland by car as his son had been much too volatile for other modes of public transportation. He had given Erdman heavy doses of the barbiturate that the pharmacist had warned him against, but it had been the only thing to keep Erdman from reviving enough to do more damage to himself and others.

By the time Albert had heard Erdman's screams and rushed outside, Erdman had taken a tire iron to the car and then to poor Edwin Knutson who had come from the barn to see what all the commotion was. Albert had to tackle Erdman to the ground and wrestle the tire iron from him; Edwin had been pinned by his neck to the shed wall and was gasping for breath when Albert rescued him from his deranged son.

Albert could only guess that Erdman had overheard Anna's rantings and had another breakdown of his own. Erdman had not been conscious enough to speak since the event and Albert knew that he needed to remove Erdman, taking him far away for help, so he let the dangerous barbiturate take effect until he could get Erdman to Eloise Hospital. The prestige of the hospital and the absolute discretion both appealed to Albert; Erdman only needed a little help to get over some of his shortcomings without everyone thinking that he was completely insane.

Albert had sworn Edwin to secrecy and had only called on Anna's brother Nels for assistance. Nels was accustomed to his sister's "delicate condition" and would keep the whole business private. Nels had taken Anna to her sister's home for a rest and had little Arvid come to his farm to stay. Edwin Knutson was left in charge of the farm with Albert's promise to give an entire year's wages for the vow to stay silent about Erdman and what had occurred.

Erdman had experienced a few problems in the past with his throat and tonsils, so the story was concocted that Erdman had been sent off to specialists for surgeries, covering over his actual stay at the mental hospital for the small, curious community. Albert now waited in the courtyard to hear from the doctors after they looked at Erdman and made a diagnosis.

An orderly came to get Albert and directed him to a waiting room outside the mental clinic. When the door opened again, a doctor walked in with Erdman beside him. Albert was surprised to see Erdman awake and so calm. He stood to embrace his son, but Erdman stared past him without seeming to recognize him. Albert looked to the doctor who calmly ushered Erdman into a chair nearby and Albert sat back down looking intently at Erdman.

"Mr. Olson, we were able to reduce Erdman's medication enough to allow us to evaluate some of his symptoms and make a plan for his treatment. I asked Erdman to join us as he is of the age of majority and should have input on his level of care. It is our greatest expectation that this course of treatment I am suggesting may affect Erdman's life positively and allow him to live his life outside of an institution." The doctor seemed sincere and direct, two qualities that Albert had come to appreciate.

"Does he understand what we are saying right now? I saw him like this after another severe breakdown and was not sure that he could even hear us. I want the very best treatment for him, and I am willing to pay whatever I need to get it." Albert glanced at Erdman who was looking down at the floor.

"I assure you that Erdman does understand us. He can follow simple directions and nod and shake his head to questions. I am wondering that whatever situation that caused his nervous breakdown might be still too overwhelming for him to speak of it or anything else just yet." The doctor knelt beside Erdman's chair. "Erdman, do you wish to stay here and try the treatments that you and I have already discussed? You understand there is the possibility it could make you well again?"

Albert was shocked to see Erdman lift his eyes from where he had been staring at the floor, look directly at the doctor, and shake his head yes. "May I ask what exactly are the treatments that you have already discussed?" Albert knew from experience with Anna that many so-called treatments only involved dangerous mixtures of potent drugs that induced a chemical trance for the patient who was then declared cured. As soon as the patient built up a tolerance for the drugs, the behaviors resumed and often increased in volatility.

"Yes. While we do work with various drugs to treat his condition the main portion of the treatment will involve infecting him with a case of malaria and then allowing that sickness to help release toxins that may be causing instability in his brain. We have the quinine necessary to treat the malaria so that it can be cured. We have a great deal of success with this newest treatment, but it will take several weeks to see results in him and cure him of the malaria. He would also be given art and music therapy which have been known to soothe as well as give the patient other outlets for their anxiety." The doctor rose from where he had knelt beside Erdman and sat behind a small desk facing Albert.

"Malaria? Don't people usually die from that?" Albert queried. This might prove to be a case where the cure was more fatal than the condition. Albert would do anything to see Erdman get help, but he would not allow the torture that he had heard of in some mental hospitals. And yet, if he did not allow them to try this treatment Erdman could be forced into an insane asylum. The horror stories of such places made Albert shudder.

"Malaria has been fatal in some cases, but it largely depends on which parasite causes the condition. By controlling this and giving immediate doses of the quinine cure we can often get the results we are seeking without a fatality. The small seizures brought on by the sickness seem to trigger corrective responses in the brain. There is one other area of treatment that I feel necessary. I think that it is best if we step into the other room as the mention of one of the parties involved seems to cause the greatest amount of anxiety for Erdman." The doctor rose from his chair and ushered Albert into an adjoining room where they could still see Erdman, but they were out of earshot.

Anna. He gets this way when they mention the poor kid's own mother, Albert thought as he followed the doctor.

"Mr. Olson, as you probably already understand, much of Erdman's current mental infirmity seems to be inherited from his mother. It is something we see on occasion and it then becomes necessary in our estimation to remove the possibility of it occurring again. While Erdman is here being treated with the malaria, we will also make sure that a small procedure is done to effectively sterilize him thus reducing the risk of continuing this in the bloodline. The latest studies show that this is one of the most effective ways to ensure less mental infirmity in the future." The doctor's matter of fact explanation staggered Albert.

You want to fix him like he's some sort of animal? Albert stared in disbelief as the doctor's words sunk into his head. "Don't you suppose that your suggestion of sterilizing him is what made him get upset again?" Albert could only imagine his own response if it were him. *And yet if I had been sterile, I never would have had to marry Anna in the first place.* The thought struck Albert like a blast of cold air to the face.

"Erdman did not seem to object to the sterilization at all. He only reacts when we mention his mother. He refers to her as "the Siren" which I am sure has more meaning then I understand at the present time. That is one of the two phrases that he has intelligibly uttered since he arrived. We will work with him to help him understand how to cope with his mother, but it may prove that some of the childhood trauma she has inflicted upon him is just too deep for intervention. All this remains to be seen if we can proceed with what I have described thus far to you."

Albert nodded his consent with resignation. He would try this, hoping against hope that Erdman could be delivered of his deepest mental and emotional wounds without succumbing to the malaria. The sterilization seemed extreme but if it was also necessary at least they could avoid this happening to their family yet again. As he rose, he asked the doctor,

"You said he used two phrases that you could understand. What was the other phrase?"

The doctor paused to think. "He keeps repeating, 'I lost Clara' followed by anguished cries."

Albert looked at his son sitting calmly in the chair staring at the lake outside the window. If only Erdman could recuperate enough for Albert to ask Clara for her help, they would see if the miraculous could be performed by her again.

Chapter 36

JUNE 28, 1926 –
SOLDIERS GROVE, WISCONSIN

The cool air in Lena Hutchins' parlor was a sanctuary from the hot and humid Wisconsin afternoon. The shades had been drawn to shut out the intense sunlight and the heat with it. A large ceiling fan overhead powered by indoor electricity was the most recent and welcome addition since the indoor privy the year before. Clara sat enjoying the cool air with a tart glass of lemonade at her side while Lena finished writing her weekly correspondence.

Usually Clara welcomed the quiet time to think to herself, but it had been torturous inside her mind since the night she had walked away from Erdman and not looked back. She had been very hopeful in the days right after their fight that Erdman would relent and come to visit or even just write her a note, but now over ten days had passed, and he had not given her a single sign of their possible reconciliation. Clara replayed the scenario and various things that she might have done differently over and over until she was worn out emotionally, mentally, and physically.

Sometimes she would think that she just had to remain resolute in her conviction that her life with Erdman as an unfaithful and deceitful husband would bring her further heartache and ruination. Other times she missed him so badly and she was so scared at facing her future with their child alone she thought she might be able to accept anything he was willing to offer as their future. These thoughts would vacillate making Clara wonder how the same person could cause so much joy and yet bring so much heartbreak to her at the same time.

Clara resolved that whatever the case was, she alone would make certain that her child did not suffer the consequences of the unfortunate circumstances she found herself in. She knew that to keep this poor child without giving it the name of its father would bring a stigma for the child and yet she couldn't bear the thought of giving her precious little one away to complete strangers never to be seen again. She had a few short months to figure out what to do while still hoping that Erdman would take her and their child back again.

"A penny for your thoughts might be too slight a price today from the look on your face, my dear." Lena had finished her writing and come to sit beside Clara on the settee. "You are so young to have the entire world upon your shoulders, Clara. Is there some way in which your old friend might help you?" Lena was always so generous and kind, but Clara knew that not even her dear friend could mend her current state of affairs. She had thought of one possible option that she tried to speak aloud.

"Lena, as you write to so many friends and family I am wondering if any of them might be looking for a nanny or a maid of some sort? I know some are very far away, even ones in Norway and I have considered traveling there but I would need a way to support myself by taking on employment." Clara thought if she could travel far enough away, she might be able to work and keep her baby telling other people that the baby's father had died in an accident. She hated the thought of the deceit she would have to live in and the fact that she would be without her own family possibly forever, but she was ready to make whatever sacrifices she needed to make for her child.

"My dear, are you planning to go by yourself or would Erdman go with you?" the kind lady asked with gentleness and without a hint of reproach.

"I am afraid that I may have to make this journey alone. I can't stay here for reasons that are too difficult for me to explain and while my hopes were that we were to be married soon I may have to face the fact that it will not happen. I only ask that you might give me suggestions of a good family and maybe a reference for employment. I would not wish to trouble you for anything else." Clara's eyes filled with the tears that had threatened numerous times in the last week. When she looked at Lena, she saw a face filled with compassion and love; she also saw a keen understanding upon the elderly lady's countenance without the judgment that understanding brought for so many others.

"I will assist you in any way that you need assistance and more. You will not need to worry as I can help you travel to Norway or wherever you decide you must go. In fact, I have considered going back myself for a visit and with you there I would be at perfect ease. Then if you decide that you really must stay on, we will make the necessary arrangements for that as well. You will never be alone, Clara." Lena drew Clara by her thin shoulders to herself and held her there as Clara let the tears that had been pent up for days fall unhindered.

Lena knew that her dear girl was probably in a family way as it was easy to see how in love she was with the young man and she would not leave a family she loved so much without very good reason. Lena bristled at the fact that Clara would be judged harshly and censured by society, while young Olson would move on as if nothing had happened, possibly doing this to the next young girl he encountered. She would see that Clara and her little one would receive good care and a good living together. She hoped that Clara's family could possibly accept her back someday as some young women lost the relations of their family permanently. She would pray for her Clara and for Erdman to decide to do the right thing by her. She knew her Samuel would agree with her decision to love the outcast and downtrodden, offering help and hope instead of condemnation.

Clara and Lena formulated a plan to travel together to Norway by mid-September if Erdman had not returned to reconcile himself to Clara. They would book passage on an ocean liner and, once in port in Oslo, they would find a private hospital for Clara's lying-in period. After the birth Clara would stay with Lena in her family home there for several months. By spring Lena would return to the United States and Clara insisted that she would find employment with a good family so she could earn a living for herself and her child.

Clara went home that evening with the knowledge that she did have an alternate plan, but she still prayed that Erdman would come for her before that time. As she often did when she visited Lena, Clara rode the evening bus from Soldiers Grove to Mt. Sterling. She stopped at the local filling station in Mt. Sterling and used their telephone to call Bernard so that he could come and pick her up there. The owner of the filling station, Ole Thorstad, had been in the war with Bernard and was a good friend of the family, so Clara knew that she was always welcome to wait there for her brother.

Clara was waiting for Bernard outside on a bench. The humidity had lessened as the day turned to evening. She had bought a cold bottle of Dr. Pepper as it was a favorite treat, but even it reminded her of the many times she had enjoyed drinking from the same bottle as Erdman, sharing it with two straws.

"Clara? Is that you?" Clara looked up to see Arvid standing beside her. He had come from the back of the building so Clara had not noticed him up to that point. He looked nervous. He continued to look behind himself as if he were expecting someone to join them. He came to sit beside her on the bench.

"Arvid! I am so happy to see you! Are you well? Is your family well?" Clara hugged the young boy and asked the questions with one particular family member in mind.

"Oh, I'm okay, I guess. I sure have missed seeing you." Arvid kicked at the dirt beneath his feet. He acted as though he were trying to evade her other question and Clara felt an alarm begin in the pit of her stomach. *Did Erdman tell him not to speak to me anymore? Is there something wrong with Erdman that he is afraid to tell me? Could Erdman be in the back of the building and that is what is making Arvid nervous?* A dozen questions circled in Clara's head at once. She tried to remain calm as she tried a different approach.

"It sure is hot this summer. I bought this Dr. Pepper to cool off, but I can never drink the whole thing by myself. Your brother always likes to share one with me. I don't suppose that you might like to share it with me since he isn't here?" Clara smiled as she extended the cold soda towards the boy. Arvid grinned, *the same exact grin as his brother,* Clara noted. He nodded his head gratefully and accepted the bottle from her.

Arvid took a long drink and then a second one, handing the bottle back to Clara. "Did you know that Erdman is really sick, and Pa had to take him far away to try and get him better?" He blurted out in one sentence and Clara felt her whole world tilt to one side. "I'm not supposed to tell anybody about Erdman, but I reckon you aren't just like anybody else. I am here with Ma and Pa because they need to get the roadster fixed and Mr. Thorstad is the very best at fixing cars. Edwin is driving the roadster down in a little while and I was to wait out here for him." Arvid reached for the bottle of soda in Clara's hand. She didn't even realize he had taken it out of her hand. She was completely dazed by what he had revealed to her.

"When did Erdman get sick?" Clara's voice was shaking, and she felt the trembling in her whole body. This could be the reason she had not heard from Erdman.

"It was almost a couple weeks ago. I think it was that Thursday night right after the real bad storms and the flooding. Clara, don't you want some more of the soda?"

It was the night of our fight and the night I walked away from him. What have I done? Clara felt a sob at the back of her throat, but she tried to hold it back because she didn't want to scare Arvid. Clara stood and watched Edwin Knutson approach the filling station with the roadster; it was badly damaged across the windshield and hood areas. *Did he have an accident?* Clara tried to gather her mind enough to pay attention to the damages to the vehicle.

Edwin noticed Clara standing there with Arvid. He looked around as he slowed the car to a stop. He hopped out and approached Clara quickly. "Miss Clara, what are you doing here?" Edwin blurted out still looking nervously about them. Before Clara had the opportunity to answer, she noticed Albert Olson standing to one side of the building with the same woman who had stared at her at the box social that summer. The woman glared at Clara standing there with Arvid.

"Arvid! Your pa and I wondered where you went. Don't talk to people you don't know." She gave Clara a very pointed look telling her she was the stranger who posed a threat to her young son. Arvid started to reply when Edwin stepped in between the woman and Clara.

"I do know her, Mrs. Olson. I asked her to meet me here. She is my friend." Edwin's voice wavered but he continued on." I didn't think that Arvid would be out here, too. I'm sorry if that upset you."

Anna Olson's pinched face showed her displeasure with Edwin. "Yes, well. Keep your 'friends' away from my son if you don't mind. Arvid, come here to Mama." She opened her arms to the boy. Arvid hesitated, looking longingly at Clara; it was obvious that he preferred her company to that of his mother's.

"Son, you heard your ma." Albert's quiet voice startled Clara. She looked into his eyes and saw momentary sympathy but then it was gone. Arvid handed the empty soda bottle back to Clara and trudged over to his parents. The three of them turned and walked back the way they had come. Only Arvid sent a glance back to Clara.

Edwin took off his cap and turned towards Clara. "I am sorry if I made you uncomfortable. I was only trying to prevent her from making a scene."

Clara's legs trembled as she sat back down on the bench. She was having difficulty breathing but she tried to voice the question screaming inside her head.

"Edwin, what happened to Erdman? Where is he?"

Just then Bernard pulled into the driveway. Edwin gently helped Clara up and walked her towards her brother's car. When they reached the car door, Edwin whispered only loud enough for Clara to hear.

"Please listen to me this time, Miss Clara. Forget about him and his family. Get in the car with your brother and return to your parents. Go and live a happy life with someone who deserves you. It is best to pretend you never knew him."

Bernard reached across the seat to grasp Clara's hand when she sat down beside him in the car. "Sister, are you all right? You look like you have just seen a ghost."

Clara nodded numbly and closed her eyes. Her mind was reeling with one question.

Erdman, where are you?

Chapter 37

JULY 2, 1926 –
VIROQUA, WISCONSIN

The early July heat emanated from the grounds of Washington Park in almost visible waves. The June breezes had left with the entrance of the new month and the heat was stifling. Volunteers were busy decorating the bandstands for the 4th of July celebration in two days; they unfurled yard after yard of red, white, and blue bunting to cover the large area. Others were setting out the chairs for the dignitaries who would attend including Frances McGovern, the 22nd Governor of the state of Wisconsin and a war hero from the recent Great War.

Clara sat on a bench under a large tree watching the bustle about her without really seeing any of it. She was too deep in her own thoughts about Erdman and her meeting today with his father. After encountering Erdman's family earlier in the week, hearing that Erdman was very ill, and seeing the incredible amount of damage to

Erdman's car, Clara's nerves were frayed by the time she reached her home on Monday evening.

Bernard had been very concerned, mentioning how he found Clara at the filling station to their father Christ. Both Christ and Dena had attempted to ask Clara what was wrong, but she evaded their questions and would run off in a torrent of tears. From this, her family assumed that Erdman had ended the relationship with Clara and the poor girl suffered from a broken heart. Both Bernard and Adolph made harsh criticisms of Erdman wanting to take their sister's part in the apparent dispute, but when they did, it only made Clara's state of mind worse and the frequent tears even more frequent.

Two days later Clara had received a note from Albert Olson in the afternoon mail. He had apologized for the nature of their last chance meeting and had asked Clara to meet him in the same park she had met Erdman in Viroqua. He explained that he wanted to give Clara more of an explanation about Erdman's condition and encouraged her to write Erdman a letter that he would deliver to Erdman himself. Clara had asked Alice to accompany her on the bus to Viroqua and now she sat waiting for Albert to arrive. Alice sat in the distance keeping a careful eye upon her sister.

"Clara, I am happy to see that you were able to meet me." Albert's voice broke through Clara's jumbled thoughts as he approached the bench where she sat. Albert removed his hat and sat down at the opposite end of the bench, an appropriate distance for anyone observing them but close enough to Clara to not be overheard. "I have to admit that I was not exactly sure if you had called it quits with Erdman and might not be interested in his welfare anymore. But I saw your face full of concern the other day, and I understood that concern to be for my son."

"I am very concerned for Erdman, Mr. Olson, and I would appreciate it greatly if you could tell me what happened to him and how he is faring currently. I have found it difficult to eat, sleep, or do much of anything else since Arvid told me that Erdman was very sick and you had to take him far away." Clara paused as she tried to breathe past the huge knot in her throat. "Please don't be upset with Arvid for telling me. He realized how concerned I was and was trying to help me. I have a great amount of affection for both of your sons."

She is obviously scared half to death about Erdman and yet she tries to appeal to me on Arvid's behalf too. This is one wonderful girl Erdman has found, Albert thought to himself as he looked into Clara's brown eyes that were brimming with tears. "I can see from your reaction that you still have feelings for Erdman, and I want you to know that he has asked for you alone several times in the past weeks."

Clara's eyes widened and several large tears slipped down her cheeks as she momentarily closed her eyes. "I wondered how Erdman felt because we had a disagreement when I saw him last and I thought that he had ended things then. I love Erdman and I want him to know I will do whatever I can to help him through this illness. Is there any way I could see him myself?"

Albert shook his head with regret. "Not at this point, my dear. It would be too dangerous for you because Erdman has a case of Malaria, and he is being treated for that as well as his throat ailments. He had to be taken all the way to specialists in Michigan to be treated, and even I am not allowed near him right now. It was all very sudden and had nothing to do with your disagreement, I am sure." Albert lied to protect her feelings as he now understood the greater part of Erdman's recent breakdown was most likely the loss of this girl. "I receive updates from the hospital by telephone. Though Erdman is not in the clear yet, he seems to be showing some improvements." Albert prayed the girl would accept his explanation and not question how Erdman contracted malaria in the first place or how she would be at risk by being exposed to him. Erdman needed the time to allow the malaria to cure his actual illness.

As Clara listened, waves of fear for Erdman washed over her. She didn't know much about malaria, but she did know that people often died from it. The reminder that part of her plan had been to tell people that her baby's father had died slammed into her with the realization that it might happen just as she had predicted. This would be a cruel hand of Fate to take Erdman from her in the way that she had so monstrously concocted to explain her own transgressions. Clara buried her head in her hands and began to sob uncontrollably.

Albert patted Clara's shoulder, attempting to comfort the distraught girl. "I am so sorry to upset you like this. I will send you notes to give you the updates on his condition that I receive. When he has recuperated enough to return, I am certain that he will wish to see you first. Did you write a letter that I can send to him for you? It may help to lift his spirits like nothing else has done. I find that you have been the very best cure for him in the past. He is very fortunate to know you." Albert noticed that her sobs had subsided into small hiccups of breath as she sat nodding beside him.

Clara reached into her purse and retrieved the letter she had written and rewritten for Erdman the night before. She placed it carefully in Albert's hands, trying to send her love with each word in the missive. Erdman simply must recover and return to her. "It is extremely difficult for me to hear this about Erdman, but thank you for taking the time to come and tell me. I will wait for your notes and pray constantly for his recovery, Mr. Olson. If there is anything else that I can do to help him, please do not hesitate to ask."

Albert smiled and hesitated for a moment. "Clara, I do think that you may need to think about what will happen if Erdman does survive but returns to us in an altered state. Many young women your age would reconsider their commitment and that is understandable as he could have infirmities for the rest of his life. I would not want you to raise his hopes only to dash them when he returns." Albert knew the young woman had the right to know what he had not known about Anna and the chance to make a choice that he had not had the chance to make. While he could not disclose all the details to her right now, he could give her the option to leave if she chose it.

Clara looked directly into Albert's eyes as she stated resolutely "Mr. Olson, I will never leave Erdman voluntarily. If God is gracious enough to grant me Erdman's life, I will gladly accept whatever infirmities that might remain. I intend to live the rest of my life making sure that he knows I love him each and every day, just as he is."

It was Albert's turn to close his eyes as his tears threatened to spill out for his son's good fortune in finding Clara. He reached to take her hand gently. "I see that you mean what you say. I also mean what I say in that I will help you in any way you might need until Erdman returns to both of us whole again. You have only to ask of me, Clara."

Clara felt her baby kick as Albert spoke. She knew that Albert would have to know about his grandchild's existence soon, but she could not formulate the words right now. She stood and turned to walk to where Alice sat nearby. She looked at Albert again and said quietly.

"Erdman must live, Mr. Olson. He has too much to live for to die right now."

Chapter 38

JULY 23, 1926 –
WESTLAND, MICHIGAN

The July morning was almost picture perfect. The azure blue sky with fluffy white clouds and a brilliant sun reflected off the clear lake to the side of Eloise Hospital. Erdman sat in a wheelchair on a veranda facing the lake. He had survived being infected by malaria, but the aftereffects continued to cause problems for him. There were times throughout the ordeal that he had begged for death to come and claim him.

The malaria meant to treat the mental infirmity diagnosed by the doctors of the Eloise Mental Hospital had caused severe symptoms that had tormented Erdman far worse than the mental condition itself. It had begun with a period of coldness as though Erdman had been thrust into a polar vortex. He had chills so violent that he had bit through his own tongue with the chattering of his teeth. He was absolutely convinced that he would never feel warm enough again.

This was followed by a fever period; his temperature ran above 105 degrees and seizures took over his body. He lost consciousness several times and had been told later that he had spent an entire three-day period in a coma barely clinging to life. His only memory of this period was the intense headaches that caused him to hear screaming without realizing that the screams were his own. The third period had been the sweating stage with fatigue so bad that he could not even open his eyes or move his limbs; it had felt as though he were trapped inside his own paralyzed body without a way of calling for help.

Then all three periods had converged taking turns in a vicious cycle that seemed to have no end. Erdman had lost a considerable amount of weight and he had jaundice due to the malaria's attack on his liver. His fatigue was so great he slept a good share of a twenty-four-hour day only to rally for a few hours and then succumb to the cycle all over again. The doctors had assured Erdman that he was recovering, and that the malaria should be doing its intended purpose of ridding his body of mental infirmity.

Now Erdman had to wait until the doctors cleared him of the parasite that had caused the malaria so they could perform the operation to sterilize him. In the first few days of his illness he had reconsidered having the operation but now he was so despondent he did not have the will to resist. He had been to numerous sessions with a specialist who tried to help him cope with the intensity of his feelings to prevent further breakdowns; the deep breathing and counting back in his head had seem to work the best for him. They had even addressed his childhood and his mother causing such detriment to his growing mind and body. He could now address some of the instances himself without having a breakdown, so they had contributed this progression to a successful recovery.

Physically Erdman could not stand for long periods of time without falling, so he often shifted back and forth from foot to foot to try and keep his balance. The blinking that had been an early warning of a breakdown before was more frequent now without a breakdown. He continued to have some intense headaches that resulted in small periods of black outs, but they grew shorter and shorter with each occurrence. Yet, the doctors continued to proclaim the success of his treatment as he did not have fits of rage.

The one subject that Erdman had not allowed anyone to touch on was the one that plagued him every waking moment and in the wee small hours of the night; he had lost Clara possibly forever. He had tried to tell himself he was better off without her. He had tried to forget she existed. He had imagined himself with myriads of other women. But nothing worked to erase the immenseness of his sense of loss. When the specialist mentioned that he cried out continually for Clara and that he had expressed numerous times he had lost her, none of the deep breathing or counting back seemed to have any effect. This was the area of concern for the doctors at the present time, and they were inside the clinic consulting about what to do next as Erdman waited on the veranda.

Erdman wore his fedora and a pair of sunglasses as the sunlight still proved too intense for his eyes. He stared out at the swans on the lake, the pure white male and female followed by six downy gray cygnets gliding across the lake, oblivious to their onlookers. The male swan caught various bugs along the surface of the water, feeding the female and each of the babies in turn. The beautiful tableau brought tears to his eyes; even these wild animals were able to care for each other and their young. What kind of a monster was he to desert Clara and their child? Clara deserved to have a husband to be solely devoted to her; she had been right to demand it of him and he had failed her in every way.

"Erdman? Son, is that you?" Albert stood a distance away on the veranda. He was still carrying his suitcase, having come straight to the hospital from the train station. Albert approached Erdman and set his suitcase on the ground as he knelt beside his son's wheelchair. Albert appeared to be examining Erdman intently as he gently put his arms around Erdman's shoulders to hug him. Erdman could hear the tell-tale sniffling and feel the slight shake of his father's body; Albert was overcome to the point of tears. Erdman lifted his hand to pat his father's back. He was surprised to feel so happy to see his father as he had so often just felt a void of emotion towards both of his parents in the past.

"It sure is good to see you again, Son," Albert began, once he had regained the ability to speak. "They sent me updates on you almost every day, and I came as soon as they said that I could." Albert pulled a chair up beside Erdman's wheelchair and sat down. "You sure did give us a scare a time or two there, my boy, but the doctors said that you will be right as rain in no time now."

"Us? Please don't try to tell me that Anna was worried about me. I hope that you didn't actually tell Arvid what was going on." Erdman looked at his father. He had learned to disassociate himself by calling his mother by her given name and thereby not allowing her such a powerful hold on his life. Even mentioning her name had him slow his breathing and concentrate on handling the emotions it made him feel. Erdman focused again on the swans in the lake until the rage had passed.

Albert shifted in his chair, watching Erdman and looking uncomfortable. No, I didn't tell Arvid why you were here other than an operation for your tonsils. I suppose you are right about your… Anna." Albert caught himself in referring to Erdman's mother and followed Erdman's lead.

Erdman smiled slightly at his father's attempt to concede. "Yet, you said "Us"? Who else did you tell that I was sick or here?" Erdman hoped his father would tell him the plain truth, as the game playing and half-truths they used to tell each other just left him with another headache.

"Well, I was going to wait a little bit before bringing the rest up, but I guess I put my foot in it, didn't I?" Albert leaned over to pat Erdman's hand as he continued. "I ran across Clara in Mt. Sterling and that poor little gal was about beside herself with worry over you. I didn't know what exactly to say, but she does know about the malaria and you being in a bad way with it. I don't want to upset you right off the bat, Son, but it was downright cruel to just let her carry on without knowing anything at all." Albert cringed while waiting for Erdman to react.

"You told Clara I was sick with malaria?" Erdman paused, letting it sink in and tried to breathe slowly. *Wait a minute. He said Clara was beside herself with worry and she wouldn't be if she didn't still care about me. Could she still be waiting for me to return and thinking I had just left with no word at all? At least she knows why I didn't come back to make amends.*

"I had to tell her something about why we sent you so far away. She has responded to each note I sent to her, and she begged me to let her come with me today. I didn't know how you would take that since she said you two had a falling out, but she is very sure that you will want to see her again. She wrote one letter for you originally and then added five more." Albert leaned down to his suitcase and pulled out the letters from a side pocket.

Erdman held out his trembling hands for the letters. He was anxious about what she might have to tell him, but he was also excited that she had written more than one. Surely, she would not take six letters to tell him that she never wished to see him again. He needed to find a quiet place by himself to read them before he made himself upset with not knowing how she felt about him, about them, and about having their child.

"She told you we had a falling out. Was that all she told you?" Erdman needed to know if Clara had gone to ask his father for help with the coming baby. Perhaps she was only interested in the money she knew Albert would offer to her. He could not believe it of her, but he still needed to know.

"Yes, she didn't say too much, but I had the feeling that maybe you had done the poor girl wrong with all your other gals. She isn't your typical kind of girl that you love and leave, and I think you know that now. I think if you put your mind to it you can still fix things with her. A girl like Clara is one in a million, Son." Albert tried to offer his son the best counsel he could, having messed up his own life in numerous ways.

She had not told his father. She kept their baby a secret so that he could return and still do the right thing by her without being forced into it. He needed to get better and get back to her soon.

"I am glad you told her, Pa. I hope that I can fix things with her. I sure am going to try." Erdman saw the smile on his father's face, full of relief and hope. Possibly these doctors were not going to have to find any more "cures" for him; he could return home and Clara would take him back again.

Albert rejoined Erdman in the solarium later that day. The natural sunlight from its many windows had been prescribed to help heal

Erdman's liver damage from the malaria. Erdman had read through all of Clara's letters that afternoon, devouring every word as if he were eating for the first time after a long fast. Clara's letters were full of her love and devotion for him. She had even asked for his forgiveness when he knew that he was completely at fault and should be asking for hers. She never mentioned their baby, possibly because she did not want anyone to intercept the letters and find their secret in black and white or because she did not know how he might react if she did. She was the one who had been deserted and alone, and yet her care and concern were only for him as she described in every loving word she had put on the papers.

One of the doctors who had been primarily responsible for Erdman's treatment had summoned Erdman and Albert to his office by way of an orderly, so they walked slowly together down the hallway from the solarium to the main part of the clinic. Erdman needed to stop and rest more than once, and at times he leaned upon his father's arm. But he had insisted on walking the distance without the aid of the wheelchair. He was now motivated to recover and return home to Clara.

The doctor looked up in surprise to see Erdman walk into his office. "Erdman, it is good to see you trying to do more without your wheelchair. But don't overdo it, as your malaria can sometimes cause relapses. You are almost to the end of the treatment we have discussed, and we have scheduled your sterilization surgery for tomorrow. If you continue to make progress in your therapies, you can expect to return home in less than two weeks. Your therapist mentioned that there seems to be still one stumbling block for you, when he mentions the young lady we have discussed in the past." The doctor was trying to put the subject of Clara forward gently which caused Erdman to smile.

"I don't think the topic of Clara will cause problems for me anymore." Erdman assured the doctor. "I am still wondering about the sterilization. Is it absolutely necessary?"

The doctor seemed surprised at Erdman's mention of Clara, but he nodded vehemently to Erdman's question. "It is absolutely necessary. We have found that the inherited traits of this particular mental infirmity will only increase with each generation. To willingly take the risk of having a child with a great propensity of derangement is unconscionable. History has shown us that allowing the hereditary traits to continue can cause someone to be deranged with the magnitude of the infamous Jack the Ripper, and the bloodline traits should be ended at all costs. We are very fortunate that you are a young man and unmarried, so you do not have any children yet."

Erdman nodded his assent while his mind ranted, *there is a child that you don't know of yet.* He knew that he needed to recover in less than the two weeks predicted and return to Clara so they could figure out what to do next.

How do I tell her that the child she is carrying could be completely deranged and it is all my fault?

Chapter 39

JULY 26, 1926 –
UTICA, WISCONSIN

More than a year had passed since the last box social for the Utica Lutheran Church. The event had been delayed twice from its original date in June because of heavy storms that had battered the area. Finally, the day dawned bright and clear for the annual event. John Fitzgibbon, a local farmer, had been selected to host the event as the hosts rotated from year to year. The Christ Olson family, everyone except Clara, eagerly anticipated the social event of the season.

Clara had mulled over several excuses for not attending the box social, but she had not come up with anything that would not cause her parents further suspicion. Dena had kept a close eye on Clara recently, noting her mood swings and fatigue. There had been a few times that Dena had been suspicious of Clara being with child, but she didn't have the heart or the courage to bring the subject directly to Clara in the hope that she was wrong. An illegitimate child was thought of as being feeble or demented, and an unwed mother had few prospects for other marriages besides the baby's father. Dena hoped that Clara's "ailment" would be resolved without more misery for the poor girl. Since the Olson boy had left her, Clara had been very forlorn and despondent. She did not need the additional heartbreak that this would bring to her and her family.

Since Clara could not think of a good reason for not attending the box social, she tried to put on a brave face and accompanied her family. She was asked to provide another box dinner, but she kept replaying in her mind how Erdman had arranged for her dinner to be purchased last year. She finally threw a lunch together at the last minute and begged one of her brothers to bid on the box when it came time for the auction.

Clara wore the yellow silk dress with the white polka dots, as it was a dress that Alice had been able to let out without people noticing. While her maternity corset hid the most predominant features of her pregnancy, she had been gaining some more curves and some of her dresses were not fitting her as well as they had. Even though she wore the yellow dress, she could not bring herself to tie another yellow ribbon around the box dinner as that had been something Erdman had kept as a keepsake of their first day together and their first kiss.

Clara rode with Bernard in his new car to the Fitzgibbon farm. The late July day was warm, but there was a gentle breeze that kept the air cooler and kept the heavy afternoon thunderstorms at bay. Clara recalled wistfully how excited she had been only a year ago and how much her life had changed in that same year period. She had not heard from Albert since he had left to visit Erdman. She wondered if she would see Erdman soon or if she would have to put her alternate plan into effect and leave with Lena for Norway by mid-September.

Clara brought her box dinner to the designated place and left it there. She had shown the box to Bernard several times so that he would know which box to bid on and she would not be put in an awkward position of having dinner with anyone else. She greeted various people as she walked along towards a row of benches in the shade, wanting a cool place to sit and think by herself. Clara noted there were a couple of young mothers sitting there in the shade with their babies. She chuckled to herself as she sat among them and admired the little ones from afar; her little one was present but unseen and unknown to almost everyone. She imagined what it might be like to be sitting here next year holding her own baby and being married to Erdman, if only he would return and marry her in time.

Clara looked at the group of young people gathered over by the barn. They were laughing and talking, the young ladies giving the gents of their choice hints about which box to buy. She knew several of the young men and young women gathered; others were new faces to her. Edwin Knutson had arrived and had found a quiet young lady to sit beside. He appeared nervous as he tried to talk with her but her quiet encouragement helped him to calm down. Clara hoped that he would not notice her sitting over by the tree. It was not that she disliked him or was angry at what he had said to her. She knew that Edwin deserved a nice sweet girl who was interested in only him, and he had wasted enough of his time on her already. Clara turned her body away from the group so that Edwin might not notice her there and come to talk to her instead of staying with the nice girl he already had engaged in conversation.

Clara saw the shadow of the man standing beside her first. She turned back to find the postal clerk, Ansgar, smiling down at her, holding two cups of lemonade. He extended one towards Clara and took a seat beside her on the bench.

"It is very warm out here and you looked as though you might enjoy a cold lemonade." Ansgar stretched his legs out in front of him as he sipped from his cup. "It appears to be a good crowd this year. I wasn't able to attend last year, but I made certain that I had the day off this year. Are you staying for the dinner, Clara?" He was hinting, and Clara knew that she should politely decline right away. Like Edwin, Ansgar deserved a nice young woman who liked only him. Clara knew that it would never be her. Her heart still belonged to Erdman, and Ansgar did not know that Clara was carrying Erdman's child. Even if Erdman never came back to her, men like Ansgar would soon consider Clara as "damaged goods". She knew what she should say to him.

"Yes, I am staying for the box dinner. There looks to be many nice dinners over there to choose from, so I am sure that mine will be meager compared to the others. My brothers like to bid on mine because they love my fattigmann cookies and I always bake them for these occasions." Clara knew what to say and yet her words came out completely different. She was tired of being set aside, tired of waiting for what might never happen, and she knew that soon she would be considered completely undesirable as a companion for any of the young men who once used to pay attention to her. She wanted one afternoon to feel like she did last year before she said goodbye to all of it.

"Fattigmann cookies? You don't say. They happen to be my favorite as well. I may have to pay close attention to which box your brothers are bidding on if that is acceptable to you?" Ansgar's eyes held the question as he looked into Clara's eyes. Clara rose from the bench, smiled at Ansgar, and gave the slightest nod of her head as she walked to where the boxes were placed for the auction to begin.

Alice noticed the exchange between the two and smiled at Clara as she took her sister's hand and stood beside her.

"Good for you, Clara. Relax and try to have a nice afternoon. Sit with me and my date, okay? I met him on our last trip to Viroqua. He is from Illinois, and he came all the way here to see me today. His name is Max Stevens and he is heavenly!" Alice paused in her rambling and glanced at Clara. Her face held regret that she hurt Clara by talking about being so happy with her beau.

"I am happy for you, Alice. No matter what happens to me and Erdman, I want you to be happy, and if this Max makes you happy then it makes me happy, too. Besides, he is very cute." Clara laughed as she whispered to her sister and hugged her tightly.

The bidding had begun, and Max bought Alice's box dinner right away to the cheering of the crowd gathered around them. Clara knew she shouldn't have encouraged Ansgar in any way, but she continued to smile in his direction as the pastor picked up her box dinner. Bernard was true to his word and placed a nice bid on Clara's box dinner but Ansgar continued to bid higher. Bernard finally had to bow out as the bid went beyond what he could pay. Ansgar had won the dinner with Clara, and she found that she was happy about it and the thought of a nice afternoon. Dena and Christ looked on with interest as Clara followed Ansgar over to where Alice and Max sat.

Ansgar placed a blanket on the ground and turned to help Clara sit down. She took his hand telling herself that she was becoming more and more awkward and she really did need his assistance. The truth of the matter was that she appreciated the attention after feeling neglected by Erdman for months. She knew that it would make Erdman very angry to see her sharing a dinner with Ansgar or any of the other eligible bachelors present, but just as quickly she told herself that if Erdman didn't want her to share her dinner with someone else he should be present himself so that she could have enjoyed the day with him. She felt a twinge of guilt knowing that Erdman had been very sick and had only just recovered, but she swatted the guilt away in her mind as if it were a pesky fly.

Clara unpacked the box dinner and handed fresh sandwiches and cheese to Ansgar. They enjoyed the dinner and laughed at the jokes Alice's beau Max told. Every time Clara glanced at Ansgar he was watching her with a smile on his face. It made her blush to receive such warm attention from him and a tiny warning kept sounding in the back of her mind. *Don't allow him to think this will ever be anything more than one dinner shared in the company of your sister and friends. Don't hurt him the way that you have been hurt by Erdman and don't do the same thing that you accused Erdman of doing to you.*

Clara enjoyed the afternoon and evening despite her misgivings. She watched as Ansgar and Max competed together in a three-legged race and came out as the champions. She enjoyed her younger sisters, Inga and Cornelia, as they sat with her and discussed the boys that they liked in hushed whispers and giggles. She saw her papa visit with the older men next to the porch and her mama come over to bring him his favorite piece of ground cherry pie. Her brothers, Bernard and Adolph, sat nearby teasing her as only big brothers could do. The sense of community in this small county was so strong. Clara knew that she was surrounded by good, honest people who worked hard and loved each other harder.

Suddenly Clara realized that for all the years that she had longed to travel the world and live in a big city far away she had not realized what a treasure her own home and the people of her community were. Soon she would have to leave with Erdman to live in a large city as he had planned or to Norway to have her baby and possibly never return. She found what she really desired now was to get married and settle down right here in Crawford County with her family and friends close by. She imagined Christ holding his first grandchild upon his knee and being the proudest bestefar ever. The thought of losing so much made her eyes water.

"Clara, are you all right? May I get you some more lemonade?" Ansgar had seen her unshed tears and immediately rushed to her assistance. He had been so attentive all afternoon but had not even attempted to hold her hand, because he didn't want her to think he was presumptuous. Clara nodded, and he rushed off to get her a fresh cup. She needed a few moments to put her thoughts back in order without him being able to almost read her mind.

Alice had been observing Clara as well; she came to sit close beside her sister. "Are you feeling unwell or lonely, Sister? I know Bernard will be happy to take you home when you are ready."

"I guess a little bit of both. Ansgar went to get some more lemonade, so I will stay until he returns. Do you mind finding Bernard for me?" Clara and Alice both understood that while it was nice to spend the afternoon with Ansgar, Clara couldn't allow him to take her home. Alice patted her sister's hand and nodded as she rose to go and search for their brother.

Ansgar returned with the cup of lemonade, handing it gently to Clara and sitting down beside her. "Clara, I understand that you might still be suffering from strong feelings towards your former beau, but I just wish for you to understand that I am happy to wait for as long as it takes. I don't want you to feel pushed into anything you are not ready for yet. If that makes you upset, then please forget I even mentioned it. Thank you for making this such a wonderful afternoon." His gentle brown eyes regarded her with such kindness and sincerity.

"Ansgar, you are one of the kindest gentlemen I have ever known. It is I who should be thanking you for the wonderful afternoon. I am honored that you would even consider me in that way. I asked my brother to take me home soon, but I didn't want to leave before saying goodbye to you." Clara knew that either way she would be leaving this place and everyone, including Ansgar, very soon. She didn't want to make him think there was hope for them, but she couldn't bring herself to send him away completely. He would understand soon enough that when she had said goodbye it possibly meant forever. Hopefully he would always remember this afternoon with fondness because she knew that she would.

Bernard came to stand beside where Clara was sitting on the blanket. He reached down and gently helped Clara to her feet and shook hands with Ansgar. Bernard had agreed to find Emma and take her home, so he left Clara standing beside the benches she had sat upon earlier. Clara was tired. She wanted to go home and take her corset off, as it was getting very uncomfortable. She sat down on a bench to wait for her brother.

Clara looked up to see Anna Olson standing a short distance away from her. She had not noticed Erdman's mother earlier in the day, and she hoped that possibly Albert and Erdman might be with her. She looked around the crowd, straining to see that one familiar face her heart longed to see but she did not see him anywhere. When Clara looked back towards Anna, she saw that the woman was staring straight at her. Anna spoke to a man who looked like a taller version of herself.

"That girl is the one who met up with our hired hand in Mt. Sterling a few weeks ago. Now she is taking up with another man today. I didn't want Arvid anywhere near her sort that day, and I am certainly glad Erdman never had anything to do with her. I know a brazen hussy when I see one!" Anna pointed her finger straight at Clara while raising her voice. The man with her shushed Anna and led her away quickly.

Clara was so humiliated, her cheeks burned with embarrassment and anger. If only Anna knew the whole truth about her precious son. Clara looked around quickly, but it appeared as if no one else had heard the woman's rant. She knew her brother would have made a ready reply to the horrid insinuations had he heard them. Bernard reappeared with Emma in tow, looking puzzled at Clara's flushed face.

As they walked towards the car Bernard whispered to her. "You know, a girl could do a whole lot worse than that Ansgar. He is a pretty stand up kind of fellow. I think he is genuinely fond of you, Clara, if you just let go of the past."

At just that moment Clara's baby decided to give its first solid kick. She paused for a moment, trying not to gasp. She shook her head at Bernard and whispered back.

"There are parts of the past that you cannot simply let go."

Chapter 40

JULY 30, 1926 –
VIROQUA, WISCONSIN

It had not been the two weeks that the doctors had predicted for Erdman's final recovery, when he and Albert stepped off the train at the station in Viroqua. It had been the better part of two days for the journey, and Erdman felt drained. It was late afternoon, The July heat was oppressive, making Erdman's fatigue even more noticeable. Albert had made plans to call Edwin to come and pick them up for their final leg of the trip home to Rising Sun.

Albert had sent Clara a quick note a few days earlier to update her on Erdman's improvements and their plans for returning home. He knew that the young woman would be worrying about them, and he wanted to alleviate any undue stress for her. Albert continued to hope that Clara and Erdman could mend their rift because she brought such hope to him and both of his sons. Albert knew that Anna already viewed Clara as a bad sort of girl, and she knew nothing about Clara's involvement with Erdman. The irony that Anna could judge anyone else, especially Clara, on her character was not lost on Albert. He had learned long ago not to fight the enigma that was his wife.

Erdman sat on a bench in the shade near the train station, waiting for Albert to return from downtown where he went to place his call. Erdman had to remove his suit jacket and roll up his shirt sleeves to prevent spiking another fever from the heat. He wore his sunglasses almost constantly to prevent the severe headaches from reoccurring. He often had to look at objects very closely to determine what they were. He liked the dark lenses of his sunglasses because they made it more difficult for people to see his frequent blinking and staring at objects and people.

Erdman had been staring at some children nearby. They played in the lawn while waiting to board their train, their laughter carrying across to Erdman as he sat trying to determine the colors of the little boy's suit jacket. Simple things like colors had become more difficult for him to detect. A young woman approached from the other side of the yard. She stood in the walkway looking directly at Erdman. He angled his head slightly to look at her better and realized he was staring back into the beautiful brown eyes that were so familiar to him.

"Clara?" Erdman felt joy and panic at the same time. She seemed transfixed where she stood her brow wrinkled slightly in concern. Erdman started to stand and felt his legs wobbling from the fatigue of his journey. Clara walked quickly to his side, gently taking his arm and guiding him to sit back down on the bench. Erdman could see her luminous brown eyes shimmering with tears as she sat down beside him.

Erdman's own emotions felt as though they were careening out of control. He took a deep breath and let it out slowly and then took another deep breath, repeating the process. The calmness he felt was almost immediate, but he realized that it must sound as if he were sighing to Clara.

"Sorry, I didn't mean to be rude. The doctors taught me to take several deep breaths to help me with my emotions, and I find that it helps me quite a bit. I didn't expect to see you here, and I was caught off guard." Erdman tried to smile at her. Now he had made it worse by suggesting that her presence was possibly unwelcome. He took another deep breath.

Clara had not spoken at all. She did not look angry or upset with him. She had looked at him this exact same way after the first time they had been intimate together, as if she were trying to see something inside him. The first time it had only made him angry, but this time he realized it was out of her concern for him and it comforted him.

"I am sorry if I seemed rude to you as well. I just realized that I have been staring at you without saying anything. It is just that I was at the point of wondering if I might ever see you again and here you are right in front of me." Clara smiled as she continued to look concerned.

"And is that a good thing that you found me?" Erdman asked tentatively, hoping that she did want to see him again and again. There was so much he needed to tell her, but he knew that she might not want to hear what he had to say after all he had done.

"It is one of the best things ever." Clara placed her hand over his hand as she continued to sit beside him. "Your pa told me that you were very sick and why you had to leave so suddenly. Then when we thought that you might not live…" Clara paused and cleared her throat, her voice full of emotion. "I have never prayed so hard for anyone in all my life. I couldn't stand the thought that my last words to you were out of anger. Did you receive my letters?"

Erdman nodded. "I read every one of them over and over. I think your letters gave me the will to finish my recovery. I need to apologize to you Clara instead of you apologizing to me. I hope that we can find a way to make up our differences and continue on."

Clara nodded quickly in agreement to his last statement. "I want that too, Erdman. I am sure you need more time for recovery at home before we make any other plans?" Her question, while simple, was complicated with the fact that she was running out of time before others discovered what she had kept secret for his sake.

"I might need a little time to get settled, but we have plans, Clara, and I want you to know that I will follow through with them if you are still willing. Is everything alright with you and everyone? I mean, are you both well?" Erdman glanced towards her belly where there was still no detectable evidence that she carried his child. How was he going to explain that their child might already carry mental infirmities and that it would be better off for everyone if they were to lose it? The thought of this caused the pangs of a migraine to begin; Erdman removed his sunglasses and rubbed at his temple with the hand not being held by Clara.

"We are both well and growing. We still have some time, Erdman, if that is what you truly wish. I don't want the pressure of our situation to make you sick again. I love you and I will be waiting for you. I think I will slip away before your father returns so that we don't need to explain our meeting to him. Send me word when we can meet again." Clara kissed his cheek gently and rose to leave.

Erdman clasped Clara's hand and brought it to hold in both of his hands. "I love you, too, Clara. You don't have to leave. My pa thinks the world of you, and he would be happy to see you. Edwin is coming to get us, and we could take you home. I can't drive you myself yet, but you could ride with us." Erdman squinted to see her, then put his sunglasses back on, so she didn't notice.

Clara smiled gently. "Thank you for offering. I would love to spend the time with you. Your pa is very nice, and I believe we will get along fine in the future. I met your mother by accident recently, and she does not like me at all. I don't think she realizes that we are a couple, but she did not want me anywhere near Arvid, let alone you. I don't want to take the risk that she might come with Edwin and Arvid to pick you up today. We have a few bridges to cross, but we will deal with that when you are feeling better. I will write to you soon."

Erdman couldn't believe what he was hearing. He wasn't even home yet, and Anna was already causing him trouble. He knew Clara was right about today, but he wanted more time with her. He kissed her hand that he still held and nodded in agreement. Clara walked away quietly as Erdman sat trying to count back in his head and breathe slowly. He knew that it was going to take a lot of his newest therapy to overcome the anxiousness and anger that one mention of Anna brought to him.

Clara walked several blocks away from the train station and Erdman. She found a quiet side street that led to the large tobacco warehouses on the edge of town. The street was lined with large oak and maple trees, and Clara found refuge under one of the trees. She sat down on the ground with her back against the tree trunk; the tears that she had tried so valiantly to hide from Erdman fell in torrents. Erdman was emaciated to the point of looking like a skeleton, his cheekbones and jaw being much more angular than she remembered. And his eyes, when he had removed his sunglasses briefly, were sunken into his skull with dark patches beneath them. He seemed to blink rapidly when he tried to focus on objects.

It was not that she now found him unattractive. It was that his current condition and "recovery" spoke volumes about just how dire his condition had been. She had not wanted him to see how shocked she was to see just how bad his sickness had been. She would not hurt him for the world, especially if it made him think that she no longer wished to be his wife. On the contrary, this only made her want to marry him more and care for him for the rest of his life. She knew he had a long road to a full recovery, and he might never regain all his former physical strength so they would have to wait a while longer to get married. She hoped that being at home would help and that they might plan for September. At least she would be able to give Lena a more definite answer that her alternate plan would not be needed after all.

Clara had estimated that her baby would be born right around Christmas so even a September wedding would still be in time. She now hoped Erdman might reconsider going back to Gale College while he still needed to recover, as the extra rigors of a new baby and college study might prove to be too much for him. Did she dare to hope that part of her recent revelations of the desire to remain among her family might actually come true? For the first time in months, the spark of hope reignited in Clara's heart. She knew that she needed to remain strong and hopeful for Erdman and for their child.

Clara wiped away her tears and stood to walk back to the downtown area. She would pick up a few items and then catch the afternoon bus back to Seneca. As she strolled past the shop windows, she noticed a beautiful white baby bonnet displayed at the mercantile. She had not purchased a single thing for her child as their future had been so unforeseeable. She left the mercantile a little while later with the beautiful baby bonnet wrapped in tissue paper and with high hopes for their future.

Chapter 41

AUGUST 10, 1926 –
SENECA, WISCONSIN

The August morning was bright with a moderate breeze. The clothing strung on the clothesline on Stoney Point Road fluttered in the breeze as if each garment had taken on a life of its own. Clara and Alice had been left at home to do the clothes washing, while Dena and Emma had taken a trip to Prairie du Chien with Christ and Bernard. Adolph had taken Cornelia and Inga to the Stoney Point School for a workday and picnic on the school grounds, so Clara and Alie were alone for the day on the family farm.

Usually Clara and Alice were two of the first people in the family to join in outings, but Clara had become more and more of a recluse after overhearing Erdman's mother at the box dinner social. Alice in turn had focused her complete attentions on Max Stevens who was away in Illinois, so she was less likely to seek the social company of others that she had in the past. Both girls had decided to do some sewing after finishing the laundry as they liked to copy patterns from the latest styles and make their own dresses, and this gave them a perfect opportunity.

Clara hung the newly washed clothing on the line; she loved the smell as it dried in the sun and fresh air. As she bent to retrieve a shirt from the basket at her feet and stretched to clip the clothespins to the shirt and the line, her baby kicked and rolled forward at the same time. This new and slightly painful sensation caused Clara to gasp and clutch her stomach as she bent over slightly. Alice ran to her side grabbing one of Clara's arms and circling her waist with Alice's other arm, guiding her to the bench.

"Clara, what happened? Are you both alright? Are you in pain?" Alice looked at her sister's pale and sweaty face with alarm. Alice had heard many stories of young women who died while pregnant or while trying to give birth, and she knew that Clara could be taking a large risk by not seeking a doctor about her condition.

Clara fanned her face with her apron and rubbed her stomach gently. "Yes, I think that we are both fine. I felt a new movement just now and it hurt just a little. Try not to worry so much Sister. Women have been having babies since the beginning of time, and I am no different. I just need to sit a bit and then we can finish."

"Women can have problems especially when they haven't been to see a doctor after this many months. Maybe there is more than one in there. Did you ever think of that? I also think that your corset may be too tight. I understand why, but I don't know if it is safe anymore." Alice shook her head slightly at her sister's nonchalant approach to impending motherhood.

There had been a time that Clara would have been annoyed by Alice's seemingly bossy attitude towards her older sister, but she knew her little sister was only showing her love and concern. "Hopefully it won't be much longer, and I can take the corset off for the duration. After I am married, I won't concern myself so much with covering it. Erdman has promised to contact me soon so we may be off to get married any time after that. One day I will be here and the next I will be gone, but only for a little while to get the ceremony out of the way. It will all turn out fine, Alice. I am sure of that." Clara had returned from meeting Erdman with a new confidence for her future, even though it had been over a week since she had seen him and she had not heard anything else.

Alice did not share her sister's confidence that Erdman would send for Clara and that they would elope. Erdman had been home only a few days when Alice heard that he had returned to selling his gin and socializing at the dance halls. He did not seem to be as much of a womanizer from the complaints Alice heard of Christine Anderson and her sort, but he certainly did not depict a soon-to-be husband and father, either. Alice had even heard that Erdman had hired a "tough", a large burly farm boy from Iowa who drove the roadster and discouraged people from stealing Erdman's ever-increasing profits by sitting in the rumble seat with Erdman's pistol in his lap.

"Have you considered writing Mr. Olson a letter and letting him know of the situation? I know he likes you very much, so he would help you get Erdman to elope if he knew that a baby is arriving in December." Alice felt strongly that it might take Mr. Olson, their own father, and the traditional shot gun to get Erdman to the actual altar.

"My goodness, no. I have never wanted to pressure Erdman into marrying me. Albert is so nice, and I want him to be a friend to me once Erdman and I are married. I would worry that he might change his mind if he knew about the baby before we are married. Erdman's mother already thinks I am not fit to be in their family. I don't need Albert to think so as well." Clara stretched her legs and stood up to return to the clothesline and their chores.

"I just thought it would be good if you had his help in this. I heard him offer you his help in any way more than once already. Don't be too proud to ask him, Clara. It wouldn't be the first time that a father needed to encourage his son to go and do the right thing by a gal. It happens far more than you realize. I think he will be more upset that you didn't tell him so that he could help you in time. Erdman could be very sick again for all that you know, and you don't have months left to wait for him to get better again. Besides, it is much better that Erdman's father finds out before our father and brothers realize what's been going on right under their noses. If they find out there is a baby and no wedding yet, it will not go well for Erdman at all. I have noticed Mama looking at you closely several times and she would be the one to figure such things out after having so many babies of her own. You might consider this as saving Erdman from future pain because Bernard and Adolph already hate him with a passion and wouldn't need much of an excuse to see him come to harm. I would just ask you to think about it, Clara." Alice joined Clara where she stood at the clothesline to resume hanging up the laundry.

Clara had been so convinced that she never wanted Erdman to feel pressured that she never realized she might be putting him into danger by allowing too much time to slip by. Alice was right about their father and brothers. They had all been very outspoken against Erdman when they believed that he had broken Clara's heart. It would not take very much to escalate their words into actions against him, far less than the realization that Erdman had gotten their sister pregnant and had not married her. Even Clara did not think she would be able to reason with her brothers at that point. She knew that Albert would never hurt Erdman and he might provide them a quicker avenue towards elopement.

Clara and Alice were quiet as they finished the chores, Alice allowing Clara to ruminate on the advice given to her. They set to work on their sewing projects. Alice started a new outfit for her next outing with Max, and Clara chose to make a dress of black and green silk, hopefully her elopement outfit as Lena had provided a perfect wedding dress already. They laughed and sang together as they cut and pieced the dresses and pinned them together. They used the sewing machine, Alice insisting that they sew Clara's dress first as she would hopefully need it very soon.

Clara modeled the almost finished dress in front of her sister. The lower cut of the waist at her hips and a large bow from the neck hid the baby well and was still very fashionable. Alice suggested getting a new black hat with a green band and wearing Clara's pearls for finishing touches.

"You will be a beautiful bride. I only wish I could be present at your wedding. I want you to be my matron of honor when I marry Max." Alice grinned at Clara letting her sister in on her own well-kept secret. Clara squealed in delight as she ran to hug her.

"I am sorry you won't be with me at my wedding, but I will be so happy to be with you at yours. I will tell you this, though, if Erdman and I have a little girl, I want to name her Alice after the very best sister in the world." This time it was Alice who squealed with delight and the sisters embraced again. "Thank you for loving me always, Sister. I think that you are right about Erdman's father and his willingness to help."

Clara knew she had just decided to take her sister's advice and appeal to Albert to help her, Erdman, and his future grandchild by finding a way for them to elope as soon as possible. Hopefully Erdman would understand why she chose this action instead of just waiting like they had planned. Alice interrupted Clara's thoughts with a declaration of her own.

"Clara, I am absolutely certain that you will have a baby girl named Alice, and she will be the luckiest little girl in the world to have you as her mama and me as her aunt."

Chapter 42

AUGUST 17, 1926 –
RISING SUN, WISCONSIN

The August afternoon was hot and humid with just a trace of a breeze. The sun shone in a brilliant blue sky dotted with puffy white clouds. Albert had determined to do more things with both of his boys and so the three had set off right after the noon lunch to fish on the Mississippi River near Ferryville, only eleven miles from their home in Rising Sun. It was a well-known spot to catch large walleye, blue gills, crappie, and perch.

Erdman had recovered enough to start driving his roadster again, so he drove with his father in the front passenger seat and Arvid holding the fishing tackle in the rumble seat. Erdman still had to wear his dark lens sunglasses much of the time, but even his eyes had recovered moderately. Erdman pulled the roadster into a parking area near the ferry dock. They could see the Little Julia Hadley, the ferry boat between Ferryville and Lansing, Iowa, chugging along the waterfront.

Albert sent Arvid with some money to purchase three cold bottles of Coca Cola from the mercantile as they unpacked the fishing poles and bait from the back of the car. He quietly studied Erdman without appearing to look at his son. Erdman had settled back into life quietly on the farm, helping with the tobacco crop, doing numerous chores outside, and helping with Arvid. He tended to steer clear of Anna most of the time, and Albert could see that Erdman was attempting to divert his former rage and emotions concerning his mother into positive areas with his little brother. Albert could not tell if Erdman had mended his relationship with Clara, as Erdman did not mention her by name even when they were alone. One of his motives for bringing the boys today was to try and ask Erdman what had happened with the girl and where their plans might be headed.

"I wrote Clara a note to tell her that you had arrived home and were still recovering. I am surprised that I haven't heard back from her yet. She was so very concerned for you, Son. Have you heard anything from her?" Albert had learned that a more direct approach suited both him and Erdman since almost losing Erdman to the malaria.

Erdman stared out at the river in front of them. He nodded slightly and cleared his throat. "Yes, I contacted her as well. She was very happy to hear from me, which made me relieved. She wanted me to take some more time to recover before we met again as she is always more concerned about me than she is about herself. A lot of women would be clamoring at a fellow because of the long absence but not Clara. She did mention that she met Anna by accident, and it didn't go very well. It doesn't really surprise me, I guess."

Albert cringed at Erdman's mention of Anna. He knew that his wife would be a major hurdle between Erdman and his happiness with Clara. "Yes, I was present for that. Anna didn't realize who Clara was to you, but she didn't react well. I don't want you to allow your mother to ruin what happiness you might have with Clara. If there is any way in which I can help the two of you, I want you to know that I will. You two might be able to start somewhere else if that is what you had in mind. I would be only too happy to help you with money or whatever you might need. You have only to ask me, Erdman."

Erdman turned his head to look at his father. His brow was knit in concentration; he was trying to form his words carefully. How did he explain to his father that he did want to marry Clara, but he did not want the child she carried because of its possible mental deformities? He had thought about taking Clara and leaving for somewhere far away but only if she would agree to have their child taken care of by means of an illegal operation or a medication to cause a miscarriage. He wanted no piece of Anna to haunt him ever again, especially hidden within his own offspring. What he didn't know was how Clara was going to respond to his idea, or even how Albert would feel about it since he still was not aware of the child.

"I was thinking about not returning to Gale in the fall. I wondered about moving away and asking Clara if she might be willing to go with me. I think if I expanded in some of the business venture I have already started, I would be able to succeed. Buddy Henks, my newest associate, tells me that he already has connections in Chicago and Minneapolis that would welcome me into what they have established. I might need some money to start, but I would be willing to pay it all back to you." Erdman felt good that he could formulate his most recent thoughts into a reasonable plan for his father.

"There will never be a need for you to repay me. I know a good investment when I see one. When do you think you might put this new plan of yours into action?" Albert had a surge of hope for

Erdman for the first time since his son had entered the hospital. He was speaking of Clara in a way that led Albert to believe the two had mended their relationship and were seeking a future together.

"Well, I would like to start sooner rather than later. One of my questions is how do I tell Clara about our marriage without the possibility of children? Most women set great store by that. She may decide she doesn't want to marry me anymore and to be honest I don't know what I will do without her." Erdman avoided telling his father about the child already present as he had a difficult time thinking about it himself.

"Son, when I spoke to Clara the first time about your illness, I felt it was important that she know that if you lived, you might never be whole again. She should have the chance to change her mind before committing the rest of her life with you. I admit I would have liked for someone to give me that opportunity before I married Anna and they didn't. Now I am glad I took that chance with Anna because it brought me you and your brother, and I wouldn't trade you for the world." Albert patted Erdman's shoulder. "Clara assured me that if God allowed you to live, she would spend every day proving to you that she loved you no matter what condition you might be in. I have told you this before, but Clara is the kind of girl that you never let go of no matter what. Talk to her and you will see that I am right."

Arvid approached carrying the bottles of soda and a box of popcorn. "Pa, are we ready to fish now?" he asked excitedly. Erdman smiled at his little brother. He followed Arvid to the bank of the river and helped him to cast his line telling him to watch the bobber and hold the fishing pole firmly. Erdman had fond of memories of Albert bringing him here to fish when he had been Arvid's age. His life had been so much simpler then. He envied his brother for his innocence and prayed that what had robbed him of his would never happen to Arvid.

Albert lit one of his favorite cigars and handed it to Erdman. The smell of the cigars drew the fish and created even more of the boyhood memory that Erdman remembered. Albert lit the second cigar for himself and the three sat for a time in companionable silence. Suddenly, there was a huge tug on Arvid's line, the bobber being pulled completely under the water's surface.

"Hey there, Son! You got yourself a biggie on the end of your line. Be patient and don't pull too hard. I will stand alongside you, but I will let you land him yourself." Albert handed his pole to Erdman and walked to where Arvid was holding his fishing pole, a look of excitement on his young face. "That's right. Let him have a little line then pull gently towards shore. Look at that, why don't you? Erdman, he is just like you were at his age." Albert winked at Erdman. Arvid pulled the large walleye to shore, grinning at his accomplishment. The large fish flopped wildly trying one last ditch effort to escape, but Albert was right there to help Arvid scoop him up in the net. Erdman laughed at the proud look on his little brother's face.

Arvid held up the huge walleye so that his father and brother could see his big catch better. Even the passengers on the nearby Little Julia Hadley were cheering from their vantage point. Albert helped Arvid remove the hook from the fish's mouth and placed the fish in the hamper to be gutted later.

"It takes a real man to reel in a fish that big without losing it. Congratulations, Brother." Erdman nodded towards Arvid who was still grinning from ear to ear. "I think he might be ready for a cigar of his own. What do you say, Pa?" It had been a rite of passage for Erdman to smoke his first cigar with his father as a boy. He was glad he could still be present to see his brother's first attempt. Arvid looked expectantly at Albert who nodded his head and reached in his pocket for another cigar.

"Your ma would skin us alive so don't say a word to her, Arvid." Albert handed the newly lit cigar to his younger son with a twinkle in his eye. "Now don't take too much at once. You have to get used to such things." Erdman knew that his father planned for Arvid to get sick on his attempt, thus preventing him from attempting it again by himself for a while. "Slow down there, Arvid." Already Arvid was coughing but he continued to try and smoke the cigar. Suddenly the boy's face turned slightly green, he dropped his fishing pole near Erdman and ran to hide behind a tree. Erdman and Albert laughed quietly at the retching noises coming from behind the tree.

"Are you okay? Don't lose your cigar! It's a Cuban!" Erdman called to his brother as his father guffawed even louder. Finally, a very pale Arvid emerged from behind the tree. He walked slowly to where his father and brother sat fishing and sat down beside them. The boy was still holding the smoldering cigar and began to try and smoke it again.

Albert was laughing so hard the tears ran down his cheeks. "That is exactly what your brother did, Arvid, after he got sick the first time. We Olson men don't give up easy, I tell you." Albert exchanged looks with Erdman who reached for the cigar in his little brother's trembling hand. No sense in making the boy very sick on such a nice day. "Don't let me catch you trying that on your own and burning down the house or barn because you thought you could." Albert's stern warning reminded Erdman of receiving the same instructions after emptying the contents of his stomach as a lad.

"Not bad for your first try. Wait until you drink too much gin." Erdman handed the fishing pole back to his brother who sat with his head between his knees. "I guess we better only start one vice for the day, though, so we will save that for another day." Suddenly it occurred to Erdman that he likely would not be present for any more of Arvid's first attempts. He would not be present to give Arvid advice for his first crush on a girl; he would not see his brother grow into a man. He would be far away starting a new life with Clara. A new ache began in Erdman.

"Erdman! There is a fish on your line!" Arvid's voice broke through Erdman's sense of sadness. Arvid leaned over to assist his brother and, though Erdman was excellent at reeling in large fish, he allowed his little brother to continue to help him. Together they landed another large walleye, adding it to the increasing number already waiting in the hamper. There would be plenty of fish to fry for supper.

It was after 5 o'clock when they packed up their gear and started for home. There were cows to be milked and chores to be done on the farm. As Erdman pulled the roadster into the driveway of the farm, he noticed his Uncle Nel's car parked by the shed. They heard the shrill screams and the breaking of glass from the car. Albert closed his eyes momentarily. "Take your brother and go to your Uncle Nel's farm until I call for you." Anna was back in a breakdown mode, and it sounded bad. Edwin came from the barn to meet Albert at the car.

"I'm sorry, Mr. Olson. She asked me to fetch the mail while I was in Rising Sun and so I brought it back with me. I should have looked closer at the letters before I handed them to her, but they were not addressed to me. She opened one and all of this began. I finally went to get her brother, but not even he is helping her calm down this time." Edwin looked towards the house where more screams punctuated by foul language could be heard.

"It's not your fault, Edwin. We usually don't get much in the way of personal letters, so I can't imagine what set her off like this. Did you happen to notice the letter she was holding?" Albert got out of the car, nodding at Erdman to turn the car around and take his brother away.

"That's just the thing, Mr. Olson. I just didn't know until it was too late, and I couldn't imagine why you received a letter from Clara." Edwin looked down at the ground, as his remorse for his part in the situation was overwhelming.

Albert heard the car door slam and saw Erdman running for the farmhouse before he could stop him. "Take the boy away." Albert commanded Edwin and followed Erdman into the house at a run. Nels held Anna by the shoulders as she lunged at Erdman repeatedly. Erdman acted as if Anna were not even present as he scanned the room quickly for the letter from Clara. It was lying on the floor over by the parlor window, and, as Erdman crossed the room to pick it up, Anna raged at him trying to free herself of her brother's firm grasp.

"That dirty little whore is trying to say you are the father of her bastard. Why would she say that, Erdman? Why?" Anna screamed, her face mottled with purple splotches from her rage. "Tell me you had nothing to do with that nasty bit of trash. Erdman, answer me!" Anna bellowed.

Erdman bent over to retrieve the letter. It was Clara's handwriting and addressed to his father. He read the missive to himself.

Dear Mr. Olson,

I know you will be surprised to hear from me and what I have to say. Please understand that I love Erdman and we are in a pinch and have to get married—if God is willing and you are willing to help us. I told Erdman a good while ago so we could get married because I do not want him in trouble, and I don't want my parents to find out before we are married. Please tell Erdman to come down one night this week so I can talk this over with him and also let me hear a few words from you.

Please be good to Erdman. I know he never meant to leave me. It is only four and one-half months left now until I will be expecting. So, I hope Erdman and I can get married this month and make our lives worthwhile. I am closing with love, and God's blessing. I hope to hear from you and see Erdman soon. You said to ask if I ever needed help, and I don't know what else to do. Please forgive me.

Clara Olson

PS – excuse the scratching as I am in haste and hoping to hear from you and see Erdman soon.

Albert watched Erdman read the letter as all the color drained from his son's face. Erdman made no comment when he had finished. He walked to where Albert stood, handed him the letter, and walked out the front door as Anna screamed profanities at his retreating back. Albert heard the roadster start, and then Erdman was gone. Albert knew he would have to read the letter he was holding, but the truth had already been written all over Erdman's face.

Chapter 43

LATER THAT DAY – RISING SUN, WISCONSIN

Albert finally resorted to a large dose of laudanum to reduce Anna to an almost comatose state. She had continued to scream and throw things after Erdman had left and Nels was tiring in his attempt to subdue her. Albert had been told by one of Anna's many doctors to not use the laudanum except in extreme circumstances, but he figured this was extreme enough as Anna had caused Erdman to flee the house and was a danger to herself. Nels had agreed to stay with the now sleeping Anna while Albert went in search of his missing son.

Albert set out in the car, driving slowly down the winding lane. The shock of Clara's news was settling in on his mind; he had a grandchild on the way and obviously his son had been aware of that fact long ago. A myriad of thoughts and emotions whirled around within him. He felt terrible that Clara had to bear much of this burden alone thus far, angry that Erdman had neglected her when he knew that she carried his child, nervous what the mental state of this child would be, and fearful what Erdman might have done to himself or others since he left the farmhouse earlier. Albert knew that he needed to locate Erdman before his son took drastic measures in his current state of mind. From there they would try to find solutions to all the other concerns.

As Albert rounded a curve in the lane leading to the highway, he glanced up the hill into a copse of trees on nearby Battle Ridge. He thought he saw movement among the trees in the twilight and hoped that he had just located his son. Erdman had often taken the old logging road just a quarter of a mile away from the farmhouse that led to the top of the ridge. Even as a boy he had run there several times when distressed at home, so it made sense that he might retreat there now as well. Albert drove the car out to Highway 27 taking a right onto the highway and then another quick right onto the logging road. He drove a half a mile out the ridge before spotting the roadster pulled off to the side. Erdman was not near the car, but Albert at least had a better idea of where to start looking for him.

Albert pulled his car behind the roadster and got out, scanning the area around him. He went to the trunk of the roadster; he knew that Erdman carried a pistol there. He was hoping that Erdman had not taken the pistol with him intending to harm himself. Albert had to dig through the scattered contents of the trunk for a few seconds before locating the pistol in its holster. Relieved that Erdman had not taken the gun, Albert shut the trunk and started walking towards the trees a short distance away.

As Albert approached the copse of trees, he heard a humming sound. He looked carefully and located Erdman sitting at the base of the largest tree with his fists balled up on either side of his head. The humming sound was Erdman's low moans as he repeatedly slammed the back of his head into the tree trunk behind him. Albert prayed that he could retrieve his son from the obvious breakdown that was occurring.

"Erdman, I am here. Can you hear me Son?" Albert knelt on the ground beside him, not touching him as he had been directed by Erdman's doctors at the mental hospital. The sense of touch seemed to worsen Erdman's breakdown and cause a violent reaction to occur.

Erdman did not respond. He continued to rock back and forth striking his head against the tree. Albert could see a wound already formed on Erdman's head; he needed to get Erdman to stop hitting his head without moving him physically. He could not determine if Erdman was purposefully striking his head or if in his rocking back and forth, he came in contact with the tree, and could not reason to remove himself from harm.

"Son, you are hitting your head in your distress. Can you move over a little bit?" Albert waited patiently and was rewarded with a sudden stop in the rocking and a lurch to one side so that Erdman lay on his side with his head on the soft ground beneath him. The moaning stopped after the contact with the tree stopped and Erdman curled into a fetal position with his fists still at his temples.

"That's a little better now, isn't it? I will wait here with you, so you know that you are not alone. Can you try some of the deep breaths? They usually help the most. I will take some myself and maybe you can just try to breathe with me." Albert took a long breath in and let it out slowly so that Erdman could hear it. He took another and repeated the process. On the third try he heard Erdman's attempt to try and take a breath followed by a fit of coughing.

"That was a good try, Son. I think you might do better if we get your face out of the dirt. I could help you sit up and you can lean on me." Albert touched Erdman's arm lightly, preparing to move his hand quickly if Erdman reacted in a negative way to his touch. Erdman started to whimper and then allowed Albert to gently pull him back into a sitting position. Erdman leaned against Albert and attempted to take another deep breath. He was more successful this time and let the breath out slowly.

"That's much better, isn't it? Your coughing reminded me of Arvid and his cigar earlier today." Albert attempted to orient Erdman back into reality by introducing a subject that would also divert his attention from his current torrent of emotions. Albert heard Erdman take another deep breath and let it out and repeat the process again. The two of them sat in silence for a long time; the only sound was the deep breathing in and out again.

The twilight turned into a clear night with the sky full of stars and a large moon overhead. Albert continued to wait, hoping that the breathing was working in a calming effect. Erdman had not spoken, but the more volatile aspects of the breakdown had subsided to a large degree.

"I didn't know what to do." Erdman's statement broke the stillness surrounding them. He took another deep breath, and Albert could hear him counting quietly. Erdman was trying to overcome his darkness by using the tools he had been given. He was valiant in his fight not to completely succumb to the overwhelming emotions that surged in his weary mind and soul.

Albert knew that his response to Erdman's statement was crucial. He would like to reprimand him for leaving this poor girl alone in a family way and not taking responsibility for his part, but at this point if he indulged in what he would like to say he might inadvertently send Erdman back into his darkness. Instead, he put his arm around Erdman's shoulders.

"Sometimes it can be hard to know what to do in these circumstances. I am willing to help you sort through things if you wish. I am sure we can come up with some reasonable solutions for everyone, especially for Clara and your child." Albert tried to introduce the subject gently so that Erdman would not retreat again. He wanted to hear his son take responsibility. "Clara is a good girl and I think we can agree that if she says there is a child that it is yours." Albert did not pose this as a question, but rather as a statement that Erdman could embrace and claim.

"Yes. I never had a doubt. She didn't even know what to do the first time." Erdman had claimed the child so they could move on with what to do about the situation at hand. The answer was obvious to Albert; the two of them needed to get married soon. Albert knew that Clara's father would react badly if there was a child and no wedding, causing an even uglier situation to occur. Albert wouldn't blame Clara's father for his reaction, but he would protect his son from the consequences likely to happen after that reaction. Anna's father had almost killed Albert when initially finding out that Erdman was on the way, and that piece of history did not need to repeat itself.

"I told Clara I would marry her a long time ago. I didn't mean it at the time, but I am willing to do that now. She needs to be willing to do something about the child if she wants that to happen." Erdman spoke slowly but clearly. He had obviously put some amount of thought into what he had planned.

Albert paused. "What exactly do you mean? There isn't much to be done about a baby once it is on the way, Son."

"You heard what the doctors at the hospital said about offspring. There are ways to still get rid of it." Erdman's voice lowered to almost a growl as he continued. "If Clara loves me and wants to get married, then she needs to agree to get rid of it so we don't have to worry about it turning into some kind of monster. I just don't know how to convince her of that."

Albert was completely aghast. He would never have imagined that Erdman would take what the doctors told him and turn it into a reason to kill his own child still in its mother's womb. He needed to try and reason with his son to see that this was not the answer.

"Erdman, those doctors can only guess about those things. They don't know everything. I just know if they had told me to get rid of you because you would inherit these mental inclinations, I wouldn't have done it because you are my son."

"I think perhaps everything would have been better if you had." Erdman's voice was flat and devoid of emotion. Albert searched his heart for another way to make his appeal to his son.

"And what about your brother? Would we have been better off without him too? Who are we to try and decide who gets to live and who doesn't? I tell you this. I would not ever change having both you and your brother. You are the two best things to ever happen to me. This has been very difficult for you and I think if we can just talk about this some more you will see things differently. Meanwhile, we need to help poor little Clara. Has she even been to see a doctor or a midwife? Having a first baby can sometimes be dangerous. We need to offer to take her for medical help to make sure that she is in good health herself. Do you want me to contact her about this?"

Erdman had sat in stony silence listening to his father's reasoning. "No, I will go to see her tomorrow. Thanks for helping me, Pa. I think I will stay at Uncle Nel's with Arvid tonight. I don't think I can go back to the house just yet." *In other words, I can't deal with Anna right now.*

Albert breathed a sigh of relief. At last Erdman sounded as if he might listen and give up this ridiculous notion of getting rid of his child. Albert would have been dismayed to hear Erdman's thoughts at that moment.

If having a baby is dangerous, then maybe something will happen without my help. If not, there are the other methods. Either way, something needs to be done with or without Clara's consent.

Chapter 44

AUGUST 18, 1926 – SENECA, WISCONSIN

Clara looked over the farmyard on Stoney Point Road from her vantage point near the hen house. A thin fog still hung low over the ridges and valleys shrouding the earth beneath it. The morning sun, rising rapidly, was burning the edges off the fog giving it an iridescent effect. Clara shuddered to herself, as it reminded her of large cobwebs and she detested spiders of any kind.

Clara had come out to the hen house to gather fresh eggs for the large breakfast to be served after morning chores. She could hear her father and brothers talking and laughing in the adjacent barn. She smiled at Bernard's bad jokes and the wonderful sound of her father's ringing laughter. Clara turned to enter the hen house and attend to her own chores. She was careful to stay a distance away from the two broody hens at the other end of the coop. Both hens were setting on nests of eggs that would soon hatch into tiny baby chicks; they were formidable foes to anyone deemed too close to their offspring. Clara smiled as she thought she understood how the broody hens must feel; she felt peckish too, and very protective of the child hidden beneath her maternity corset.

Clara had gathered most of the eggs, when Inga flew through the hen house door causing a flurry of activity and cackling from the disturbed hens. Clara glanced quickly towards the broody hens to make certain they did not fly off their nests and attack her impetuous little sister.

"Inga! What's gotten into you? You know better than to upset broody hens. If I weren't standing guard, they would have attacked you. You need to be more careful next time." Clara still faced the angry hens as she backed towards the door and her sister. As she approached Inga, Clara reached in front of her little sister and carefully opened the door for their escape. Inga stood rooted in place causing Clara to give her a slight shove, propelling her out the door to safety.

Clara was irritated as she turned to face her still silent little sister. One look at Inga's face told Clara that something had scared the young girl. She was pale and tears stood in her eyes as her mouth hung slightly open in shock. Clara initially assumed her sister was just frightened by the angry hens, until Inga turned towards the lane in front of the house and pointed at something Clara could not see.

"Clara, he's over there and he wanted me to come and get you. He doesn't look right, though. Don't go over there, Clara. Let's go find Papa and the boys and make him go away." Inga's eyes were wide as she clutched Clara's arm, nearly knocking the egg basket out of her hands.

Clara set the egg basket down on the ground and clutched Inga's shoulders with both hands. "Who is out there, Inga? What has you so scared, Honey?" Clara hugged Inga close to herself and felt the girl trembling.

"I came out to the front yard to pick some violets for everyone's breakfast plates and Erdman was standing there. He walked down from the road, but he wouldn't come to the house or the barn. He acted strangely, blinking and shaking his head at me. When I asked him what he wanted, he shouted at me to come and get you and make sure you come out there alone. I don't think Papa would like this one bit." Inga looked around as if she were searching for Christ nearby.

Clara was startled at Inga's news. Possibly Erdman was here to talk about eloping and that was his reason for secrecy. She didn't know why he would be mean to her little sister when usually he was so charming to her, but Inga might have surprised him and then plagued him with questions as she was wont to do. Inga calling Papa and the boys from the barn was the last thing Clara needed to happen.

"Inga, I know how much you like Erdman and he likes you ever so much as well. He has been very sick, Sweetie and that is probably why you think he looks different. I am going out to meet him right now. Please promise me that you won't go get Papa or the boys. Now be a good girl and take the eggs into Mama for me." She hugged Inga again, took off her chore apron, and placed it in the top of the egg basket handing it to her sister.

Clara walked through the back yard towards the front yard. She crossed in front of the windows on the opposite side of the house from the kitchen to avoid detection by her mother and sisters. As Clara rounded the last corner, she noticed the roadster parked far down the lane and assumed Erdman must be waiting there for her as he was not near the front yard where Inga had found him. Clara walked towards the roadster, trying to straighten her hair as she went.

Erdman opened the driver's side door and got out of the car as Clara came near. She walked straight towards him with her arms out in front of her so that she could embrace him. His face was expressionless, and he stood like a statue as she wrapped her arms around his waist and leaned against him hugging him tightly. His familiar scents of cologne and hair pomade tingled in her nose and made her heart leap. He slowly put his arms around her and rested his chin on the top of her head. Clara had not realized until this moment how much she had missed his closeness and his embrace. She took a step back to look up at him while standing on her tiptoes to place a gentle kiss on his lips. Her kiss deepened as he responded in kind, caressing her mouth with his own and rubbing the small of her back with his hands.

Clara was breathless when Erdman stepped away from her. She had closed her eyes during their kiss and upon opening them saw that he was staring at her with a hard, determined look on his face. Her bliss at seeing him evaporated in confusion and hurt. Certainly, he had not come to fight with her when they had just made up and been separated for so long.

"I am so happy to see you, but I admit I am confused as you don't look happy to see me. Has something happened?" Clara asked quietly, preparing her heart for yet another one of his many delays in their plans. She didn't know how long she could continue in what seemed a constant cycle of deep passion followed by desolating rejection.

"Why did you write the letter?" His curt, direct question threw Clara off balance mentally. Obviously, he was more than upset that she wrote the letter to Albert. She scrambled to think of something to say in her defense as he continued to stare at her. She was distracted by watching him blink his eyes rapidly and shift from one foot to the other and she found that she was staring back at him, angering him even more.

"I asked you a question. Obviously, you did not understand it. Do I need to use smaller words for you?" His words dripped with sarcasm. He was trying to humiliate her and bully her into acquiescence. This was a bad side of Erdman that had scared Clara in the past. Now it only caused her to retaliate and form a counterattack much like the broody hens she had left in the hen house.

"I understood you just fine. What I don't understand is how you expect me to know what is going on when you leave me without word for weeks at a time. I suppose I am to just sit here hoping that you might show up sooner or later. But we both know how that has worked out thus far. I don't know if you understand that we are running out of time. I finally asked your pa for help because I was worried that you might be sick again and unable to answer a letter addressed to you. I am sorry if that made you angry, but I need help as I didn't get into this by myself." Clara stood with her hands on her hips toe to toe with him.

"Yes, I see that. The problem is that my pa didn't receive the letter, my ma did. There has been the devil to pay since yesterday. Anna is insistent that she has personally seen you in the company of various men and that I shouldn't assume to take any responsibility for your condition nor offer any solutions to you as it is quite possible that I am not the father. My pa is insisting that you seek medical attention immediately so we can determine how to proceed. I thought I told you to never contact my family and yet that is exactly what you did."

Clara felt dizzy and weak. She should not have listened to Alice and written the letter to Albert. How could everything that had looked so bright and promising suddenly go wrong? Everything in her wanted to sink to the ground in a torrent of tears, but another part of her would not give Erdman that satisfaction. She noticed his odd way of referring to his mother by her given name, but in the tumult of emotions she could not think about his strangeness.

"What is it that you want me to do, Erdman? I never dreamed that your ma would intercept my letter, as it was addressed only to your pa. I did not mean to cause you any harm, but you seem to think that I did. I do not need any medical attention, as women have been giving birth for thousands of years without it. If that is your pa's offer of help, then I refuse it." Clara knew she needed to hold fast for the sake of her child even as her world seem to be falling apart.

"What kind of help were you seeking from him, Clara? Did you want his money?" Erdman's blunt questions cut through Clara like a sharp knife. "I told you we would still elope, and you were the one who said to wait a little longer until I recovered. The next thing I know you are making demands of my family." Erdman's eyes were hard and unyielding. "If we get married, Clara, it will be on my terms and you will obey them. Do you understand that?"

"I was scared. I have done most of this by myself. Then I thought I was going to lose you, that you were going to die. I didn't want to live without you, Erdman. I don't want money or anything else from your pa. I only thought he could help us elope and that everything would be fine after that, but I can see I was wrong. You know that you are the father of our child but if you deny even that then I will leave, and you will never have to see me again." Clara was drained as she turned to walk away from him once again.

Erdman took two long strides and grabbed her arm spinning her to face him. "One of my terms is that you won't ever walk away from me again. You just about killed me that night, Clara, and I won't survive a repeat of it. I find that as much as I might want to deny it, I can't seem to live without you either, so I guess we are stuck with one another for life."

Clara gasped as he pulled her roughly into his chest. He acted as though he was going to kiss her, putting his fingers in her hair and yanking her head back causing sharp pain to her scalp and neck. He froze in place as he felt the abrupt series of kicks hard through her corset and clothing, kicks that landed on his stomach that was pulled tightly to her own. There was a momentary look of fear in his eyes as the kicking from his child increased in intensity and repetition. Clara watched as his realization dawned across his face.

"You had best remove your hands from my daughter right now." Christ's voice was nearby when Clara turned her head to look. Her pa stood a few feet away, flanked on either side by Bernard and Adolph. Bernard was still holding the pitchfork he had been using in the haymow and the three men glared at Erdman, daring him to challenge them. "Clara, you come here to me right now. You go home and stay there, Boy. Don't bother my daughter anymore. You already broke her heart once and that is one too many times."

"Papa. No." Clara could not conceive of her father having worse timing than this. She looked pleadingly at her father, but the look on his face told her that if she did not comply soon, Erdman might be injured or worse.

"Erdman, please go now before anything else happens. Write to me if you wish to continue our conversation. I love you." Clara barely whispered the words trying to conceal the meaning from her angry father and brothers.

Erdman nodded at her and began to back away from them, keeping a close eye especially on Bernard until he reached the door of the car. Clara walked to her father. He put a protective arm around her shoulders without taking his eyes off Erdman's retreat. Erdman started the car and turned it around in the road as Clara watched in helplessness.

"Clara, follow me." Christ's words were a firm command as he turned back towards the barn. Bernard and Adolph continued to stand at the edge of the driveway, watching the roadster until they couldn't see it anymore.

"The dumb fool has a patched tire that isn't going to last him long. I hope he has a flat as he runs home to his mama," Adolph remarked to Bernard as the two brothers turned to follow their pa and sister back to the barn.

Chapter 45

AUGUST 18, 1926 – SENECA, WISCONSIN

Clara had followed her father to the barn as he had commanded. She had never heard him speak in the tone he had used with her when he caught her with Erdman and sent Erdman away. Clara sat on a milking stool in the barn waiting for her father to speak. He had continued to go about his chores in silence since they entered the barn, and Clara now wondered exactly what parts of the conversation Christ had overheard. She could only imagine their next conversation if Christ had overheard Erdman denying their child was his.

Bernard and Adolph returned to the barn giving sympathetic looks to their sister. Clara assumed she would not have their sympathy if they had heard what had transpired between her and Erdman. She would have to be careful in answering her father and brothers until she knew the extent of their knowledge. She hated being deceptive with her family, and she was sorely tempted to just tell her father everything and bear the consequences. But Erdman had mentioned the possibility of their elopement right before they were interrupted, and she knew that chance would be completely ruined by an outraged father and vengeful brothers.

Christ came to sit beside Clara with a determined look on his face. He stared down at his old chore boots for a time, trying to decide how to begin. Clara wanted to begin for him, but she knew better than to disrespect her father by speaking about the matter before he was ready.

"Clara, I am finding myself angry and confused. I thought you had called it quits with this boy quite a while ago, and here he is grabbing you and yanking on your hair as if he was going to tear it right out of your head. Why would you even want to meet him when he asked you? Don't be upset with your little sister. She went in the house as you told her to, but she was frightened by his strange behavior and came to get me. She was absolutely right to do so. I don't want to even think what might have happened if I hadn't come just as he was grabbing you." Christ slapped the chore gloves he was holding in his hands upon his knees, angry that his daughter had been handled in such a rough way.

Inwardly, Clara breathed a momentary sigh of relief. Her father had not heard the conversation leading up to when she had walked away from Erdman and he had grabbed her. She would still need to be cautious in her answers to him, but the main secret had not been revealed. She looked at her father's face. He was looking at her with eyes so full of love and compassion that it made her heart want to burst. Whatever her father might do, she knew it would be because he loved her, her mother, and her siblings.

"Papa I know the whole thing has been difficult for everyone and I am so sorry. Erdman and I did have a falling out, and I thought he had left me for good. What I didn't know was that he had taken very ill and was actually in a hospital all that time. It was a big misunderstanding between us, and we are trying to fix things now. I still love him, Papa." Clara reached over and placed her hand upon her father's calloused hand. She would give anything to see those wonderful work worn hands holding his first grandchild. She hoped that if she and Erdman could still elope, her family might accept Erdman and their child as part of their loving family.

Christ closed his eyes and shook his head slowly. "I did not just witness you fixing things with him," he said. "I saw him react in anger towards you and put his hands on you in anger. Clara, I know that you are convinced that he loves you as you love him, but I do not see that in his actions. I would give anything for your happiness, Daughter, but not if it means looking the other way while he hurts you. I don't think you should see him anymore. I know that you are a grown woman and I cannot demand it of you, but I ask you because I am your papa."

"I know that it probably looked bad to you, but it wasn't what you thought. Papa, I want to do as you ask because I love and respect you, but I am asking you to just give me a little more time. I think it will get better soon and we will put all of this behind us. I don't want to see all of you treat Erdman badly if we end up getting married someday." Clara's pleading eyes were locked upon her father's eyes as he listened to her plea.

Bernard interrupted the conversation because he could not bear to watch Clara defend this reprobate any longer.

"You don't want us to treat him badly? Clara, he treats you badly, and we should not be putting up with this. I have asked Papa more than once to let me go and have a talk with him, and Papa has held me back for your sake alone. Now they say he has hired a thug named Buddy Henks from Iowa to be his bodyguard. This Henks fellow has ties with criminals down in Chicago. There is no telling what they are up to, Sister, and you should not be any part of it."

"Bernard I am surprised at you, listening to the town gossips and taking sides against your own sister. Papa, please. Let me try and talk to Erdman and if it doesn't work out, I will do as you say. Tell Bernard he must continue to stay away from Erdman. Please." Clara knew this was her last appeal, and if her father did not agree she would have to plan to leave for Norway soon. She would leave Erdman and all of them behind, possibly forever. Her heart hurt at the thought of it.

Christ stared down at his hands for a long time. He wanted to command his daughter to never see the worthless boy again and allow Bernard and Adolph to pay Erdman a visit to inform him. It was in this decision that he faced the possibility that he might risk losing Clara to Erdman forever if she chose him over her family. The thought of never seeing his precious daughter again was more than he could bear. Against all his better judgement and the small voice in the back of his mind warning him to not proceed, Christ looked at Clara and nodded.

"One more time, Clara, then you will do as you promise. Bernard, you know what I expect." Christ sat as Clara threw her arms around her father in joy and Bernard stomped off. Christ hoped against hope that he had just made the right decision, one they could all live with from here on to eternity.

Chapter 46

AUGUST 25, 1926 – RISING SUN, WISCONSIN

The dog days of summer were supposed to have passed by August eleventh, but in late August in Crawford County it was still sweltering. The heat was so intense at times that an egg could fry right on cement, something Arvid had tried with one of the eggs from the henhouse. It was difficult to work in the tobacco fields by early afternoon, so Albert had switched to working his extra farm hands into the night when the blistering temperatures would cool off slightly. They would set out large lanterns so the workers could see by the dim light and work into the wee hours of the morning when the sun would return with its full intensity.

Erdman sat at the kitchen table in front of a fan and the open windows in his white sleeveless t shirt and pants. It was early afternoon, and there would be a rest period before everyone returned to the tobacco fields. Albert was still sleeping, and Arvid was in the barn enjoying some new puppies with Edwin. Erdman did not know where Anna was, but as long as she kept away from him that was all that mattered.

Edwin had returned from the post office earlier and quietly handed Erdman a letter from Clara. Edwin was very careful about delivering any mail to the family, making sure that a repeat of Anna's latest breakdown was not repeated. Albert had continued to give Anna liberal doses of the laudanum as it calmed her more than anything he had discovered in the past, so the family had settled into an uneasy peace.

Erdman stared at the outside of the envelope as he consumed several glasses of bourbon. He was unsure that he wanted to know what Clara had written in the letter after the incident with her father and brothers last week. He had been so consumed in getting answers from Clara that he had not noticed their approach, a potentially dangerous situation for him by the way her brother held a pitchfork and her father had spoken. It was Clara herself who had come to his rescue, allowing him time to make a rapid escape.

Erdman had told Clara that there was still a possibility for their elopement, but they had been interrupted before he could give her all his terms. He was now regretting that he had mentioned that chance to her. He had taken time to think things over in the last week. He had the opportunity to return to the college or to make his way to Chicago with his father's blessings and, most importantly, with his financing. In both scenarios, Clara proved to be mostly a liability to him, his narcissistic side seeing only her inconvenient morals rather than all the traits that had drawn him to her in the first place.

Then there was the matter of the child Clara still carried. Erdman did not have any doubt that the child was his, making it even more of a danger to him than she or her family were. Erdman believed what the doctors at Eloise had told him about the strong possibility that any of his offspring would possess the genetic potential for derangement and this child, if allowed to survive, would prove to be a major downfall for him. From the moment that he had felt the child kicking him through Clara's body pressed against him, he knew he had to make certain it did not survive. This could prove to be difficult if, due to her sentimentality, Clara would not cooperate with him in ridding them of the excrescence.

He had consulted with a pharmacist in Viroqua who seemed very suspicious of Erdman's questions about difficult pregnancies. He had pretended to have a frail wife and to have needed to know what things they could avoid, preventing the loss of their child due to miscarriage. The concerned pharmacist made a list that included Vitamin C, Black Cohosh, and Cinnamon. Erdman had purchased quantities of each at another pharmacy and considered mixing it with loose tea leaves for Clara to drink. If she wanted to get married, she would need to do what he told her to do and drink the concoction.

Erdman's new "assistant", Buddy, had advised Erdman to use something he called Pennyroyal. It was in the mint family and could be crushed to add to the other ingredients. Buddy knew of several prostitutes that kept this abortifacient on hand when an inconvenience cropped up in their line of work. It sometimes caused the death of the mother as well, but most people found the risk worth taking and Erdman added the Pennyroyal to the list. Buddy had been invaluable in his expertise and availability for tasks that were otherwise distasteful to Erdman, and this was just one more time that Buddy's underhanded knowledge might save the day for Erdman.

Erdman used a knife he kept in his boot to slit open the envelope that had been lying in front of him. Clara's beautiful script filled the page. Even the paper held her scent, making Erdman long for her to be near. He chided himself, telling himself that allowing her to influence him was the start of all his problems in the first place. Erdman poured another drink and began to read.

My dearest E,

I don't have words to express how sorry I am for what occurred this past week when you came to visit me. I know that you were already upset with me, and then it must have been even more upsetting to have my father and brothers interrupt us. I have spoken at length with them, and they now understand that I won't hold with them making any threats towards you, so you have nothing to concern yourself with in that regard.

We had spoken of our plans again right before their interruption, and I write to tell you that I am still willing to meet your terms, as you put it, so that we can proceed. You have only to contact me with the details of when and where, and I will ready myself to meet all your conditions.

Since you declared that you can't seem to live without me just like I can't seem to live without you, I guess we are stuck with each other as you put it. I love you but if you have changed your mind about us, then you have only to let me know. I do not want you forced into this nor do I want your father's money. I only wish us to be happy and raise our child together.

If that has changed for you, then I have another plan that I can carry through and you will not need to concern yourself with either of us again. I have limited time left to choose my second option so we will need to proceed soon or part ways for always.

Your friend always,

C

Erdman read the letter twice through trying to understand what she was saying about choosing a second option. She didn't have any other options unless she were to run away from her family on her own. He knew that Clara would not be able to make that break with them by herself. Did she have someone else willing to take her away or, even worse, marry her and raise the child he had sired right here in front of him?

Anna kept talking about the postal clerk from Seneca and seeing Clara at the box social in a compromising embrace. Could this be the one time that Anna was correct, and Clara had convinced the fawning idiot to accept her as damaged goods? Or possibly she was running out of time because she had seduced the postal clerk as well and could now convince him that she carried his child? Erdman's logic began to follow that of other immoral people, to accuse an otherwise innocent person of exactly what the immoral person would do in their situation, thereby making them guilty of it.

Jealousy surged in him for the first time in a long time. Clara was his possession. He would do with her whatever he wanted, but he would never allow her to leave him for someone else. She needed to submit to him and allow him to decide what their future would be without declaring that she would leave him if she did not agree. Clara would soon find out that he was her only option.

Erdman would have to put some quick plans into place and reply to Clara's letter. It might be a good idea for him to consult with Buddy again to gain more of his insight and formulate a secondary plan himself in case Clara decided not to cooperate with his conditions. Erdman emptied the remainder of the bourbon into his glass. Finally, his life was taking shape again after the mess that Clara had made of it and he could see a future for himself, a future with or without Clara.

Chapter 47

SEPTEMBER 2, 1926 –
SOLDIERS GROVE, WISCONSIN

The intense heat and humidity of August had finally surrendered to the cooler temperatures and gentle breezes of September. The late afternoon sun illuminated the leaves of the stately maple trees in Lena Hutchins' back yard, the dappled light casting shadows upon Lena and Clara as they sat drinking tea and enjoying the weather. Clara had come to visit Lena with the specific purpose of helping the elderly woman prepare for her trip to Norway, but it always seemed that Lena was the one to provide Clara with assistance in various ways.

"My nephew and his wife will be meeting me in Chicago, and we will be traveling by train to New York City. From there we will board a steamer for Oslo. I still have time to purchase the steamer ticket for you, my dear, if you find you should need it at the last minute. I am happy that Erdman has decided to make good on his promises to you, but I am sad that you will not be accompanying me to Norway after all. Has Erdman let you know when he will be ready to elope? I do not want to waste a single minute of our times together, as I wonder that each one might be our last. When I return, you will be a married mother with a small baby, too busy with your own household to come and visit your old friend very often." Lena sighed and took another sip of her tea from the delicate cup hand painted in Norway.

"Erdman has not given me the specifics yet," Clara replied, "but I hope it will be soon. As for visiting you, my dearest friend, I will be only too happy to come and bring my wee one often for you to hold and cuddle to your heart's content. I will never forget all that you have given me, especially your understanding and friendship. I wish that I could go with you, but I am very happy that we will be married soon and will raise our child here among family and friends. I think that is what Erdman is still planning, but to tell the truth, I cannot be sure of it right now. Wherever I am, you can be sure that I will send you news often and visit whenever it is possible." Clara set her teacup on the small table beside her and knelt beside her friend's chair. She hugged Lena tightly; each understanding that they might be parted by distance for a time but not by love.

"Clara, I wish that any of my sweet babes lost in infancy might have grown to adulthood, but I love you as though you were one of them. Please assure me that this plan of Erdman's is what you truly want so that I may know my girl is in good care and happy. If there is any part of you in doubt now or in the future, you only need to contact me by telegram, and I will send for you right away." Lena returned Clara's embrace as she fought a nagging sense of doubt about Erdman's intentions.

"For all the rough beginning," Clara said, "I think that we shall end up very happy together. I wish that Erdman might be more excited about our baby, but it might just be nervousness on his part and not an aversion to fatherhood. I keep expecting Erdman to be more like my own papa with his children, and perhaps I will have to accept that he is nothing like my papa. Was your Samuel excited about children?"

"Oh, my, yes. Samuel would follow me about like a mother hen trying to keep me and each one of our babies safe. It devastated him to lose them, as much or more than it devastated me. Our son lived to six months of age before he died of diphtheria, and it was Samuel who would walk the floor holding him when he cried at night. What makes you think that Erdman is not excited about the child?" Lena placed her hand upon Clara's back as she sat in front of Lena on the ground. She rubbed Clara's shoulders lightly, remembering the aches and pains of pregnancy and the way her Samuel would alleviate them with massage.

"Erdman has not said that he doesn't want a baby, but he doesn't seem interested either. He felt the baby kicking for the first time the last time I saw him, and he looked terrified and then angry. I was hoping experiencing that might make him feel more enthusiastic about fatherhood, but I might be expecting too much from him at this point. I have the most wonderful papa in the world, and it isn't fair for me to expect the same from him." Clara sighed as Lena's ministrations helped the cramping in her back to cease.

Lena grimaced behind Clara. *Terrified, yes. Angry, no. Why would this young man respond this way to his own child and to the beautiful young woman he claims to love?* Something still nagged at Lena, but she could not name it, nor did she wish to put a damper on their delightful afternoon together. *Lord, please make this young man worthy of my precious Clara and her little baby.*

"Speaking of your papa, when will you let your parents know of all your plans and that they are to be grandparents?" Lena hoped that Clara would confide in her parents soon so they could help her decide what to do. From what she knew of Christ and Dena Olson, they were good people who loved their children and would accept Clara no matter the circumstances. Perhaps if Clara did not feel pressured into marrying Erdman as a way to redeem herself, she might end up with someone more worthy of her.

"Erdman and I have agreed that we will elope quietly. I will leave them a note so they won't worry and when we return as a married couple, we can let them in on our other little secret coming in December. My parents did something similar so I am certain they will understand and accept it afterwards. I would worry that my father and brothers might hurt Erdman if they found out before we eloped, so I have stayed quiet. I have wanted to tell everything to my parents so many times. I look forward to the day when I can just tell them as I have told you." Clara started to rise slowly, gathering her things to leave for the evening bus to Mt. Sterling. She hugged Lena one more time, knowing that the elderly woman's age might make it be the last time she would see her before heaven.

Clara rode the bus back to Mt. Sterling with a large lump in her throat. She would miss her dear friend and confidante, but she was convinced her future belonged with Erdman. Clara got off the bus outside Ole Thorstad's filling station and looked to see if there was still a light on in the office. She always used the telephone there to call Bernard and ask him to come and get her. As she walked towards the office, she heard a car pull in the driveway behind her. Clara turned in time to see Erdman in the driver's seat of the roadster with a stranger sitting in the passenger seat beside him.

"Hey there, Stranger. Are you going my way?" Erdman called out to her as he pulled the car alongside her. He jumped out of the driver's side door and ran around it, scooping Clara up in a bear hug, lifting her off the ground. He smelled strongly of spirits as he put her feet back on the ground, tipping her head back with both of his hands to kiss her.

Clara was surprised at his sudden appearance and his passionate demeanor. This was the exact opposite of his behavior the last time she had seen him, as though their last altercation had not even occurred. There were so many times that he seemed to vacillate between the two extremes that she never knew what to expect next. During this musing, she realized that he had been talking to her between passionate kisses.

"So, what do you say, Bright Eyes? Do you want to come with me to the dance hall or do you want to wait here for that fearsome brother of yours? I have lots of business to do tonight as I am saving up for a big trip soon or I would find some time to get you all to myself. It's been way too long Baby." He kissed her again. She noticed that although he held her in his arms, he kept a small distance between their torsos, so they did not touch. She wondered if he was trying to distance himself from feeling the movement he had felt before, so she stepped closer to him wrapping her arms around his waist tightly. He paused a moment, chuckled, and stepped back out of her embrace putting the small distance between them again. He turned towards the stranger still sitting in the passenger seat of the roadster.

"Isn't my girl a beauty? I tell you what, Buddy, my Clara is the best gal ever. I may even make an honest woman out of her one of these days." Erdman laughed loudly and the stranger joined him in laughing. Clara's face burned with humiliation. Who was this stranger and how did he know personal details of her life with Erdman?

"Who is your friend? I don't believe I have met him." Clara tried to get Erdman to look at her eyes as she spoke to him, but he kept glancing away from her and blinking rapidly. He clutched her to himself again lowering his mouth on hers in a savage kiss. Clara tried to respond to the kiss so she would not anger him, but the intense pressure on her lips began to hurt, so she finally stepped back

Erdman still gripped her arms. "Why, that's just Buddy. He is my new business associate. I need to make good money in my business, if I am to be a married man. Buddy helps me sell the hooch and makes sure that no one decides to take what's mine." Erdman leaned down near Clara's ear and growled. "You see, no one ever takes what is mine and gets away with it. I always keep what belongs to me, Clara."

"Well, I guess that you need to go make what is yours then, and I won't keep you from it. I will wait here for Bernard. It wouldn't be a good idea for the two of you to run into each other. I will wait for you to send word and come for me. I love you, Erdman." Clara reached up to move the lock of Erdman's hair that fell onto his forehead. She moved her hand in a gentle motion alongside his face and gave him a gentle kiss. Their eyes met for a moment, and Clara saw the Erdman that she knew and loved looking back at her with longing. He closed his eyes, and when he opened them again the moment was gone.

"Don't worry about me and your brother. I may just have a little surprise for him the next time we meet. I will send you a note soon, so be ready to go. Remember, Clara, you will need to meet my conditions if this is going to work out for us, but don't worry,

Baby, I have got you." He flashed his grin that she loved so much and kissed her again.

Erdman turned back to walk to his car. "Come on, Buddy! We have tons of thirsty people, and that hooch doesn't sell itself. Everyone is mourning the fact that the great Rudolph Valentino just died, and they need our liquid courage." He hopped back in the car and drove off leaving Clara standing alone wondering what exactly had just happened.

Clara turned back to the filling station office to call her brother. She just wanted to go home and hoped that the Erdman that she knew and loved would send for her soon.

Chapter 48

SEPTEMBER 9, 1926 – SENECA, WISCONSIN

*I*t was a perfect fall day. The temperature was in the middle 70's with a gentle breeze. The sun was bright in the azure sky reflecting on all the tree leaves causing them to shimmer. Clara had done all her chores inside and found beating the rugs on the clothesline an excellent excuse to be outside enjoying the weather. She held the carpet beater in one hand, giving the carpet in front of her a whack, sending dust motes swirling into the air around her.

Clara had waited the entire week since encountering Erdman and his odd friend Buddy in Mt. Sterling. She had watched for the afternoon mail each day hoping that the word from Erdman about their elopement would arrive. Clara tried to be patient but the child in her womb continued to grow, and soon she would not be able to conceal it from her family and the outside world. There were several times during that week Clara had thought about contacting Lena and leaving for Norway with her. She knew her friend would welcome her, and she would have a way to make a new life for herself. Each time Clara considered this alternative she would remind herself that Erdman did love her, and he would do as he had promised.

Clara had just finished with the last rug when Bernard drove up the lane. She knew that he had been to the post office and would have the afternoon mail with him. Clara tried to steel herself against the likelihood that there would not be a letter from Erdman. She watched as her brother approached and held out an envelope towards her. Clara accepted the envelope and smiled at Bernard, putting the envelope on the top of the pile she was carrying back to the house. She did not want to seem over eager to her brother who was still upset that their father had told him to leave Erdman alone.

Clara walked nonchalantly back to the house and put the pile of rugs down on the parlor floor. She glanced down at the envelope and saw that the handwriting was indeed Erdman's. This was most likely what she had been waiting months to receive. Clara carried the letter upstairs to her room where she could read it without her mother and sisters looking on.

Alice was in their shared bedroom changing the sheets on the beds. Clara crossed to the small chair next to the open window and sat down upon the chair to read the letter. Alice looked at Clara's face and put the sheets she was holding back down on the bed. Alice crossed to where Clara sat, putting her hand on her sister's shoulder and positioning herself to glance at the missive over Clara's shoulder.

"So, is this it, then?" Alice asked. Both she and Clara knew the exact meaning of her question. Clara looked up from her reading, smiled, and nodded. Clara then continued to read.

Dear Friend,

I suppose you think me awfully neglectful, but I haven't. I have been to the hospital for a while, had a couple of operations. I have decided the time for us is right to show action. Now, we'll not leave for good but will go and get the ceremony over with and then come back in a week or two and let them know if they don't know. You'll have to coax your brother to take you down to Seneca to the dance Sept. 9ᵗʰ and I'll get you there. We will go up to Hendrum, Minnesota, which is the same as Winona. Do not take any more clothes than what you wear, as taking more will cause suspicion and try to get as much cash as possible as that is necessary if we wish to make a pleasant trip of it. I have some myself of course.

I will be at Seneca between 9 and 10 o'clock and when you see me, leave the hall alone and walk up the street alone until I find you and remember that everything is on the QT also write a note and leave some place where it can be found in a day or so and say that you are going away for a while but not to worry as you'll be back someday but don't mention why you were going nor mention my name. If you can't come to the dance, leave a lantern in your window so I know you are there, sneak out of the house about 12:00 and come towards the road. If I am not there, keep on going until I meet you. Don't let anyone see you. Please destroy this letter and all my other letters and act hard towards me to your folks.

Do as I have asked you to do and everything will be OK. If you don't your chance might be shot and I might make a scarce hubby, so if you wish to avoid the disgrace do as I say and keep mum.

See you on the 9th.

As ever,

As usual.

P.S. Remember do as I say and destroy all letters.

Clara reread the letter several times. The words sounded unlike so many of the other letters that Erdman had written to her; these words were so impersonal and almost cold. She knew that he had planned on marrying in Minnesota because the state did not have the three-day waiting period that Wisconsin did, and they could get married right away. She had never heard of Hendrum before, so she went to fetch a geography book from the parlor, bringing it back to the bedroom.

"What are you searching for, Sister? Why do you need to learn geography now of all things?" Alice asked incredulously. She thought Clara's reaction to the elopement letter and her behavior more than a little odd. "Don't you think you should worry more about packing and what you are going to wear? When does he want you to leave?"

Clara continued to search the map of Minnesota before her, but she could not find Hendrum on it. Perhaps Erdman had made a mistake or Hendrum was too small to be listed. Either way Alice was right, she had a lot to do before she met him. Clara put the book down on the small desk and walked to her bed. She reached underneath the bed for the box of special mementos, pulling out the many love letters Erdman had written to her over the past year. Why did he want her to burn them? She would love to take the time to reread them, but she needed to prepare herself and it was better to have the author of the letters rather than just the letters themselves.

"Clara, did you hear me?" Alice followed Clara out of their bedroom and down the stairs to the kitchen and the woodstove.

Clara selected two of the missives, the one she had just received and another one and took the rest and shoved them into the fire in the stove. "Why on earth are you burning his letters? Clara, did he leave you again?"

Clara turned to face Alice, taking her hand as she spoke. "Shh. He asked me to burn the letters to help keep our secret, and they are only letters after all. Come and help me, please. He wants me to meet him tonight." Clara walked out of the kitchen and back up the stairs towards their bedroom with Alice following close behind.

Alice closed the bedroom door behind them. "Tonight? How in the world are you going to do all you need to by tonight?" She watched helplessly as Clara went to their closet and brought out a pasteboard box, setting it open on her bed.

"Lena bought me a beautiful ivory gown that I knew would be my wedding dress. I will wear my black green silk tonight and pack one other as well; I think the yellow silk one with the white polka dots. I was wearing that dress the first day we met, and Erdman still carries the yellow silk ribbon from the box dinner I packed. I can ask Papa if I may go into town with him this afternoon and pick up a few new things to take along. I can't believe it's finally happening Alice." Clara crossed to hug her sister, then sat down at the desk and began to write a note. "I will hide this under the lamp. Don't tell the folks that you know about any of this and let them find it tomorrow after I'm gone."

Clara busied herself with packing a few more things in the box, then picked up her small purse and went in search of her father. Christ agreed to take her with him to Seneca as he was taking the short trip to go to the hardware store, and he always welcomed the company of his precious Clara. Christ and Clara told jokes to each other and laughed together as they rode in the wagon to Seneca. Christ was relieved to see Clara happy and smiling again after a rough couple of weeks since the day he had ordered Erdman to leave the farm.

Clara made several purchases at the mercantile. She purchased a new satin slip and some new hosiery. She selected a new tan hat to go with her recently purchased overcoat and shoes. She purchased some needles, thread, and safety pins and then her one gift to herself, a small bottle of perfume to celebrate her wedding. Soon Clara was ready to join Christ for their journey home.

As she rode in the wagon, Clara leaned her head against Christ's shoulder for a moment. "Thank you, Papa. I know the past few weeks have been difficult for all of us, but you are always so good to me. I hope the future will be much better."

Christ smiled down at his daughter. "Your mama and I only wish you to be healthy and happy, Daughter. I wish a wonderful future for you, Clara." Christ looked into the beautiful brown eyes that reminded him so much of his own mother.

When Clara returned to her bedroom, she added her purchases to the pasteboard box which was now overflowing. She decided to carry the perfume bottle in her small purse along with the money she had saved, seven dollars total. Clara wrapped corset strings around the box to keep it shut and added a yellow ribbon to the outside with her new tan hat. She carefully hid the box back under her bed and went downstairs.

"Mama, I thought Alice and I could make some fattigman cookies before supper. Papa and the boys will enjoy them coming in from the tobacco fields." Clara donned her apron at Dena's nod of approval, and she and Alice set to work. When they pulled the cookies out of the heated oil and sprinkled them with the powdered sugar, Clara stuck her pointer finger in the sugar and dabbed it on Alice's nose. *I love you, Sister.*

Alice's eyes held tears as she dabbed Clara's nose in turn. *I love you too.* When Clara returned, she would be married with a home of her own, and things would never be quite the same again. Clara and Alice finished the cookies and helped Dena and their sisters prepare the evening meal for their father and brothers.

Soon it was time for dinner and Clara looked around at the family she loved so much gathered round the large farmhouse table. There was a part of her that did not want to leave this big, noisy, loving family, but she knew that life brought many changes and one must accept them. She longed for the future when Erdman and their child would join her and this noisy bunch for the occasional family meal.

Everyone held hands as Papa led their daily meal prayer.

I Jesu navn går vi til bords
In Jesus' name to the table we go
Og spiser, drikker på ditt ord
To eat and drink according to his word
Deg, Gud, til ære, oss til gavn
To God the honor, us the gain,
Så får vi mat i Jesu navn.
So we have food in Jesus' name.
Amen.

Clara knew that she could not ask Bernard to take her to Seneca that evening. If Bernard had any idea that Erdman would be there, he would forget Papa's admonition and hurt her bridegroom. Erdman would just have to come to the farm for her; she would set up the usual light to signal him and slip out unnoticed.

Clara kissed her papa and mama goodnight. She managed to hug her sisters before retiring to her bedroom to wait for Erdman. Her brothers would be alerted to something very unusual occurring if she extended the affection to them as well, so she teased them both in her sisterly manner and left it at that. She hoped that Bernard could let bygones be bygones when she returned with Erdman as a married woman. She knew Bernard's heart was bigger than his anger, and she was eager for him to know that he would be an uncle as he loved little children.

Alice joined Clara in their bedroom and the two sisters sat hugging and whispering on Clara's bed. They laughed a lot and cried a little knowing that the time for Clara to leave was coming soon.

Alice saw the headlights blink on and off from outside. "Remember, if it is a girl her name is Alice." She hugged Clara tightly as Clara sent the signal back to Erdman and prepared to leave. Their father had just shut the downstairs lights off and Clara carefully crept down the dark stairs.

"Who is there?" Christ's concerned voice came to Clara in the darkness.

"It's just me Papa. I am only getting a breath of fresh air. I will be right back." Clara replied. She continued in the darkness to the front door and down the lane.

I love you Papa and Mama. I will be home soon.

Chapter 49

SEPTEMBER 9, 1926 – RISING SUN, WISCONSIN

Erdman sat in the kitchen eating a quick sandwich before he left for the dance in Seneca. Albert had left the house a few hours earlier to meet a business associate in Prairie du Chien and was due home soon. Erdman did not like leaving Arvid home alone with Anna, so he had decided to wait a few more minutes for his father's return. Anna bustled about the kitchen making her usual mess, and Erdman did his best to ignore her completely.

Erdman was eager to get underway now that his plans were settled. He had listened to Buddy and written a letter to Clara asking her to meet him in Seneca that night. Buddy had been extremely helpful, even helping Erdman phrase the letter when he became stuck on what to tell Clara about their meeting. Buddy had agreed to accompany Erdman tonight and protect him from Clara's overgrown brother if it came to a physical altercation. Erdman rather hoped that it might come to fisticuffs as Bernard was no match for the street fighter, Buddy, who kept extra dirks hidden in his boots. It might be nice to see Bernard Olson get roughed up and put in his place for once.

As for Clara, she would be so focused on eloping that she would agree to Erdman's other conditions including getting rid of the child once and for all. Buddy had given Erdman several more suggestions in the event that Clara became uncooperative, but Erdman did not anticipate using any of them. Once Clara agreed with his plan, he would give her the first concoction to drink and drive her as far as Minnesota to miscarry the child. After she had recovered, they would discuss their next move including the possibility of getting married and moving straight to Minneapolis. Erdman did not want to risk having Clara come back to her family and change her mind about leaving permanently; it was better for her to think that she would be returning for now only to find out later she would be gone for good.

Buddy had already been in contact with the bootleggers from both Minneapolis and Chicago. Once they learned of Erdman's successful venture in Crawford County, they were immediately interested in Erdman coming to work for them. Erdman would take Clara and join Buddy in Chicago within a few weeks. From there his dreams of houses, cars, and money would come true, and Clara would be there to reap the benefits as well.

Erdman took a swig of the gin beside him to wash down the dry sandwich. He had started drinking by midafternoon telling himself it was celebratory of his upcoming nuptials and ignoring the nagging feelings about the child. He could not afford to be sentimental when it came to this matter. What was one small insignificant creature compared to his entire life? In fact, he was doing the world a service in this, and any feelings of remorse or guilt should be ignored.

Anna approached the table, sitting in a chair beside him. He cringed slightly, trying to breathe slowly. Her presence alone brought surges of anger to the surface. He would be happy to leave this house and never lay eyes on her again.

"Have you heard anything more about your situation?" Her whiny voice grated in his ears. The laudanum Albert had given her before he left was wearing off. Erdman wondered where his father kept the medicine in case she needed another dose before Albert returned. He even ventured to think of what might happen if she found the medicine herself. She was completely addicted to the substance by this point and might easily overdose herself if it were left with her. That thought made Erdman smile as he reached to pour more gin into his glass. That would be another reason to celebrate this day.

"Everything is handled, and that is all you need to know." These were the first words Erdman had spoken directly to Anna in months. "Where does Pa keep your medicine? I think it might be time for more."

"I'm glad to see that gal did not trap you. Marriage is bad enough without being stuck with a child who is not your own. You're lucky I never told Albert that he's not your real pa. I was already with child from my wild and wanton ways, and my family set out to find someone who would be honorable enough to get married once he thought you were his. Albert fell right in line and never asked a single question. He's stupid like that, unlike you and me." Anna picked up the bottle of gin and took a long drink.

Erdman rose from the chair without answering Anna. Of course, she would have one final torture for him, something to remember her by forever. But he wouldn't. He would leave this house tonight and never look back again. It was time to go and find Clara.

Erdman started the roadster, waving to Arvid who came to the barn door holding a puppy. At the last moment, Erdman jumped out of the car and ran to hug his little brother goodbye. He returned to the car and drove off towards Mt. Sterling where he would meet Buddy and head to the dance in Seneca. Buddy was waiting for him at the filling station and soon they were on their way.

"So, tonight's the big night," Buddy mused aloud as they drove along Highway 27. Buddy reached into the glove compartment and withdrew a pistol putting it into the pocket of his coat. "I hope that little gal decides to cooperate because she is going to be trouble otherwise."

"Leave her to me. Just make sure her big brother doesn't get involved. If he does, make it look like an accident. Remember, we are drawing her way down the street and away from any witnesses roaming around." Erdman spoke the plan aloud to remind himself rather than Buddy, who nodded in agreement. "It's just like the Rudolph Valentino movie, The Sheik. He abducts the girl and carries her off, and she gives herself over to him."

"Well, if you are Rudolph Valentino then I am Douglas Fairbanks." Buddy laughed and took a drink from his hip flask. He handed the flask to Erdman. "Here, have a little more of what you call liquid courage."

By the time Erdman reached Seneca, he felt the strong influence of the alcohol taking effect. He drove to his usual spot in the alley behind the dance hall and spotted several young men already waiting for him on the opposite street corner. He offered his usual samples of gin, exchanged niceties, and sold quite a bit of his stock. Buddy looked up and down the street and alley for any sign of Bernard Olson, keeping his hand on the pistol in his pocket.

The appointed time came and went without the appearance of Clara. Erdman decided to check inside the dance hall, climbing the steps to the second floor two at a time. Clara was nowhere in sight. Apparently, she had been unable to get to Seneca, forcing Erdman to take the risk of showing up at her father's farm again.

There was a very good band from Iowa playing dance music inside the dance hall. Erdman decided he would take one last dance as a bachelor and looked around for a partner. Christine Olson was sitting to one side of the room with her pretty cousin Marie. Erdman grinned as he approached the ladies and asked Marie to dance with him. They left Christine to pout over his deliberate shunning of her company.

The band began to play 'Oh Katherina', and Erdman led Marie into the steps of the foxtrot, one of his favorite dances. "So, are you teaching at the school again this year, Marie?" Erdman noticed his words came out a little slurred, and he missed one step and then another.

Marie smiled politely. "Yes, it is almost time to go back to the life of a spinster teacher. Ouch!" she stopped as Erdman missed another step and landed on her foot. "Are you all right, Erdman?"

"Sorry. I guess I am a little distracted tonight. I think I will go back outside and see how my hooch sales are going. Thanks for the dance, Marie." *Rudolph Valentino indeed, more like Charlie Chaplin,* Erdman thought to himself as he walked to the exit and down to the alley below.

Buddy had continued the gin sales, continuing to keep watch for Clara and her brother. "I take it she wasn't waiting in the dance hall like she was instructed. You might want to work on keeping that little doll in hand, or she is going to start thinking she's the boss instead of you." Buddy chuckled in a way that let Erdman know he was being serious. "Now what are you going to do?"

Erdman's head was hurting from the alcohol and his mounting frustration with Clara. "I will have to go and see if she is waiting at the farm. You can hunker down in the rumble seat in case her brothers are around. She is most definitely going to find out who is the boss around here soon enough." Erdman couldn't help but think this was one more way of Clara's attempts to control him, and the thought pushed at the rage that Anna had loosed with her latest revelation earlier.

It was nearly midnight when Erdman started the roadster with Buddy hiding in the rumble seat and drove it back up Highway 27 towards Stoney Point Road. He took the left hand turn rather sharply, causing Buddy to swear at him vehemently from the back. He slowed the roadster to a crawl when he approached the lane to the farmhouse. The house was dark and quiet. Erdman flashed the headlights once and waited, listening for any movement.

The shutters moved on the second-floor window of Clara's bedroom. She had seen his signal and sent hers. It remained quiet as Erdman waited for Clara to appear. The only sounds were those of coyotes in the distance. The night was very dark with a dim sliver of moon, but he could soon see Clara's lone figure walking down the lane towards him.

Erdman got out of the car to greet her as she drew near. He leaned down to kiss her and felt the large box she was carrying in front of her. "Clara, I told you not to bring anything so you wouldn't raise suspicions." He whispered in a growl near her ear.

Clara started at the sound of his voice and turned to peer at him in the darkness. "Have you been drinking, Erdman? I just brought a few things as a girl likes to be pretty when she gets married."

Erdman grabbed the pasteboard box she was holding to put it in the back. He noticed the yellow ribbon hanging off the side of the box and stopped for a moment. She was just being a girl who was excited about getting married, even to the point of remembering the yellow ribbon. He needed to be calm with her so she would be more agreeable to his conditions, and he had already started off badly in her eyes. "I see you brought me another yellow ribbon for my collection." His observation brought a small giggle from her and a passionate kiss. He opened the passenger side door and helped her in, then tossed the box in the back on top of the hiding Buddy.

Erdman looked around one last time before starting the car again. They were very near to making a clean getaway, and he didn't want any last-minute surprises. Everything remained quiet so he started the car and turned it around quickly at the end of the lane. He drove rapidly down Stoney Point Road towards Highway 27.

He turned left onto Highway 27 and headed towards Mt. Sterling. Erdman and Buddy had planned to pick up Buddy's car on the return trip, and then Buddy would wait in the lane at the farm while he took Clara to their spot on the logging road and explained the rest of the conditions to her. Once he and Clara were underway to Minnesota, Buddy would head for Chicago and meet them again in a few weeks. Buddy felt he should remain at the farm for a few hours in case Clara's brothers showed up unexpectedly and Erdman needed backup.

Clara sighed as she snuggled closer to Erdman. "I was beginning to wonder if this day would ever come. I love you so much, Erdman." She rested her head against his shoulder.

"Oh, boy! Can we wait for the smooching until after I leave the car?" Buddy popped up from his hiding place in the rumble seat causing Clara to shriek and Erdman to swerve towards the ditch.

"What is he doing here?" Clara screamed, not realizing that she was still next to Erdman's ear. He gave her a small shove sending her back across the seat and away from his already ringing head. She landed with a thud against the opposite door, whimpering at the contact.

"Clara! Stop screaming! Buddy went with me to Seneca to do business tonight. We are dropping him off at his car in Mt. Sterling." Erdman squeezed his eyes shut several times trying to get the ringing to stop in his head. He could hear Clara crying softly from the opposite side of the seat.

Erdman pulled the car over in the filling station driveway in Mt. Sterling. Buddy hopped out and came to the driver's side. "I will meet up with you in a few hours, and we will go from there. Remember who's boss," Buddy cautioned with another chuckle.

Erdman massaged his temples trying everything to alleviate the pounding in his head. He heard Clara's sniffles as she continued to cry quietly beside him. "Are you all right Clara?" He forced himself to ask the question. "I didn't mean to hurt you. You screamed right next to me, and I have a very bad headache."

Clara shifted in the seat, scooting next to him again. She turned his head to face her and replaced his fingers at his temples with her own. "I'm sorry. I didn't know." She massaged gently, kissing his forehead occasionally, and soon much of his headache was gone.

"Thank you. It is much better now." Erdman leaned forward to place a gentle kiss on Clara's lips. She smiled at him as he started the car again and drove back out to the highway. "We are going to stop near Rising Sun so we can talk about what to do next."

"Talk? Hmmm. I am not quite sure that you just want to talk, Erdman, but it has been a long time and I guess that I like to "talk" too." She giggled softly and rested her head back on his shoulder again. She was so sweet when she was like this. If only she would remain this way, what he had to tell her would be so much easier.

Soon Erdman reached the old logging road just past Lone Pine Lane and the farm. He took the right-hand turn and continued to drive out to their usual spot near the copse of trees on Battle Ridge. The farmhouse below was aglow with light, meaning that Albert had returned home and was still in the dining room. The thought of Albert brought a myriad of questions and anger. Was Anna telling the truth and the man that Erdman had always known as his father was a well-meaning stranger? Erdman tried to take several deep breaths, but his chest felt like a heavy stone was weighing it down. He glanced at Clara as she lifted her head from his shoulder and began to kiss the side of his face and his chin.

Clara was convinced that he had brought her back to this spot for some lovemaking before they left for Minnesota. Part of him felt like obliging her, but the main part of him felt crushed and angry at what Anna had told him. He gave Clara a few small kisses in return, hoping that his feelings for her would distract him from the other feelings he was battling. But he continued to feel flat and dead inside.

"Erdman, sweetie, is something the matter? Do you have another headache?" Clara paused in her kisses to massage the back of his neck, something that had always helped to calm him in the past. This time he felt trapped by her embrace and suffocated by her closeness. He gently pulled her hands from behind his neck and nudged her across the seat. It was time to have this out.

"I told you that I brought you here to talk, and I meant that we were going to talk, Clara. We have plenty of time for other things later." He saw her nod and adjust her red sweater and tan coat back into place.

"I just missed you so much. What did you need to tell me?" Clara held his right hand in both of her hands. He suddenly realized that she was most likely expecting him to produce one of the wedding rings they had picked out at the jewelers in La Crosse last April. He hadn't even considered a ring in the midst of his planning to elope with her. The oddity of that struck him and made him wonder just how badly he wanted to marry her after all. Leaving for a new life in Chicago would be so much easier without worrying about her or the child.

"I told you before that I had conditions that you need to agree to before we can leave to elope. I know you love me and want to spend our future together. I have told you before that my dream is to live somewhere like Chicago, and recently several opportunities have presented themselves. I am leaving for Chicago for good, and I want you to agree to come with me. I am sure we can make a go of it there, and you will have a nice house, cars, clothes, and whatever else you might desire including me." Erdman withdrew his hand from her hands and took her gently by the left shoulder. "I know we will be happy, Baby."

Clara had remained quiet and looked at him with concern. "Do you mean we are just going to leave for Chicago after we get married? Aren't we going to return here first for the rest of our things at least? What about our families? What will they think when we just run off and don't come back at all?" She didn't sound angry, which made Erdman think she was ready to agree to the first condition.

"Honey, I will be your family from now on. You and I will always have each other, and I know I can make you happy. We have had way too many things try to break us apart to allow anything to happen now, Clara. We are almost there. Your family will never accept me, and Anna will never accept you. This really is the best way." Erdman rubbed Clara's shoulder and leaned to kiss her earlobe.

"I can see what you mean, and I am willing to live with you wherever you want. Do we have to just leave suddenly and never come back? What about our baby? You want us to raise our baby without any grandparents, aunts or uncles? I was just thinking the other day how excited my papa will be when we have been married and can tell them about their first grandchild. I would hate to take all of that away from them, Erdman."

Erdman paused and closed his eyes. The throbbing in his head had resumed. Clara seemed to accept living far away but would she accept his next condition?

"That's the thing, Honey. I have been thinking, and it certainly isn't a good time for us to be having any babies. There will be a lot of moving around at first and the places we need to go to sell hooch, well, you definitely can't bring a baby along. I have been told by my pa that since you haven't even been to see a doctor yet, that this baby probably won't be right if it even lives to be born. We can't have a sickly child weighing us down, Clara. The other part is the danger to you, since the kid isn't right and I can't allow anything to hurt you. You will see that this is really for the best too. This way you will know I want to marry you and not because I got you in the family way." Erdman could feel the tension mounting in Clara's body as she sat in silence beside him.

"This isn't something that you can just undo, Erdman. Who in the world gave you the idea that we shouldn't have our baby? Was it this new friend of yours? I don't like him, and I haven't even known him very long." Clara's body shook with sobs at the realization of what he was telling her.

"Now don't blame Buddy. He has nothing to do with this. I know it is a lot for you to accept, but the sooner you do the sooner we can go and get hitched and move on with our lives. I have been doing some studying on this and I even have a tea for you to drink that will cause you to miscarry the sickly thing. You need to start drinking it now and by the time we reach Minnesota in the morning it should start to take effect. I will be right there with you. Don't worry, Bright Eyes, I've got you." Erdman reached into the back and brought forth the thermos filled with the tea infused with abortifacients. He started to pour the tea into the attached cup when Clara stopped him.

"The sickly thing? You just called our baby a thing! Are you trying to tell me that this is the rest of your conditions so that we can get married? You want me to murder our child and run off and marry you without thinking twice about it? I knew that you were not excited about our child like a normal father would be, but this is beyond that. If this is your condition, to choose you or to choose my baby, what makes you think I would choose you?" Clara was yelling by the time she finished speaking, her rage shaking her body more violently than the crying had.

"This is not negotiable, Clara. If you don't have an induced miscarriage, then I will refuse to marry you. This little town will not be kind to an unwed woman and her moronic sickly little reject. Most likely your own family will shun you although they should be used to your moronic reject of a brother."

Clara slapped him with all her might, making Erdman's head spin and causing him to see the brilliant little pinpricks of light that had once plagued him. "I will not marry you now or ever, Erdman Olson. I told you that I had another option available to me, and I can see that I was a fool to wait for you. Don't ever try to contact me again. Goodbye." Clara darted out of the car door, grabbed her box from the rumble seat and walked briskly down the logging road towards the highway.

"No! You don't get to walk away from me again! I told you that no one takes what is mine!" Erdman was in a full-blown rage as he exited the car to pursue her.

More than half an hour had passed as Buddy Henks sat inside his car waiting for Erdman and Clara to reappear. Finally, he saw the headlights of the roadster slowly approaching from the highway. Buddy jumped out of his car and ran to the driver's side door, ready to chide Erdman for taking his own sweet time amorously reuniting with the girl while he waited. Buddy looked in the car, and the first thing he saw was the blood everywhere; all over Erdman and all over the passenger side door of the car. What he didn't see was Clara anywhere.

"Erdman, what have you done with her?" Buddy shouted as Erdman calmly looked straight ahead towards the farmhouse.

"There's been a change of plans. I am going to need your help with a couple of loose ends." Erdman answered his friend in a calm, flat voice, devoid of all emotion.

Chapter 50

SEPTEMBER 10, 1926 – RISING SUN, WISCONSIN

Albert Olson sat at his dining room table sipping a glass of bourbon. He had returned from a visit to Prairie du Chien to find Erdman gone and Anna in the barn with Arvid and Edwin Knutson. Anna sat in the middle of a pile of puppies yapping and tugging on the hem of her dress. She laughed and scooped up one of the puppies to kiss. Even Albert had to smile at the picture of joy she created. She had followed Albert to the house, asking him for a dose of her laudanum and fell fast asleep soon afterwards.

It was almost one o'clock in the morning and Albert could not sleep. He had told Erdman that he was visiting a friend in Prairie du Chien, when, in reality, he had visited a doctor and midwife seeking their assistance for Clara and the baby. He had hired the pair to check on Clara and provide care including the delivery of her child with absolute secrecy. Albert planned to secure a flat in Prairie du Chien for Clara to stay in while she was confined in the later stages of her pregnancy. Albert still hoped that Erdman would come to see the brilliance of the plan and end up marrying Clara and claiming his child as his own.

Meanwhile Erdman was outside in the barn taking care of his "loose ends". He had stored a suitcase of clothes in the barn earlier, anticipating picking it up when he and Clara met Buddy back at the farm. Now he used the extra clothing as part of his subterfuge. He washed all the blood off his body and hid his bloody clothing in the burn barrel. He couldn't burn the clothing yet, because the fire would attract his father's attention in the house. He piled trash over the clothing so that anyone ready to burn the trash would just light a fire without checking what lay hidden at the bottom.

While Erdman cleaned himself, Buddy had changed the front tire on the roadster so that Erdman could make a faster getaway if needed, but it also hid the fact that his front tire had been patched recently and it left tire marks accordingly. Buddy had offered to take the roadster back to the woods and clean it, then take care of the rest of the mess that Erdman had created on Battle Ridge. Erdman was insistent on accompanying Buddy back to the logging road at first, but Buddy told him that he needed to create an alibi by going into the house with Albert. Buddy would take care of the roadster first, then bring it back and store it in the shed and return to the logging road with his vehicle so it would be out of sight by daylight. Erdman needed to stay away from the logging road completely and never return to the copse of trees on Battle Ridge.

From there, they created a plan for Erdman to remain at the house and claim that he had not seen Clara last night because he had been in Seneca. Erdman would wait for his parents to take him back to college in a few days and would then catch a bus to meet Buddy a few weeks later when everything had calmed down. Erdman would try to convince everyone that Clara had asked him for money and that she must have taken off to have her baby elsewhere. While her parents would be upset, it was a plausible story if Erdman could stick to it. Buddy was amazed at how relatively calm Erdman was in light of what he had just done. It was a sure sign that Erdman would do well with the criminal underground he was about to join in Chicago.

Buddy drove the roadster slowly back up the lane towards Highway 27 keeping the headlights off. He took a right onto the highway and then another quick right onto the logging road. He was able to turn the headlights on from there and drive the rest of the way to the area Erdman had described.

Buddy was a seasoned criminal, but he was not prepared for the sight of the savagery that had taken place. The pasteboard box of clothing was still lying in the road where Clara had apparently dropped it in her attempt to flee. She had been dragged backwards towards the roadster, then beaten viciously as evidenced by the tracks and spots of blood. Buddy wondered if Erdman had attempted to shove her back in the passenger side of the roadster to abduct her and if she had tried to run again; this time to the front of the vehicle down the hill towards the farmhouse. The poor thing hadn't run very far when she was felled from behind. A gravel shovel was still lying there beside her lifeless body. Buddy had his work cut out for him to get rid of the evidence that anything had occurred here. Even working quickly, it would take him well past dawn.

Erdman went to the corn crib and took a bottle of gin from the hidden storehouse there. He took several large gulps, then proceeded to the back door of the house. Albert looked up as he entered the kitchen.

"I was wondering when you might be home, Son. It must have been a busy night at the dance. Did you stop to see Clara afterwards? I have an idea to run past you about your situation, and I think you will agree that it might work for everyone. I waited up for you so Anna wouldn't overhear us." Albert shifted in his seat so that he could see Erdman, who was still in the kitchen.

Erdman took several deep breaths to calm his rapidly beating heart. He decided to busy himself by making a sandwich from the leftovers he had used earlier. He brought the sandwich, along with the bottle of gin, and came to the dining room table where Albert was seated. Erdman stopped at the radio and turned it on to cover the conversation at the table.

"It was a big crowd at Seneca tonight, and I ended up staying late but selling everything. I didn't have time to stop for Clara, but she has been acting a little odd lately and may have not wanted to see me anyway. I appreciate you trying to help us, but this is something we need to handle between the two of us. Clara realizes now that she shouldn't have tried to involve you in this. I have told her that I plan to return to Gale after all, and she can join me there if she wishes. I think I will help you out with the tobacco this weekend and go back to the college Sunday evening if that works for you." Erdman glanced at the mail still lying on the dining room table, picked up a Montgomery Ward catalog and began to thumb through it.

Albert tried to contain his surprise at Erdman's sudden switch in plans. He couldn't fault the boy for trying to go back to school, but he still wondered if it was to evade his responsibility to Clara. If Clara agreed to go to Prairie du Chien after Erdman left for school, Albert could effectively take care of her and his grandchild, making sure they were both safe and sound. Hopefully, Erdman would decide to come down from college and get married before the baby was due, but at least he had stopped his crazy talk about getting rid of the child. Albert knew that Erdman detested feeling forced into anything, so this version of the plan would work just as well as the one he had formulated that morning. He nodded his agreement and patted Erdman's shoulder.

"Did you see Edwin outside? I guess he went out for the evening, and he hasn't returned yet. I wondered if he might be out in the barn or the shed. I guess I will head up for bed as it will be a long day in the fields tomorrow. Good night, Son."

Erdman looked up from the catalog when Albert mentioned Edwin being outside. Where was the little worm and what might he have seen tonight? Erdman might have another loose end in the form of the hired hand to wrap up before he made his escape on Sunday.

Chapter 51

SEPTEMBER 10, 1926 – SENECA, WISCONSIN

It was just before dawn when Christ Olson awoke with a jolt. He had drifted in and out of sleep the entire night, having a bad dream about searching for Clara. He suddenly realized that he had heard Clara leave the house, but he had not heard her return. He was so tired from all the work in the tobacco fields that he must have fallen into a deep sleep and missed her. The sense of uneasiness from his dreams returned to him as he rolled to his side and faced Dena.

"Ma, did you hear Clara come back in the house last night? I didn't hear her, and that isn't like her to be out so late." Christ gently woke Dena with a pat to her shoulder. "I had a terrible dream about searching all over for her and finding her face down on one of the hills towards Rising Sun. I can't seem to shake the feeling. Can you just go and check on her in the girls' room?" Christ was sure that he was being silly, but he needed to know that his girl was fast asleep in her bed.

"Yah, I think I heard Clara last night, but I will go and check. I told you not to eat all that dessert before you went to bed last night. It gives you bad dreams every time." Dena rose from their bed and put her robe on, tying it around her plump waist. She opened their bedroom door and Christ could hear her open the door to the bedroom that Clara shared with Alice. Christ waited a moment then he could hear a discussion between Dena and Alice. He did not hear Clara's voice, so he rose and hurried down the hall.

Dena's voice was loud by the time that Christ entered the room and when he looked at Clara's untouched bed, he understood what made Dena so upset. Soon Bernard and Adolph came to join them, being drawn by their mother's upset tone.

"Alice, what do you mean that Clara did not come home last night? Where in the world could she be? Clara doesn't just take off like that. Pa, what are we going to do?" Dena's voice got progressively louder with each question that she asked. Soon Emma, Cornelia, and Inga were in the room as well and everyone seemed to be talking at once.

"QUIET! I need to think." Christ shouted into the hubbub going on around him. The family members were immediately silent, and all of them turned to look at their patriarch. Where could Clara have gone? Why wouldn't she tell them she was leaving if she wasn't planning to come back? Surely, she would leave word for them.

Christ spied the note sticking out from underneath the lamp at about the same time as Bernard saw it. Bernard picked up the note and, with trembling hands, gave it to his father to read to everyone.

Dear Folks,

I know you all will be surprised to see me gone as I am leaving this evening. I will have to go tonight. I did not know I

*was going until this afternoon but could not make up my mind
to go till now, when I am leaving. Please do not worry about
me as I will not be gone very long. If anyone asks about me tell
them that I have gone to La Crosse. Again, I must tell you do
not worry about me as I am taken good care of and will be back
soon. Don't take it too seriously as it will mean nothing-only a
little surprise. I will be back soon from my trip.*

    Your daughter,

    Clara

The sense of unease increased in Christ's heart. What did Clara
mean that she was going on a trip that she discovered only yesterday?
He feared that his daughter had just run off with Erdman Olson and
would return married to him. That would be the one thing that Clara
would not tell him about because she knew that her papa would object
strongly. That boy had never come to introduce himself to Christ, let
alone ask for his blessing despite Christ's entreaties that Erdman do so.

"Let's not stand around gathering flies. Ma, you and the girls go
get breakfast started, Bernard and Adolph walk down the lane to see
if there any tracks left behind, and I will check the barn and sheds
to see if Clara might be there." Christ knew he would not find Clara
in his barn, but it got him out of that room and into an open space
so he could breathe again.

Everyone stood for a few more moments staring at each other in
shock before they left the room to do what Christ told them. Alice
lingered behind to say a quick prayer for her family and for her sister
wherever she might be.

Bernard and Adolph headed down the lane to the road. Adolph
was looking all over the ground around them for any sign of their

sister, but Bernard walked to a small grassy area just to the right of their lane. Bernard knew this was where Erdman often parked his roadster waiting for Clara to walk down the lane to him. Bernard chided himself for not paying more attention yesterday after he had handed Clara the letter from the post office. He realized now that the letter was most likely the plan to run off with that good for nothing scoundrel. When Bernard arrived at the grassy area, he found fresh tire tracks in the mud leading in and out of the grass and headed down Stoney Point Road towards the highway. Clara's footprints were still there as well, as she had joined him there like she always did.

Adolph came to see what Bernard was staring at in the mud. "Well, I'll be, would you look at that? The front tire is still patched on the idiot's car. Looks like we have our answer." Adolph looked at his brother who had remained silent up to this point. Bernard clenched his hand into a fist and struck it in the palm of the other with a loud smack. He turned to hurry back to their pa in the barn with Adolph following close behind.

When Christ heard about the boys' discovery, his sense of unease grew to dread. "It is time to go over to Rising Sun and see what they know about this. Bernard, I am trusting you to do this as I can't be peaceful with them right now. Just go ask about your sister and see if they know where their son might be this morning. I am afraid that they are together far off by now." Christ closed his eyes shut and the boys watched as tears trickled down their father's face. Bernard and Adolph both patted their father's shoulders and waited for him to regain his composure again.

"Whatever you learn, come back to tell me out here in the barn. We must not upset your Ma more than she is already. Adolph, come help me do the chores." Christ turned slowly and headed for the barn with his head down and his shoulders slumped. Adolph raised an eyebrow at Bernard and followed his father towards the barn.

Bernard went to his car and started it. He tried to clear his mind of the overwhelming sense of guilt that he had not been able to stop his sister from making the biggest mistake of her life. He would try to be peaceful with Mr. and Mrs. Olson but, when he saw Erdman again, not even Christ would be able to contain him.

Bernard made the drive from Seneca to Rising Sun. He passed through Mt. Sterling, he passed the Utica Lutheran Church, and soon he was making the right-hand turn onto Lone Pine Lane. The odd tracks from the patched tire had led him back to this spot and the tracks continued onto the lane almost crossing themselves as if the roadster had been driven back and forth several times.

Bernard pulled into the driveway. The farm was quiet as it was only an hour past dawn. Bernard headed for the front door and knocked on it. He was greeted at the door by a middle-aged woman in her robe. Bernard was a little shocked, as he knew his own mama would never answer the door in this state of dress.

"Good morning, Mrs. Olson. My name is Bernard Olson, and I was wondering if you knew where your son Erdman might be this morning?"

The woman glared at Bernard and said sharply, "Erdman is still sleeping in his bed as any sane person is at this hour of the morning. Why did you want to know?"

Bernard did not mention that the woman herself was not in her bed sleeping as she suggested that any sane person would do. Obviously, they did not know that Erdman was missing yet, probably somewhere with his sister. Well, it was time for the nasty woman to discover he was missing.

"Could you go and see if he is awake? I need to talk with him about something very important. Please, Mrs. Olson."

Anna motioned for Bernard to step inside the door and wait in the kitchen for her to return. Bernard noticed the mess in the kitchen that appeared to be the beginning of their breakfast. He waited for the woman to react to her son's absence, so he was more than surprised when she returned after a few minutes. "He is awake now and he will be down in a minute. Wait there."

Bernard thought he had misheard her somehow. "Erdman is upstairs? He is coming down?" How could be upstairs if Clara had run off with him? Something was very wrong.

"Yes, I told you he was asleep. You told me it was important." Anna glared at him again with impatience. She returned to her mess in the kitchen, stopping long enough to pour a cup of coffee and bring it to the dining room table. She dumped a large amount of sugar in the coffee and stirred it then she left it sitting there without offering any to Bernard.

Bernard turned when he heard footsteps on the stairs. Erdman came into view looking groggy and grumpy. Bernard seethed at the sight of him but tried to remain calm so that he could learn of Clara's whereabouts. Erdman looked briefly startled to see Bernard standing in the kitchen, but he walked past Bernard and seated himself in front of the cup of coffee at the dining room table. Bernard followed Erdman and stood at the end of the table, not having been invited by anyone to sit.

"Erdman, I came to see you about Clara. We woke up this morning and she was gone. She left last night, and we thought you came to get her. Do you know where she might be?" Bernard had tried to be as polite as he could be, wanting instead to pick Erdman up and toss him across the room.

"Nope. I haven't seen your sister since I was asked so graciously to leave by your pa the last time we met. I wouldn't be surprised if she up and decided to take a little trip. She can be unpredictable, you know." Erdman looked at Bernard over the coffee he was drinking. Each drink was a loud slurp as though he was deliberately trying to annoy Bernard.

"Clara is usually very predictable, and she hasn't traveled by herself before this. I think you know more than you may be telling me. My parents are very worried for her, so your help would be greatly appreciated by them." Bernard ground his teeth at having to ask nicely for Erdman's help.

"If my son tells you that he doesn't know where your sister is then he doesn't know. Obviously, you don't believe him so I will take you around the house so that you can see for yourself we aren't hiding her in the closet or the basement somewhere." Anna interrupted the discussion and grabbed Bernard's arm to lead him around the house. He tried to free himself of her grasp, but she continued to lead him throughout the house to prove that Clara was not present. Erdman sat grinning at the sight from his chair at the dining room table.

Anna returned Bernard to the spot where he had been standing a few minutes before. She behaved as though she were taking him on a Sunday stroll instead of helping to search for Bernard's missing sister. Erdman continued to drink his coffee as he watched. Bernard felt his patience slipping away. He would try a different tactic to get his information.

"Listen, Erdman. I followed fresh car tire tracks from our house straight up to your house. The front tire is different and yours has been patched. You can either decide to help me or I can go and get the sheriff and he can ask you these questions. Clara could be in danger if she isn't with you, and I would think that you of all people would be concerned for her." Bernard shifted to lean on the chair in front of him, getting closer to where Erdman sat.

Erdman stood slowly and motioned for Bernard to follow him outside. "You are also welcome to look at my car. I don't know what you were looking at, but I don't have a patched tire." Erdman opened a shed containing his car. Bernard walked to the front and saw a brand-new tire replacing the patched tire. He couldn't believe his eyes. What had Erdman done with the tire and more importantly what had Erdman done with his sister?

Erdman continued. "You know I care about Clara, so it is unfair of you to suggest that I don't. In fact, I do know something about this, but I didn't wish to say it in front of my mother. Clara came to me after the display you all put on in front of us, and she begged me to help her get away from your family. She just couldn't take it anymore. I tried to talk her out of it, but I certainly wasn't going to let her hitchhike. I gave her a ride to Viroqua last night and I gave her some money to take the bus. You will find Clara if she wants you to find her. I would suggest that all of you be a little less hostile from now on. I didn't want to say anything in front of my family, so they won't think badly of Clara. After all, it's not her fault."

Bernard could not believe the pack of lies that Erdman just let roll off his tongue as though it was nothing.

"If you went to Viroqua, then why do the tire tracks only come from the direction of our farm and not from the other way?" Bernard knew Erdman was lying and he wanted Erdman to know that he knew.

"I was trying to cover up the fact that I came from Viroqua, so I drove past our farm and turned around crossing over where I had been several times. Go home and tell your parents that Clara will be home when she decides to come home and not before. You know, she was the most scared of you, Bernard. She said that you came home from the war very different and it frightened her." Erdman's eyes squinted at Bernard as if he had told him a big secret.

Bernard felt as though he would vomit. Clara had never been afraid of him; she had always turned to him when she needed protection from anything. Bernard had a desperate feeling that his little sister was in big trouble somewhere, and he needed to find her soon.

"Clara has never been afraid of me, but I think that from here on you should be. If I find that you have done anything to harm her in the least, there will be no place on earth to hide from me, Erdman. You had better get on your knees and pray that I find her soon and safe!" Bernard shouted the last part, his voice echoing inside the shed.

"I think you had better leave right now before you say anything else to my son." Albert had come from the barn when he heard the shouting and stood holding a crowbar. Edwin Knutson stood beside Albert looking sympathetic. Edwin also showed surprise when he glanced down at the new front tire on the roadster; obviously it had been changed overnight without the help of the hired hand. Bernard shook his head at Erdman and walked past them to his car. He drove slowly back up the lane towards the road. How was he going to explain this to his parents? Where in the world was his sister?

Little did Bernard know that less than a half mile away in the woods, his little sister had just been buried below the copse of trees on Battle Ridge. Buddy Henks had unceremoniously dumped Clara's body in a shallow grave. She was face down in Rising Sun.

Chapter 52

SEPTEMBER 12, 1926 – RISING SUN, WISCONSIN

Erdman had helped Albert with the tobacco crop for the next few days, just as he had promised, and was now readying himself to take the trip back to Galesville. Word had spread rapidly all over the county that Clara Olson was missing. The Crawford County Sheriff had made a brief stop at the farm, and Albert had assured him that Erdman did not know where the girl was at the present time. Albert had spoken so glowingly of Clara that it convinced the sheriff there was not the animosity that Christ Olson and his sons claimed between the two families.

Erdman had stayed on the farm for the following days knowing that he would only attract undue attention from the gossips in Seneca, Mt. Sterling, and Rising Sun. Buddy had left him a cryptic message, "Task completed. Don't return. Meet me in a few weeks." And then Buddy had left for Chicago. Erdman was relieved that there had not been more visits from Bernard Olson or his father.

Erdman had asked Albert if Edwin Knutson could drive him back to the college as Edwin had done numerous times in the past. Erdman wanted everything to appear as normal on the outside as possible. He also wanted to learn from Edwin about his whereabouts on the night of the 9th and if Edwin had witnessed anything on the 10th. The long drive to Galesville would provide an excellent opportunity to tie up any other possible loose ends.

It was dusk as Edwin drove the roadster down the lane with Erdman beside him in the passenger seat. Erdman had not brought his usual bottle of gin for the trip, so Edwin braced himself for the possibility that he would have to converse with him. Edwin was very worried about Clara, and he was suspicious about Erdman's involvement. He wanted to glean any information that he could from Erdman and hand it over to Bernard Olson and the Sheriff. So, the two adversaries plotted to extract information from each other without being obvious.

There was an uneasy silence in the car until they reached Highway 35 in Ferryville. Erdman looked at the Mississippi River stretched out before them and remarked, "Have you ever wanted to travel and see the world? I have been thinking about it lately. I am wondering if that is what Clara decided to do. She wanted out of this county and to see the world." Erdman glanced at Edwin to gauge his reaction when he mentioned Clara.

"I think she wanted to leave, but I don't think she would have gone alone. I hope that she sends word to her family soon. Folks are saying that Clara's poor mother is almost sick from worry over her. It doesn't seem at all like her to worry folks." Edwin was careful to not say anything about Erdman being involved.

"Possibly she wasn't alone, or she had someone to meet up with her. I know you were out and about Thursday evening. Did you hear anything from her? She always counted you as a good friend." Erdman was calculated in giving small pieces of information while trying to extract information from Edwin.

"I came home from Soldiers Grove. I met a young lady named Olga at the last box social, and we have been keeping company ever since. I came home very late because we had taken a trip to Prairie du Chien, and the movie we saw let out later than usual. I took her back to Soldiers Grove, and we spent time together there before I came back. I wish that I had seen or heard from Clara so that I could help her poor family find her." Edwin gave an honest account of his evening, but also let Erdman know that he had returned to the farm very late and therefore not witnessed any of the events of that night.

"Ah yes, the box dinner social. I was not able to attend this year, but I was told that Clara did, and she kept company with the postal clerk from Seneca. I know that I saw them dancing together at the dance hall one night as well. Perhaps they should be checking with that guy as to her whereabouts. He may have her hidden away somewhere trying to sneak off with her." Again, Erdman shifted the responsibility for Clara's disappearance onto someone else.

Edwin was interested in Erdman's theory that someone may have hidden Clara away for a later meeting and escape. He was also certain that it was not Ansgar.

"Ansgar bought Clara's box dinner that day, but they weren't keeping company. Clara has never as much as looked at another man since she met you. I am sure Ansgar would have been very happy if Clara had considered him in that way, but she didn't. He has been helping Clara's family try to find her by sending out notices everywhere, so I don't think he hid her away somewhere. What I don't understand is why Clara would just leave so suddenly. She received a letter that afternoon and by that night she was gone." Edwin hinted that he knew about the letter and its contents. Bernard and Alice Olson were both telling everyone that Erdman had sent that letter.

Erdman scoffed. "You know what I think? Clara is gone for a while, and she will be back if and when she decides to return. All this excitement over nothing is getting very tiresome. She left them a note for pity's sake!" In his irritation Erdman had revealed that he knew all about Clara's note to her parents. "It isn't a good idea for these people to run around and stir up trouble for me or my folks. I have business associates who would be all too willing to help shut up a few of these loud mouths, so I guess they need to keep quiet and let this alone until she decides to return." Erdman's threat was clear-stay quiet or get hurt.

Edwin knew he had pushed as far as he should. He was convinced that Erdman had something to do with Clara leaving. He hoped that Erdman would get Clara soon and bring her back to her family, provoking him further would just cause him to keep her away longer.

"I hope Clara knows everyone is thinking of her, especially today. It has been a hard day for her family," Edwin stated, intending to end their conversation as they were nearing their destination.

"What's so special about today?" Erdman asked with irritation. He was ready to leave this little worm behind.

"Why, Erdman, surely you know that today is Clara's 22nd birthday. She has never missed a birthday celebration with her family," Edwin responded.

The rest of the car ride was in complete silence, as both men had a lot to think over for very different reasons.

Chapter 53

SEPTEMBER 24, 1926 –
SENECA, WISCONSIN

The weeks following Clara's disappearance were one of the longest time periods ever known to the Christ Olson family. Neighbors had come from near and far to assist Christ and the boys in harvesting the remainder of the tobacco crop, many women from the Utica Lutheran Church brought gifts of food and help, and the entire community said daily prayers for Clara's safe return to her family.

The family suffered through the unknown. Where was their Clara, and why did she not send word to them? Dena, who was usually so busy from sunup to sundown, had taken to sitting in her rocker by the window watching for Clara. She believed that Clara needed to see her mama watching for her just as Dena had always done when a family member was away for the day. Then surely her daughter would come home to her.

All the Olson girls suffered from nightmares about strangers coming to their house and taking them away just as they were convinced someone had done to Clara. Alice suffered additional remorse for knowing more information than she had divulged on the day Clara left. Alice had told her parents about Erdman's last letter to Clara, the request to burn his other letters, and the absolute secrecy he required.

Bernard and Adolph continued to comb the county for any signs of their little sister but found not a single trace of her. Arthur had been contacted in Milwaukee to see if Clara had been there or had been seen there by people who knew her. Still, it was if Clara had vanished off the face of the earth after entering that car in the middle of the night.

Though the entire family suffered in various ways, it was probably Christ who suffered the most. He replayed conversations with Clara in his mind again and again, trying to gain a clue as to where she might have gone. Christ still went through the day to day work that he had always done, but he did it as a man who was not there. His mind was constantly searching for his daughter. Many of the locals said that Christ had seemed to age twenty years overnight.

After two weeks of agony, Christ decided that he was going to try and get some more answers from Albert and Anna Olson. The tripe that Erdman had told Bernard about Clara fleeing her family because she was afraid of them was preposterous. Clara always sought the solace of her family; she would not run away willingly. Christ knew that Clara did not fear him.

Dena had surprised Christ by asking to accompany him on the trip to Rising Sun. She felt that perhaps she could appeal to Anna Olson mother-to-mother and ask her to help them. At this point, Christ was willing to try any tactic necessary, so he and Dena left their farm for Rising Sun around two o'clock in the afternoon. Christ borrowed Bernard's car and drove Dena the eleven miles to the Albert Olson farm.

The farmyard was quiet as Christ parked the car. He quickly squeezed Dena's hand to offer her encouragement and exited the car to open his wife's car door. The two walked together to the front door where Christ knocked. Anna Olson answered the door, looking surprised to see them.

"We are very sorry to bother you, Mrs. Olson, but we wanted to talk to you and your husband about our daughter Clara. She has been gone for two weeks now and we have had no word of her whereabouts or when she might return." Dena was quiet in voice, but her eyes pleaded for help from the other woman.

"My husband isn't home right now. He has gone to Prairie du Chien on business. You can come in and sit at the table with me if you like. I really don't know how I can help you, though. Erdman already told your son everything he knew and that was that he didn't know where she had taken off to." Anna showed Christ and Dena to seats at the table. She usually offered guests a place in the fancy parlor she had decorated, but she felt these people were not exactly guests.

"We understand that Erdman told our Bernard that Clara had run off because she was afraid of us, and I beg your pardon, but I just don't believe that for a second. Clara wouldn't run away from her family. We have waited two weeks as my wife said, and we are very worried about her as you can imagine if it were your child." Christ tried to contradict what Erdman said in such a way as to gain Anna's sympathy and not her animosity.

Anna nodded her agreement. "Yes, I would be worried too. if that were my child. I don't think Erdman told your son the whole reason that Clara wanted to leave, however. I don't think Clara is afraid of you. I think she is afraid of what you will think of her."

Dena looked confused. "Why would our Clara be afraid of what we would think of her? She has always been a good girl and a wonderful daughter. Do you know anything else that we don't, Mrs. Olson? I beg you to tell me as I can't hardly eat or sleep with worry for my child."

Anna paused as she looked at Dena. The dark circles under Dena's eyes spoke of her sleepless nights worrying about her child. "Well, I probably shouldn't say this, but I can't stand for you to worry yourself sick. A little over a month ago Clara sent us a letter claiming that we needed to insist that Erdman marry her. When we asked Erdman why she would say this, he insisted that he bore no responsibility in the issue with Clara. You see, my son had been very ill, and he was even away in a hospital having surgeries for a good deal of time. I know for a fact that Clara saw a number of men around the county because I saw her myself with at least two of them."

Christ was growing impatient with Anna's prattle about his daughter. "I still don't understand. Why would Clara insist that your son marry her? They had a huge falling out and we thought they had called it quits. This doesn't explain why Clara would leave or why she would be afraid of what we would think of her."

Anna sighed dramatically as she looked towards Christ. How dull could these ignorant country people be? "Let me put it this way. Clara left suddenly because Erdman would not marry her. She was running out of time. I expect she will return after the New Year with a child and no man. I am sure you now understand why she thought you might be disappointed and angry with her. It wasn't Erdman's responsibility because he has not even been home for a good deal of time."

Dena gasped aloud and Christ felt as if he had been mule kicked in the gut. Their daughter was pregnant, and they found out via the mother of the possible father of the child. Clara had written them a letter to tell them and Erdman, but she had never mentioned a word to her own parents. Christ didn't know what else to say, but he knew he needed to get Dena out of this house before she broke down in front of this odious woman who sat looking at them with a disdainful look upon her face.

"I see. I thank you for your assistance. If you will excuse us, we will be leaving now. Come, Mama." Christ stood and helped a shocked and immobile Dena to her feet. She followed him woodenly to the door and out to the car. Anna stood at her front door watching them as they left down the lane.

Christ drove the car down the lane and pulled it over to the side after he had rounded a corner out of sight of Anna Olson. He reached to take Dena's hand again. She stared out of the window at Battle Ridge in front of them without speaking. After a few moments, Dena spoke.

"Is it true, Pa? Has our girl run off to have a child and she was too afraid to tell us?" Dena's voice was barely audible. The news she had just received had taken all her remaining strength.

"She might be with child, but our Clara would never be afraid of us. There is more to this story, I think, and we are going to have to search it out for ourselves. Let's go home and decide what to do next, Mama." Christ drove the remainder of the trip in silence as both grieved the loss of their daughter's innocence. Still, they knew they would love and accept Clara no matter the circumstances, if only she would return home to her family.

Bernard was waiting for them when they returned home. He jogged from the barn out to the car to speak with his father. "Pa,

Mrs. Lena Hutchins sent word that she needs to see you today. She has heard about Clara and thinks she might have more information that will prove helpful. I will drive you over there right away."

Christ nodded his head in agreement. "Let me see Mama into the house and we will leave." Christ gently helped Dena to the house and left instructions for the girls to fix her a strong cup of tea. Dena returned to her rocking chair by the window and rocked back and forth with her eyes closed. Christ knew she was praying that Clara would come home.

Bernard drove Christ to Soldiers Grove. On the way Christ told Bernard what Anna Olson had revealed to them. Bernard's face turned white and then beet red in anger. Christ knew Bernard's anger was not towards his little sister, but towards Erdman and his pack of lies.

A servant showed Christ and Bernard into Lena Hutchins' parlor. She treated them as honored guests in contrast to how they had been received by Anna Olson. The elderly lady sat in a rocking chair with a blanket over her lap. She tried to stand when Christ entered, but she sank weakly back into the chair. Both Christ and Bernard made certain that she was safely seated again and not in danger of falling.

"Mr. Olson, thank you for coming to see me on such short notice. I adore our Clara so much. When I heard today that she was missing and that all of you were so worried, I thought I might have some additional information that might assist you. I apologize that I am in an altered condition today; I took the news about Clara rather hard and my heart has been giving me trouble." Lena's face lit up with her mention of Clara. Christ could see that she adored his daughter.

"Thank you for asking to see us, Mrs. Hutchins. I am sorry that you are feeling poorly. You said you might have more information?"

Christ was trying to be polite, but he yearned for anything that might bring Clara home to him.

"Yes, I had traveled with Clara before as you are aware, and I had offered to help Clara with her current circumstances. We had made a plan to travel to Norway so that Clara could stay there and possibly return to you in the future if you would allow it." Lena was trying to be delicate about Clara's condition and her family's possible response to it.

"I assure you, Mrs. Hutchins, that we not only would have allowed Clara to return, but her whole family would welcome her and her child." Christ wanted to be clear that he loved his daughter no matter what and would love his grandchild as well.

Lena nodded approvingly. "Yes, that is just how I thought it would be. I tried to convince Clara that her family would be loving and accepting of her circumstance as well. She spoke so highly of all of you that I feel I already know you."

"Mrs. Hutchins, if you tried to convince Clara of this, do you think she left because she was afraid of how we would treat her once we knew?" Christ asked the question and dreaded the answer at the same time.

"Oh my, no. Clara was not afraid for herself. She would have run off with Erdman because she hoped once they were married that you would not hurt him, that you would accept him into your family. She did what she did for him. I would have guessed that they would be back before now and that is what worried me today. Clara told me he asked her to elope, so she didn't need to go to Norway with me. I assured her that if she changed her mind at any time, she had only to send a telegram and I would send for her." Lena's eyes were bright with tears.

Bernard and Christ exchanged looks of alarm. Christ needed to be certain he understood Lena. "You say she would have gone away with you and not gone off by herself? That makes much more sense to me. I thank you for helping my daughter. You have been more than kind."

"I am absolutely certain she would not have gone off by herself. I heard that Erdman had remained here for a time, and I wondered if he had taken her somewhere to wait for him. I don't understand why he would do that rather than just elope and bring her back to her family right away. My mind keeps coming back to his odd behavior, and I am very uneasy. I want you to know that I have already contacted my lawyer, and he is to establish an account today to assist you in the search for Clara. My nephew suggested contacting private investigators, and I am insistent that I will pay for them as well. Please accept my help to bring our girl back to us." Lena patted Christ's hand that rested on the arm of the sofa.

Christ's eyes were full of tears as he nodded his acceptance. "Thank you. I won't refuse anything that might help us to find Clara. Your information has been very helpful. I will send a telegram with updates to Norway for you."

Lena shook her head. "I won't be going anywhere until we have Clara home again. If I may indulge myself, I do want to mention one more thing. Clara was talking about fathers, and she said that she couldn't expect Erdman or anyone to be as good of a father as her own. Your daughter loves you very much."

Christ wiped at the tears in his eyes as he stood to leave. He thanked Lena once again and left for the car with Bernard. Once they were on the way home, Bernard said what they were both thinking.

"Pa, if Clara wouldn't have left by herself, then where in the world is she? If she is by herself now, is she still in need of her family?" Both men were starting to dread the answers to those questions.

Christ was firm in his answer to his son. "The next step is for me to have a talk with Erdman."

Chapter 54

SEPTEMBER 26, 1926 –
GALESVILLE, WISCONSIN

The Sunday morning sun was bright in Erdman's eyes as he rolled over in his bed to try and go back to sleep. He had gone to a football game in Minneapolis with a large group of college chums the day before, and he drank way too much for his own good. His return to Gale College had been a success; Erdman was welcomed back by the administration, staff, and most of the students. He had even volunteered to be a tour guide for the annual open house sponsored by the college which began that afternoon.

Erdman eyes felt gritty as he attempted to open them. He was in a state of partial dress and unsure of how he even arrived back in his dorm room. The celebration after the football game was a continuation of the drinking he had done before and during the game. Erdman had decided that he might only have a month or so of college life left before he left for Chicago, so he would live it up while he could.

Someone stirred beside him, throwing an arm over his chest as he lay on his back. Erdman attempted to open his eyes again, trying to see who was in the bed with him. He had no memory of bringing anyone back to his room and no memory of doing anything else. He turned his head to the side where the sleeping figure lay and tried to focus his still blurry eyes. A mass of black curls covered the head against his shoulder, and a familiar scent of perfume wafted over him. Lilla lay nestled beside him, still asleep.

Confusion smothered Erdman as he tried to rack his brain for any memory of what had occurred the previous night. He vaguely recalled arriving back in Galesville and taking the gang of college boys to his favorite speakeasy, the one that Lilla frequented. His memory stalled there, and he could not remember anything beyond entering the speakeasy. What in the world had happened and why on earth was Lilla in his bed? Erdman recalled that in all his previous trysts with Lilla she had never slept in the bed with him. She always insisted on remaining awake while he slept.

"Relax. I left you relatively innocent." Lilla's voice drifted to him as she lifted her head off his shoulder and looked into his eyes. "You look like you just saw someone come back from the dead." She chuckled as she rose and put his shirt on over the slip she wore. She walked slowly to the mirror sitting on the top of his bureau to look at her reflection. "Yikes! I guess I look almost as rough as you do."

"How did you get here? How did I get here? What happened?" Erdman's voice was curt and raspy. He was not prepared to have to deal with Lilla and her games again. The last time they had been together he had beaten her half to death, and he did not wish for a repeat. After being accepted back into the college and trying to weather the storm over Clara's disappearance back in Rising Sun,

Erdman knew he needed to proceed with great caution when it came to Lilla.

Lilla sat down on the bed beside him. "You came strolling into the speakeasy last night, and it was like nothing bad had ever happened between us. It was cute the way you kept professing your undying love for me. You almost had me believing the whole thing until you slipped and called me Clara. I guess some things will never change between us."

Erdman winced at the intense pain in his head as he sat up and leaned against the headboard. "That does not explain why you are here with me or what happened." He looked at her and noticed a scar running down the side of her face. He wondered if he had put it there.

"You were pretty bad off and getting loud with your chums around. You kept referring to me as Clara and then crying. I wasn't sure what you were going to say next, so I knew that I had to get you out of there. I allowed you to think I was your little sweetheart to keep you from saying what you had started to say in front of everyone. You followed me here like a lamb and I got you to lie down by lying down beside you. I don't know what happened to her, but it sounds as if she didn't fare any better than I did at your hands. I carry a knife with me now in case you are in a mind to try that again." Lilla stood and began to dress, keeping her eye on Erdman.

"I am not sure what you are talking about. Clara is fine. She is meeting me in a few weeks after escaping her crazy family. I think it is best that you leave right away. Clara and I are getting married soon, and I wouldn't want her to think that I had been unfaithful to her. I don't know what your current game is, Lilla, but I am not playing." Erdman ran his hand through his hair attempting to look much calmer than he felt. What had he been saying to her?

"Whatever you wish, Erdman. I didn't do this to play a game with you. As far as I am concerned, I hope I never see you again. I did it because I owe your father a debt of gratitude; he made sure I was taken care of after you left me for dead. He paid all my hospital bills and has been sending me money ever since. He is a good and honorable man. I did it to protect him from more harm, not you. As for Clara, I hope she is where you say she is now and not on the Battle Ridge you mentioned last night. Not even I would wish that on her. Goodbye, Erdman. I hope you get exactly what you deserve." Lilla picked up her coat and her purse and walked out of the door, leaving Erdman to contemplate what had just happened.

He knew he had just experienced another close call. He would have to be vigilant against drinking to excess. Obviously he had partially confessed to Lilla what had occurred on Battle Ridge. If he was going to stay alive and stay out of prison, he was going to have to do better than this.

Erdman looked much improved later that afternoon as he led tour groups around the college campus. His dazzling smile and boyish charm had captivated more than one of the newest female students in his groups. He had led his fourth group through the entire tour when one of his chums from the previous day, Knute Halverson, approached him with a grin.

"Hey, Erdman, do you feel as bad as I do right now? I think we had a little too much yesterday. Speaking of which, they are looking for you in the Quad right now. I guess you have people wanting to buy more of your hooch for later this evening. I will take over for you here." Knute stepped forward, smiling at the young ladies in the group.

Erdman thanked Knute and headed for the large courtyard area of the campus. It was always good news when people sought him out to buy large quantities of his gin. Erdman arrived at the Quad and looked at the various people milling around. He wondered which party was looking for his gin. He decided to just stand and wait to determine who it might be.

An older looking man approached him from the side and before Erdman knew what happened, Christ Olson was standing there in front of him. Erdman's first response was to flee, but his face must have betrayed him as Christ grasped him by the shoulder to restrain him. Christ did not look angry, but he looked very determined.

"I suppose you know why I have come to see you Erdman. You need to tell me what you have done with my Clara." Christ's voice was barely above a whisper. He was trying to not make a scene in the crowd of people around them.

"Look, I already talked to your son, and I told him what I am telling you. I don't know where Clara is, and I don't have anything more to say about it. If you came all this way for that, then you just wasted your time." Erdman turned to leave, but Christ's hand remained on his shoulder with a firm grip.

"I didn't bring Bernard with me this time, as the two of you don't get on with each other. I thought you might be more willing to talk to just me. I know that you had something to do with Clara leaving and I can prove it, so you best just get on with telling me the truth." Christ's voice gained a little more volume, causing the people close by to turn and look.

"You can't prove nothing on me. Clara left you of her own free will, and she will return if and when she wants to. I have nothing to do with it." Erdman reached up to try and break free of Christ's grasp on his shoulder causing the older man to increase the strength of his grip.

"I can prove it and you know it. Alice saw your last letter. She thought you were eloping, so she didn't come forward right away. She saw the instructions to burn the letters, and she helped Clara pack that day. You came and got my daughter and all I want to know is if you are willing to admit that and if she is safe. Clara knows I don't hold any claims on her as she is a grown woman, so she wouldn't just run off." Christ kept his hand on Erdman's shoulder and led him towards a quiet area of trees where they could talk more freely without being overheard.

"There are probably quite a few things you don't know about your daughter including the fact that she would run off because she didn't want to live there anymore. I don't blame her for that. You need to just leave her alone." Erdman tried to counter the information that Christ had with the lie that Clara had wanted to run away from her family.

"Well, I do know that my daughter was in a family way and she wanted you to marry her as you are the father of her child. I also know that Clara had planned to leave for Norway with Mrs. Hutchins to raise your child there if you didn't marry her, so she would not have just run away. She had all the plans set up, and the only reason she would change them is if you told her that you were going to marry her. So, you did come and get my Clara that night, didn't you?" Christ knew the truth and there was no way for Erdman to slip from it.

"I did." Erdman spoke the two words of truth quietly. His mind was reeling from the revelation that Clara had planned to leave for Norway quietly instead of running off with another man as he had accused her of. In admitting he was there that night Erdman knew he needed a cover for what had occurred after he had picked Clara up from the farmhouse.

"I picked Clara up and took her to the bus station in Viroqua. She caught a bus to St. Paul to wait for me there. I gave her $50 for food and lodging. I still don't know for certain that her baby is mine, and we needed to figure that out before getting married. We even talked of just moving on from St Paul and not returning to Crawford County, so that is what is still being decided." Erdman laid on one lie after another trying to cover for himself and buy himself some time.

"Well, if that is the case then I want to encourage you to do the right thing by my daughter. I promise that we will not hold anything thus far against you if you will only go get my girl and bring her home. Please tell Clara to send me word. Her mama is sick with worry over her. I want to offer you a house with land, six cows, a team of horses, and $500 as a wedding gift for the two of you. We love Clara and only want what is best for her. She has chosen you, Erdman, and I am willing to accept that and let bygones be bygones." Christ's earnest eyes pleaded with Erdman. This father was willing to humble himself mightily when it came to his child.

"I will tell her and let her decide if she wishes to return. We can't get married right away, but I already told her I am willing to still marry her if she can prove the baby is mine. I think I can get her and bring her back by Thursday if that is what she wants to do." Erdman was cruel. His lies to the hopeful father were promises to return what he could never bring back.

"I only ask that you come to the car and tell Oliver Helgerson what you just told me. It has been too many weeks of people saying this and that and no one getting any of it right. I know my Clara will want to come home, and she will be welcomed with open arms and so will you, Son." Christ led Erdman to a car parked nearby. Oliver and Andrew Helgerson had driven Christ to Galesville and would serve as

Christ's witnesses to the agreement with Erdman. Erdman followed through as he did not see any other immediate means of escape.

Christ let go of Erdman's shoulder with the admonition, "Bring my girl home by Thursday night as we have agreed. If you don't, I will send the sheriff here as you have admitted to taking her away. Just follow through and everything will be fine." Christ climbed in the car, and Oliver drove away leaving Erdman standing in the street.

Knute Halverson found Erdman still standing in the street. "Olson, what happened? Who was the old guy? It was the young fellow with him that wanted to buy the gin." So that was how Christ had lured Erdman to him. Erdman needed to be careful as the old man was cagey.

"Yeah, he was some old hick offering me a herd of cows to marry his little cow of a daughter." Erdman laughed raucously. "I am going to need a ride to the bus station in the morning. I will give you ten bucks for the ride, Halverson."

Erdman had precious little time to spare in making his escape. He went to see President Lokensgard and withdrew from Gale College that day. He packed up all his belongings in a box to ship to his father in Rising Sun. He wrote a letter to Christ Olson telling him that where Clara was would never be Christ's concern again and not to look for them, they were never coming home. He sent a telegram to Buddy asking him to pick him up from the bus station in Chicago and provide him a place to lay low for a while. He would leave for Chicago and start his new life a little sooner than he had planned.

Late that night, the fellows in the dormitory heard the sobbing coming from Erdman Olson's room. He was crying, not for what he had done, not for the people he would devastate, not even for the fact that he had accused Clara of being unfaithful and Clara had not planned to run off with another. She was completely innocent of his accusations. He cried because he was all alone and the only person to ever love him and take care of him was still hidden from the world on Battle Ridge.

Chapter 55

SEPTEMBER 30, 1926 – SENECA, WISCONSIN

The late September weather had turned gloomy. Christ Olson looked out at the overcast skies as he trudged back to his farmhouse for breakfast. The turmoil of the churning gray clouds mirrored Christ's thoughts and emotions. This was the day that Clara was set to return; he and Erdman had agreed upon it. The rest of the family were more optimistic, but Christ struggled with doubts that his precious Clara would ever return to her family.

Dena had breakfast on the table when Christ entered the kitchen. The girls had been scurrying about and Christ could tell they were excited about their sister's return. He didn't want his current foul mood to interfere with the respite of joy Dena had had since he had returned from Galesville on Sunday and told her about his agreement with Erdman.

Christ tried to eat the breakfast set before him, but all his food tasted dry and bland. He knew this was not due to the cook; Dena was among the very best. It was due to the continuing sense of dread that would not leave him since he had the dream the night Clara disappeared. How happy he would be to find out he had been a superstitious old Norwegian and to see his daughter walk in their front door once again.

There would still be the matter of the coming child and a hurried wedding to attend to, but Christ knew that he would be so relieved to hug Clara in his arms that these things were mere trifles in the whole scheme of things. It was funny how a near tragedy could help to prioritize what was truly important.

Christ sipped at the hot black coffee in his saucer and looked at the expectant faces of his daughters and wife. *Please, God. Just let our Clara come home today.* His thoughts brought a catch in his throat, and he set the coffee aside next to most of the remains of his breakfast.

Dena cleared her throat, a sure sign that she was going to ask something of him.

"Papa, the girls and I thought it might be pleasant to bake Clara's favorite treats and have a little party set for this afternoon. I know we don't want to encourage running off like this, but perhaps just a small celebration because we missed her birthday?" Dena smiled for the first time in three weeks.

"Yah, sure Mama. I think that would be nice. Keep it for just the family though, okay?" Christ knew it would be hard enough to face the possibility that Clara would not return today without a large gathering of people there to witness it.

"And Erdman, too? We probably should include him from now on." Dena looked into Christ's eyes with a plea to include Clara's beau for her sake. Dena had recently taken to praying for Erdman aloud during her prayer time at night, and she was asking Christ to help her extend the olive branch of peace to their new potential son-in-law.

"Yah, I suppose him, too." Christ conceded. At this point he would throw Erdman his own party if he would only bring their daughter back safe and sound.

"Papa! No! After all Erdman has done?" Bernard who was normally so quiet leaped to his feet in objection.

"Bernard, I know you have taken all of this with your sister in a hard way. I understand that, Son. I promised Erdman that if he brought your sister home today, I would let bygones be bygones, and I need to be a man of my word." Christ reached his hand towards his son, but Bernard backed away towards the door.

"I know you are a man of your word, Papa. You have always lived that. I am afraid to say that Erdman Olson is not a man of his word and all of this is for nothing. I am sorry, Mama. I don't wish to make you upset, but I have seen this Erdman lie again and again." Tears coursed down Bernard's face as he turned and left through the kitchen door.

Dena's face turned pale as she looked at Christ. She had not considered that Erdman was lying to them again. Christ stood and came to hug Dena tightly.

"You get your treats for Clara ready, Mama; I am sure that she will have been longing for them. I will go back and work in the barn for a while. Adolph, will you run into Seneca after a bit and pick up the mail?" Christ hugged Dena again and followed Bernard out the kitchen door.

As Christ approached the barn door, he could see Bernard standing outside a stall with his arms resting at the top of the gate and his head buried in his arms. His shoulders were shaking slightly, so Christ waited a few minutes to give his son some time. Bernard had not shown such emotion even after experiencing many of the horrors of the War. He had stored all the atrocities and his feelings concerning them inside himself. Whatever Bernard was feeling currently, he was feeling it very deeply, and Christ respected his son enough to let him express what he needed to without recrimination.

"I will go back in the house and apologize to Mama and the girls. I just needed to get myself in order first." Bernard still faced away from Christ but had sensed his father's quiet presence. "I have prayed and prayed that I am wrong about this and Clara will come running in the door today, but I just can't shake the awful feeling that she is gone and is never coming home, Papa." Bernard put his head back down on his arms as his sobs shook his entire body.

Christ knew that his son was feeling exactly the way he was feeling at that moment. Christ walked over and put his hand on Bernard's back.

"You feel the way you feel, and you don't have to apologize to anyone for that, Son. It is good if you can tell me these things, because you have tried to keep them all to yourself for too long and it is too heavy a burden to bear all alone. I have had that very same sense about your sister, and I hope that we are both wrong. I guess we will have to wait and see this afternoon. Promise me that you won't try to keep all of this to yourself anymore, Bernard." Christ patted Bernard's back as the sobs subsided.

"That's just the thing, Pa. When I couldn't handle all the thoughts and feelings racing around in my head, it was always Clara who listened to me. She has always been the one to listen and know what to say. I have felt this overwhelming sense of loss ever since I left Albert Olson's farmhouse that first morning, and I couldn't tell her.

I don't want to upset Mama, so I will go in and try to encourage her even if I don't feel encouraged. It is exactly what Clara would do if she were here right now." Bernard wiped the tears from his face with his handkerchief and turned towards his father. Christ enveloped his son in an embrace and held him tightly.

The two of them worked together for the next few hours, looking up at any sound from the lane that might announce Clara's arrival. Adolph had left an hour earlier for Seneca, so when they heard Bernard's car return it was not a surprise. Christ continued to work on the leather harness he was mending at his workbench.

"Papa, this came in the mail for you." Adolph stood in the doorway of the barn holding a small envelope. He came and handed the letter to his father as Bernard joined them at the workbench. Christ's hands trembled as he opened the letter without a return address.

> *I am leaving Gale college after tonight. You will not be able to find me or Clara from here on. Where she is, is my business and none of your concern from now on. After dealing with all your lip, I don't much care how upset your family is.*
>
> *Don't try to drag my family into this here mess. They don't know anything about it. I wouldn't make too much fuss if I were you as it sure doesn't look good for your daughter having to run off from her own family in the middle of the night.*
>
> *I believe she is still all right, but I can't really say and won't tell you where she is. I don't like the idea of the sheriff being called on me, so I am going. I would be a fool to wait around here for the sheriff to show up. There's a good chance that was the last time you will ever see either one of us again.*
>
> *E. Olson—Galesville, Wisconsin*

Christ would have collapsed on the ground if Bernard and Adolph had not caught him. Clara was gone. He wanted to lie down and never get back up again. He knew that Dena was in the house with the girls, still preparing for Clara's return.

He would go and hire the private detectives that Mrs. Hutchins had suggested. He would go and appeal to the Crawford County Sheriff and District Attorney yet again. He would leave no stone unturned in the search for his daughter. But first he would go in the house and tell Dena, then offer her and his family any encouragement and strength that he could give. As Bernard had just reminded him, *'That is exactly what Clara would do if she were here.'*

Chapter 56

NOVEMBER 26, 1926 –
PRAIRIE DU CHIEN, WISCONSIN

Thanksgiving Day dawned cold and blustery. The wind carried sharp bits of sleet that stung Christ Olson's face as he walked towards the Crawford County Courthouse. Bernard drove to Prairie du Chien, bringing his father to a meeting with Sheriff Harry Underwood, District Attorney J.S. Earl, and Judge C.H. Speck.

Since the day that Erdman had failed to bring Clara home, Christ had hired a private detective. Captain John Sullivan was a retired police officer and known nationally as a crime fighter. He had agreed immediately to begin a search for Clara as he had two daughters of his own who were close in age to Christ's missing daughter. Captain Sullivan searched in maternity wards of hospitals, hotels, and even in brothels for any place that Erdman might have stashed Clara. No trace of Clara had been found in all of Wisconsin, Minnesota, Iowa, or Illinois. He did find records of Erdman having been in Eloise

Mental Hospital in Michigan, which caused even more distress to the already overburdened Christ. After over two months of intense searching, Captain Sullivan had asked Christ to join him for the meeting with the officials at the courthouse that day.

Christ thought Dena might object to him leaving on Thanksgiving morning, but she hadn't raised any objections. Dena had resumed her seat in her rocking chair by the front window ever since Christ had told her that Erdman was not bringing their daughter back to them. She would mend clothes and rock, waiting for any sign of her Clara to return. Their oldest daughter Minnie had come home from La Crosse to help Emma and the girls with the daily chores that had been done previously by their mother. Minnie planned a small dinner for later in the day, but none of the family was in a festive enough mood to celebrate the holiday.

Christ reached the steps of the courthouse and paused. Captain Sullivan approached him from the top of the stairs, and Bernard came from the street where he had parked the car. Captain Sullivan extended his hand and shook Christ's hand with a firm grip.

"Thank you for meeting me here, Christ. I think this time we might have enough evidence to get them to listen. Hopefully after today we will get more results." Captain Sullivan referred to the fifteen times that Christ had already been to see the District Attorney. Each time, he was sent away because they believed that Clara had just run off with her lover. Since Clara was over the age of consent, running off with Erdman was not an illegal act and they would not pursue the search for either one of them any further.

"Thank you, John, for all you have done for us so far. No one else will listen when I tell them that my Clara would not have done this to her family. There has been a lot of talk about her in town and most of it is not good. I guess I should be glad that Mama isn't of a mind to go out of the house much, as it shelters her from some of the worst of it." Christ shook his head sadly as Bernard looked stonily at the ground. Most of the gossip about Clara had been fueled by Anna Olson saying that Clara had been with numerous men besides Erdman and had probably just up and run off with one of them after getting pregnant. If it wasn't enough of a hardship on their family to have their daughter missing, the busybodies of the community had added the disgraceful tarnishing of Clara's good name to the family's burdens.

"I wish there were an easier way to say this, Christ, but what I will try to prove today is what we have suspected for some time. Erdman Olson murdered your daughter back in September and that is why there isn't any evidence of her leaving Crawford County. I know that has to be hard to hear out loud, but if I can get them to issue Erdman's arrest warrant, I promise that I will not rest until he is brought to justice." Captain Sullivan put his hand on Christ's shoulder. "No father should ever have to endure what you are, Christ, and for that I am truly sorry."

"It is a pain like no other, John. Even just knowing where she is right now would help so that we could bring her home to her final rest. People haven't been too helpful in searching for her around us because they believe she ran off. The boys and I think that it is probably much closer by than we realize since Erdman didn't have time to go far that night. Let's hope that we get results today and then deal with the next part tomorrow." Christ started to climb the courthouse steps slowly with Bernard and Captain Sullivan on either side.

The meeting lasted several hours, and Captain Sullivan brought his very best investigative work. When they concluded, the officials all agreed; there was enough evidence for Christ to file a murder complaint against Erdman Sanford Olson. The complaint was drawn up as an arrest warrant and sworn that day. Erdman was now a fugitive from the law.

When Christ and Bernard returned to the farm in Seneca that afternoon, they had no idea what a sensation would be caused. Early the next day, a reporter from a local paper found the arrest warrant with the details and sent the story of Clara out on the wire. By the end of the first day the telephone at the Christ Olson farmhouse was ringing almost non-stop, and reporters from all over the state began to gather in Seneca, Rising Sun, and Prairie du Chien. Soon the story would be spread nationally and then internationally.

Christ, Adolph, and Bernard had repeatedly searched the woods around their farm by themselves. The day after Thanksgiving, Bernard asked at the local VFW for volunteers to help in the search for his sister. The word spread, and over six hundred people came to help that day. A blizzard was forecast for the following day, and the search would be complicated by several feet of snow and driving winds.

On the next day, over one thousand people arrived ready to search the hills and valleys in a blizzard. They searched in areas around Seneca and Rising Sun. Even many of the reporters joined the search party as they spread the word about Clara's story.

Dena continued her vigil of watching for Clara. She insisted that the lamp be left in the front window each night to light the way home for her daughter. Christ would sit with her in the evenings, holding her hand. That evening Dena turned to Christ, who was dozing as he sat beside her. He had been searching in a blizzard all day.

"Papa, they are searching for Clara still?" Dena whispered softly.

"Yes, Mama, we will bring her home." Christ answered wearily.

"We both know our Clara is already home. She is in Heaven, Papa." Dena closed her eyes as tears fell for the first time since Clara had disappeared.

"Yes, Mama, she is." Christ held his wife as they wept together.

Chapter 57

DECEMBER 1, 1926 –
RISING SUN, WISCONSIN

More than one blizzard raged as people continued to search for Clara. Another massive storm was building on the horizon over the Mississippi River as over one hundred volunteers gathered near the Albert Olson farm in Rising Sun. The consensus was that Erdman would not have been able to travel a large distance away and to return to his home at the time he did on the early morning of September 10th.

Albert Olson observed the numerous men traipsing in the woods all around his farm. He was sickened that Christ Olson had gone so far as to swear out a murder warrant on Erdman when it was obvious that Erdman and Clara had run off together. Erdman had written a short note to his parents telling them that he needed to leave because Christ Olson had threatened him. Erdman sent most of his belongings back with the letter and instructed Albert to give the things to Arvid when he grew older. He had also given them an ominous warning that they would not see him again unless it was in a coffin. Albert was certain that Erdman would change his mind and bring Clara and the baby home after time had passed. Albert had even gone to the trouble of setting up a link to Erdman's bank account so that Erdman could draw money off the account without being tracked by the authorities.

Numerous cars were parked down the lane from the farmhouse, and Albert could hear the voices of the search parties as he went about his daily chores. He had ordered that Arvid stay home from school and stay inside the house until some of the initial melee had settled down. Anna remained relatively calm as she continued to take large amounts of laudanum. She had panicked when the search parties initially appeared, insisting that Edwin Knutson and Arvid hide in the basement for a good part of an afternoon until Albert arrived home to unlock the basement door and release them.

Albert saw men trudging through the snow at the top of Battle Ridge. It irritated him that so many people had already assumed his son was a murderer and were out there looking for Clara's body. A reward of over $3000 had been offered for Erdman's arrest; Albert had torn down the reward poster from one of the postings in Mt. Sterling. He knew that he needed to remain cooperative with the law and with the local citizens as anything else would make it look as if Erdman was guilty.

The group of men gathered in lines along Battle Ridge looked down at the farmhouse below. They could see Albert Olson and Edwin Knutson going about their daily chores as if nothing out of the ordinary had occurred. One of Clara's cousins, Clarence Allen, was walking just below a copse of trees facing the Albert Olson farm.

An old logging road lay a few hundred feet behind him as he walked along in a straight line parallel to Battle Ridge. He was one of over one hundred volunteers who had shown up from the American Legion in Gays Mills. Many of the war veterans and their families were devoting copious amounts of time in the search for Clara in respect for Bernard Olson who had asked for assistance.

The wind howled as Clarence and the others walked along trying to see any traces of Clara in the snow. Clarence tripped over a large root near the copse of trees and almost landed on his face in the snow. He righted himself at the last moment and continued the treacherous terrain with caution. There was a slope going towards the Olson farmhouse and the last thing Clarence wanted to do was to slide down the slope right towards the farmyard where Albert Olson was working and watching them.

This particular wooded area had been a focus in the previous searches as well as wooded sites around the Christ Olson farm in Seneca. The private detective, Captain Sullivan, speculated that Erdman would not be strong enough to carry Clara a far distance without assistance. The men continued to return each day even though no one had discovered a single trace of Clara in the vicinity. Sometimes it was easy to believe what Albert and Anna Olson insisted was the truth; they would never find a body because Clara had run off. But then they only had to look at the sorrow of Christ Olson and his family to know they must continue to search.

The search was called off just as the sun started to set. Charles Bowen, a local woodsman, had volunteered to head the search party near Rising Sun. Charles was a gifted tracker and knew most of the area well. He was giving instructions for starting the next day when someone teased Clarence Allen about falling.

"I thought old Clarence was going to fall and roll right down the hill to Albert Olson. You should have seen Clarence's face when he started to trip." The man next to Clarence was entertaining the group with the story.

"Yah, I didn't see those tree roots in time and almost ended up visiting at the Olson's. I'm sure Albert would have rolled out the red carpet in welcome for me." Clarence agreed as he chuckled with the rest of the group.

The next morning when Charles Bowen returned to Battle Ridge with an even larger group of men, he had one place in mind to search. It had bothered him all the previous night that Clarence Allen had tripped over tree roots in the location Clarence had described. Charles knew that the copse of trees had large roots but the roots above ground ran to the sides of the trees and not down the slope behind them. If Clarence had tripped on roots above the ground there, it would be because someone had been digging in the area.

Charles retraced the path taken by Clarence the day before. He edged his way partially down the slope and between the trees. Sure enough, there were roots above the ground just as Clarence had described them. Charles carefully looked over the snow-covered area. He walked slowly and stooped after a few steps to take a closer look. The ground just below the snow had been overturned causing the ground and the snow to turn yellow from the minerals in the dirt.

Charles took a large stick and carefully began to brush the snow cover away. Two more men who were close by saw what Charles was doing and came over to join him. The more snow that was brushed away revealed an area that had been dug up recently including tree roots that had been hacked away and were now sticking above the ground. Charles used the stick to gently prod the excavated area.

He was methodically working his way across the small area when he struck something several inches down in the dirt. Charles knelt to the ground and carefully dug at the area with his hand. He unearthed the heel of a woman's boot sticking up in the snow.

Charles called to the men around him. "Someone needs to call the police. We have just found Clara Olson."

A man from the search party ran to get his car and head for a telephone in nearby Rising Sun. Two other men laid branches around the small area where the body lay. Charles Bowen and the other searchers knew not to dig around the body anymore until the police and the coroner had arrived.

The police and the coroner were summoned and came very quickly. They found a huge group of men standing around the site, watching over Clara in silent vigil. Most of these men, veterans and old farmers alike, had tears in their eyes for the poor girl they had just found. Not a single one of them would leave her, as the coroner and police began to dig around the body. Several young men assisted with careful shoveling until they were able to see that she was lying face down in the shallow grave. A long rattan basket was brought, and they placed Clara inside it with the dirt of the area still clinging to her. Her left hand was over her abdomen and the other lay off to her side. One of the older men gently placed the right hand near her abdomen as they lifted her from her hidden grave into the basket. Tiny pearls from her necklace lay strewn about the grave and the men bent down to retrieve each one and place it in the basket with her.

It was early afternoon when Albert Olson looked up to see at least two hundred men gathered at the copse of trees on Battle Ridge. He watched as they silently and solemnly escorted the long basket back towards the logging road. Something or someone was in that basket and, for the first time since Clara had disappeared, Albert experienced dread at the coming news.

A long line of cars followed the police car to a funeral home in Mt. Sterling. All the volunteers continued to keep watch over Clara as they followed and waited outside in the cold and snow. A police guard was placed at the entrance of the funeral home and not even the funeral home director was allowed admittance. Still hundreds of men gathered outside and all of them waited in hushed silence. They were still watching over Clara until her papa arrived.

A police officer arrived at the Christ Olson farm near Seneca with the grim news; a body had been found on Battle Ridge near Rising Sun. Christ left Dena with Adolph and the girls while he traveled with Bernard to Mt. Sterling. The police let Christ and Bernard inside the funeral home to identify Clara's clothing still on her remains. It was all there: the black green silk dress, a red sweater, new Mary Jane shoes with boots over them, a tan overcoat, and the most telling of all, the pieces of the pearl necklace Christ and Dena had given Clara for her confirmation.

Christ nodded silently at the police officer and turned to leave. Bernard caught Christ as he fainted at the top of the steps and carried his father towards the car with the help of the throng of silent onlookers. The grief of the crowd was palpable as Christ came to and began to cry.

"My Clara! Oh, my little Clara is gone!" Christ's voice carried out through the early evening sky and reverberated in each heart gathered there.

Bernard led his father the rest of the way to the car. They would return home to Dena with the news that Clara and her baby had been found just as Christ had seen it in his dream, face down in Rising Sun.

Chapter 58

DECEMBER 3, 1926 –
PRAIRIE DU CHIEN, WISCONSIN

The news that young Clara Olson's body had been found in a shallow grave on Battle Ridge spread like wildfire in the small communities of Crawford County. Crowds continued to gather at the funeral home in Mt. Sterling where Clara's remains had been taken. The state pathologist, Dr. Charles Hunting, was called to come from Madison to perform the autopsy and testify at an inquest later in the day. The Crawford County Sheriff decided to take Clara's remains from the funeral home in Mt. Sterling to the Otteson Funeral Home in Prairie du Chien in the early morning hours of December 3rd before the crowds began to gather again in the daylight.

Police guards were once again placed outside the doors of the funeral home in Prairie du Chien. Officials were waiting anxiously for Dr. Hunting to arrive on the first train from Madison. News reporters sent out stories on the telegraph and swarmed the area around the funeral home in Prairie du Chien. The newly elected

District Attorney, Arthur Curran, listened to the public outcry for justice for Clara Olson. Many citizens were extremely upset that the former district attorney had made Christ Olson appeal fifteen times before swearing the arrest warrant, thereby allowing Erdman Olson to elude the authorities.

The public sentiment had shifted from a judgmental opinion that a wayward Clara had run off with a lover to a sympathetic opinion of their hometown sweetheart being an innocent victim of a brutal murderer. The men of the search party who found her also circulated the fact that Clara's purse had been found empty of all money. Alice Olson told her father that she was certain Clara had taken at least seven dollars in cash with her. Erdman Olson was a murderer and a thief and many in the community called for "hill country justice", a phrase that meant they would rather see him dead by lynching than brought to justice in a court system that had already dismally failed Clara Olson.

Dr. Charles Hunting stepped off the morning train from Madison and was immediately surrounded by throngs of people. He hurried towards the uniformed police officers standing at the door of the car sent to take him to the funeral home. Something told him this morning that this day would be taxing, and he had assumed it was because he had been called to perform the always difficult task of an autopsy on a young murder victim. The distress of the people in the community was obvious to him making it easy for him to involve himself in their sentiment for the young woman, but Dr. Hunting considered himself a man of science, and he was determined not to let the public sentiment influence his findings in any way.

Sheriff Underwood was waiting for him when he entered the back seat of the car. The Sheriff watched the masses gathering outside the window with a grim look on his face.

"Good to see you, Dr. Hunting. Thank you for coming on such short notice. As you can see, we have quite a public spectacle brewing over this investigation. The subject has been secured at the local funeral home, and all the evidence from the site has been brought over as well. Please let me know if you require anything else from me. I will be stationed close by helping to regulate the crowds outside. Judge Speck will be waiting to take your testimony later today. Hopefully, we will have you back on the evening train to Madison."

"I didn't realize that this was such a publicized case. I have not read any accounts of it on purpose as I do not wish to have any information that might unduly affect my findings. After performing the autopsy, I would like to speak to the Coroner who was at the site to listen to his details of the site and positioning of the remains. Other than this, I should have sufficient equipment with me in my boxes." Dr. Hunting looked from the Sheriff beside him to the funeral home entrance that had just appeared outside his window. Dr. Hunting exited the car and entered the funeral home with the assistance of the guards placed at the entrance.

Once inside the funeral home, Dr. Hunting followed the assistant to the prep room where everything was waiting for his autopsy examination to begin. Dr. Hunting removed his overcoat and suitcoat and donned a large apron and gloves. The assistant situated himself on a stool next to the prep table to take the necessary dictation of the autopsy notes.

Dr. Hunting saw the remains of a young woman on the stainless-steel table before him. She had been placed face down just as she had been found at the gravesite. The clay mud and dirt still clung to her in large chunks as the Coroner had been careful to not remove anything that might potentially be evidence in the case. Dr Hunting carefully began to remove some of the larger chunks of earth clinging to the young woman. He determined she was in her early twenties and in apparent good health before her death.

As he progressed Dr. Hunting found several key pieces of information. There had been a skull fracture to the left side of her cranium that caused a two-inch triangular piece of her skull to fall out upon the table. Someone had hit her in the back of head with a huge amount of force several times causing her death. The force necessary was not even possible with a fall from a great height; someone had struck her with great amounts of rage and power. The most likely instrument of death would have been a pipe, club, or the handle of a shovel or axe. The victim had also been beaten badly before the death blows were delivered.

The young woman had been about six months pregnant with what appeared to be a healthy baby girl. The child did not show any outward abnormalities and had succumbed to death after her mother died. Even Dr. Huntley, who prided himself in his clinical professionalism, was shaken that someone would brutalize a pregnant woman, killing both her and her unborn child.

Probably the most compelling evidence had been saved by the young woman herself. She had stored two letters, neatly folded into tight triangles, in the bodice of her undergarments next to her heart. Dr. Hunting painstakingly removed the blood and debris from the outside of the letters and tried to unfold them carefully to dry. The handwriting and much of the content of both letters were still visible. Both letters were to Clara Olson, the victim, from Erdman Olson, the accused. She had saved a letter from early in the summer with his promises to marry her after becoming intimate with her, and the last letter he had written to her with his plans to elope on September 9th.

Dr. Hunting took several hours to finish the exam and prepare his report for the inquest. He asked the guards at the door to call for the Sheriff so that he could escort the doctor over to the courthouse. Sheriff Underwood appeared soon after, and the two men set out for the Crawford County Courthouse.

Dr. Hunting appeared before Judge Speck to give his testimony early that afternoon. He gave a concise account of the date and time of Clara Olson's murder as well as the likely cause. He then finished with entering the letters found on Clara's remains as evidence. When he had finished testifying, he prepared to leave by the back door for the train station.

As he neared the back door, he found an older gentleman with overalls and a worn sweater waiting near the door. The grief-stricken countenance of the man assured Dr. Hunting that this man must be the poor young woman's father. This same man had sat silently in the courtroom listening to the pathologist's account of his daughter's murder. In a sudden and uncustomary rush of compassion, the doctor removed his hat and nodded at the grieving Christ Olson as he passed him in the hallway. Dr. Hunting continued to the train station, with the personal thoughts of his discoveries swirling about in his mind.

Clara herself showed us what happened that night and who did this awful thing to her. I pray for justice for this brave young woman and her baby and for the grieving family left behind.

Clara's body was taken from the funeral home to Christ Olson's house that night. Someone had donated a light gray casket and a beautiful wreath of white roses for her wake and funeral. Alice stayed up all night sewing beautiful white dresses for her beloved sister and her tiny baby niece. Dena sat in the parlor overnight beside Clara's casket so that her girl would not be alone. The time would soon come for the family to gather and say their final goodbyes. Christ Olson grieved his precious daughter and the granddaughter that he would never hold as Clara had once imagined.

Chapter 59

DECEMBER 6, 1926 –
PRAIRIE DU CHIEN, WISCONSIN

Another blizzard had hit Crawford County with deep snow and howling winds. The inquest into Clara Dorothea Olson's murder by Erdman Sanford Olson was scheduled to begin at 9 a.m. but had to be postponed until 10:30 a.m. to allow the fifteen witnesses called to testify to reach the Crawford County courthouse. By the time the inquest began, another 500 people had gathered and filled the courtroom, the hallways, and the yard outside.

Christ, Bernard, and Alice were all called to testify and had set out by car three hours earlier than planned to make the scheduled time. Dena stayed at home beside Clara's casket and Adolph, Emma, and Minnie helped the younger siblings complete the chores on the farm and make the final arrangements for Clara's funeral. Another son, Arthur, who lived in Milwaukee was scheduled to come home that day, but the weather had delayed him.

A massive crowd greeted Christ and Alice as they exited the car in front of the courthouse. Bernard went to try and find a place to park the car; all the streets were full of cars, wagons and even sleighs. Finally, one of the sheriff's deputies saw Bernard trying to park his car and found a place in the lot reserved for public officials for him. Bernard hurried back towards the courthouse to join his father and sister. He knew that numerous people had been called to testify including Albert and Anna Olson. Bernard did not relish seeing them again and certainly did not want his sister and bereaved father to have to endure them.

Bernard found Christ and Alice at the top of the courthouse steps. Their progress had been slowed by all the people in the crowd trying to offer condolences and encouragement to their family. There was also a large assemblage of reporters who tried to get Christ to stop and talk with them. District Attorney Curran had told the family to be very cautious in what they told the reporters and general public so they would not jeopardize the case against Erdman.

Albert and Anna Olson had obviously not been given the same directions by the District Attorney or they had chosen to ignore them. Bernard noticed a large group of reporters gathered around them just inside the entrance as he entered the building with his father and sister. He recognized Anna Olson's shrill grating voice as she answered their questions.

"Of course, all of this against Erdman is completely false. He is not to blame for the indiscretions of a woman years older than he is who made poor choices and tried to wrangle our son into an unwanted relationship. Her father then went to Erdman's college and made threats against him, so he ran because he is scared for his life." Anna's voice trailed off slightly when she looked up from the reporter in front of her and saw the bereaved father standing a few feet away. Christ paused for just a moment to make eye contact with Albert Olson, then led Alice down the hallway away from the reporters.

An officer of the court came down the hallway to meet them. He shook Christ's hand and offered his condolences for the family's loss. He informed them that they would be taken to an anteroom and held there by guard until it was their turn to testify. Each group of witnesses would be guarded, and the groups would not be allowed to speak to each other. Bernard was relieved to hear that they would be spared any more of Anna Olson's opinions about Clara; he had had more than enough from that entire family of liars. He had wondered numerous times since Clara had been found if the Olson family had been involved in hiding her only one quarter of a mile away from where he stood that first morning, and that Anna had distracted him by leading him all over the house when she knew exactly where his sister was. Bernard believed there was a place in Hell reserved for all of them, and he would personally like to send Erdman on his way there if only they could find him.

"I would like to hear what Erdman's parents have to say for themselves, but I guess this is the best way to do this." Christ sat near a pot belly stove in the small waiting room warming his hands. "Although, after hearing just a little bit of what Erdman's mother had to say as we were coming in the door, I think I have heard enough from them."

"Papa, I am so glad we don't have to be near those terrible people at all. To be telling such lies about Clara and knowing that she has just been found almost in their backyard. I hope they get what is coming to them." Alice shuddered as she leaned near her father and rested her head on his shoulder. "I will be glad to get this done and go home to Mama. She needs us with her right now."

"Your mama told me how important it was to her that we come to testify for Clara today. We shouldn't wish ill tidings on others, Alice. They are missing their son and that makes them act like that. At least we have Clara home with us now, and he is still out there somewhere." Christ patted Alice's shoulder as he hugged her.

"He is out there because he ran away after murdering my sister. They may have helped him or at least helped him hide what he did. Now they are trying to tell people that Clara was the bad person. I wish very bad tidings for them, Papa." Bernard stared straight ahead at the calendar on the wall instead of looking at his father.

"Bernard, your mama talked to me about this just last night. I know that Erdman killed your sister and there is a part of my heart that wants vengeance for that, but any time we seek revenge it is only harmful to us and not to the other party. That bitterness will hold us hostage if we allow it to do so. It will not bring your sister back to us, and it will not even harm Erdman. It will only fester in our hearts and hurt us. I think you need time yet, Son, but I hope you will see your mama's wisdom in this. I have faith in three things: the Bible, the law, and my family. Revenge has no room in there." Christ stood as the court officer opened the door.

Bernard remained silent. He and his brothers had already made a vow unknown to their father. They would try to find Erdman Olson before the law did and exact justice the way they saw it. His father could talk about forgiveness if that is what helped him. Bernard had killed before in the war and he could do it again. He would find Erdman Olson and not leave a trace for anyone else to ever find. Albert and Anna Olson would know the grief of never having their son's remains recovered.

Christ was sworn in and seated before the judge. District Attorney

Curran began with several preliminary questions including name and address. His next question was about Christ's children, how many he had and their names.

"I have five girls and four boys now. They are Bernard, Arthur, Adolph, Minnie, Emma, Alice." Christ broke into a sob as he tried to say Clara's name several times. The District Attorney patted his shoulder to comfort him.

"You had a daughter named Clara as well?" The DA asked Christ gently.

"Yah, my Clara is gone now." Christ said quietly and cleared his throat. He would try and be brave for Clara's sake.

The District Attorney continued to ask Christ questions about the night that Clara left the farmhouse and how she came up missing the following day. He then proceeded to ask questions of Alice and Bernard pertaining to their knowledge of the events surrounding Clara's disappearance. After a long series of questions and details, their testimony had been given and they were sent back to the small anteroom to wait. A court officer brought them coffee and sandwiches for lunch.

The other witnesses were each questioned, and it was late in the afternoon when the judge called for Christ, Bernard and Alice to return to the courtroom. They were the only witnesses who had remained until the end of the inquest, and the judge decided to allow them to hear the verdict as it was announced from the bench.

It is the finding of this inquest that Clara Dorothea Olson was beaten to death by Erdman Sanford Olson in the early morning hours of September 10, 1926. Erdman Sanford Olson is hereby charged with murder in the first degree.

Chapter 60

DECEMBER 8, 1926 –
SENECA, WISCONSIN

The early morning sun glistened across the fresh snow, making the hills sparkle. Heavy snow and icicles still hung from the tree branches after the blizzard from the day before. Christ Olson stood inside the barn door surveying the snow around him; *Clara always loved the fresh snow and making snow angels.*

Yesterday had been an extremely difficult day for the entire family but it seemed to have aged Christ an additional ten years overnight. Despite the blizzard that raged around them, they had laid his precious Clara to her final rest in the cemetery at the Utica Lutheran Church. They had hesitated to hold her funeral yesterday, in the middle of one of the worst blizzards Crawford County had seen in a century, but all the arrangements had been set for that day and it seemed pointless to cancel the plans. Christ had assumed that it would be a very small turnout, and he was fine with just his family attending the services and burial.

They had started out with a small service in the parlor for just the family with the Reverend Finstad conducting. Six young men from Clara's confirmation class had asked to be allowed to be her pall bearers. They reverently took Clara from her home for the final time and into the hearse that would take her to the church. Christ, Dena, and the family followed behind the hearse through the heavy snow. By the time they reached the left turn onto Highway 27, there were cars lining both sides of the road as far as the eye could see. Over one hundred and fifty cars joined the procession from Seneca to the church.

The Utica Lutheran Church had a capacity of nearly one hundred and fifty people and yet over three hundred people stood in the church with another three hundred people waiting outside in the blizzard conditions. At first Christ was offended that so many people had come to gawk at his poor unfortunate daughter, who had been portrayed all over the newspapers for weeks. As he entered the church, Christ could feel compassion, reverence, and respect coming from friends and neighbors and even complete strangers. These people were there to honor Clara and to stand with her family through this difficult time. Even this morning that recollection brought fresh tears to his eyes.

Finally, Clara was taken to the cemetery located on the left side of the churchyard. The black dirt of the freshly dug grave stuck out in the white snow all around it. There was silence from the massive crowd gathered around as the family huddled together to whisper their goodbyes. Christ wept openly; he could not contain his grief with the stoic silence that was expected of a man and the head of the household.

The choir that Clara had so enjoyed being a member of sang a final song as the men began to fill in the grave. Christ recognized the song as *We Shall Sleep but not Forever.*

When we see a precious blossom,
That we tended with such care,
Rudely taken from our bosom,
How our aching hearts despair!
Round its little grave we linger,
Till the setting sun is low,
Feeling all our hopes have perished,
With the flow'r we cherished so.

Refrain

We shall sleep, but not forever,
In the lone and silent grave:
Blessèd be the Lord that taketh,
Blessèd be the Lord that gave.
In the bright eternal city,
Death can never, never come!
In His own good time He'll call us,
From our rest, to home, sweet home.

People began to disperse leaving Christ, Dena and the family to make their way home. As they left the churchyard, Christ noticed a car parked in the field across from the cemetery. Arthur commented that the man seated in the car had been there when they first arrived and had not moved from the spot. Christ had a very good idea who was sitting in that car.

When they returned to the farm, they had received a note from Lena Hutchins' nephew that stated the elderly lady had risen that day to attend Clara's funeral and had a stroke; she had passed away by the day's end. Christ couldn't help but think that it was just like the sweet elderly woman to go to Heaven that day to check on her Clara and the little one there.

Dena had finally slept that night, but Christ had risen before dawn, going out to the barn to sit and reflect. Mingling with his tremendous grief was an unexplainable peace because Clara had finally been found and brought home. She was no longer missing and alone. He had prayed numerous times for God to give him even the smallest sign that they would be able to survive this terrible loss and to know that Clara was at rest. He patiently waited each day knowing that he was bound to recognize this sign from the Almighty when it came.

The thought of the snow and Clara gave Christ the idea to hitch up the sleigh and ride the few miles to Clara's grave in the churchyard. He knew it would somehow comfort him to see her grave and speak aloud some of the things he had wanted to tell her. He knew that the boys would automatically know where he had gone when they came to the barn and found him gone.

Christ made the short trip and parked the sleigh on the right side of the church. He walked around the church as the morning sun rose a little higher, revealing the figure of a man kneeling in the snow beside Clara's grave. Christ looked to see the same car that had been parked in the field the day before, pulled off to the side of the road. Though the man wore a hat and a heavy coat Christ already knew who he was.

Albert Olson looked up from placing roses on Clara's grave to see Christ standing a few yards away staring at him. Albert stood quickly and backed away from the grave so that Christ could approach without standing near him.

"I am so sorry. I did not wish to intrude. I did not think that any of her family would be out here so early this morning. I know that

I don't have any right to be here at all." Albert turned to leave, until Christ held up his hand to stop him.

"I think you do have a right because this is also your grandchild's grave as well as mine. Clara would appreciate you being here." Christ spoke in almost a whisper as the words of forgiveness and peace were difficult to form, but Dena had been right, he must try to forgive.

Tears streamed down Albert Olson's face. "Clara was very important to me. She was one of the kindest people I have ever known. I will grieve her and our grandchild the rest of my life."

"Yah, me too." Christ's statement was simple and complete. The two fathers spent the next hour in companionable silence and solace before they left for their own homes again.

Christ arrived home in time for breakfast. He saw his little Inga already playing in the snow with Bernard and Arthur as he pulled into the lane.

"Papa come see what I made for Clara! She can look down from Heaven this morning and smile!" Inga hugged her father tightly as Christ looked around the farmyard. There were dozens of perfectly made snow angels lying side by side in the snow. Inga had made them, and her brothers had patiently pulled her up from each one so she wouldn't ruin them, just like Clara had taught her to do. Christ knew immediately that this was the sign he had been praying for, angels everywhere now that Clara was at rest. Their family would grieve, but they would go on living a peaceful and happy life as a tribute to Clara.

Christ placed a kiss on Inga's forehead and smiled at his sons as tears of joy ran down his cheeks. "I am sure Clara is smiling."

Chapter 61

APRIL 6, 1927 –
RISING SUN, WISCONSIN

Spring had made a sudden appearance again in the hills of Crawford County. The barren trees that had stood stark against the winter sky now had new green buds forming, and the grass began to turn green almost overnight. These were signs from nature that life continued despite harrowing circumstances.

In the months since Clara and her child had been discovered in their shallow grave on Battle Ridge, the Crawford County Sheriff had numerous tips of where to find Erdman Olson. He had been sighted in Minnesota, North Dakota, and various cities in Wisconsin. Each time a sighting was reported, Bernard Olson would pack up and leave on the next train to try and discover whether the sighting was real. Each time Bernard would return home with the news that the reported person was not Erdman.

In March, a local hunter had found Clara's belongings hidden under foliage and wedged between a sapling and a tree stump. The deep snow had melted revealing a small trace of color from the yellow ribbon Clara had tied to the corset strings around the pasteboard box. The box was only a few hundred yards further out on Battle Ridge on land belonging to Erdman's uncle, Nels Severson. The public outcry that Erdman had not been found renewed as Christ and Alice were called to Prairie du Chien to identify Clara's belongings as the ones she had taken with her on the night she had disappeared.

Anna continued to protest Erdman's innocence. She talked incessantly to reporters who still came to the farmhouse regularly. Albert had asked the reporters to disregard most of what Anna was telling them as she was unwell and her recollections of events concerning Clara were not accurate. Most of the reporters complied, but sometimes there would be an outrageous story produced to sell more papers and often Anna was quoted in the story.

Edwin Knutson had just returned to the farm after a leave of absence following the inquest into Clara's murder. Edwin had an emotional breakdown and his father had to come and collect him, taking him back to Stanley, Wisconsin, to recuperate. Albert was saddened that yet another person had been so tragically affected by the events surrounding Erdman and Clara. He continued to pay Edwin even while he was away from the farm, knowing that Edwin had seen and heard things while on their farm that no one else should have to endure.

Albert worked the farm quietly, spent more time doing things with Arvid, and visited Clara's grave at least once a week with fresh flowers. He saw Christ visiting his daughter and grandchild occasionally, and the two spent respectful silent times together. They never mentioned Erdman and what either thought had happened; they were there to honor Clara's life and they would not allow anything to diminish that.

Albert knew that both Bernard and Arthur Olson were intent on capturing Erdman and bringing him to some form of justice. Everything in him wanted to defend his son as ferociously as he had in the beginning, but after Clara's battered body was found so close to their home, Albert knew he needed answers that only Erdman could give him. Albert also knew that Erdman might never return, and his questions would go unanswered.

Albert was still sitting at the kitchen table just after the evening meal when he noticed a truck driving up Lone Pine Lane. He was growing accustomed to the frequent visits of police officers, newspaper reporters, and nosey onlookers. At least this time they had been able to finish their meal before being interrupted by the knock at the front door. Albert steeled himself to patiently endure the continuous line of questions, some of which bordered on absurd. He looked towards the window that had a clear view of the front door, but no one appeared after he heard the truck doors open and close.

Suddenly Albert heard a noise at the back door. It startled him because he knew that Anna and Arvid were both upstairs and Edwin had left for Seneca over an hour before. The door opened as Albert stormed through the kitchen, ready to confront whoever was bold enough to just enter his house uninvited.

"Pa, it's me." Albert would not have recognized Erdman standing there if Erdman had not spoken. Erdman had dyed his hair blonde and had grown a mustache and slight beard. He had gained at least thirty pounds, giving him the appearance of a much older man than his actual nineteen years. Erdman had even had dental work done which changed the look of his mouth and jaw line. Albert stood frozen in place staring at his son as though he had just seen a ghost.

Buddy Henks stood in the doorway behind Erdman looking around the room nervously. Both men had pistols holstered at their waists, and Buddy kept his hand covering his pistol as he continued to look around.

"Erdman, I told you not to just go busting in here. You don't know when there might be other folks lingering about who don't need to know that you are here." Buddy looked nervously towards Albert, who had not moved since Erdman opened the door. "Is there anyone else in the house beside you, Pops?"

Albert glared at the man for using a familiarity with him. "Anna and Arvid are both upstairs, and the hired hand's not home right now, No one else is present in **my house** at this time." Albert emphasized the two words to help the hooligan understand who was in charge around here. Buddy ignored Albert's statement as if he had not spoken at all.

"I will go back out and hide the truck in one of the sheds while you and your pa get reacquainted." Buddy turned and left, closing the door behind him. Erdman watched Albert's face, carefully gauging his father's reaction to his sudden reappearance.

"I bet you thought you would never see me again, huh, Pa? Honestly, I didn't plan on ever returning, but I had to leave Chicago and thought to stop in on my way through. Did you say Arvid is upstairs?" Erdman did not attempt to hug his father, and Albert found himself oddly relieved.

"Yes, we can call him down here in a few minutes. You need to take it easy on him; it will be quite a shock to see you." Albert found himself stalling Erdman's reunion with his little brother until he sought a few answers to the myriad of questions he had for his older son. "You say you were in Chicago all this time but now you had to leave?" Albert motioned for Erdman to follow him back to the kitchen table where he had been seated. Erdman took his old place at the table just to Albert's left and grinned at his father still staring at him.

"Yup. I planned to meet up with Buddy in Chicago before everything else. I have been living the high life there and needed a change, so the Wild West is next on the agenda. There is a call for businessmen to sell alcohol in Montana and Nevada. The associates I work with now are sending me to branch out their business there. I figured that the heat has died down around these parts, and I regretted leaving without talking to Arvid, so here I am. Is there any hooch in the cupboard? I could use a stiff drink or two." Erdman stared out the window towards Battle Ridge in the twilight.

He regrets not talking to Arvid. Is that all he regrets? Albert stood and crossed to the cupboard taking down a bottle of bourbon and two glasses. He had not drunk as much of the alcohol lately, but he found in the current circumstances he was going to need a drink or two as well. He came back to the table and poured the bourbon in both glasses.

"There has been a very intense search conducted for you since you ran off. I don't know if you have kept up with the local news, but they found Clara and your baby in December and indicted you for murder. I doubt that it is safe for you to remain here for very long as it is common to have the police or reporters show up unannounced." Albert had mixed emotions about wanting his son to stay and wanting this version of Erdman to leave as soon as possible.

"All of that is unfortunate but, like I always say, the past is in the past. You can't undo it when it's done. Best to just leave it alone. I noticed that you had linked an account with money to my old account. Pretty smart move, and I have used most of the funds in there. I could use some more travel money so I can get out of your hair and leave you in peace." Erdman drained the bourbon from his glass and reached for the bottle to pour more into his glass.

Albert understood that Erdman was not going to be forthcoming about anything that had occurred concerning Clara. He had come home to get more money, not because he had a filial attachment to any other member of his family or because he felt remorse for anything he had done. There was even a slight tone of threat when Erdman suggested that it was best to leave Clara's murder alone. Albert now understood that the best thing he could do was to give Erdman the money and get him out of the house before more harm came to innocent bystanders.

Buddy entered through the back door just as Anna and Arvid came down the stairs to see who had arrived. Arvid stopped on the stairs and stared at his brother, causing Erdman to laugh and making him sound more like the son that Albert knew. Erdman stood and held his arms out to his little brother as Arvid raced down the rest of the steps with Anna right behind him.

"Erdman! It is you! You look so different I couldn't be sure. Where have you been and why did you leave?" Arvid threw himself at Erdman, almost knocking his brother over with his bear hug. Anna came to stand beside her sons, beaming as if she had just been named mother of the year.

"We knew that you would come home to us, Erdman. I have told all these silly people that you did nothing wrong and would come home to set the record straight. I never stopped believing it was true." Anna glanced at Albert with a triumphant look as she patted Erdman's back.

"I did not come here to set anything straight. I have no interest in what you or any of these other green hicks think anymore. I came back to see Arvid and talk to him. If you want to remain in the room with us, then be silent." Erdman did not even look at Anna as he addressed her in a matter of fact tone. Anna looked as if she had just been slapped. For the first time, Albert felt pity for her.

"I can't stay long, Arvid, but I wanted to tell you that after a while, when I am settled out West, I can send for you to come and live with me if you want. You don't have to grow up here in this backwater hole like I did. Would you like that?" Erdman grinned at his little brother and hugged him again.

Arvid looked at his father before answering his brother. "Well, I guess a visit would be okay, but this is my home and yours too, Brother. Can't you just come home to stay? I know you didn't hurt anybody, so you could just come and explain that."

Erdman and Buddy both laughed aloud, making Arvid wince. "I am afraid that isn't going to happen, Little Brother. I have moved on to better things and want to offer the same to you. Maybe when you are older with a little hair on your chest you will be more interested. Just remember that you aren't stuck here." Erdman ruffled Arvid's hair roughly, making the boy start to back away. Albert decided to intercede.

"I have quite a bit of cash on hand in the safe if you need to leave soon. I can send more to the hidden account when you get established. I have had to be careful as the authorities are still watching my bank accounts and mail for clues regarding your whereabouts." Albert would offer instant cash and then tempt Erdman with the possibility of receiving more cash in the future to prevent Erdman or Buddy leaving him, Anna, and Arvid for dead when they left. He hated to suspect his own son of doing him harm, but self-preservation was of the highest priority to his son and, if Erdman decided he no longer needed them, he might wish to do away with them just as he had with Clara. Albert recognized the truth that he had dreaded. Erdman had killed Clara and their child so that he could be free of them.

"Yeah, that works for me. I have a little task to take care of outside and then I will be ready to go if you have what I need ready. Buddy here could probably use a sandwich and a drink while he is waiting for me to return." Erdman nodded towards Buddy who looked nervous that Erdman was venturing outdoors.

"I will come with you." Arvid offered, much to Albert's dismay.

"Not this time. I will be back soon, Arvid, and you can tell me all about the girls that are chasing after you and the ones who already caught you." Erdman laughed at his brother's blush of embarrassment. He turned and opened the back door, pausing to look around before he exited.

Anna took Arvid back upstairs as Albert prepared a sandwich for their unwelcome visitor. He brought the sandwich back to the table along with a clean glass for some of the bourbon. Buddy continued to stare out of the window towards Battle Ridge as he picked up the sandwich and took a bite.

"I told him we shouldn't take a chance and stop here but he was dead set on it. There is not much to do once his mind is made up." Buddy took another bite with a quick swallow of the bourbon.

"He is taking a big chance as not only all of the law is hunting him, but Bernard and Arthur Olson are hunting him as well. He will not fare well if they find him here." Albert wanted the threat of the sudden appearance of the Olson brothers to make Buddy eager to depart.

"It wouldn't be the first time we have dodged Bernard. He has been only a few minutes behind us on two different occasions. We have had to leave fast before, and we will have to again." Buddy shook his head nonchalantly.

"Is that why he had to leave Chicago? Is Bernard that close to finding him?" Albert grew more uneasy about Bernard tracking Erdman here and a gun battle ensuing with his family right in the middle of it.

"Nope. We had to leave Chicago last night because another girl was beaten to death and it doesn't look good for Erdman to stick around when they start asking questions about what happened. Erdman insists it wasn't him this time, but he said that last time too." Buddy shoved the rest of the sandwich in his mouth preparing to leave as soon as Erdman returned.

Albert felt sick to his stomach. Buddy knew all about Clara, and now there was another girl dead.

"What exactly did Erdman tell you about what happened?" Albert asked the vague question but both men knew exactly what he meant.

"He didn't have to tell me anything. I had a front row seat. Who do you think cleaned up his mess up there while he came down here with you? That poor girl tried to get away from him and come down here to you, but she didn't make it but a few steps. Bad business, all of it. Now, this next one has happened. I am seeing he gets to Montana, then I am returning to Chicago. I am not going to see this keep happening time after time." Buddy drained his glass and Albert refilled it.

"Is he out on Battle Ridge right now? Is he missing Clara that badly that he returned here?" Albert's hands were shaking as he gestured towards the ridge.

"He is out there by where he left her, of that I am sure. I don't think it is because he misses her, though, or even feels badly about what happened to her. He seems to relish thinking about what happened out there." Buddy took another sip as he looked at Albert's reaction.

"Why would he want to return there? Wasn't it an accident? I was convinced he loved Clara and lost his temper somehow." Albert asked the questions but realized that he didn't want the answers anymore; they were too awful to hear.

"I thought it was an accident at first, too. He seemed crazy about the girl and told me she was running off with us after he got rid of the baby. Then when I went back out there to take care of burying her, I found a perfectly dug grave already waiting just beyond where I found her. The fact is that poor girl never stood a chance. She was never leaving Battle Ridge alive. He planned it, and he likes to relive it in his mind. Truth be told, Mr. Olson, something is terribly wrong with your son, and it will continue on." Buddy stopped as he heard Erdman open the back door.

Albert got to his feet somehow and managed to retrieve cash from his safe and hand it to Erdman. Arvid came to say goodbye, and soon Erdman was gone just as suddenly as he had arrived.

Albert lay awake the entire night thinking about what Buddy had revealed to him. If only he could have helped Clara when she ran for the house, if only he had committed Erdman to an institution, if only there was a way to turn back time and give Clara another chance. He would give anything to do all of it over again, including giving his own son over to the authorities when asked to do so. He would look for the opportune time to send the authorities after Erdman and prevent this from happening to anyone else.

Chapter 62

AUGUST 10, 1945 – STANLEY, WISCONSIN

Almost nineteen years had passed since Clara's death, and Erdman Olson had not been captured by the authorities. Bernard Olson had continued to search for Erdman for years, and the reward money for his capture had built to over ten thousand dollars. Law enforcement officers had followed clues as far as Norway, but Erdman seemed to keep one step ahead of them.

The world had changed since Clara's death. The second World War began in 1939 with the United States joining the Allied forces against Nazi Germany in 1941 after the Japanese forces bombed Pearl Harbor. Many more young men went off to fight in Europe and the South Pacific, and numerous ones never returned home. Edwin Knutson had been one of the luckier ones. He had fought in Europe and saw the liberation of Poland in May of 1945 before returning later that year to his childhood home.

Edwin had been experiencing terrible nightmares since his return from the war. His wife Olga, the same shy, sweet girl he had met at the box dinner social in July of 1926 and later married in 1938, grew very concerned over the frequency of his nightmares and how they seemed to affect Edwin. Olga begged Edwin to go to a doctor or a local priest and talk to them about his experiences in Poland to help him alleviate his nervous condition. Edwin had ignored most of Olga's pleas, but the recent nightmares had increased in intensity, causing him to wonder if he would have another emotional breakdown just like the one he had already experienced in 1926 after Clara's death.

Edwin made the choice to visit with a kindly local priest. He had seen too many of his fellow veterans be medicated by doctors and end up in a worse state, being addicted to the drugs prescribed for the terrors of the mind and heart. Like so many others with him, Edwin had witnessed the atrocities of war including the concentration camps where over six million people had been murdered.

Father Mackenzie was an older man in his late sixties. He welcomed Edwin into his small office near the chapel and confessionals. Edwin took a seat across from the priest and fought the nausea and sweating that his nerves produced. Father Mackenzie handed him a cup of hot tea and sat down, smiling patiently.

"It seems so good to be able to offer tea once again. There were so many items rationed for a time that tea was indeed a luxury. Your wife told me that you have been having some nightmares? I want you to know that you may discuss anything you wish, and of course, you know that it will be strictly confidential just like a confession." Father Mackenzie smiled and sipped his tea waiting for Edwin to speak.

"Yes, I guess that the war has taken a toll on me like so many others. I was in Poland and saw just how badly one human can treat another and still justify their actions. Many of the smaller villages that we liberated were virtually empty of every man, woman, and child. Even the elderly and infirm were not spared from experiencing the horrors of the concentration camps. So many people lost. And yet, though it sounds crazy, I am not certain that this experience alone is what has been causing the nightmares. I don't dream about the war at all." Edwin shook his head slightly and looked down at his feet. He knew deep down that it was not his war experiences causing the nervousness to reappear.

"May I ask what you do dream about if you can recall it? Sometimes just talking about it out loud with someone else is the start to healing the heart and causing the nightmares to cease." Father Mackenzie patted Edwin's shoulder gently.

"Well, Father, I dream about a young woman named Clara who was found murdered right next to the farm in Rising Sun where I worked as a hired hand. She was a sweet young lady, and I admired her very much and counted her as a friend. Knowing that she was murdered and knowing who murdered her has weighed upon me for many years." Edwin could still see Clara in his mind's eye just as she was in his dreams, running from Erdman and calling for his help.

"I think I have read some things about that murder in Crawford County back in 1926. I thought they never caught her murderer, but you say you know who it is? Was it someone you knew?" The priest's questions were gentle as he tried to get Edwin to tell him more.

"Yes, I knew Erdman Olson and I knew that he killed Clara. The night he killed her, I returned to the Olson farm to see Erdman cleaning blood off himself out near the barn. He didn't realize I was there to witness it. He asked where I was that night later, and I lied to him because I was afraid of what he might do to me. I had failed

Clara by not arriving in time to rescue her and then by not turning Erdman into the authorities right away. I was just too frightened of him at the time." Tears ran down Edwin's cheeks at the admission that no one else but this priest had ever heard.

"Oh my, I see. I can see you feel remorse for that. Do you think that is what has caused your nightmares?" The priest's gentle eyes remained on Edwin without the judgment Edwin had dreaded. He had tormented himself for years about letting Erdman get away, but that wasn't the full compass of what he knew as the truth of the burden he carried.

"I think that it is part of it, Father. The rest is that I have carried a secret for years and the weight of it is almost more than I can bear at times. It was a very necessary secret, one that I promised to keep, and I will still keep it, but I thought I might be able to share part of the burden with you." Edwin stood at a precipice. No one else living knew what he knew about what happened to Erdman Olson.

"By all means if you feel it will help you to tell me, then please go on." The priest leaned closer so that Edwin could speak softly.

"Well, if you read about Clara's story then you probably already know that Erdman Olson escaped the law and ran off. They hunted for him all over the country for years. What the authorities didn't know was that Erdman returned twice to the farm where he lived as a boy and to the place where he had murdered Clara on Battle Ridge just past Rising Sun.

"The first time he returned was in April of 1927. I was not present that time. I only knew of it because Erdman's younger brother Arvid confessed to me afterwards that Erdman had been there. Arvid also confessed that while he and Erdman had been very close as brothers growing up, Arvid was now very frightened of Erdman and thought his father Albert was frightened, too. Apparently, Erdman offered to send for Arvid, but Arvid did not want to go with him. Albert had sent Erdman away with more money.

Arvid also admitted that while Erdman was there at the farm, he left to go up on Battle Ridge to the spot where he had killed Clara. Arvid snuck out of the farmhouse that night and followed Erdman. Arvid insisted that Erdman stood at the spot where he had dug a shallow grave and talked to the poor dead girl. He blamed Clara for all his misfortunes and even relived the moments right before she died, exclaiming he would kill her again if he could. Arvid had been terrified to hear this and ran back to the house before his brother discovered him. I tried to reassure young Arvid that I would not let his brother harm him, but I had been so useless to Clara that I didn't know if I could protect him."

"Erdman returned to Rising Sun a second time in August of 1937. I was in the barn finishing chores after supper when I saw him walk towards the farmhouse. I wanted to run away but I had promised Arvid that I would protect him, and I would not let him down as I had Clara. I stayed hidden in the barn and waited for an opportunity."

"It wasn't very long until I saw Erdman leave the house and head towards the woods. I knew from Arvid's account of Erdman's previous visit exactly where Erdman was headed. I also knew that this was the opportunity I needed if only I was man enough to take it. Only a few thoughts of Clara trying to run away as Erdman chased her down had me grabbing a nearby axe and heading for the top of Battle Ridge facing Rising Sun."

"I crept quietly towards the spot where Clara had been found, and there was Erdman standing over it with his back towards me. He was talking to Clara as if she were still standing there.

'*I suppose it makes you happy that I have been a fugitive all this time. My only crime ever was to think that you were important enough for me to change who I was for you. You were just like Anna and all the rest of them, a manipulative piece of trash not worthy of my notice. Just so you know, you haven't been my only one, Clara, just my first successful one. I tried to kill Lilla before you, but she ended up surviving it, so I perfected my skill with you. Now there have been several others but none of them have been as exciting as you were. I think it was the way you fought me and then cried and begged me to let you go. Even as you tried to run away from me to get my pa, you provided a level of excitement I have not achieved since. I told you, Clara. No one gets the chance to walk away from me more than once.*'

"My head spun, and I thought I was going to vomit listening to Erdman's proud admission. He had planned to kill Clara, and he was continuing to kill others. He might be planning to return to the farmhouse and kill his family and me. I had to stop him. This had to end."

"My heart was pounding so hard that I was certain that Erdman would hear it and turn around to discover my hiding place nearby. I couldn't breathe for the fear as I stood slowly from where I was crouched."

"Clara had the terror of seeing what was coming as Erdman had chased her down, but Erdman did not have the same experience. Just as I started to move, Albert Olson stepped out from behind a stand of trees and struck Erdman in the back of the head with a shovel. He stood over his son with tears running down his cheeks, as I stood staring at the two of them before me. Albert crouched down to check if Erdman was still breathing, but I could tell from the wound on Erdman's head that he was already dead."

'I couldn't allow him to live anymore. I didn't want you or Bernard Olson to have to bear the burden of doing what had to be done. I tried to turn him in several times, but he always got away. He told me once that it would have been better if he were never born, and I guess he may have been right.'

"Albert remained kneeling beside his son's body as he sobbed in grief. I walked to place my hand on his shoulder as the initial shock wore off. We remained there beside Erdman for at least half an hour. Together we selected a place in one of the larger swamp areas located on the farm and sunk the car Erdman drove to the farm in the swamp. We buried Erdman's body close by the swamp where the vegetation and murky water would hide it forever. Albert made certain that Erdman was placed face down in Rising Sun just as Clara was so many years ago."

"Both Albert and I vowed that we would not tell anyone of what had happened until one of us had passed away. Later that year, Anna consulted with a psychic who predicted that Erdman had been killed by two men and his body was close to Rising Sun. Albert made certain that the psychic was paid off well to keep all his other predictions quiet."

"I know that I endured the horrors of the war, Father, but it somehow seemed secondary to seeing the evil that had lurked so near to home while Erdman Olson still lived. I recently heard that Albert passed away last year while I was still in Europe. I think that is what triggered all of this to come back to me. As you can understand, I need for my wife and everyone else to think that it was the war that caused this."

"You see, Arvid has grown into a fine young man. He is a pillar in the community of Rising Sun, known by everyone for his kindness and generosity to all. He stayed on the farm and has helped turn it into one of the finest farms in Crawford County. Arvid is the complete opposite of his brother and should never be judged for what Erdman did. The story of what happened might only serve to injure him, and that would add more harm to all the harm that Erdman has already done. This is the main reason that I ask you to keep my secret, Father, so that no one else is ever hurt by Erdman Olson again."

"Now I need to do what Clara's father and mother have done since they lost her. They have let all the anger and sorrow go and have gone on to live their lives as a tribute to Clara. I couldn't rescue Clara, but I would be able to honor her life with living my own in a manner worthy of her. If you are willing to listen to me from time to time, Father, I think I could do just that."

Father Mackenzie nodded in agreement. The world might never know everything that happened, but the best thing to do was to live each day in peace and let both families live their lives in peace.

EPILOGUE

There have been people in Rising Sun who say that Clara can still be found in the early morning hours wandering the hills crying for Erdman, but only a few understand that she knows exactly where he is. Clara is at peace and rest. It is Erdman who will always be hidden from the world, face down in Rising Sun.

ACKNOWLEDGEMENTS

I want to the thank the many people who gave me encouragement, advice, support, and a never-ending supply of patience while I wrote this, my debut novel. Your impact goes so much farther than you will ever know.

There were people to come alongside me on this initial journey: Sherry Allbaugh, who showed so much mutual interest in Clara's story (including taking a road trip to Rising Sun) and reading my first attempts, Lorrie Pauls, who read and reread the rough draft and gave me valuable input as my sister/friend, Lauren Stinton, who began as my student long ago and became my teacher and mentor, and numerous friends who sent me encouragement along the way.

Thank you to Marilyn J. Martin, copy editor extraordinaire, who took my rough draft and made it smooth and easier to read. Thank you, Marilyn, for the wise counsel and the ability to relate to some of the intricacies of the subplots and character developments.(I wrote this for you without using the semi-colon, though I have proclaimed myself the Queen of them.)

Ghislain Viau, of Creative Publishing Book Design, you took my work, put it in the proper format for publishing and created a cover design that is a work of heart and a work of art. It was exactly what I envisioned, Ghislain. Thank you for your patient answers to my many questions. It was all "well received", to borrow your own gracious words.

At the very center of my heart is the gratitude for the love and support of a wonderful family: my mother, Charlotte Bindl, who listened as I read portions and offered her support and encouragement. My daughters, Michelle Breininger and Alyssa Montiel who both read all my work and offered their input and their love in each word. Thanks to my son in laws, Nate Breininger and Sam Montiel for being part of this crazy adventure and to my new grandson, Riley John, for being such a sweet little man who Grammy adores. I love you all.

And last, but not least, thank you to my husband and my best friend, John. You listened to every word I wrote, listened to every idea and doubt, and supported each one with the love and dedication that I have always found in you alone.